RABINDRANATH TAGORE was a Bengali poet, writer, song writer and composer, playwright, essayist, painter and humanist. Born on 7 May 1861, Rabindranth, the youngest son of Maharshi Debendranath Tagore — a prominent exponent of the Brahmo Samaj — was educated at home and later sent to England for higher studies. On his return to India, he began to write satirical verses on the socio-political climate in a colonised India. Political dissent, class inequities, gender prejudices, revolt, the fight for freedom, and more were recurrent themes in his vast oeuvre.

In 1891, Tagore moved to East Bengal to supervise his family's vast estates. Around this time, his writing was deeply influenced by his proximity to the village folk.

In 1901, in a bid to blend the best of Indian and Western traditions, he founded an experimental school at Shantiniketan, now a university town with the renowned Visva-Bharati University.

In 1910, his collection of poems *Gitanjali* was published. In 1913, he received the Nobel Prize for Literature. Amongst his notable works is the poetry collection *Sonar Tari* (1894), the play *Chitrangada* (1892), several volumes of short stories and novels like *Gora* (1910), *Ghare-Baire* (1916), and *Yogayog* (1929). He also composed over 2,000 songs, popularly known as Rabindra Sangeet.

He died at the age of 80 on 7 August 1941 in Calcutta and left behind a rich, powerful literary legacy.

The Lost Jewels And Other Stories

Rabindranath Tagore

Om Books International

This edition first published in 2023 by

Om Books International

Corporate & Editorial Office
A-12, Sector 64, Noida 201 301
Uttar Pradesh, India
Phone: +91 120 477 4100
Email: editorial@ombooks.com
Website: www.ombooksinternational.com

Sales Office
107, Ansari Road, Darya Ganj,
New Delhi 110 002, India
Phone: +91 11 4000 9000
Email: sales@ombooks.com
Website: www.ombooks.com

Compiled by: Simran Kaur

ISBN, 978-93-53764-43-2

Printed in India

10 9 8 7 6 5 4 3 2 1

Contents

1

The Hungry Stones

My kinsman and myself were returning to Calcutta from our Puja trip when we met the man in a train. From his dress and bearing we took him at first for an up-country Mahomedan, but we were puzzled as we heard him talk. He discoursed upon all subjects so confidently that you might think the Disposer of All Things consulted him at all times in all that He did. Hitherto we had been perfectly happy, as we did not know that secret and unheard-of forces were at work, that the Russians had advanced close to us, that the English had deep and secret policies, that confusion among the native chiefs had come to a head. But our newly-acquired friend said with a sly smile, "There happen more things in heaven and earth, Horatio, than are reported in your newspapers." As we had never stirred out of our homes before, the demeanour of the man struck us dumb with wonder. Be the topic ever so trivial, he would quote science, or comment on the Vedas, or repeat quatrains from some Persian poet; and as we had no pretence to a knowledge of science or the Vedas or Persian, our admiration for him went on increasing, and my kinsman, a theosophist, was firmly convinced that our fellow-passenger must have been supernaturally inspired by some strange "magnetism" or "occult power," by an "astral body" or something of that kind. He listened to the tritest saying that fell from the lips of our extraordinary companion with devotional rapture, and secretly took down notes of his conversation. I fancy that the extraordinary man saw this, and was a little pleased with it.

When the train reached the junction, we assembled in the waiting-room for the connection. It was then, 10 P.M., and as the train, we heard, was likely to be very late, owing to something wrong in the lines, I spread my bed on the table and was about to lie down for a comfortable doze, when the extraordinary person deliberately set about spinning the following yarn. Of course, I could get no sleep that night.

When, owing to a disagreement about some questions of administrative policy, I threw up my post at Junagarh, and entered the service of the Nizam of Hyderabad, they appointed me at once, as a strong young man, collector of cotton duties at Barich.

Barich is a lovely place. The Susta "chatters over stony ways and babbles on the pebbles," tripping, like a skilful dancing girl, in through the woods below the lonely hills. A – flight of 150 steps rises from the river, and above that flight, on the river's brim and at the foot of the hills, there stands a solitary marble palace. Around it there is no habitation of man – the village and the cotton mart of Barich being far off.

About 250 years ago the Emperor Mahmud Shah II. had built this lonely palace for his pleasure and luxury. In his days jets of rose-water spurted from its fountains, and on the cold marble floors of its spray-cooled rooms young Persian damsels would sit, their hair dishevelled before bathing, and, splashing their soft naked feet in the clear water of the reservoirs, would sing, to the tune of the guitar, the ghazals of their vineyards.

The fountains play no longer; the songs have ceased; no longer do snow-white feet step gracefully on the snowy marble. It is but the vast and solitary quarters of cess-collectors like us, men oppressed with solitude and deprived of the society of women. Now, Karim Khan, the old clerk of my office, warned me repeatedly not to take up my abode there. "Pass the day there, if you like," said he, "but never stay the night." I passed it off with a light laugh. The servants said that they would work till dark, and go away at night. I gave my ready assent. The house had such a bad name that even thieves would not venture near it after dark.

At first the solitude of the deserted palace weighed upon me like a nightmare. I would stay out, and work hard as long as possible, then, return home at night jaded and tired, go to bed and fall asleep.

Before a week had passed, the place began to exert a weird fascination upon me. It is difficult to describe or to induce people to believe; but I felt as if the whole house was like a living organism slowly and imperceptibly digesting me by the action of some stupefying gastric juice.

Perhaps the process had begun as soon as I set my foot in the house, but I distinctly remember the day on which I first was conscious of it.

It was the beginning of summer, and the market being dull I had no work to do. A little before sunset I was sitting in an arm-chair near the water's edge below the steps. The Susta had shrunk and sunk low; a broad patch of sand on the other side glowed with the hues of evening; on this side the pebbles at the bottom of the clear shallow waters were glistening. There was not a breath of wind anywhere, and the still air was laden with an oppressive scent from the spicy shrubs growing on the hills close by.

As the sun sank behind the hill-tops a long dark curtain fell upon the stage of day, and the intervening hills cut short the time in which light and shade mingle at sunset. I thought of going out for a ride, and was about to get up when I heard a foot-fall on the steps behind. I looked back, but there was no one.

As I sat down again, thinking it to be an illusion, I heard many footfalls, as if a large number of persons were rushing down the steps. A strange thrill of delight, slightly tinged with fear, passed through my frame, and though there was not a figure before my eyes, methought I saw a bevy of joyous maidens coming down the steps to bathe in the Susta in that summer evening. Not a sound was in the valley, in the river, or in the palace, to break the silence, but I distinctly heard the maidens' gay and mirthful laugh, like the gurgle of a spring gushing forth in a hundred cascades, as they ran past me, in quick playful pursuit of each other, towards the river, without noticing me at all. As they were invisible to me, so I was, as it were, invisible to them. The river was perfectly calm, but I felt that its still, shallow, and clear waters were stirred suddenly by the splash of many an arm jingling with bracelets, that the girls laughed and dashed and spattered water at one another, that the feet of the fair swimmers tossed the tiny waves up in showers of pearl.

I felt a thrill at my heart – I cannot say whether the excitement was due to fear or delight or curiosity. I had a strong desire to see them more clearly, but naught was visible before me; I thought I could catch all that they said if I only strained my ears; but however hard I strained them, I heard nothing but the chirping of the cicadas in the woods. It seemed as if a dark curtain of 250 years was hanging before me, and I would fain lift a corner of it tremblingly and peer through, though the assembly on the other side was completely enveloped in darkness.

The oppressive closeness of the evening was broken by a sudden gust of wind, and the still surface of the Susta rippled and curled like the hair of a nymph, and from the woods wrapt in the evening gloom there came forth a simultaneous murmur, as though they were awakening from a black dream. Call it reality or dream, the momentary glimpse of that invisible mirage reflected from a far-off world, 250 years old, vanished in a flash. The mystic forms that brushed past me with their quick unbodied steps, and loud, voiceless laughter, and threw themselves into the river, did not go back wringing their dripping robes as they went. Like fragrance wafted away by the wind they were dispersed by a single breath of the spring.

Then, I was filled with a lively fear that it was the Muse that had taken advantage of my solitude and possessed me – the witch had evidently come to ruin a poor devil like myself making a living by collecting cotton duties. I decided to have a good dinner – it is the empty stomach that all sorts of incurable diseases find an easy prey. I sent for my cook and gave orders for a rich, sumptuous dinner, redolent of spices and ghee.

Next morning the whole affair appeared a queer fantasy. With a light heart I put on a sola hat like the Sahebs, and drove out to my work. I was to have written my quarterly report that day, and expected to return late; but before it was dark I was strangely drawn to my house – by what I could not say – I felt they were all waiting, and that I should delay no longer. Leaving my report unfinished I rose, put on my sola hat, and startling the dark, shady, desolate path with the rattle of my carriage, I reached the vast silent palace standing on the gloomy skirts of the hills.

On the first floor the stairs led to a very spacious hall, its roof stretching wide over ornamental arches resting on three rows of massive pillars, and groaning day and night under the weight of its own intense solitude. The day had just closed, and the lamps had not yet been lighted. As I pushed the door open a great bustle seemed to follow within, as if a throng of people had broken up in confusion, and rushed out through the doors and windows and corridors and verandas and rooms, to make its hurried escape.

As I saw no one I stood bewildered, my hair on end in a kind of ecstatic delight, and a faint scent of attar and unguents almost effaced by age lingered in my nostrils. Standing in the darkness of that vast desolate hall between the rows of those ancient pillars, I could hear the gurgle of fountains plashing on the marble floor, a strange tune on the guitar, the jingle of ornaments and the tinkle of anklets, the clang of bells tolling the hours, the distant note of nahabat, the din of the crystal pendants of chandeliers shaken by the breeze, the song of bulbuls from the cages in the corridors, the cackle of storks in the gardens, all creating round me a strange unearthly music.

Then, I came under such a spell that this intangible, inaccessible, unearthly vision appeared to be the only reality in the world – and all else a mere dream. That I, that is to say, Srijut So-and-so, the eldest son of So-and-so of blessed memory, should be drawing a monthly salary of Rs. 450 by the discharge of my duties as collector of cotton duties, and driving in my dog-cart to my office every day in a short coat and sola hat, appeared to me to be such an astonishingly ludicrous illusion that I burst into a horse-laugh, as I stood in the gloom of that vast silent hall.

At that moment my servant entered with a lighted kerosene lamp in his hand. I do not know whether he thought me mad, but it came back to me at once that I was in very deed Srijut So-and-so, son of So-and-so of blessed memory, and that, while our poets, great and small, alone could say whether inside or outside the earth there was a region where unseen fountains perpetually played and fairy guitars, struck by invisible fingers, sent forth an eternal harmony, this at any rate was certain, that I collected duties at the cotton market at Barich, and earned thereby Rs. 450 per mensem as my salary. I laughed in great glee at my curious illusion, as I sat over the newspaper at my camp-table, lighted by the kerosene lamp.

After I had finished my paper and eaten my Mughlai dinner, I put out the lamp, and lay down on my bed in a small side-room. Through the open window a radiant star, high above the Avalli Hills skirted by the darkness of their woods, was gazing intently from millions and millions of miles away in the sky at Mr. Collector lying on a humble camp-bedstead. I wondered and felt amused at the idea, and do not know when I fell asleep or how long I slept; but I suddenly awoke with a start, though I heard no sound and saw no intruder – only the steady bright star on the hilltop had set – and the dim light of the new moon was stealthily entering the room through the open window, as if ashamed of its intrusion.

I saw nobody, but felt as if some one was gently pushing me. As I awoke she said not a word, but beckoned me with her five fingers bedecked with rings to follow her cautiously. I got up noiselessly, and, though not a soul save myself was there in the countless apartments of that deserted palace with its slumbering sounds and waking echoes, I feared at every step lest any one should wake up. Most of the rooms of the palace were always kept closed, and I had never entered them.

I followed breathless and with silent steps my invisible guide – I cannot now say where. What endless dark and narrow passages, what long corridors, what silent and solemn audience-chambers and close secret cells I crossed!

Though I could not see my fair guide, her form was not invisible to my mind's eye, an Arab girl, her arms, hard and smooth as marble, visible through her loose sleeves, a thin veil falling on her face from the fringe of her cap, and a curved dagger at her waist! Me thought that one of the thousand and one Arabian Nights had been wafted to me from the world of romance, and that at the dead of night I was wending my way through the dark narrow alleys of slumbering Baghdad to a trysting-place fraught with peril.

At last my fair guide stopped abruptly before a deep blue screen, and seemed to point to something below. There was nothing there, but a sudden dread froze the blood in my heart – methought I saw there on the floor at the foot of the screen a Negro eunuch dressed in rich brocade – sitting and dozing with outstretched legs, with a naked sword on his lap. My fair guide lightly tripped over his legs and held up a fringe of the screen. I could catch a glimpse of a part of the room spread with a Persian carpet – some one was sitting inside on a bed – I could not see her, but only caught a glimpse of two exquisite feet in gold-embroidered slippers, hanging out from loose saffron-coloured pajamas and placed idly on the orange-coloured velvet carpet. On one side there was a bluish crystal tray on which a few apples, pears, oranges, and bunches of grapes in plenty, two small cups and a gold-tinted decanter were evidently awaiting the guest. A fragrant intoxicating vapour, issuing from a strange sort of incense that burned within, almost overpowered my senses.

As with trembling heart I made an attempt to step across the outstretched legs of the eunuch, he woke up suddenly with a start, and the sword fell from his lap with a sharp clang on the marble floor.

A terrific scream made me jump, and I saw I was sitting on that camp-bedstead of mine sweating heavily; and the crescent moon looked pale in the morning light like a weary sleepless patient at dawn; and our crazy Meher Ali was crying out, as is his daily custom, "Stand back! Stand back!" while he went along the lonely road.

Such was the abrupt close of one of my Arabian Nights; but there were yet a thousand nights left.

Then, followed a great discord between my days and nights. During the day I would go to my work worn and tired, cursing the bewitching night and her empty dreams, but as night came my daily life with its bonds and shackles of work would appear a petty, false, ludicrous vanity.

After nightfall I was caught and overwhelmed in the snare of a strange intoxication. I would then, be transformed into some unknown personage of a bygone age, playing my part in unwritten history; and my short English coat and tight breeches did not suit me in the least. With a red velvet cap on my head, loose pajamas, an embroidered vest, a long flowing silk gown, and coloured handkerchiefs scented with attar, I would complete my elaborate toilet, sit on a high-cushioned chair, and replace my cigarette with a many-coiled narghileh filled with rose-water, as if in eager expectation of a strange meeting with the beloved one.

I have no power to describe the marvellous incidents that unfolded themselves, as the gloom of the night deepened. I felt as if in the curious apartments of that vast edifice the fragments of a beautiful story, which I could follow for some distance, but of which I could never see the end, flew about in a sudden gust of the vernal breeze. And all the same I would wander from room to room in pursuit of them the whole night long.

Amid the eddy of these dream-fragments, amid the smell of henna and the twanging of the guitar, amid the waves of air charged with fragrant spray, I would catch like a flash of lightning the momentary glimpse of a fair damsel. She it was who had saffron-coloured pajamas, white ruddy soft feet in gold-embroidered slippers with curved toes, a close-fitting bodice wrought with gold, a red cap, from which a golden frill fell on her snowy brow and cheeks.

She had maddened me. In pursuit of her I wandered from room to room, from path to path among the bewildering maze of alleys in the enchanted dreamland of the nether world of sleep.

Sometimes in the evening, while arraying myself carefully as a prince of the blood-royal before a large mirror, with a candle burning on either side, I would see a sudden reflection of the Persian beauty by the side of my own. A swift turn of her neck, a quick eager glance of intense passion and pain glowing in her large dark eyes, just a suspicion of speech on her dainty red lips, her figure, fair and slim, crowned with youth like a blossoming creeper, quickly uplifted in her graceful tilting gait, a dazzling flash of pain and craving and ecstasy, a smile and a glance and a blaze of jewels and silk, and she melted away. A wild gust of wind, laden with all the fragrance of hills and woods, would put out my light, and I would fling aside my dress and lie down on my bed, my eyes closed and my body thrilling with delight, and there around me in the breeze, amid all the perfume of the woods and hills, floated through the silent gloom many a caress and many a kiss and many a tender touch of hands, and gentle murmurs in my ears, and fragrant breaths on my brow; or a sweetly-perfumed kerchief was wafted again and again on my cheeks. Then, slowly a mysterious serpent would twist her stupefying coils about me; and heaving a heavy sigh, I would lapse into insensibility, and then, into a profound slumber.

One evening I decided to go out on my horse – I do not know who implored me to stay – but I would listen to no entreaties that day. My English hat and coat were resting on a rack, and I was about to take them down when a sudden whirlwind, crested with the sands of the Susta and the dead leaves of the Avalli Hills, caught them up, and whirled them round and round, while a loud peal of merry laughter rose higher and higher, striking all the chords of mirth till it died away in the land of sunset.

I could not go out for my ride, and the next day I gave up my queer English coat and hat for good.

That day again at dead of night I heard the stifled heart-breaking sobs of some one – as if below the bed, below the floor, below the stony foundation of that gigantic palace, from the depths of a dark damp grave – a voice piteously cried and implored me, "Oh, rescue me! Break through these doors of hard illusion, deathlike slumber and fruitless dreams, place me by your side on the saddle, press me to your heart, and, riding through hills and woods and across the river, take me to the warm radiance of your sunny rooms above!"

Who am I? Oh, how can I rescue thee? What drowning beauty, what incarnate passion shall I drag to the shore from this wild eddy of dreams? O lovely ethereal apparition! Where didst thou flourish and when? By what cool spring, under the shade of what date-groves, wast thou born – in the lap of what homeless wanderer in the desert? What Bedouin snatched thee from thy mother's arms, an opening bud plucked from a wild creeper, placed thee on a horse swift as lightning, crossed the burning sands, and took thee to the slave-market of what royal city? And there, what officer of the Badshah, seeing the glory of thy bashful blossoming youth, paid for thee in gold, placed thee in a golden palanquin, and offered thee as a present for the seraglio of his master? And O, the history of that place! The music of the sarangi, the jingle of anklets, the occasional flash of daggers and the glowing wine of Shiraz poison, and the piercing flashing glance! What infinite grandeur, what endless servitude! The slave-girls to thy right and left waved the chamar as diamonds flashed from their bracelets; the Badshah, the king of kings, fell on his knees at thy snowy feet in bejewelled shoes, and outside the terrible Abyssinian eunuch, looking like a messenger of death, but clothed like an angel, stood with a naked sword in his hand! Then, O, thou flower of the desert, swept away by the blood-stained dazzling ocean of grandeur, with its foam of jealousy, its rocks and shoals of intrigue, on what shore of cruel death wast thou cast, or in what other land more splendid and more cruel?

Suddenly at this moment that crazy Meher Ali screamed out, "Stand back! Stand back! All is false! All is false!" I opened my eyes and saw that it was already light. My chaprassi came and handed me my letters, and the cook waited with a salam for my orders.

I said, "No, I can stay here no longer." That very day I packed up, and moved to my office. Old Karim Khan smiled a little as he saw me. I felt nettled, but said nothing, and fell to my work.

As evening approached I grew absent-minded; I felt as if I had an appointment to keep; and the work of examining the cotton accounts seemed wholly useless; even the Nizamat of the Nizam did not appear to be of much worth. Whatever belonged to the present, whatever was moving and acting and working for bread seemed trivial, meaningless, and contemptible.

I threw my pen down, closed my ledgers, got into my dog-cart, and drove away. I noticed that it stopped of itself at the gate of the marble palace just at the hour of twilight. With quick steps I climbed the stairs, and entered the room.

A heavy silence was reigning within. The dark rooms were looking sullen as if they had taken offence. My heart was full of contrition, but there was no one to whom I could lay it bare, or of whom I could ask forgiveness. I wandered about the dark rooms with a vacant mind. I wished I had a guitar to which I could sing to the unknown, "O fire, the poor moth that made a vain effort to fly away has come back to thee! Forgive it but this once, burn its wings and consume it in thy flame!"

Suddenly, two tear-drops fell from overhead on my brow. Dark masses of clouds overcast the top of the Avalli Hills that day.

The gloomy the sooty waters of the Susta were waiting in terrible suspense and in an ominous calm. Suddenly land, water, and sky shivered, and a wild tempest-blast rushed howling through the distant pathless woods, showing its lightning-teeth like a raving maniac who had broken his chains. The desolate halls of the palace banged their doors, and moaned in the bitterness of anguish.

The servants were all in the office, and there was no one to light the lamps. The night was cloudy and moonless. In the dense gloom within I could distinctly feel that a woman was lying on her face on the carpet below the bed – clasping and tearing her long dishevelled hair with desperate fingers. Blood was trickling down her fair brow, and she was now laughing a hard, harsh, mirthless laugh, now bursting into violent wringing sobs, now rending her bodice and striking at her bare bosom, as the wind roared in through the open window, and the rain poured in torrents and soaked her through and through.

All night there was no cessation of the storm or of the passionate cry. I wandered from room to room in the dark, with unavailing sorrow. Whom could I console when no one was by? Whose was this intense agony of sorrow? Whence arose this inconsolable grief?

And the mad man cried out, "Stand back! Stand back!! All is false! All is false!"

I saw that the day had dawned, and Meher Ali was going round and round the palace with his usual cry in that dreadful weather. Suddenly it came to me that perhaps he also had once lived in that house, and that, though he had gone mad, he came there every day, and went round and round, fascinated by the weird spell cast by the marble demon.

Despite the storm and rain I ran to him and asked, "Ho, Meher Ali, what is false?"

The man answered nothing, but pushing me aside went round and round with his frantic cry, like a bird flying fascinated about the jaws of a snake, and made a desperate effort to warn himself by repeating, "Stand back! Stand back!! All is false! All is false!!"

I ran like a mad man through the pelting rain to my office, and asked Karim Khan, "Tell me the meaning of all this!"

What I gathered from that old man was this, That at one time countless unrequited passions and unsatisfied longings and lurid flames of wild blazing pleasure raged within that palace, and that the curse of all the heart-aches and blasted hopes had made its every stone thirsty and hungry, eager to swallow up like a famished ogress any living man who might chance to approach. Not one of those who lived there for three consecutive nights could escape these cruel jaws, save Meher Ali, who had escaped at the cost of his reason.

I asked, "Is there no means whatever of my release?" The old man said, "There is only one means, and that is very difficult. I will tell you what it is, but first you must hear the history of a young Persian girl who once lived in that pleasure-dome. A stranger or a more bitterly heart-rending tragedy was never enacted on this earth."

Just at this moment the coolies announced that the train was coming. So soon? We hurriedly packed up our luggage, as the train steamed in. An English gentleman, apparently just aroused from slumber, was looking out of a first-class carriage endeavouring to read the name of the station. As soon as he caught sight of our fellow-passenger, he cried, "Hallo," and took him into his own compartment. As we got into a second-class carriage, we had no chance of finding out who the man was nor what was the end of his story.

I said, "The man evidently took us for fools and imposed upon us out of fun. The story is pure fabrication from start to finish." The discussion that followed ended in a lifelong rupture between my theosophist kinsman and myself.

2

THE VICTORY

She was Princess Ajita. And the court poet of King Narayan had never seen her. On the day he recited a new poem to the king he would raise his voice just to that pitch which could be heard by unseen hearers in the screened balcony high above the hall. He sent up his song towards the star-land out of his reach, where, circled with light, the planet who ruled his destiny shone unknown and out of ken.

He would espy some shadow moving behind the veil. A tinkling sound would come to his ear from afar, and would set him dreaming of the ankles whose tiny golden bells sang at each step. Ah, the rosy red tender feet that walked the dust of the earth like God's mercy on the fallen! The poet had placed them on the altar of his heart, where he wove his songs to the tune of those golden bells. Doubt never arose in his mind as to whose shadow it was that moved behind the screen, and whose anklets they were that sang to the time of his beating heart. Manjari, the maid of the princess, passed by the poet's house on her way to the river, and she never missed a day to have a few words with him on the sly. When she found the road deserted, and the shadow of dusk on the land, she would boldly enter his room, and sit at the corner of his carpet. There was a suspicion of an added care in the choice of the colour of her veil, in the setting of the flower in her hair.

People smiled and whispered at this, and they were not to blame. For Shekhar the poet never took the trouble to hide the fact that these meetings were a pure joy to him.

The meaning of her name was the spray of flowers. One must confess that for an ordinary mortal it was sufficient in its sweetness. But Shekhar made his own addition to this name, and called her the Spray of Spring Flowers. And ordinary mortals shook their heads and said, Ah, me!

In the spring songs that the poet sang the praise of the spray of spring flowers was conspicuously reiterated; and the king winked and smiled at him when he heard it, and the poet smiled in answer. The king would put him the question,

"Is it the business of the bee merely to hum in the court of the spring?"

The poet would answer, "No, but also to sip the honey of the spray of spring flowers."

And they all laughed in the king's hall. And it was rumoured that Princess Ajita also laughed at her maid's accepting the poet's name for her, and Manjari felt glad in her heart.

Thus, truth and falsehood mingle in life – and to what God builds man adds his own decoration.

Only those were pure truths which were sung by the poet. The theme was Krishna, the lover god, and Radha, the beloved, the Eternal Man and the Eternal Woman, the sorrow that comes from the beginning of time, and the joy without end. The truth of these songs was tested in his inmost heart by everybody from the beggar to the king himself. The poet's songs were on the lips of all. At the merest glimmer of the moon and the faintest whisper of the summer breeze his songs would break forth in the land from windows and courtyards, from sailing-boats, from shadows of the wayside trees, in numberless voices.

Thus, passed the days happily. The poet recited, the king listened, the hearers applauded, Manjari passed and repassed by the poet's room on her way to the river – the shadow flitted behind the screened balcony, and the tiny golden bells tinkled from afar.

Just then, set forth from his home in the south a poet on his path of conquest. He came to King Narayan, in the kingdom of Amarapur. He stood before the throne, and uttered a verse in praise of the king. He had challenged all the court poets on his way, and his career of victory had been unbroken.

The king received him with honour, and said,

"Poet, I offer you welcome."

Pundarik, the poet, proudly replied, "Sire, I ask for war."

Shekhar, the court poet of the king did not know how the battle of the muse was to be waged. He had no sleep at night. The mighty figure of the famous Pundarik, his sharp nose curved like a scimitar, and his proud head tilted on one side, haunted the poet's vision in the dark.

With a trembling heart Shekhar entered the arena in the morning. The theatre was filled with the crowd.

The poet greeted his rival with a smile and a bow. Pundarik returned it with a slight toss of his head, and turned his face towards his circle of adoring followers with a meaning smile.

Shekhar cast his glance towards the screened balcony high above, and saluted his lady in his mind, saying, "If I am the winner at the combat to-day, my lady, thy victorious name shall be glorified."

The trumpet sounded. The great crowd stood up, shouting victory to the king. The king, dressed in an ample robe of white, slowly came into the hall like a floating cloud of autumn, and sat on his throne.

Pundarik stood up, and the vast hall became still. With his head raised high and chest expanded, he began in his thundering voice to recite the praise of King Narayan. His words burst upon the walls of the hall like breakers of the sea, and seemed to rattle against the ribs of the listening crowd. The skill with which he gave varied meanings to the name Narayan, and wove each letter of it through the web of his verses in all manner of combinations, took away the breath of his amazed hearers.

For some minutes after he took his seat his voice continued to vibrate among the numberless pillars of the king's court and in thousands of speechless hearts. The learned professors who had come from distant lands raised their right hands, and cried, Bravo!

The king threw a glance on Shekhar's face, and Shekhar in answer raised for a moment his eyes full of pain towards his master, and then, stood up like a stricken deer at bay. His face was pale, his bashfulness was almost that of a woman, his slight youthful figure, delicate in its outline, seemed like a tensely strung veena ready to break out in music at the least touch.

His head was bent, his voice was low, when he began. The first few verses were almost inaudible. Then, he slowly raised his head, and his clear sweet voice rose into the sky like a quivering flame of fire. He began with the ancient legend of the kingly line lost in the haze of the past, and brought it down through its long course of heroism and matchless generosity to the present age. He fixed his gaze on the king's face, and all the vast and unexpressed love of the people for the royal house rose like incense in his song, and enwreathed the throne on all sides. These were his last words when, trembling, he took his seat, "My master, I may be beaten in play of words, but not in my love for thee."

Tears filled the eyes of the hearers, and the stone walls shook with cries of victory.

Mocking this popular outburst of feeling, with an august shake of his head and a contemptuous sneer, Pundarik stood up, and flung this question to the assembly, "What is there superior to words?" In a moment the hall lapsed into silence again.

Then, with a marvellous display of learning, he proved that the Word was in the beginning, that the Word was God. He piled up quotations from scriptures, and built a high altar for the Word to be seated above all that there is in heaven and in earth. He repeated that question in his mighty voice, "What is there superior to words?"

Proudly he looked around him. None dared to accept his challenge, and he slowly took his seat like a lion who had just made a full meal of its victim. The pandits shouted, Bravo! The king remained silent with wonder, and the poet Shekhar felt himself of no account by the side of this stupendous learning. The assembly broke up for that day.

Next day, Shekhar began his song. It was of that day when the pipings of love's flute startled for the first time the hushed air of the Vrinda Forest. The shepherd women did not know who was the player or whence came the music. Sometimes it seemed to come from the heart of the south wind, and sometimes from the straying clouds of the hilltops. It came with a message of tryst from the land of the sunrise, and it floated from the verge of sunset with its sigh of sorrow. The stars seemed to be the stops of the instrument that flooded the dreams of the night with melody. The music seemed to burst all at once from all sides, from fields and groves, from the shady lanes and lonely roads, from the melting blue of the sky, from the shimmering green of the grass. They neither knew its meaning nor could they find words to give utterance to the desire of their hearts. Tears filled their eyes, and their life seemed to long for a death that would be its consummation.

Shekhar forgot his audience, forgot the trial of his strength with a rival. He stood alone amid his thoughts that rustled and quivered round him like leaves in a summer breeze, and sang the Song of the Flute. He had in his mind the vision of an image that had taken its shape from a shadow, and the echo of a faint tinkling sound of a distant footstep.

He took his seat. His hearers trembled with the sadness of an indefinable delight, immense and vague, and they forgot to applaud him. As this feeling died away Pundarik stood up before the throne and challenged his rival to define who was this Lover and who was the Beloved. He arrogantly looked around him, he smiled at his followers and then, put the question again, "Who is Krishna, the lover, and who is Radha, the beloved?"

Then, he began to analyse the roots of those names, and various interpretations of their meanings. He brought before the bewildered audience all the intricacies of the different schools of metaphysics with consummate skill. Each letter of those names he divided from its fellow, and then, pursued them with a relentless logic till they fell to the dust in confusion, to be caught up again and restored to a meaning never before imagined by the subtlest of word-mongers.

The pandits were in ecstasy; they applauded vociferously; and the crowd followed them, deluded into the certainty that they had witnessed, that day, the last shred of the curtains of Truth torn to pieces before their eyes by a prodigy of intellect. The performance of his tremendous feat so delighted them that they forgot to ask themselves if there was any truth behind it after all.

The king's mind was overwhelmed with wonder. The atmosphere was completely cleared of all illusion of music, and the vision of the world around seemed to be changed from its freshness of tender green to the solidity of a high road levelled and made hard with crushed stones.

To the people assembled their own poet appeared a mere boy in comparison with this giant, who walked with such ease, knocking down difficulties at each step in the world of words and thoughts. It became evident to them for the first time that the poems Shekhar wrote were absurdly simple, and it must be a mere accident that they did not write them themselves. They were neither new, nor difficult, nor instructive, nor necessary.

The king tried to goad his poet with keen glances, silently inciting him to make a final effort. But Shekhar took no notice, and remained fixed to his seat.

The king in anger came down from his throne – took off his pearl chain and put it on Pundarik's head. Everybody in the hall cheered. From the upper balcony came a slight sound of the movements of rustling robes and waist-chains hung with golden bells. Shekhar rose from his seat and left the hall.

It was a dark night of waning moon. The poet Shekhar took down his MSS from his shelves and heaped them on the floor. Some of them contained his earliest writings, which he had almost forgotten. He turned over the pages, reading passages here and there. They all seemed to him poor and trivial – mere words and childish rhymes!

One by one he tore his books to fragments, and threw them into a vessel containing fire, and said, "To thee, to thee, O my beauty, my fire! Thou hast been burning in my heart all these futile years. If my life were a piece of gold it would come out of its trial brighter, but it is a trodden turf of grass, and nothing remains of it but this handful of ashes."

The night wore on. Shekhar opened wide his windows. He spread upon his bed the white flowers that he loved, the jasmines, tuberoses and chrysanthemums, and brought into his bedroom all the lamps he had in his house and lighted them. Then, mixing with honey the juice of some poisonous root he drank it and lay down on his bed.

Golden anklets tinkled in the passage outside the door, and a subtle perfume came into the room with the breeze. The poet, with his eyes shut, said,

"My lady, have you taken pity upon your servant at last and come to see him?"

The answer came in a sweet voice, "My poet, I have come."

Shekhar opened his eyes – and saw before his bed the figure of a woman.

His sight was dim and blurred. And it seemed to him that the image made of a shadow that he had ever kept throned in the secret shrine of his heart had come into the outer world in his last moment to gaze upon his face.

The woman said,

"I am Princess Ajita."

The poet with a great effort sat up on his bed.

The princess whispered into his ear, "The king has not done you justice. It was you who won at the combat, my poet, and I have come to crown you with the crown of victory."

She took the garland of flowers from her own neck, and put it on his hair, and the poet fell down upon his bed stricken by death.

3

Once There Was a King

"Once upon a time there was a king."

When we were children there was no need to know who the king in the fairy story was. It didn't matter whether he was called Shiladitya or Shaliban, whether he lived at Kashi or Kanauj. The thing that made a seven-year-old boy's heart go thump, thump with delight was this one sovereign truth, this reality of all realities, "Once there was a king."

But the readers of this modern age are far more exact and exacting. When they hear such an opening to a story, they are at once critical and suspicious. They apply the searchlight of science to its legendary haze and ask, "Which king?"

The story-tellers have become more precise in their turn. They are no longer content with the old indefinite, "There was a king," but assume instead a look of profound learning, and begin, "Once there was a king named Ajatasatru."

The modern reader's curiosity, however, is not so easily satisfied. He blinks at the author through his scientific spectacles, and asks again, "Which Ajatasatru?"

"Every schoolboy knows," the author proceeds, "that there were three Ajatasatrus. The first was born in the twentieth century B.C., and died at the tender age of two years and eight months. I deeply regret that it is impossible to find, from any trustworthy source, a detailed account of his reign. The second Ajatasatru is better known to historians. If you refer to the new Encyclopedia of History..."

By this time the modern reader's suspicions are dissolved. He feels he may safely trust his author. He says to himself, "Now we shall have a story that is both improving and instructive."

Ah! How we all love to be deluded! We have a secret dread of being thought ignorant. And we end by being ignorant after all, only we have done it in a long and roundabout way.

There is an English proverb, "Ask me no questions, and I will tell you no lies." The boy of seven who is listening to a fairy story understands that perfectly well; he withholds his questions, while the story is being told. So the pure and beautiful falsehood of it all remains naked and innocent as a babe; transparent as truth itself; limpid as a fresh bubbling spring. But the ponderous and learned lie of our moderns has to keep its true character draped and veiled. And if there is discovered anywhere the least little peep-hole of deception, the reader turns away with a prudish disgust, and the author is discredited.

When we were young, we understood all sweet things; and we could detect the sweets of a fairy story by an unerring science of our own. We never cared for such useless things as knowledge. We only cared for truth. And our unsophisticated little hearts knew well where the Crystal Palace of Truth lay and how to reach it. But today we are expected to write pages of facts, while the truth is simply this,

"There was a king."

I remember vividly that evening in Calcutta when the fairy story began. The rain and the storm had been incessant. The whole of the city was flooded. The water was knee-deep in our lane. I had a straining hope, which was almost a certainty, that my tutor would be prevented from coming that evening. I sat on the stool in the far corner of the veranda looking down the lane, with a heart beating faster and faster. Every minute I kept my eye on the rain, and when it began to grow less I prayed with all my might, "Please, God, send some more rain till half-past seven is over." For I was quite ready to believe that there was no other need for rain except to protect one helpless boy one evening in one corner of Calcutta from the deadly clutches of his tutor.

If not in answer to my prayer, at any rate according to some grosser law of physical nature, the rain did not give up.

But, alas! Nor did my teacher.

Exactly to the minute, in the bend of the lane, I saw his approaching umbrella. The great bubble of hope burst in my breast, and my heart collapsed. Truly, if there is a punishment to fit the crime after death, then, my tutor will be born again as me, and I shall be born as my tutor.

As soon as I saw his umbrella I ran as hard as I could to my mother's room. My mother and my grandmother were sitting opposite one another playing cards by the light of a lamp. I ran into the room, and flung myself on the bed beside my mother, and said,

"Mother dear, the tutor has come, and I have such a bad headache; couldn't I have no lessons today?"

I hope no child of immature age will be allowed to read this story, and I sincerely trust it will not be used in text-books or primers for schools. For what I did was dreadfully bad, and I received no punishment whatever. On the contrary, my wickedness was crowned with success.

My mother said to me, "All right," and turning to the servant added, "Tell the tutor that he can go back home."

It was perfectly plain that she didn't think my illness very serious, as she went on with her game as before, and took no further notice. And I also, burying my head in the pillow, laughed to my heart's content. We perfectly understood one another, my mother and I.

But Everyone must know how hard it is for a boy of seven years old to keep up the illusion of illness for a long time. After about a minute I got hold of grandmother, and said, "Granny, do tell me a story."

I had to ask this many times. Granny and mother went on playing cards, and took no notice. At last mother said to me, "Child, don't bother. Wait till we've finished our game." But

I persisted, "Granny, do tell me a story." I told mother she could finish her game tomorrow, but she must let Granny tell me a story there and then.

At last mother threw down the cards and said, "You had better do what he wants. I can't manage him." Perhaps she had it in her mind that she would have no tiresome tutor on the morrow, while I should be obliged to be back to those stupid lessons.

As soon as ever mother had given way, I rushed at Granny. I got hold of her hand, and, dancing with delight, dragged her inside my mosquito curtain on to the bed. I clutched hold of the bolster with both hands in my excitement, and jumped up and down with joy, and when I had got a little quieter, said, "Now, Granny, let's have the story!"

Granny went on, "And the king had a queen." That was good to begin with. He had only one.

It is usual for kings in fairy stories to be extravagant in queens. And whenever we hear that there are two queens, our hearts begin to sink. One is sure to be unhappy. But in Granny's story that danger was past. He had only one queen.

We next hear that the king had not got any son. At the age of seven I didn't think there was any need to bother if a man had had no son. He might only have been in the way.

Nor are we greatly excited when we hear that the king has gone away into the forest to practise austerities in order to get a son. There was only one thing that would have made me go into the forest, and that was to get away from my tutor!

But the king left behind with his queen a small girl, who grew up into a beautiful princess.

Twelve years pass away, and the king goes on practising austerities, and never thinks all this while of his beautiful daughter. The princess has reached the full bloom of her youth. The age of marriage has passed, but the king does not return. And the queen pines away with grief and cries, "Is my golden daughter destined to die unmarried? Ah me! What a fate is mine."

Then, the queen sent men to the king to entreat him earnestly to come back for a single night and take one meal in the palace. And the king consented.

The queen cooked with her own hand, and with the greatest care, sixty-four dishes, and made a seat for him of sandal-wood, and arranged the food in plates of gold and cups of silver. The princess stood behind with the peacock-tail fan in her hand. The king, after twelve years' absence, came into the house, and the princess waved the fan, lighting up all the room with her beauty. The king looked in his daughter's face, and forgot to take his food.

At last he asked his queen, "Pray, who is this girl whose beauty shines as the gold image of the goddess? Whose daughter is she?"

The queen beat her forehead, and cried, "Ah, how evil is my fate! Do you not know your own daughter?"

The king was struck with amazement. He said at last, "My tiny daughter has grown to be a woman."

"What else?" the queen said with a sigh. "Do you not know that twelve years have passed by?"

"But why did you not give her in marriage?" asked the king.

"You were away," the queen said. "And how could I find her a suitable husband?"

The king became vehement with excitement. "The first man I see tomorrow," he said, "when I come out of the palace shall marry her."

The princess went on waving her fan of peacock feathers, and the king finished his meal.

The next morning, as the king came out of his palace, he saw the son of a Brahmin gathering sticks in the forest outside the palace gates. His age was about seven or eight.

The king said, "I will marry my daughter to him."

Who can interfere with a king's command? At once the boy was called, and the marriage garlands were exchanged between him and the princess.

At this point I came up close to my wise Granny and asked her eagerly, "What then?"

In the bottom of my heart there was a devout wish to substitute myself for that fortunate wood-gatherer of seven years old. The night was resonant with the patter of rain. The earthen, lamp by my bedside was burning low. My grandmother's voice droned on as she told the story. And all these things served to create in a corner of my credulous heart the belief that I had been gathering sticks in the dawn of some indefinite time in the kingdom of some unknown king, and in a moment garlands had been exchanged between me and the princess, beautiful as the Goddess of Grace. She had a gold band on her hair and gold earrings in her ears. She had a necklace and bracelets of gold, and a golden waist-chain round her waist, and a pair of golden anklets tinkled above her feet.

If my grandmother were an author how many explanations she would have to offer for this little story! First of all, everyone would ask why the king remained twelve years in the forest? Secondly, why should the king's daughter remain unmarried all that while? This would be regarded as absurd.

Even if she could have got so far without a quarrel, still there would have been a great hue and cry about the marriage itself. First, it never happened. Secondly, how could there be a marriage between a princess of the warrior caste and a boy of the priestly Brahmin caste? Her readers would have imagined at once that the writer was preaching against our social customs in an underhand way. And they would write letters to the papers..

So I pray with all my heart that my grandmother may be born a grandmother again, and not through some cursed fate take birth as her luckless grandson.

So with a throb of joy and delight, I asked Granny, "What then?"

Granny went on, then, the princess took her little husband away in great distress, and built a large palace with seven wings, and began to cherish her husband with great care.

I jumped up and down in my bed and clutched at the bolster more tightly than ever and said, "What then?"

Granny continued, The little boy went to school and learnt many lessons from his teachers, and as he grew up his class-fellows began to ask him, "Who is that beautiful lady who lives with you in the palace with the seven wings?"

The Brahmin's son was eager to know who she was. He could only remember how one day he had been gathering sticks, and a great disturbance arose. But all that was so long ago, that he had no clear recollection.

Four or five years passed in this way. His companions always asked him, "Who is that beautiful lady in the palace with the seven wings?" And the Brahmin's son would come back from school and sadly tell the princess, "My school companions always ask me who is that beautiful lady in the palace with the seven wings, and I can give them no reply. Tell me, oh, tell me, who you are!"

The princess said, "Let it pass to-day. I will tell you some other day." And every day the Brahmin's son would ask, "Who are you?" and the princess would reply, "Let it pass to-day. t will tell you some other day." In this manner four or five more years passed away.

At last the Brahmin's son became very impatient, and said, "If you do not tell me to-day who you are, O beautiful lady, I will leave this palace with the seven wings." Then, the princess said, "I will certainly tell you tomorrow."

Next day the Brahmin's son, as soon as he came home from school, said, "Now, tell me who you are." The princess said, "Tonight I will tell you after supper, when you are in bed."

The Brahmin's son said, "Very well "; and he began to count the hours in expectation of the night. And the princess, on her side, spread white flowers over the golden bed, and lighted a gold lamp with fragrant oil, and adorned her hair, and dressed herself in a beautiful robe of blue, and began to count the hours in expectation of the night.

That evening when her husband, the Brahmin's son, had finished his meal, too excited almost to eat, and had gone to the golden bed in the bed-chamber strewn with flowers, he said to himself, "Tonight I shall surely know who this beautiful lady is in the palace with the seven wings."

The princess took for her the food that was left over by her husband, and slowly entered the bed-chamber. She had to answer that night the question, who was the beautiful lady who lived in the palace with the seven wings. And as she went up to the bed to tell him she found a serpent had crept out of the flowers and had bitten the Brahmin's son. Her boy-husband was lying on the bed of flowers, with face pale in death.

My heart suddenly ceased to throb, and I asked with choking voice, "What then?" Granny said, "Then …"

But what is the use of going on any further with the story? It would only lead on to what was more and more impossible. The boy of seven did not know that, if there were some "What then?" after death, no grandmother of a grandmother could tell us all about it.

But the child's faith never admits defeat, and it would snatch at the mantle of death itself to turn him back. It would be outrageous for him to think that such a story of one teacherless evening could so suddenly come to a stop. Therefore, the grandmother had to call back her story from the ever-shut chamber of the great End, but she does it so simply, it is merely by floating the dead body on a banana stem on the river, and having some incantations read by a magician. But in that rainy night and in the dim light of a lamp death loses all its horror in the mind of the boy, and seems nothing more than a deep slumber of a single night. When the story ends the tired eyelids are weighed down with sleep. Thus, it is that we send the little body of the child floating on the back of sleep over the still water of time, and then, in the morning read a few verses of incantation to restore him to the world of life and light.

4

Homecoming

Phatik Chakravorti was ringleader among the boys of the village. A new mischief got into his head. There was a heavy log lying on the mud-flat of the river waiting to be shaped into a mast for a boat. He decided that they should all work together to shift the log by main force from its place and roll it away. The owner of the log would be angry and surprised, and they would all enjoy the fun. Everyone seconded the proposal, and it was carried unanimously.

But just as the fun was about to begin, Makhan, Phatik's younger brother, sauntered up, and sat down on the log in front of them all without a word. The boys were puzzled for a moment. He was pushed, rather timidly, by one of the boys and told to get up, but he remained quite unconcerned. He appeared like a young philosopher meditating on the futility of games. Phatik was furious. "Makhan," he cried, "if you don't get down this minute, I'll thrash you!"

Makhan only moved to a more comfortable position.

Now, if Phatik was to keep his regal dignity before the public, it was clear he ought to carry out his threat. But his courage failed him at the crisis. His fertile brain, however, rapidly seized upon a new manoeuvre which would discomfit his brother and afford his followers an added amusement. He gave the word of command to roll the log and Makhan over together. Makhan heard the order, and made it a point of honour to stick on. But he overlooked the fact, like those who attempt earthly fame in other matters, that there was peril in it.

The boys began to heave at the log with all their might, calling out, "One, two, three, go." At the word" go" the log went; and with it went Makhan's philosophy, glory and all.

All the other boys shouted themselves hoarse with delight. But Phatik was a little frightened. He knew what was coming. And sure enough Makhan rose from Mother Earth blind as Fate and screaming like the Furies. He rushed at Phatik and scratched his face and beat him and kicked him and then, went crying home. The first act of the drama was over.

Phatik wiped his face, and sat down on the edge of a sunken barge on the river bank, and began to chew a piece of grass. A boat came up to the landing, and a middle-aged man, with grey hair and dark moustache, stepped on shore. He saw the boy sitting there doing nothing, and asked him where the Chakravortis lived. Phatik went on chewing the grass, and said, "Over there," but it was quite impossible to tell where he pointed. The stranger asked him again. He swung his legs to and fro on the side of the barge, and said, "Go and find out," and continued to chew the grass as before.

But now a servant came down from the house, and told Phatik his mother wanted him. Phatik refused to move. But the servant was the master on this occasion. He took Phatik up roughly, and carried him, kicking and struggling in impotent rage.

When Phatik came into the house, his mother saw him. She called out angrily, "So you have been hitting Makhan again?"

Phatik answered indignantly, "No, I haven't; who told you that?"

His mother shouted, "Don't tell lies! You have."

Phatik said suddenly, "I tell you, I haven't. You ask Makhan!" But Makhan thought it best to stick to his previous statement. He said, "Yes, mother. Phatik did hit me."

Phatik's patience was already exhausted. He could not bear this injustice. He rushed at Makhan, and hammered him with blows, "Take that," he cried, "and that, and that, for telling lies."

His mother took Makhan's side in a moment, and pulled Phatik away, beating him with her hands. When Phatik pushed her aside, she shouted out, "What! You little villain! Would you hit your own mother?"

It was just at this critical juncture that the grey-haired stranger arrived. He asked what was the matter. Phatik looked sheepish and ashamed.

But when his mother stepped back and looked at the stranger, her anger was changed to surprise. For she recognised her brother, and cried, "Why, Dada! Where have you come from?"

As she said these words, she bowed to the ground and touched his feet. Her brother had gone away soon after she had married, and he had started business in Bombay. His sister had lost her husband while he was in Bombay. Bishamber had now come back to Calcutta, and had at once made enquiries about his sister. He had then, hastened to see her as soon as he found out where she was.

The next few days were full of rejoicing. The brother asked after the education of the two boys. He was told by his sister that Phatik was a perpetual nuisance. He was lazy, disobedient, and wild. But Makhan was as good as gold, as quiet as a lamb, and very fond of reading. Bishamber kindly offered to take Phatik off his sister's hands, and educate him with his own children in Calcutta. The widowed mother readily agreed. When his uncle asked Phatik if he would like to go to Calcutta with him, his joy knew no bounds, and he said, "Oh, yes, Uncle!" in a way that made it quite clear that he meant it.

It was an immense relief to the mother to get rid of Phatik. She had a prejudice against the boy, and no love was lost between the two brothers. She was in daily fear that he would either drown Makhan some day in the river, or break his head in a fight, or run him into some danger or other. At the same time, she was somewhat distressed to see Phatik's extreme eagerness to get away.

Phatik, as soon as all was settled, kept asking his uncle every minute when they were to start. He was on pins and needles all day long with excitement, and lay awake most of the night. He bequeathed to Makhan, in perpetuity, his fishing-rod, his big kite and his marbles. Indeed, at this time of departure his generosity towards Makhan was unbounded.

When they reached Calcutta, Phatik made the acquaintance of his aunt for the first time. She was by no means pleased with this unnecessary addition to her family. She found her own three boys quite enough to manage without taking any one else. And to bring a village lad of fourteen into their midst was terribly upsetting. Bishamber should really have thought twice before committing such an indiscretion.

In this world of human affairs there is no worse nuisance than a boy at the age of fourteen. He is neither ornamental, nor useful. It is impossible to shower affection on him as on a little boy; and he is always getting in the way. If he talks with a childish lisp he is called a baby, and if he answers in a grown-up way he is called impertinent. In fact any talk at all from him is resented. Then, he is at the unattractive, growing age. He grows out of his clothes with indecent haste; his voice grows hoarse and breaks and quavers; his face grows suddenly angular and unsightly. It is easy to excuse the shortcomings of early childhood, but it is hard to tolerate even unavoidable lapses in a boy of fourteen. The lad himself becomes painfully self-conscious. When he talks with elderly people he is either unduly forward, or else so unduly shy that he appears ashamed of his very existence.

Yet it is at this very age when in his heart of hearts a young lad most craves for recognition and love; and he becomes the devoted slave of any one who shows him consideration. But none dare openly love him, for that would be regarded as undue indulgence, and therefore, bad for the boy. So with scolding and chiding, he becomes very much like a stray dog that has lost his master.

For a boy of fourteen his own home is the only paradise. To live in a strange house with strange people is little short of torture, while the height of bliss is to receive the kind looks of women, and never to be slighted by them.

It was anguish to Phatik to be the unwelcome guest in his aunt's house, despised by this elderly woman, and slighted on every occasion. If she ever asked him to do anything for her, he would be so overjoyed that he would overdo it; and then, she would tell him not to be so stupid, but to get on with his lessons.

The cramped atmosphere of neglect in his aunt's house oppressed Phatik so much that he felt that he could hardly breathe. He wanted to go out into the open country and fill his lungs and breathe freely. But there was no open country to go to. Surrounded on all sides by Calcutta houses and walls, he would dream night after night of his village home, and long to be back there. He remembered the glorious meadow where he used to fly his kite all day long; the broad river-banks where he would wander about the livelong day singing and shouting for joy; the narrow brook where he could go and dive and swim at any time he liked. He thought of his band of boy companions over whom he was despot; and, above all, the memory of that tyrant mother of his, who had such a prejudice against him, occupied him day and night. A kind of physical love like that of animals; a longing to be in the presence of the one who is loved; an inexpressible wistfulness during absence; a silent cry of the inmost heart for the mother, like the lowing of a calf in the twilight this love, which was almost an animal instinct, agitated the shy, nervous, lean, uncouth and ugly boy. No one could understand it, but it preyed upon his mind continually.

There was no more backward boy in the whole school than Phatik. He gaped and remained silent when the teacher asked him a question, and like an overladen ass patiently suffered all the blows that came down on his back. When other boys were out at play, he stood wistfully by the window and gazed at the roofs of the distant houses. And if by chance he espied children playing on the open terrace of any roof, his heart would ache with longing.

One day he summoned up all his courage, and asked his uncle, "Uncle, when can I go home?"

His uncle answered, "Wait till the holidays come."

But the holidays would not come till November, and there was a long time still to wait.

One day Phatik lost his lesson-book. Even with the help of books he had found it very difficult indeed to prepare his lesson. Now it was impossible. Day after day the teacher would cane him unmercifully. His condition became so abjectly miserable that even his cousins were ashamed to own him. They began to jeer and insult him more than the other boys. He went to his aunt at last, and told her that he had lost his book.

His aunt pursed her lips in contempt, and said, "You great clumsy, country lout. How can I afford, with all my family, to buy you new books five times a month?"

That night, on his way back from school, Phatik had a bad headache with a fit of shivering. He felt he was going to have an attack of malarial fever. His one great fear was that he would be a nuisance to his aunt.

The next morning Phatik was nowhere to be seen. All searches in the neighbourhood proved futile. The rain had been pouring in torrents all night, and those who went out in search of the boy got drenched through to the skin. At last, Bishamber asked help from the police.

At the end of the day, a police van stopped at the door before the house. It was still raining and the streets were all flooded. Two constables brought out Phatik in their arms and placed him before Bishamber. He was wet through from head to foot, muddy all over, his face and eyes flushed red with fever, and his limbs all trembling. Bishamber carried him in his arms, and took him into the inner apartments. When his wife saw him, she exclaimed, "What a heap of trouble this boy has given us. Hadn't you better send him home?"

Phatik heard her words, and sobbed out loud, "Uncle, I was just going home; but they dragged me back again."

The fever rose very high, and all that night the boy was delirious. Bishamber brought in a doctor. Phatik opened his eyes flushed with fever, and looked up to the ceiling, and said vacantly, "Uncle, have the holidays come yet? May I go home?"

Bishamber wiped the tears from his own eyes, and took Phatik's lean and burning hands in his own, and sat by him through the night. The boy began again to mutter. At last his voice became excited,

"Mother," he cried, "don't beat me like that! Mother! I am telling the truth!"

The next day Phatik became conscious for a short time. He turned his eyes about the room, as if expecting some one to come. At last, with an air of disappointment, his head sank back on the pillow. He turned his face to the wall with a deep sigh.

Bishamber knew his thoughts, and, bending down his head, whispered, "Phatik, I have sent for your mother."

The day went by. The doctor said in a troubled voice that the boy's condition was very critical.

Phatik began to cry out, "By the mark! Three fathoms. By the mark – four fathoms. By the mark." He had heard the sailor on the river-steamer calling out the mark on the plumb-line. Now he was himself plumbing an unfathomable sea.

Later in the day, Phatik's mother burst into the room like a whirlwind, and began to toss from side to side and moan and cry in a loud voice.

Bishamber tried to calm her agitation, but she flung herself on the bed, and cried, "Phatik, my darling, my darling."

Phatik stopped his restless movements for a moment. His hands ceased beating up and down. He said, "Eh?"

The mother cried again, "Phatik, my darling, my darling."

Phatik very slowly turned his head and, without seeing anybody, said, "Mother, the holidays have come."

5

My Lord, The Baby

I

Raicharan was twelve years old when he came as a servant to his master's house. He belonged to the same caste as his master, and was given his master's little son to nurse. As time went on the boy left Raicharan's arms to go to school. From school he went on to college, and after college he entered the judicial service. Always, until he married, Raicharan was his sole attendant.

But, when a mistress came into the house, Raicharan found two masters instead of one. All his former influence passed to the new mistress. This was compensated for by a fresh arrival. Anukul had a son born to him, and Raicharan by his unsparing attentions soon got a complete hold over the child. He used to toss him up in his arms, call to him in absurd baby language, put his face close to the baby's and draw it away again with a grin.

Presently the child was able to crawl and cross the doorway. When Raicharan went to catch him, he would scream with mischievous laughter and make for safety. Raicharan was amazed at the profound skill and exact judgment the baby showed when pursued. He would say to his mistress with a look of awe and mystery, "Your son will be a judge some day."

New wonders came in their turn. When the baby began to toddle, that was to Raicharan an epoch in human history. When he called his father Baba and his mother Ma-ma and Raicharan Channa, then, Raicharan's ecstasy knew no bounds. He went out to tell the news to all the world.

After a while, Raicharan was asked to show his ingenuity in other ways. He had, for instance, to play the part of a horse, holding the reins between his teeth and prancing with his feet. He had also to wrestle with his little charge, and if he could not, by a wrestler's trick, fall on his back defeated at the end, a great outcry was certain.

About this time, Anukul was transferred to district on the banks of the Padma. On his way through Calcutta he bought his son a little go-cart. He bought him also a yellow satin waistcoat, a gold laced cap, and some gold bracelets and anklets. Raicharan was wont to take these out, and put them on his little charge with ceremonial pride, whenever they went for a walk.

Then, came the rainy season, and day after day the rain poured down in torrents. The hungry river, like an enormous serpent, swallowed down terraces, villages, cornfields, and covered with its flood the tall grasses and wild casuarinas on the sand-banks. From time to time there was a deep thud, as the river-banks crumbled. The unceasing roar of the main current could be heard from far away. Masses of foam, carried swiftly past, proved to the eye the swiftness of the stream.

One afternoon the rain cleared. It was cloudy, but cool and bright. Raicharan's little despot did not want to stay in on such a fine afternoon. His lordship climbed into the go-cart. Raicharan, between the shafts, dragged him slowly along till he reached the rice-fields on the banks of the river. There was no one in the fields, and no boat on the stream. Across the water, on the farther side, the clouds were rifted in the west. The silent ceremonial of the setting sun was revealed in all its glowing splendour. In the midst of that stillness the child, all of a sudden, pointed with his finger in front of him and cried, "Channa! Pitty fow."

Close by on a mud-flat stood a large kadamba tree in full flower. My lord, the baby, looked at it with greedy eyes, and Raicharan knew his meaning. Only a short time before he had made, out of these very flower balls, a small go-cart and the child had been so entirely happy dragging it about with a string, that for the whole day Raicharan was not made to put on the reins at all. He was promoted from a horse into a groom.

But Raicharan had no wish that evening to go splashing knee-deep through the mud to reach the flowers. So he quickly pointed his finger in the opposite direction, calling out, "Oh, look, baby, look! Look at the bird." And with all sorts of curious noises he pushed the go-cart rapidly away from the tree.

But a child, destined to be a judge, cannot be put off so easily. And besides, there was at the time nothing to attract his eyes. And you cannot keep up for ever the pretence of an imaginary bird.

The little Master's mind was made up, and Raicharan was at his wits' end. "Very well, baby," he said at last, "you sit still in the cart, and I'll go and get you the pretty flower. Only mind you don't go near the water."

As he said this, he made his legs bare to the knee, and waded through the oozing mud towards the tree.

The moment Raicharan had gone, his little Master went off at racing speed to the forbidden water. The baby saw the river rushing by, splashing and gurgling as it went. It seemed as though the disobedient wavelets themselves were running away from some greater Raicharan with the laughter of a thousand children. At the sight of their mischief, the heart of the human child grew excited and restless. He got down stealthily from the go-cart and toddled off towards the river. On his way he picked up a small stick, and leant over the bank of the stream pretending to fish. The mischievous fairies of the river with their mysterious voices seemed inviting him into their play-house.

Raicharan had plucked a handful of flowers from the tree, and was carrying them back in the end of his cloth, with his face wreathed in smiles. But when he reached the go-cart, there was no one there. He looked on all sides and there was no one there. He looked back at the cart and there was no one there.

In that first terrible moment his blood froze within him. Before his eyes the whole universe swam round like a dark mist. From the depth of his broken heart he gave one piercing cry, "Master, Master, little Master."

But no voice answered Channa. No child laughed mischievously back; no scream of baby delight welcomed his return. Only the river ran on, with its splashing, gurgling noise as before, as though it knew nothing at all, and had no time to attend to such a tiny human event as the death of a child.

As the evening passed by Raicharan's mistress became very anxious. She sent men out on all sides to search. They went with lanterns in their hands, and reached at last the banks of the Padma. There they found Raicharan rushing up and down the fields, like a stormy wind, shouting the cry of despair,

Master, Master, little Master!

When they got Raicharan home at last, he fell prostrate at his mistress's feet. They shook him, and questioned him, and asked him repeatedly where he had left the child; but all he could say was, that he knew nothing.

Though everyone held the opinion that the Padma had swallowed the child, there was a lurking doubt left in the mind. For a band of gypsies had been noticed outside the village that afternoon, and some suspicion rested on them. The mother went so far in her wild grief as to think it possible that Raicharan himself had stolen the child. She called him aside with piteous entreaty and said, "Raicharan, give me back my baby. Oh! Give me back my child. Take from me any money you ask, but give me back my child!"

Raicharan only beat his forehead in reply. His mistress ordered him out of the house.

Anukul tried to reason his wife out of this wholly unjust suspicion, "Why on earth," he said, "should he commit such a crime as that?"

The mother only replied, "The baby had gold ornaments on his body. Who knows?"

It was impossible to reason with her after that.

II

Raicharan went back to his own village. Up to this time he had had no son, and there was no hope that any child would now be born to him. But it came about before the end of a year that his wife gave birth to a son and died.

An overwhelming resentment at first grew up in Raicharan's heart at the sight of this new baby. At the back of his mind was resentful suspicion that it had come as a usurper in place of the little Master. He also thought it would be a grave offence to be happy with a son of his own after what had happened to his master's little child. Indeed, if it had not been for a widowed sister, who mothered the new baby, it would not have lived long.

But a change gradually came over Raicharan's mind. A wonderful thing happened. This new baby in turn began to crawl about, and cross the doorway with mischief in its face. It also showed an amusing cleverness in making its escape to safety. Its voice, its sounds of laughter and tears, its gestures, were those of the little Master. On some days, when Raicharan listened to its crying, his heart suddenly began thumping wildly against his ribs, and it seemed to him that his former little Master was crying somewhere in the unknown land of death because he had lost his Channa.

Phailna (for that was the name Raicharan's sister gave to the new baby) soon began to talk. It learnt to say Baba and Mama with a baby accent. When Raicharan heard those familiar sounds the mystery suddenly became clear. The little Master could not cast off the spell of his Channa, and therefore, he had been reborn in his own house.

The arguments in favour of this were, to Raicharan, altogether beyond dispute,

(i) The new baby was born soon after his little master's death.

(ii) His wife could never have accumulated such merit as to give birth to a son in middle age.

(iii) The new baby walked with a toddle and called out Baba and Mama. There was no sign lacking which marked out the future judge.

Then, suddenly Raicharan remembered that terrible accusation of the mother. "Ah," he said to himself with amazement, "the mother's heart was right. She knew I had stolen her child." When once he had come to this conclusion, he was filled with remorse for his past neglect. He now gave himself over, body and soul, to the new baby, and became its devoted attendant. He began to bring it up, as if it were the son of a rich man. He bought a go-cart, a yellow satin waistcoat, and a gold-embroidered cap. He melted down the ornaments of his dead wife, and made gold bangles and anklets. He refused to let the little child play with any one of the neighbourhood, and became himself its sole companion day and night. As the baby grew up to boyhood, he was so petted and spoilt and clad in such finery that the village children would call him "Your Lordship," and jeer at him; and older people regarded Raicharan as unaccountably crazy about the child.

At last the time came for the boy to go to school. Raicharan sold his small piece of land, and went to Calcutta. There he got employment with great difficulty as a servant, and sent Phailna to school. He spared no pains to give him the best education, the best clothes, the best food. Meanwhile he lived himself on a mere handful of rice, and would say in secret, "Ah! My little Master, my dear little Master, you loved me so much that you came back to my house. You shall never suffer from any neglect of mine."

Twelve years passed away in this manner. The boy was able to read and write well. He was bright and healthy and good-looking. He paid a great deal of attention to his personal appearance, and was specially careful in parting his hair. He was inclined to extravagance and finery, and spent money freely. He could never quite look on Raicharan as a father, because, though fatherly in affection, he had the manner of a servant. A further fault was this, that Raicharan kept secret from Everyone that himself was the father of the child.

The students of the hostel, where Phailna was a boarder, were greatly amused by Raicharan's country manners, and I have to confess that behind his father's back Phailna joined in their fun. But, in the bottom of their hearts, all the students loved the innocent and tender-hearted old man, and Phailna was very fond of him also. But, as I have said before, he loved him with a kind of condescension.

Raicharan grew older and older, and his employer was continually finding fault with him for his incompetent work. He had been starving himself for the boy's sake. So he had grown physically weak, and no longer up to his work. He would forget things, and his mind became dull and stupid. But his employer expected a full servant's work out of him, and would not brook excuses. The money that Raicharan had brought with him from the sale of his land was exhausted. The boy was continually grumbling about his clothes, and asking for more money.

III

Raicharan made up his mind. He gave up the situation where he was working as a servant, and left some money with Phailna and said, "I have some business to do at home in my village, and shall be back soon."

He went off at once to Baraset where Anukul was magistrate. Anukul's wife was still broken down with grief. She had had no other child.

One day, Anukul was resting after a long and weary day in court. His wife was buying, at an exorbitant price, a herb from a mendicant quack, which was said to ensure the birth of a child. A voice of greeting was heard in the courtyard. Anukul went out to see who was there. It was Raicharan. Anukul's heart was softened when he saw his old servant. He asked him many questions, and offered to take him back into service.

Raicharan smiled faintly, and said in reply, "I want to make obeisance to my mistress."

Anukul went with Raicharan into the house, where the mistress did not receive him as warmly as old master. Raicharan took no notice of this, but folded his hands, and said, "It was not the Padma that stole your baby. It was I."

Anukul exclaimed, "Great God! Eh! What! Where is he?

Raicharan replied, "He is with me. I will bring him the day after tomorrow."

It was Sunday. There was no magistrate's court sitting. Both husband and wife were looking expectantly along the road, waiting from early morning for Raicharan's appearance. At ten o'clock he came, leading Phailna by the hand.

Anukul's wife, without a question, took the boy into her lap, and was wild with excitement, sometimes laughing, sometimes weeping, touching him, kissing his hair and his forehead, and gazing into his face with hungry, eager eyes. The boy was very good-looking and dressed like a gentleman's son. The heart of Anukul brimmed over with a sudden rush of affection.

Nevertheless the magistrate in him asked, "Have you any proofs?"

Raicharan said, "How could there be any proof of such a deed? God alone knows that I stole your boy, and no one else in the world."

When Anukul saw how eagerly his wife was clinging to the boy, he realised the futility of asking for proofs, It would be wiser to believe. And then, where could an old man like Raicharan get such a boy from? And why should his faithful servant deceive him for nothing?

"But," he added severely, "Raicharan, you must not stay here."

"Where shall I go, Master?" said Raicharan, in a choking voice, folding his hands; "I am old. Who will take in an old man as a servant?"

The mistress said, "Let him stay. My child will be pleased. I forgive him."

But Anukul's magisterial conscience would not allow him. "No," he said, "he cannot be forgiven for what he has done."

Raicharan bowed to the ground, and clasped Anukul's feet. "Master," he cried, "Let me stay. It was not I who did it. It was God."

Anukul's conscience was worse stricken than ever, when Raicharan tried to put the blame on God's shoulders.

"No," he said, "I could not allow it. I cannot trust you any more. You have done an act of treachery."

Raicharan rose to his feet and said, "It was not I who did it."

"Who was it then?" asked Anukul.

Raicharan replied, "It was my fate."

But no educated man could take this for an excuse. Anukul remained obdurate.

When Phailna saw that he was the wealthy magistrate's son, and not Raicharan's, he was angry at first, thinking that he had been cheated all this time of his birthright. But seeing Raicharan in distress, he generously said to his father, "Father, forgive him. Even if you don't let him live with us, let him have a small monthly pension."

After hearing this, Raicharan did not utter another word. He looked for the last time on the face of his son; he made obeisance to his old master and mistress. Then, he went out, and was mingled with the numberless people of the world.

At the end of the month Anukul sent him some money to his village. But the money came back. There was no one there of the name of Raicharan.

6

The Kingdom of Cards

I

Once upon a time there was a lonely island in a distant sea where lived the Kings and Queens, the Aces and the Knaves, in the Kingdom of Cards. The Tens and Nines, with the Twos and Threes, and all the other members, had long ago settled there also. But these were not twice-born people, like the famous Court Cards.

The Ace, the King, and the Knave were the three highest castes. The fourth caste was made up of a mixture of the lower Cards. The Twos and Threes were lowest of all. These inferior Cards were never allowed to sit in the same row with the great Court Cards.

Wonderful indeed were the regulations and rules of that island kingdom. The particular rank of each individual had been settled from time immemorial. Everyone had his own appointed work, and never did anything else. An unseen hand appeared to be directing them wherever they went according to the Rules.

No one in the Kingdom of Cards had any occasion to think, no one had any need to come to any decision, no one was ever required to debate any new subject. The citizens all moved along in a listless groove without speech. When they fell, they made no noise. They lay down on their backs, and gazed upward at the sky with each prim feature firmly fixed for ever.

There was a remarkable stillness in the Kingdom of Cards. Satisfaction and contentment were complete in all their rounded wholeness. There was never any uproar or violence. There was never any excitement or enthusiasm.

The great ocean, crooning its lullaby with one unceasing melody, lapped the island to sleep with a thousand soft touches of its wave's white hands. The vast sky, like the outspread azure wings of the brooding mother-bird, nestled the island round with its downy plume. For on the distant horizon a deep blue line betokened another shore. But no sound of quarrel or strife could reach the Island of Cards, to break its calm repose.

II

In that far-off foreign land across the sea, there lived a young Prince whose mother was a sorrowing queen. This queen had fallen from favour, and was living with her only son on the seashore. The Prince passed his childhood alone and forlorn, sitting by his forlorn mother, weaving the net of his big desires. He longed to go in search of the Flying Horse, the jewel in the Cobra's hood, the Rose of Heaven, the Magic Roads, or to find where the Princess Beauty was sleeping in the Ogre's castle over the thirteen rivers and across the seven seas.

From the Son of the Merchant at school, the young Prince learnt the stories of foreign kingdoms. From the Son of the Kotwal, he learnt the adventures of the Two Genii of the Lamp. And when the rain came beating down, and the clouds covered the sky, he would sit on the threshold facing the sea, and say to his sorrowing mother, "Tell me, mother, a story of some very far-off land."

And his mother would tell him an endless tale she had heard in her childhood of a wonderful country beyond the sea where dwelt the Princess Beauty. And the heart of the young Prince would become sick with longing, as he sat on the threshold, looking out on the ocean, listening to his mother's wonderful story, while the rain outside came beating down and the grey clouds covered the sky.

One day, the Son of the Merchant came to the Prince, and said boldly, "Comrade, my studies are over. I am now setting out on my travels to seek my fortunes on the sea. I have come to bid you good-bye."

The Prince said, "I will go with you."

And the Son of Kotwal said also, "Comrades, trusty and true, you will not leave me behind. I also will be your companion."

Then, the young Prince said to his sorrowing mother, "Mother, I am now setting out on my travels to seek my fortune. When I come back once more, I shall surely have found some way to remove all your sorrow."

So the Three Companions set out on their travels together. In the harbour were anchored the twelve ships of the merchant, and the Three Companions got on board. The south wind was blowing, and the twelve ships sailed away, as fast as the desires which rose in the Prince's breast.

At the Conch Shell Island they filled one ship with conchs. At the Sandal Wood Island they filled a second ship with sandal-wood, and at the Coral Island they filled a third ship with coral.

Four years passed away, and they filled four more ships, one with ivory, one with musk, one with cloves, and one with nutmegs.

But when these ships were all loaded a terrible tempest arose. The ships were all of them sunk, with their cloves and nutmeg, and musk and ivory, and coral and sandalwood and conchs. But the ship with the Three Companions struck on an island reef, hurled them safe ashore, and itself broke in pieces.

This was the famous Island of Cards, where lived the Ace and King and Queen and Knave, with the Nines and Tens and all the other members – according to the Rules.

III

Up till now there had been nothing to disturb that island stillness. No new thing had ever happened. No discussion had ever been held.

And then, of a sudden, the Three Companions appeared, thrown up by the sea – and the Great Debate began. There were three main points of dispute.

Firstly, to what caste should these unclassed strangers belong? Should they rank with the Court Cards? Or were they merely lower-caste people, to be ranked with the Nines and Tens? No precedent could be quoted to decide this weighty question.

Secondly, what was their clan? Had they the fairer hue and bright complexion of the Hearts, or was theirs the darker complexion of the Clubs? Over this question there were interminable disputes. The whole marriage system of the island, with its intricate regulations, would depend on its nice adjustment.

Thirdly, what food should they take? With whom should they live and sleep? And should their heads be placed south-west, north-west, or only north-east? In all the Kingdom of Cards a series of problems so vital and critical had never been debated before.

But the Three Companions grew desperately hungry. They had to get food in some way or other. So while this debate went on, with its interminable silence and pauses, and while the Aces called their own meeting, and formed themselves into a Committee, to find some obsolete dealing with the question, the Three Companions themselves were eating all they could find, and drinking out of every vessel, and breaking all regulations.

Even the Twos and Threes were shocked at this outrageous behaviour. The Threes said, "Brother Twos, these people are openly shameless!" And the Twos said, "Brother Threes, they are evidently of lower caste than ourselves!"

After their meal was over, the Three Companions went for a stroll in the city.

When they saw the ponderous people moving in their dismal processions with prim and solemn faces, then, the Prince turned to the Son of the Merchant and the Son of the Kotwal, and threw back his head, and gave one stupendous laugh.

Down Royal Street and across Ace Square and along the Knave Embankment ran the quiver of this strange, unheard-of laughter, the laughter that, amazed at itself, expired in the vast vacuum of silence.

The Son of the Kotwal and the Son of the Merchant were chilled through to the bone by the ghostlike stillness around them. They turned to the Prince, and said, "Comrade, let us away. Let us not stop for a moment in this awful land of ghosts."

But the Prince said, "Comrades, these people resemble men, so I am going to find out, by shaking them upside down and outside in, whether they have a single drop of warm living blood left in their veins."

IV

The days passed one by one, and the placid existence of the Island went on almost without a ripple. The Three Companions obeyed no rules nor regulations. They never did anything correctly either in sitting or standing or turning themselves round or lying on their back. On the contrary, wherever they saw these things going on precisely and exactly according to the Rules, they gave way to inordinate laughter. They remained unimpressed altogether by the eternal gravity of those eternal regulations.

One day the great Court Cards came to the Son of the Kotwal and the Son of the Merchant and the Prince.

"Why," they asked slowly, "Are you not moving according to the Rules?"

The Three Companions answered, "Because that is our Ichcha."

The great Court Cards with hollow, cavernous voices, as if slowly awakening from an age-long dream, said together, "Ichcha! And pray who is Ichcha?"

They could not understand who Ichcha was then, but the whole island was to understand it by-and-by.

The first glimmer of light passed the threshold of their minds when they found out, through watching the actions of the Prince, that they might move in a straight line in an opposite direction from the one in which they had always gone before. Then, they made another startling discovery, that there was another side to the Cards which they had never yet noticed with attention. This was the beginning of the change.

Now that the change had begun, the Three Companions were able to initiate them more and more deeply into the mysteries of Ichcha. The Cards gradually became aware that life was not bound by regulations. They began to feel a secret satisfaction in the kingly power of choosing for themselves.

But with this first impact of Ichcha the whole pack of cards began to totter slowly, and then, tumble down to the ground. The scene was like that of some huge python awaking from a long sleep, as it slowly unfolds its numberless coils with a quiver that runs through its whole frame.

V

Hitherto the Queens of Spades and Clubs and Diamonds and Hearts had remained behind curtains with eyes that gazed vacantly into space, or else remained fixed upon the ground.

And now, all of a sudden, on an afternoon in spring the Queen of Hearts from the balcony raised her dark eyebrows for a moment, and cast a single glance upon the Prince from the corner of her eye.

"Great God," cried the Prince, "I thought they were all painted images. But I am wrong. They are women after all."

Then, the young Prince called to his side his two Companions, and said in a meditative voice, "My comrades! There is a charm about these ladies that I never noticed before. When I saw that glance of the Queen's dark, luminous eyes, brightening with new emotion, it seemed to me like the first faint streak of dawn in a newly created world."

The two Companions smiled a knowing smile, and said, "Is that really so, Prince?

And the poor Queen of Hearts from that day went from bad to worse. She began to forget all rules in a truly scandalous manner. If, for instance, her place in the row was beside the Knave, she suddenly found herself quite accidentally standing beside the Prince instead. At this, the Knave, with motionless face and solemn voice, would say, "Queen, you have made a mistake."

And the poor Queen of Hearts' red cheeks would get redder than ever. But the Prince would come gallantly to her rescue and say, "No! There is no mistake. From to-day I am going to be Knave!"

Now it came to pass that, while Everyone was trying to correct the improprieties of the guilty Queen of Hearts, they began to make mistakes themselves. The Aces found themselves elbowed out by the Kings. The Kings got muddled up with the Knaves. The Nines and Tens assumed airs as though they belonged to the Great Court Cards. The Twos and Threes were found secretly taking the places specially reserved for the Fours and Fives. Confusion had never been so confounded before.

Many spring seasons had come and gone in that Island of Cards. The Kokil, the bird of Spring, had sung its song year after year. But it had never stirred the blood as it stirred it now. In days gone by the sea had sung its tireless melody. But, then, it had proclaimed only the inflexible monotony of the Rule. And suddenly its waves were telling, through all their flashing light and luminous shade and myriad voices, the deepest yearnings of the heart of love!

VI

Where are vanished now their prim, round, regular, complacent features? Here is a face full of love-sick longing. Here is a heart beating wild with regrets. Here is a mind racked sore with doubts. Music and sighing, and smiles and tears, are filling the air. Life is throbbing; hearts are breaking; passions are kindling.

Everyone is now thinking of his own appearance and comparing himself with others. The Ace of Clubs is musing to himself, that the King of Spades may be just passably good-looking. "But," says he, "when I walk down the street you have only to see how people's eyes turn towards me." The King of Spades is saying, "Why on earth is that Ace of Clubs always straining his neck and strutting about like a peacock? He imagines all the Queens are dying of love for him, while the real fact is" here he pauses, and examines his face in the glass.

But the Queens were the worst of all. They began to spend all their time in dressing themselves up to the Nines. And the Nines would become their hopeless and abject slaves. But their cutting remarks about one another were more shocking still.

So the young men would sit listless on the leaves under the trees, lolling with outstretched limbs in the forest shade. And the young maidens, dressed in pale-blue robes, would come walking accidentally to the same shade of the same forest by the same trees, and turn their eyes as though they saw no one there, and look as though they came out to see nothing at all. And then, one young man more forward than the rest in a fit of madness would dare to go near to a maiden in blue. But as he drew near, speech would forsake him. He would stand there tongue-tied and foolish, and the favourable moment would pass.

The Kokil birds were singing in the boughs overhead. The mischievous South wind was blowing; it disarrayed the hair, it whispered in the ear, and stirred the music in the blood. The leaves of the trees were murmuring with rustling delight. And the ceaseless sound of the ocean made all the mute longings of the heart of man and maid surge backwards and forwards on the full spring tide of love.

The Three Companions had brought into the dried-up channels of the Kingdom of Cards the full flood-tide of a new life.

VII

And though the tide was full, there was a pause as though the rising waters would not break into foam but remain suspended for ever. There were no outspoken words, only a cautious going forward one step and receding two. All seemed busy heaping up their unfulfilled desires like castles in the air, or fortresses of sand. They were pale and speechless, their eyes were burning, their lips trembling with unspoken secrets.

The Prince saw what was wrong. He summoned Everyone on the Island and said, "Bring hither the flutes and the cymbals, the pipes and drums. Let all be played together, and raise loud shouts of rejoicing. For the Queen of Hearts this very night is going to choose her Mate!"

So the Tens and Nines began to blow on their flutes and pipes; the Eights and Sevens played on their sackbuts and viols; and even the Twos and Threes began to beat madly on their drums.

When this tumultuous gust of music came, it swept away at one blast all these sighings and mopings. And then, what a torrent of laughter and words poured forth! There were daring proposals and mocking refusals, and gossip and chatter, and jests and merriment. It was like the swaying and shaking, and rustling and soughing, in a summer gale, of a million leaves and branches in the depth of the primeval forest.

But the Queen of Hearts, in a rose-red robe, sat silent in the shadow of her secret bower, and listened to the great uproarious sound of music and mirth, that came floating towards her. She shut her eyes, and dreamt her dream of love. And when she opened them she found the Prince seated on the ground before her gazing up at her face. And she covered her eyes with both hands, and shrank back quivering with an inward tumult of joy.

And the Prince passed the whole day alone, walking by the side of the surging sea. He carried in his mind that startled look, that shrinking gesture of the Queen, and his heart beat high with hope. That night the serried, gaily-dressed ranks of young men and maidens waited with smiling faces at the Palace Gates. The Palace Hall was lighted with fairy lamps and festooned with the flowers of spring. Slowly the Queen of Hearts entered, and the whole assembly rose to greet her. With a jasmine garland in her hand, she stood before the Prince with downcast eyes. In her lowly bashfulness she could hardly raise the garland to the neck of the mate she had chosen. But the Prince bowed his head, and the garland slipped to its place. The assembly of youths and maidens had waited her choice with eager, expectant hush. And when the choice was made, the whole vast concourse rocked and swayed with a tumult of wild delight. And the sound of their shouts was heard in every part of the Island, and by ships far out at sea. Never had such a shout been raised in the Kingdom of Cards before.

And they carried the Prince and his Bride, and seated them on the throne, and crowned them then, and there in the Ancient Island of Cards.

And the sorrowing Mother Queen, on the far-off island shore on the other side of the sea, came sailing to her son's new kingdom in a ship adorned with gold.

And the citizens are no longer regulated according to the Rules, but are good or bad, or both, according to their Ichcha.

7

THE DEVOTEE

I

At a time, when my unpopularity with a part of my readers had reached the nadir of its glory, and my name had become the central orb of the journals, to be attended through space with a perpetual rotation of revilement, I felt the necessity to retire to some quiet place and endeavour to forget my own existence.

I have a house in the country some miles away from Calcutta, where I can remain unknown and unmolested. The villagers there have not, as yet, come to any conclusion about me. They know I am no mere holiday-maker or pleasure-seeker; for I never outrage the silence of the village nights with the riotous noises of the city. Nor do they regard me as an ascetic, because the little acquaintance they have of me carries the savour of comfort about it. I am not, to them, a traveller; for, though I am a vagabond by nature, my wandering through the village fields is aimless. They are hardly even quite certain whether I am married or single; for they have never seen me with my children. So, not being able to classify me in any animal or vegetable kingdom that they know, they have long since given me up and left me stolidly alone.

But quite lately I have come to know that there is one person in the village who is deeply interested in me. Our acquaintance began on a sultry afternoon in July. There had been rain all the morning, and the air was still wet and heavy with mist, like eyelids when weeping is over.

I sat lazily watching a dappled cow grazing on the high bank of the river. The afternoon sun was playing on her glossy hide. The simple beauty of this dress of light made me wonder idly at man's deliberate waste of money in setting up tailors' shops to deprive his own skin of its natural clothing.

While I was watching and lazily musing, a woman of middle age came and prostrated herself before me, touching the ground with her forehead. She carried in her robe some bunches of flowers, one of which she offered to me with folded hands. She said to me, as she offered it, "This is an offering to my god."

She went away. I was so taken aback as she uttered these words, that I could hardly catch a glimpse of her before she was gone. The whole incident was entirely simple, but it left a deep impression on my mind; and as I turned back once more to look at the cattle in the field, the zest of life in the cow, who was munching the lush grass with deep breaths, while she whisked off the flies, appeared to me fraught with mystery. My readers may laugh at my foolishness, but my heart was full of adoration. I offered my worship to the pure joy of living, which is God's own life. Then, plucking a tender shoot from the mango tree, I fed the cow with it from my own hand, and as I did this I had the satisfaction of having pleased my god.

The next year when I returned to the village it was February. The cold season still lingered on. The morning sun came into my room, and I was grateful for its warmth. I was writing, when the servant came to tell me that a devotee, of the Vishnu cult, wanted to see me. I told him, in an absent way, to bring her upstairs, and went on with my writing. The devotee came in, and bowed to me, touching my feet. I found that she was the same woman whom I had met, for a brief moment, a year ago.

I was able now to examine her more closely. She was past that age when one asks the question whether a woman is beautiful or not. Her stature was above the ordinary height, and she was strongly built; but her body was slightly bent owing to her constant attitude of veneration. Her manner had nothing shrinking about it. The most remarkable of her features were her two eyes. They seemed to have a penetrating power which could make distance near.

With those two large eyes of hers, she seemed to push me as she entered.

"What is this?" she asked. "Why have you brought me here before your throne, my god? I used to see you among the trees; and that was much better. That was the true place to meet you."

She must have seen me walking in the garden without my seeing her. For the last few days, however, I had suffered from a cold, and had been prevented from going out. I had, perforce, to stay indoors and pay my homage to the evening sky from my terrace. After a silent pause the devotee said to me, "O my god, give me some words of good."

I was quite unprepared for this abrupt request, and answered her on the spur of the moment,

Good words I neither give nor receive. I simply open my eyes and keep silence, and then, I can at once both hear and see, even when no sound is uttered. Now, while I am looking at you, it is as good as listening to your voice.

The devotee became quite excited as I spoke, and exclaimed, "God speaks to me, not only with his mouth, but with his whole body."

I said to her, "When I am silent I can listen with my whole body. I have come away from Calcutta here to listen to that sound."

The devotee said, "Yes, I know that, and therefore, I have come here to sit by you."

Before taking her leave, she again bowed to me, and touched my feet. I could see that she was distressed because my feet were covered. She wished them to be bare.

Early next morning I came out, and sat on my terrace on the roof. Beyond the line of trees southward I could see the open country chill and desolate. I could watch the sun rising over the sugar-cane in the East, beyond the clump of trees at the side of the village. Out of the deep shadow of those dark trees the village road suddenly appeared. It stretched forward, winding its way to some distant villages on the horizon, till it was lost in the grey of the mist.

That morning it was difficult to say whether the sun had risen or not. A white fog was still clinging to the tops of the trees. I saw the devotee walking through the blurred dawn, like a mist-wraith of the morning twilight. She was singing her chant to God, and sounding her cymbals.

The thick haze lifted at last; and the sun, like the kindly grandsire of the village, took his seat amid all the work that was going on in home and field.

When I had just settled down at my writing-table, to appease the hungry appetite of my editor in Calcutta, there came a sound of footsteps on the stair, and the devotee, humming a tune to herself, entered. and bowed before me. I lifted my head from my papers.

She said to me, "My god, yesterday I took as sacred food what was left over from your meal."

I was startled, and asked her how she could do that.

"Oh," she said, "I waited at your door in the evening, while you were at dinner, and took some food from your plate when it was carried out."

This was a surprise to me, for everyone in the village knew that I had been to Europe, and had eaten with Europeans. I was a vegetarian, no doubt, but the sanctity of my cook would not bear investigation, and the orthodox regarded my food as polluted.

The devotee, noticing my sign of surprise, said, "My god, why should I come to you at all, if I could not take your food?"

I asked her what her own caste people would say. She told me she had already spread the news far and wide all over the village. The caste people shook their heads, but agreed that she must go her own way.

I found out that the devotee came from a good family in the country, and that her mother was well-to-do, and desired to keep her daughter. But she preferred to be a mendicant. I asked her how she made her living. She told me that her followers had given her a piece of land, and that she begged her food from door to door. She said to me, "The food which I get by begging is divine."

After I had thought over what she said, I understood her meaning. When we get our food precariously as alms, we remember God the giver. But when we receive our food regularly at home, as a matter of course, we are apt to regard it as ours by right.

I had a great desire to ask her about her husband. But as she never mentioned him even indirectly, I did not question her.

I found out very soon that the devotee had no respect at all for that part of the village where the people of the higher castes lived.

"They never give," she said, "a single farthing to God's service; and yet they have the largest share of God's glebe. But the poor worship and starve."

I asked her why she did not go and live among these godless people, and help them towards a better life. "That," I said with some unction, "would be the highest form of divine worship."

I had heard sermons of this kind from time to time, and I am rather fond of copying them myself for the public benefit, when the chance comes.

But the devotee was not at all impressed. She raised her big round eyes, and looked straight into mine, and said,

"You mean to say that because God is with the sinners, therefore, when you do them any service you do it to God? Is that so?"

"Yes," I replied, "that is my meaning."

"Of course," she answered almost impatiently, "Of course, God is with them, otherwise, how could they go on living at all? But what is that to me? My god is not there. My god cannot be worshipped among them; because I do not find him there. I seek him where I can find him."

As she spoke, she made obeisance to me. What she meant to say was really this. A mere doctrine of God's omnipresence does not help us. That God is all-pervading – this truth may be a mere intangible abstraction, and therefore, unreal to ourselves. Where I can see him, there is his reality in my soul.

I need not explain that all the while she showered her devotion on me she did it to me not as an individual. I was simply a vehicle of her divine worship. It was not for me either to receive it or to refuse it, for it was not mine, but God's.

When the devotee came again, she found me once more engaged with my books and papers.

"What have you been doing," she said, with evident vexation, "That my god should make you undertake such drudgery? Whenever I come, I find you reading and writing."

"God keeps his useless people busy," I answered, "otherwise they would be bound to get into mischief. They have to do all the least necessary things in life. It keeps them out of trouble."

The devotee told me that she could not bear the encumbrances, with which, day by day, I was surrounded. If she wanted to see me, she was not allowed by the servants to come straight upstairs. If she wanted to touch my feet in worship, there were my socks always in the way. And when she wanted to have a simple talk with me, she found my mind lost in a wilderness of letters.

This time, before she left me, she folded her hands, and said, "My god! I felt your feet in my breast this morning. Oh, how cool! And they were bare, not covered. I held them upon my head for a long time in worship. That filled my very being. Then, after that, pray what was the use of my coming to you yourself? Why did I come? My Lord, tell me truly – wasn't it a mere infatuation?"

There were some flowers in my vase on the table. While she was there, the gardener brought some new flowers to put in their place. The devotee saw him changing them.

"Is that all?" she exclaimed. "Are you done with the flowers? Then, give them to me."

She held the flowers tenderly in the cup of her hands, and began to gaze at them with bent head. After a few moments' silence she raised her head again, and said to me, "You never look at these flowers; therefore, they become stale to you. If you would only look into them, then, your reading and writing would go to the winds."

She tied the flowers together in the end of her robe, and placed them, in an attitude of worship, on the top of her head, saying reverently, "Let me carry my god with me."

While she did this, I felt that flowers in our rooms do not receive their due meed of loving care at our hands. When we stick them in vases, they are more like a row of naughty schoolboys standing on a form to be punished.

The devotee came again the same evening, and sat by my feet on the terrace of the roof.

"I gave away those flowers," she said, "as I went from house to house this morning, singing God's name. Beni, the head man of our village, laughed at me for my devotion, and said, "Why do you waste all this devotion on him? Don't you know he is reviled up and down the countryside?' Is that true, my god? Is it true that they are hard upon you?"

For a moment I shrank into myself. It was a shock to find that the stains of printers' ink could reach so far.

The devotee went on, "Beni imagined that he could blow out the flame of my devotion at one breath! But this is no mere tiny flame, it is a burning fire. Why do they abuse you, my god?"

I said, "Because I deserved it. I suppose in my greed I was loitering about to steal people's hearts in secret."

The devotee said, "Now you see for yourself how little their hearts are worth. They are full of poison, and this will cure you of your greed."

"When a man," I answered, "has greed in his heart, he is always on the verge of being beaten. The greed itself supplies his enemies with poison."

"Our merciful God," she replied, "beats us with his own hand, and drives away all the poison. He who endures God's beating to the end is saved."

II

That evening the devotee told me the story of her life. The stars of evening rose and set behind the trees, as she went on to the end of her tale.

"My husband is very simple. Some people think that he is a simpleton; but I know that those who understand simply, understand truly. In business and household management he was able to hold his own because his needs were small, and his wants few, he could manage carefully on what we had. He would never meddle in other matters, nor try to understand them.

"Both my husband's parents died before we had been married long, and we were left alone. But my husband always needed some one to be over him. I am ashamed to confess that he had a sort of reverence for me, and looked upon me as his superior. But I am sure that he could understand things better than I, though I had greater powers of talking.

"Of all the people in the world he held his Guru Thakur (spiritual master) in the highest veneration. Indeed it was not veneration merely but love; and such love as his is rare."

"Guru Thakur was younger than my husband. Oh! How beautiful he was!

"My husband had played games with him when he was a boy; and from that time forward he had dedicated his heart and soul to this friend of his early days. Thakur knew how simple my husband was, and used to tease him mercilessly.

"He and his comrades would play jokes upon him for their own amusement; but he would bear them all with long-suffering.

"When I married into this family, Guru Thakur was studying at Benares. My husband used to pay all his expenses. I was eighteen years old when he returned home to our village.

"At the age of fifteen I had my child. I was so young I did not know how to take care of him. I was fond of gossip, and liked to be with my village friends for hours together. I used to get quite cross with my boy when I was compelled to stay at home and nurse him. Alas! My child-god came into my life, but His playthings were not ready for him. He came to the mother's heart, but the mother's heart lagged behind. He left me in anger; and ever since I have been searching for him up and down the world.

"The boy was the joy of his father's life. My careless neglect used to pain my husband. But his was a mute soul. He has never been able to give expression to his pain.

"The wonderful thing was this, that in spite of my neglect the child used to love me more than any one else. He seemed to have the dread that I would one day go away and leave him. So even when I was with him, he would watch me with a restless look in his eyes. He had me very little to himself, and therefore, his desire to be with me was always painfully eager. When I went each day to the river, he used to fret and stretch out his little arms to be taken with me. But the bathing ghat was my place for meeting my friends, and I did not care to burden myself with the child.

"It was an early morning in August. Fold after fold of grey clouds had wrapped the mid-day round with a wet clinging robe. I asked the maid to take care of the boy, while I went down to the river. The child cried after me as I went away."

"There was no one there at the bathing ghat when I arrived. As a swimmer, I was the best among all the village women. The river was quite full with the rains. I swam out into the middle of the stream some distance from the shore."

"Then, I heard a cry from the bank, 'Mother!' I turned my head and saw my boy coming down the steps, calling me as he came. I shouted to him to stop, but he went on, laughing and calling. My feet and hands became cramped with fear. I shut my eyes, afraid to see. When I opened them, there, at the slippery stairs, my boy's ripple of laughter had disappeared for ever.

"I got back to the shore. I raised him from the water. I took him in my arms, my boy, my darling, who had begged so often in vain for me to take him. I took him now, but he no more looked in my eyes and called 'Mother'.

"My child-god had come. I had ever neglected him. I had ever made him cry. And now all that neglect began to beat against my own heart, blow upon blow, blow upon blow. When my boy was with me, I had left him alone. I had refused to take him with me. And now, when he is dead, his memory clings to me and never leaves me.

"God alone knows all that my husband suffered. If He had only punished me for my sin, it would have been better for us both. But He knew only how to endure in silence, not how to speak.

"When I was almost mad with grief, Guru Thakur came back. In earlier days, the relation between him and my husband had been that of boyish friendship. Now, my husband's reverence for his sanctity and learning was unbounded. He could hardly speak in his presence, his awe of him was so great."

"My husband asked his Guru to try to give me some consolation. Guru Thakur began to read and explain to me the scriptures. But I do not think they had much effect on my mind. All their value for me lay in the voice that uttered them. God makes the draught of divine life deepest in the heart for man to drink, through the human voice. He has no better vessel in His hand than that; and He Himself drinks His divine draught out of the same vessel.

"My husband's love and veneration for his Guru filled our house, as incense fills a temple shrine. I showed that veneration, and had peace. I saw my god in the form of that Guru. He used to come to take his meal at our house every morning. The first thought that would come to my mind on waking from sleep was that of his food as a sacred gift from God. When I prepared the things for his meal, my fingers would sing for joy.

"When my husband saw my devotion to his Guru, his respect for me greatly increased. He noticed his Guru's eager desire to explain the scriptures to me. He used to think that he could never expect to earn any regard from his Guru himself, on account of his stupidity; but his wife had made up for it.

"Thus, another five years went by happily, and my whole life would have passed like that; but beneath the surface some stealing was going on somewhere in secret. I could not detect it; but it was detected by the God of my heart. Then, came a day when, in a moment our whole life was turned upside down.

"It was a morning in midsummer. I was returning home from bathing, my clothes all wet, down a shady lane. At the bend of the road, under the mango tree, I met my Guru Thakur. He had his towel on his shoulder and was repeating some Sanskrit verses as he was going to take his bath. With my wet clothes clinging all about me I was ashamed to meet him. I tried to pass by quickly, and avoid being seen. He called me by my name.

"I stopped, lowering my eyes, shrinking into myself. He fixed his gaze upon me, and said, 'How beautiful is your body!'

"All the universe of birds seemed to break into song in the branches overhead. All the bushes in the lane seemed ablaze with flowers. It was as though the earth and sky and everything had become a riot of intoxicating joy.

"I cannot tell how I got home. I only remember that I rushed into the room where we worship God. But the room seemed empty. Only before my eyes those same gold spangles of light were dancing which had quivered in front of me in that shady lane on my way back from the river.

"Guru Thakur came to take his food that day, and asked my husband where I had gone. He searched for me, but could not find me anywhere.

"Ah! I have not the same earth now any longer. The same sunlight is not mine. I called on my god in my dismay, and he kept His face turned away from me.

"The day passed, I know not how. That night I had to meet my husband. But the night is dark and silent. It is the time when my husband's mind comes out shining, like stars at twilight. I had heard him speak things in the dark, and I had been surprised to find how deeply he understood.

"Sometimes, I am late in the evening in going to rest on account of household work. My husband waits for me, seated on the floor, without going to bed. Our talk at such times had often begun with something about our Guru.

"That night, when it was past midnight, I came to my room, and found my husband sleeping on the floor. Without disturbing him I lay down on the ground at his feet, my head towards him. Once he stretched his feet, while sleeping, and struck me on the breast. That was his last bequest.

"Next morning, when my husband woke up from his sleep, I was already sitting by him. Outside the window, over the thick foliage of the jack-fruit tree, appeared the first pale red of the dawn at the fringe of the night. It was so early that the crows had not yet begun to call.

"I bowed, and touched my husband's feet with my forehead." He sat up, starting as if waking from a dream, and looked at my face in amazement. I said,

"I have made up my mind. I must leave the world. I cannot belong to you any longer. I must leave your home.

"Perhaps my husband thought that he was still dreaming. He said not a word."

"Ah! Do hear me!" I pleaded with infinite pain. "Do hear me and understand! You must marry another wife. I must take my leave."

"My husband said, 'What is all this wild, mad talk? Who advises you to leave the world?'

"I said, 'My Guru Thakur.'

"My husband looked bewildered. 'Guru Thakur!' he cried. 'When did he give you this advice?'

"In the morning," I answered, 'Yesterday, when I met him on my way back from the river.'

His voice trembled a little. He turned, and looked in my face, and asked me, 'Why did he give you such a behest?'

"I do not know, I answered. 'Ask him! He will tell you himself, if he can.'

"My husband said, 'It is possible to leave the world, even when continuing to live in it. You need not leave my home. I will speak to my Guru about it.'

'Your Guru,' I said, 'may accept your petition; but my heart will never give its consent. I must leave your home. From henceforth, the world is no more to me.'

"My husband remained silent, and we sat there on the floor in the dark. When it was light, he said to me, 'Let us both come to him.'

"I folded my hands and said, 'I shall never meet him again.'

"He looked into my face. I lowered my eyes. He said no more. I knew that, somehow, he had seen into my mind, and understood what was there. In this world of mine, there were only two who loved me best – my boy and my husband. That love was my god, and therefore, it could brook no falsehood. One of these two left me, and I left the other. Now I must have truth, and truth alone."

She touched the ground at my feet, rose and bowed to me, and departed.

8

The Vision

I

When I was a very young wife, I gave birth to a dead child, and came near to death myself. I recovered strength very slowly, and my eyesight became weaker and weaker.

My husband at this time was studying medicine. He was not altogether sorry to have a chance of testing his medical knowledge on me. So he began to treat my eyes himself.

My elder brother was reading for his law examination. One day, he came to see me, and was alarmed at my condition.

"What are you doing?" he said to my husband. "You are ruining Kumo's eyes. You ought to consult a good doctor at once."

My husband said irritably, "Why! What can a good doctor do more than I am doing? The case is quite a simple one, and the remedies are all well known."

Dada answered with scorn, "I suppose you think there is no difference between you and a professor in your own Medical College."

My husband replied angrily, "If you ever get married, and there is a dispute about your wife's property, you won't take my advice about Law. Why, then, do you now come advising me about Medicine?"

While they were quarrelling, I was saying to myself that it was always the poor grass that suffered most when two kings went to war. Here was a dispute going on between these two, and I had to bear the brunt of it.

It also seemed to me very unfair that, when my family had given me in marriage, they should interfere afterwards. After all, my pleasure and pain are my husband's concern, not theirs.

From that day forward, merely over this trifling matter of my eyes, the bond between my husband and Dada was strained.

To my surprise one afternoon, while my husband was away, Dada brought a doctor in to see me. He examined my eyes very carefully, and looked grave. He said that further neglect would be dangerous. He wrote out a prescription, and Dada sent for the medicine at once. When the strange doctor had gone, I implored my Dada not to interfere. I was sure that only evil would come from the stealthy visits of a doctor.

I was surprised at myself for plucking up courage to speak to my brother like that. I had always hitherto been afraid of him. I am sure also that Dada was surprised at my boldness. He kept silence for a while, and then, said to me, "Very well, Kumo. I won't call in the doctor any more. But when the medicine comes you must take it."

Dada then, went away. The medicine came from the chemist. I took it – bottles, powders, prescriptions and all – and threw it down the well!

My husband had been irritated by Dada's interference, and he began to treat my eyes with greater diligence than ever. He tried all sorts of remedies. I bandaged my eyes as he told me, I wore his coloured glasses, I put in his drops, I took all his powders. I even drank the cod-liver oil he gave me, though my gorge rose against it.

Each time he came back from the hospital, he would ask me anxiously how I felt; and I would answer, "Oh! Much better." Indeed I became an expert in self-delusion. When I found that the water in my eyes was still increasing, I would console myself with the thought that it was a good thing to get rid of so much bad fluid; and, when the flow of water in my eyes decreased, I was elated at my husband's skill.

But after a while the agony became unbearable. My eyesight faded away, and I had continual headaches day and night. I saw how much alarmed my husband was getting. I gathered from his manner that he was casting about for a pretext to call in a doctor. So I hinted that it might be as well to call one in.

That he was greatly relieved, I could see. He called in an English doctor that very day. I do not know what talk they had together, but I gathered that the Saheb had spoken very sharply to my husband.

He remained silent for some time after the doctor had gone. I took his hands in mine, and said, "What an ill-mannered brute that was! Why didn't you call in an Indian doctor? That would have been much better. Do you think that man knows better than you do about my eyes?"

My husband was very silent for a moment, and then, said with a broken voice, "Kumo, your eyes must be operated on."

I pretended to be vexed with him for concealing the fact from me so long.

"Here you have known this all the time," said I, "and yet you have said nothing about it! Do you think I am such a baby as to be afraid of an operation?"

At that he regained his good spirits, "There are very few men," said he, "who are heroic enough to look forward to an operation without shrinking."

I laughed at him, "Yes, that is so. Men are heroic only before their wives!"

He looked at me gravely, and said, "You are perfectly right. We men are dreadfully vain."

I laughed away his seriousness, "Are you sure you can beat us women even in vanity?"

When Dada came, I took him aside, "Dada, that treatment your doctor recommended would have done me a world of good; only unfortunately I mistook the mixture for the lotion. And since the day I made the mistake, my eyes have grown steadily worse; and now an operation is needed."

Dada said to me, "You were under your husband's treatment, and that is why I gave up coming to visit you."

"No," I answered. "In reality, I was secretly treating myself in accordance with your doctor's directions."

Oh! What lies we women have to tell! When we are mothers, we tell lies to pacify our children; and when we are wives, we tell lies to pacify the fathers of our children. We are never free from this necessity.

My deception had the effect of bringing about a better feeling between my husband and Dada. Dada blamed himself for asking me to keep a secret from my husband, and my husband regretted that he had not taken my brother's advice at the first.

At last, with the consent of both, an English doctor came, and operated on my left eye. That eye, however, was too weak to bear the strain; and the last flickering glimmer of light went out. Then, the other eye gradually lost itself in darkness.

One day my husband came to my bedside. "I cannot brazen it out before you any longer," said he, "Kumo, it is I who have ruined your eyes."

I felt that his voice was choking with tears, and so I took up his right hand in both of mine and said, "Why! You did exactly what was right. You have dealt only with that which was your very own. Just imagine, if some strange doctor had come and taken away my eyesight. What consolation should I have had then? But now I can feel that all has happened for the best; and my great comfort is to know that it is at your hands I have lost my eyes. When Ramchandra found one lotus too few with which to worship God, he offered both his eyes in place of the lotus. And I have dedicated my eyes to my god. From now, whenever you see something that is a joy to you, then, you must describe it to me; and I will feed upon your words as a sacred gift left over from your vision."

I do not mean, of course, that I said all this there and then, for it is impossible to speak these things on the spur of the moment. But I used to think over words like these for days and days together. And when I was very depressed, or if at any time the light of my devotion became dim, and I pitied my evil fate, then,

I made my mind utter these sentences, one by one, as a child repeats a story that is told. And so I could breathe once more the serener air of peace and love.

At the very time of our talk together, I said enough to show my husband what was in my heart.

"Kumo," he said to me, "the mischief I have done by my folly can never be made good. But I can do one thing. I can ever remain by your side, and try to make up for your want of vision as much as is in my power."

"No," said I. "That will never do. I shall not ask you to turn your house into an hospital for the blind. There is only one thing to be done – you must marry again."

As I tried to explain to him that this was necessary, my voice broke a little. I coughed, and tried to hide my emotion, but he burst out saying,

"Kumo, I know I am a fool, and a braggart, and all that, but I am not a villain! If ever I marry again, I swear to you – I swear to you the most solemn oath by my family god, Gopinath – may that most hated of all sins, the sin of parricide, fall on my head!"

Ah! I should never, never have allowed him to swear that dreadful oath. But tears were choking my voice, and I could not say a word for insufferable joy. I hid my blind face in my pillows, and sobbed, and sobbed again. At last, when the first flood of my tears was over, I drew his head down to my breast.

"Ah!" said I," why did you take such a terrible oath? Do you think I asked you to marry again for your own sordid pleasure? No! I was thinking of myself, for she could perform those services which were mine to give you when I had my sight."

"Services!" said he, "Services! Those can be done by servants. Do you think I am mad enough to bring a slave into my house, and bid her share the throne with this my goddess?"

As he said the word, "Goddess," he held up my face in his hands, and placed a kiss between my brows. At that moment the third eye of divine wisdom was opened, where he kissed me, and verily I had a consecration.

I said in my own mind, "It is well. I am no longer able to serve him in the lower world of household cares. But I shall rise to a higher region. I shall bring down blessings from above. No more lies! No more deceptions for me! All the littlenesses and hypocrisies of my former life shall be banished for ever!"

That day, the whole day through, I felt a conflict going on within me. The joy of the thought, that after this solemn oath it was impossible for my husband to marry again, fixed its roots deep in my heart, and I could not tear them out. But the new Goddess, who had taken her new throne in me, said, "The time might come when it would be good for your husband to break his oath and marry again." But the woman, who was within me, said, "That may be; but all the same an oath is an oath, and there is no way out." The Goddess, who was within me, answered, "That is no reason why you should exult over it." But the woman, who was within me, replied, "What you say is quite true, no doubt; all the same he has taken his oath." And the same story went on again and again. At last the Goddess frowned in silence, and the darkness of a horrible fear came down upon me.

My repentant husband would not let the servants do my work; he must do it all himself. At first it gave me unbounded delight to be dependent on him thus, for every little thing. It was a means of keeping him by my side, and my desire to have him with me had become intense since my blindness. That share of his presence, which my eyes had lost, my other senses craved. When he was absent from my side, I would feel as if I were hanging in mid-air, and had lost my hold of all things tangible.

Formerly, when my husband came back late from the hospital, I used to open my window and gaze at the road. That road was the link which connected his world with mine. Now when I had lost that link through my blindness, all my body would go out to seek him. The bridge that united us had given way, and there was now this unsurpassable chasm. When he left my side the gulf seemed to yawn wide open. I could only wait for the time when he should cross back again from his own shore to mine.

But such intense longing and such utter dependence can never be good. A wife is a burden enough to a man, in all conscience, and to add to it the burden of this blindness was to make his life unbearable. I vowed that I would suffer alone, and never wrap my husband round in the folds of my all-pervading darkness.

Within an incredibly short space of time I managed to train myself to do all my household duties by the help of touch and sound and smell. In fact I soon found that I could get on with greater skill than before. For sight often distracts rather than helps us. And so it came to pass that, when these roving eyes of mine could do their work no longer, all the other senses took up their several duties with quietude and completeness.

When I had gained experience by constant practice, I would not let my husband do any more household duties for me. He complained bitterly at first that I was depriving him of his penance.

This did not convince me. Whatever he might say, I could feel that he had a real sense of relief when these household duties were over. To serve daily a wife who is blind can never make up the life of a man.

II

My husband at last had finished his medical course. He went away from Calcutta to a small town to practise as a doctor. There in the country I felt with joy, through all my blindness, that I was restored to the arms of my mother. I had left my village birthplace for Calcutta when I was eight years old. Since then, ten years had passed away, and in the great city the memory of my village home had grown dim. As long as I had eyesight, Calcutta with its busy life screened from view the memory of my early days. But when I lost my eyesight I knew for the first time that Calcutta allured only the eyes, it could not fill the mind. And now, in my blindness, the scenes of my childhood shone out once more, like stars that appear one by one in the evening sky at the end of the day.

It was the beginning of November when we left Calcutta for Harsingpur. The place was new to me, but the scents and sounds of the countryside pressed round and embraced me. The morning breeze coming fresh from the newly ploughed land, the sweet and tender smell of the flowering mustard, the shepherd-boy's flute sounding in the distance, even the creaking noise of the bullock-cart, as it groaned over the broken village road, filled my world with delight. The memory of my past life, with all its ineffable fragrance and sound, became a living present to me, and my blind eyes could not tell me I was wrong. I went back, and lived over again my childhood. Only one thing was absent, my mother was not with me.

I could see my home with the large peepal trees growing along the edge of the village pool. I could picture in my mind's eye my old grandmother seated on the ground with her thin wisps of hair untied, warming her back in the sun as she made the little round lentil balls to be dried and used for cooking. But somehow I could not recall the songs she used to croon to herself in her weak and quavering voice. In the evening, whenever I heard the lowing of cattle, I could almost watch the figure of my mother going round the sheds with lighted lamp in her hand. The smell of the wet fodder and the pungent smoke of the straw fire would enter into my very heart. And in the distance I seemed to hear the clanging of the temple bell wafted up by the breeze from the river bank.

Calcutta, with all its turmoil and gossip, curdles the heart. There, all the beautiful duties of life lose their freshness and innocence. I remember one day, when a friend of mine came in, and said to me, "Kumo, why don't you feel angry? If I had been treated like you by my husband, I would never look upon his face again."

She tried to make me indignant, because he had been so long calling in a doctor.

"My blindness," said I, "was itself a sufficient evil. Why should I make it worse by allowing hatred to grow up against my husband?"

My friend shook her head in great contempt, when she heard such old-fashioned talk from the lips of a mere chit of a girl. She went away in disdain. But whatever might be my answer at the time, such words as these left their poison; and the venom was never wholly got out of the soul, when once they had been uttered.

So you see Calcutta, with its never-ending gossip, does harden the heart. But when I came back to the country all my earlier hopes and faiths, all that I held true in life during childhood, became fresh and bright once more. God came to me, and filled my heart and my world. I bowed to him, and said,

"It is well that thou has taken away my eyes. Thou art with me."

Ah! But I said more than was right. It was a presumption to say, "Thou art with me." All we can say is this, "I must be true to thee." Even when nothing is left for us, still we have to go on living.

III

We passed a few happy months together. My husband gained some reputation in his profession as a doctor. And money came with it.

But there is a mischief in money. I cannot point to any one event but, because the blind have keener perceptions than other people, I could discern the change which came over my husband along with the increase of wealth.

He had a keen sense of justice when he was younger, and had often told me of his great desire to help the poor when once he obtained a practice of his own. He had a noble contempt for those in his profession who would not feel the pulse of a poor patient before collecting his fee. But now I noticed a difference. He had become strangely hard. Once when a poor woman came, and begged him, out of charity, to save the life of her only child, he bluntly refused. And when I implored him myself to help her, he did his work perfunctorily.

While we were less rich my husband disliked sharp practice in money matters. He was scrupulously honourable in such things. But since he had got a large account at the bank he was often closeted for hours with some scamp of a landlord's agent, for purposes which clearly boded no good.

Where has he drifted? What has become of this husband of mine, the husband I knew before I was blind; the husband who kissed me that day between my brows, and enshrined me on the throne of a Goddess? Those whom a sudden gust of passion brings down to the dust can rise up again with a new strong impulse of goodness. But those who, day by day, become dried up in the very fibre of their moral being; those who by some outer parasitic growth choke the inner life by slow degrees – such men reach one day a deadness which knows no healing.

The separation caused by blindness is the merest physical trifle. But, ah! It suffocates me to find that he is no longer with me, where he stood with me in that hour when we both knew that I was blind. That is a separation indeed!

I, with my love fresh and my faith unbroken, have kept to the shelter of my heart's inner shrine. But my husband has left the cool shade of those things that are ageless and unfading. He is fast disappearing into the barren, waterless waste in his mad thirst for gold.

Sometimes the suspicion comes to me that things are not so bad as they seem, that perhaps I exaggerate because I am blind. It may be that, if my eyesight were unimpaired, I should have accepted the world as I found it. This, at any rate, was the light in which my husband looked at all my moods and fancies.

One day an old Musalman came to the house. He asked my husband to visit his little grand-daughter. I could hear the old man say, "Babu, I am a poor man; but come with me, and Allah will do you good." My husband answered coldly, "What Allah will do won't help matters; I want to know what you can do for me."

When I heard it, I wondered in my mind why God had not made me deaf as well as blind. The old man heaved a deep sigh, and departed. I sent my maid to fetch him to my room. I met him at the door of the inner apartment, and put some money into his hand.

"Please take this from me," said I, "for your little grand-daughter, and get a trustworthy doctor to look after her. And pray for my husband."

But the whole of that day I could take no food at all. In the afternoon, when my husband got up from sleep, he asked me, "Why do you look so pale?"

I was about to say, as I used to do in the past,

"Oh! It's nothing," but those days of deception were over, and I spoke to him plainly.

"I have been hesitating," I said, "For days together to tell you something. It has been hard to think out what exactly it was I wanted to say. Even now I may not be able to explain what I had in my mind. But I am sure you know what has happened. Our lives have drifted apart."

My husband laughed in a forced manner, and said, "Change is the law of nature."

I said to him, "I know that. But there are some things that are eternal."

Then, he became serious.

"There are many women," said he, "who have a real cause for sorrow. There are some whose husbands do not earn money. There are others whose husbands do not love them. But you are making yourself wretched about nothing at all."

Then, it became clear to me that my very blindness had conferred on me the power of seeing a world which is beyond all change. Yes! It is true. I am not like other women. And my husband will never understand me.

IV

Our two lives went on with their dull routine for some time. Then, there was a break in the monotony. An aunt of my husband came to pay us a visit.

The first thing she blurted out after our first greeting was this, "Well, Kumo, it's a great pity you have become blind; but why do you impose your own affliction on your husband? You must get him to marry another wife."

There was an awkward pause. If my husband had only said something in jest, or laughed in her face, all would have been over. But he stammered and hesitated, and said at last in a nervous, stupid way, "Do you really think so? Really, aunt, you shouldn't talk like that."

His aunt appealed to me, "Was I wrong, Kumo?"

I laughed a hollow laugh.

"Had not you better," said I, "consult some one more competent to decide? The pickpocket never asks permission from the man whose pocket he is going to pick."

"You are quite right," she replied blandly. "Abinash, my dear, let us have our little conference in private. What do you say to that?"

After a few days my husband asked her, in my presence, if she knew of any girl of a decent family who could come and help me in my household work. He knew quite well that I needed no help. I kept silence.

"Oh! There are heaps of them," replied his aunt. "My cousin has a daughter who is just of the marriageable age, and as nice a girl as you could wish. Her people would be only too glad to secure you as a husband."

Again there came from him that forced, hesitating laugh, and he said, "But I never mentioned marriage."

"How could you expect," asked his aunt, "a girl of decent family to come and live in your house without marriage?"

He had to admit that this was reasonable, and remained nervously silent.

I stood alone within the closed doors of my blindness after he had gone, and called upon my god and prayed, "O God, save my husband."

When I was coming out of the household shrine from my morning worship a few days later, his aunt took hold of both my hands warmly.

"Kumo, here is the girl," said she, "we were speaking about the other day. Her name is Hemangini. She will be delighted to meet you. Hemo, come here and be introduced to your sister."

My husband entered the room at the same moment. He feigned surprise when he saw the strange girl, and was about to retire. But his aunt said, "Abinash, my dear, what are you running away for? There is no need to do that. Here is my cousin s daughter, Hemangini, come to see you. Hemo, make your bow to him."

As if taken quite by surprise, he began to ply his aunt with questions about the when and why and how of the new arrival.

I saw the hollowness of the whole thing, and took Hemangini by the hand and led her to my own room. I gently stroked her face and arms and hair, and found that she was about fifteen years old, and very beautiful.

As I felt her face, she suddenly burst out laughing and said, "Why! What are you doing? Are you hypnotising me?"

That sweet ringing laughter of hers swept away in a moment all the dark clouds that stood between us. I threw my right arm about her neck.

"Dear one," said I, "I am trying to see you." And again I stroked her soft face with my left hand.

"Trying to see me?" she said, with a new burst of laughter. "Am I like a vegetable marrow, grown in your garden, that you want to feel me all round to see how soft I am?"

I suddenly bethought me that she did not know I had lost my sight. "Sister, I am blind," said I.

She was silent. I could feel her big young eyes, full of curiosity, peering into my face. I knew they were full of pity. Then, she grew thoughtful and puzzled, and said, after a short pause,

"Oh! I see now. That was the reason your husband invited his aunt to come and stay here."

"No!" I replied, "you are quite mistaken. He did not ask her to come. She came of her own accord."

Hemangini went off into a peal of laughter. "That's just like my aunt," said she. "Oh! Wasn't it nice of her to come without any invitation? But now she's come, you won't get her to move for sometime, I can assure you!"

Then, she paused, and looked puzzled.

"But why did father send me?" she asked. "Can you tell me that?"

The aunt had come into the room while we were talking. Hemangini said to her, "When are you thinking of going back, Aunt?"

The aunt looked very much upset.

"What a question to ask!" said she, "I've never seen such a restless body as you. We've only just come, and you ask when we're going back!"

"It is all very well for you," Hemangini said, "for this house belongs to your near relations. But what about me? I tell you plainly I can't stop here." And then, she held my hand and said, "What do you think, dear?"

I drew her to my heart, but said nothing. The aunt was in a great difficulty. She felt the situation was getting beyond her control; so she proposed that she and her niece should go out together to bathe.

"No! We two will go together," said Hemangini, clinging to me. The aunt gave in, fearing opposition if she tried to drag her away.

Going down to the river Hemangini asked me, "Why don't you have children?"

I was startled by her question, and answered, "How can I tell? My god has not given me any. That is the reason."

"No! That's not the reason," said Hemangini quickly. "You must have committed some sin. Look at my aunt. She is childless. It must be because her heart has some wickedness. But what wickedness is in your heart?"

The words hurt me. I have no solution to offer for the problem of evil. I sighed deeply, and said in the silence of my soul, "My god! Thou knowest the reason."

"Gracious goodness," cried Hemangini, "What are you sighing for? No one ever takes me seriously."

And her laughter pealed across the river.

V

I found out after this that there were constant interruptions in my husband's professional duties. He refused all calls from a distance, and would hurry away from his patients, even when they were close at hand.

Formerly, it was only during the mid-day meals and at night time that he could come into the inner apartment. But now, with unnecessary anxiety for his aunt's comfort, he began to visit her at all hours of the day. I knew at once that he had come to her room, when I heard her shouting for Hemangini to bring in a glass of water. At first the girl would do what she was told; but later on she refused altogether.

Then, the aunt would call, in an endearing voice, "Hemo! Hemo! Hemangini." But the girl would cling to me with an impulse of pity. A sense of dread and sadness would keep her silent. Sometimes she would shrink towards me like a hunted thing, who scarcely knew what was coming.

About this time my brother came down from Calcutta to visit me. I knew how keen his powers of observation were, and what a hard judge he was. I feared my husband would be put on his defence, and have to stand his trial before him. So I endeavoured to hide the true situation behind a mask of noisy cheerfulness. But I am afraid I overdid the part, it was unnatural for me.

My husband began to fidget openly, and asked how long my brother was going to stay. At last, his impatience became little short of insulting, and my brother had no help for it but to leave. Before going he placed his hand on my head, and kept it there for some time. I noticed that his hand shook, and a tear fell from his eyes, as he silently gave me his blessing.

I well remember that it was an evening in April, and a market-day. People who had come into the town were going back home from market. There was the feeling of an impending storm in the air; the smell of the wet earth and the moisture in the wind were all-pervading. I never keep a lighted lamp in my bedroom, when I am alone, lest my clothes should catch fire, or some accident happen. I sat on the floor in my dark room, and called upon the God of my blind world.

"O my lord," I cried, "Thy face is hidden. I cannot see. I am blind. I hold tight this broken rudder of a heart till my hands bleed. The waves have become too strong for me. How long wilt thou try me, my god, how long?"

I kept my head prone upon the bedstead and began to sob. As I did so, I felt the bedstead move a little. The next moment Hemangini was by my side. She clung to my neck, and wiped my tears away silently. I do not know why she had been waiting that evening in the inner room, or why she had been lying alone there in the dusk. She asked me no question. She said no word.

She simply placed her cool hand on my forehead, and kissed me, and departed.

The next morning Hemangini said to her aunt in my presence, "If you want to stay on, you can. But I don't. I'm going away home with our family servant."

The aunt said there was no need for her to go alone, for she was going away also. Then, smilingly and mincingly she brought out, from a plush case, a ring set with pearls.

"Look, Hemo," said she, "what a beautiful ring my Abinash brought for you." Hemangini snatched the ring from her hand. "Look, aunt," she answered quickly, "Just see how splendidly I aim." And she flung the ring into the tank outside the window.

The aunt, overwhelmed with alarm, vexation, and surprise, bristled like a hedgehog. She turned to me, and held me by the hand.

"Kumo," she repeated again and again, "Don't say a word about this childish freak to Abinash. He would be fearfully vexed."

I assured her that she need not fear. Not a word would reach him about it from my lips.

The next day before starting for home Hemangini embraced me, and said, "Dearest, keep me in mind; do not forget me."

I stroked her face over and over with my fingers, and said, "Sister, the blind have long memories."

I drew her head towards me, and kissed her hair and her forehead. My world suddenly became grey. All the beauty and laughter and tender youth, which had nestled so close to me, vanished when Hemangini departed. I went groping about with arms outstretched, seeking to find out what was left in my deserted world.

My husband came in later. He affected a great relief now that they were gone, but it was exaggerated and empty. He pretended that his aunt's visit had kept him away from work.

Hitherto there had been only the one barrier of blindness between me and my husband. Now another barrier was added – this deliberate silence about Hemangini. He feigned utter indifference, but I knew he was having letters about her.

It was early in May. My maid entered my room one morning, and asked me, "What is all this preparation going on at the landing on the river? Where is Master going?"

I knew there was something impending, but I said to the maid, "I can't say."

The maid did not dare to ask me any more questions. She sighed, and went away.

Late that night my husband came to me.

"I have to visit a patient in the country," said he. "I shall have to start very early tomorrow morning, and I may have to be away for two or three days."

I got up from my bed. I stood before him, and cried aloud, "Why are you telling me lies?"

My husband stammered out, "What – what lies have I told you?"

I said, "You are going to get married."

He remained silent. For some moments there was no sound in the room. Then, I broke the silence,

"Answer me," I cried. "Say, yes."

He answered, "Yes," like a feeble echo.

I shouted out with a loud voice, "No! I shall never allow you. I shall save you from this great disaster, this dreadful sin. If I fail in this, then, why am I your wife, and why did I ever worship my god?"

The room remained still as a stone. I dropped on the floor, and clung to my husband's knees.

"What have I done?" I asked. "Where have I been lacking? Tell me truly. Why do you want another wife?"

My husband said slowly, "I will tell you the truth. I am afraid of you. Your blindness has enclosed you in its fortress, and I have now no entrance. To me you are no longer a woman. You are awful as my god. I cannot live my everyday life with you. I want a woman – just an ordinary woman – whom I can be free to chide and coax and pet and scold."

Oh, tear open my heart and see! What am I else but that – just an ordinary woman? I am the same girl that I was when I was newly wed – a girl with all her need to believe, to confide, to worship.

I do not recollect exactly the words that I uttered. I only remember that I said, "If I be a true wife, then, may God be my witness, you shall never do this wicked deed, you shall never break your oath. Before you commit such sacrilege, either I shall become a widow, or Hemangini shall die."

Then, I fell down on the floor in a swoon. When I came to myself, it was still dark. The birds were silent. My husband had gone.

All that day I sat at my worship in the sanctuary at the household shrine. In the evening a fierce storm, with thunder and lightning and rain, swept down upon the house and shook it. As I crouched before the shrine, I did not ask my god to save my husband from the storm, though he must have been at that time in peril on the river. I prayed that whatever might happen to me, my husband might be saved from this great sin.

Night passed. The whole of the next day I kept my seat at worship. When it was evening there was the noise of shaking and beating at the door. When the door was broken open, they found me lying unconscious on the ground, and carried me to my room.

When I came to myself at last, I heard some one whispering in my ear, "Sister."

I found that I was lying in my room with my head on Hemangini's lap. When my head moved, I heard her dress rustle. It was the sound of bridal silk.

O my god, my god! My prayer has gone unheeded! My husband has fallen!

Hemangini bent her head low, and said in a sweet whisper, "Sister, dearest, I have come to ask your blessing on our marriage."

At first my whole body stiffened like the trunk of a tree that has been struck by lightning. Then, I sat up, and said, painfully, forcing myself to speak the words, "Why should I not bless you? You have done no wrong."

Hemangini laughed her merry laugh.

"Wrong!" said she. "When you married it was right; and when I marry, you call it wrong!"

I tried to smile in answer to her laughter. I said in my mind, "My prayer is not the final thing in this world. His will is all. Let the blows descend upon my head; but may they leave my faith and hope in God untouched."

Hemangini bowed to me, and touched my feet. " May you be happy," said I, blessing her, "and enjoy unbroken prosperity."

Hemangini was still unsatisfied.

"Dearest sister," she said, "a blessing for me is not enough. You must make our happiness complete. You must, with those saintly hands of yours, accept into your home my husband also. Let me bring him to you."

I said, "Yes, bring him to me."

A few moments later I heard a familiar footstep, and the question, "Kumo, how are you?"

I started up, and bowed to the ground, and cried, "Dada!"

Hemangini burst out laughing.

"You still call him elder brother?" she asked. "What nonsense! Call him younger brother now, and pull his ears and tease him, for he has married me, your younger sister."

Then, I understood. My husband had been saved from that great sin. He had not fallen.

I knew my Dada had determined never to marry. And since my mother had died, there was no sacred wish of hers to implore him to wedlock. But I, his sister, by my sore need had brought it to pass. He had married for my sake.

Tears of joy gushed from my eyes, and poured down my cheeks. I tried, but I could not stop them. Dada slowly passed his fingers through my hair. Hemangini clung to me, and went on laughing.

I was lying awake in my bed for the best part of the night, waiting with straining anxiety for my husband's return. I could not imagine how he would bear the shock of shame and disappointment.

When it was long past the hour of midnight, slowly my door opened. I sat up on my bed, and listened. They were the footsteps of my husband. My heart began to beat wildly. He came up to my bed, held my hand in his.

"Your Dada," said he, "Has saved me from destruction. I was being dragged down and down by a moment's madness.

An infatuation had seized me, from which I seemed unable to escape. God alone knows what a load I was carrying on that day when I entered the boat. The storm came down on the river, and covered the sky. In the midst of all my fears I had a secret wish in my heart to be drowned, and so disentangle my life from the knot in which I had tied it. I reached Mathurganj. There I heard the news which set me free. Your brother had married Hemangini. I cannot tell you with what joy and shame I heard it. I hastened on board the boat again. In that moment of self-revelation I knew that I could have no happiness except with you. You are a goddess."

I laughed and cried at the same time, and said, "No, no, no! I am not going to be a goddess any longer. I am simply your own little wife. I am just an ordinary woman."

"Dearest," he replied, "I have also something I want to say to you. Never again put me to shame by calling me your god."

On the next day the little town became joyous with the sound of conch shells. But nobody made any reference to that night of madness, when all was so nearly lost.

9

THE BABUS OF NAYANJORE

I

Once upon a time, the Babus of Nayanjore were famous landholders. They were noted for their princely extravagance. They would tear off the rough border of their Dhaka muslin, because it rubbed against their skin. They could spend many thousands of rupees over the wedding of a kitten. On a certain grand occasion it is alleged that in order to turn night into day they lighted numberless lamps and showered silver threads from the sky to imitate sunlight. Those were the days before the flood. The flood came. The line of succession among these old-world Babus, with their lordly habits, could not continue for long. Like a lamp with too many wicks burning, the oil flared away quickly, and the light went out.

Kailas Babu, our neighbour, is the last relic of this extinct magnificence. Before he grew up, his family had very nearly reached its lowest ebb. When his father died, there was one dazzling out burst of funeral extravagance, and then, insolvency. The property was sold to liquidate the debt. What little ready money was left over was altogether insufficient to keep up the past ancestral splendours.

Kailas Babu left Nayanjore, and came to Calcutta. His son did not remain long in this world of faded glory. He died, leaving behind him an only daughter.

In Calcutta, we are Kailas Babu's neighbours. Curiously, enough our own family history is just the opposite to his. My father got his money by his own exertions, and prided himself on never spending a penny more than was needed. His clothes were those of a working man, and his hands also. He never had any inclination to earn the title of Babu by extravagant display, and I myself his only son, owe him gratitude for that. He gave me the very best education, and I was able to make my way in the world. I am not ashamed of the fact that I am a self-made man. Crisp bank-notes in my safe are dearer to me than a long pedigree in an empty family chest.

I believe this was why I disliked seeing Kailas Babu drawing his heavy cheques on the public credit from the bankrupt bank of his ancient Babu reputation. I used to fancy that he looked down on me, because my father had earned money with his own hands.

I ought to have noticed that no one showed any vexation towards Kailas Babu except myself. Indeed, it would have been difficult to find an old man who did less harm than he. He was always ready with his kindly little acts of courtesy in times of sorrow and joy. He would join in all the ceremonies and religious observances of his neighbours. His familiar smile would greet young and old alike. His politeness in asking details about domestic affairs was untiring. The friends who met him in the street were perforce ready to be button-holed, while a long string of questions of this kind followed one another from his lips,

My dear friend, I am delighted to see you. Are you quite well? How is Shashi? And Dada – is he all right? Do you know, I've only just heard that Madhu's son has got fever. How is he? Have you heard? And Han Charan Babu – I have not seen him for a long time – I hope he is not ill. What's the matter with Rakkhal? And, er – er, how are the ladies of your family?

Kailas Babu was spotlessly neat in his dress on all occasions, though his supply of clothes was sorely limited. Every day he used to air his shirts and vests and coats and trousers carefully, and put them out in the sun, along with his bed-quilt, his pillowcase, and the small carpet on which he always sat. After airing them he would shake them, and brush them, and put them on the rock. His little bits of furniture made his small room decent, and hinted that there was more in reserve if needed. Very often, for want of a servant, he would shut up his house for a while. Then, he would iron out his shirts and linen with his own hands, and do other little menial tasks. After this he would open his door and receive his friends again.

Though Kailas Babu, as I have said, had lost all his landed property, he had still some family heirlooms left. There was a silver cruet for sprinkling scented water, a filigree box for otto of roses, a small gold salver, a costly ancient shawl, and the old-fashioned ceremonial dress and ancestral turban. These he had rescued with the greatest difficulty from the money-lenders' clutches. On every suitable occasion he would bring them out in state, and thus, try to save the world-famed dignity of the Babus of Nayanjore. At heart the most modest of men, in his daily speech he regarded it as a sacred duty, owed to his rank, to give free play to his family pride. His friends would encourage this trait in his character with kindly good-humour, and it gave them great amusement.

The neighbourhood soon learnt to call him their Thakur Dada. They would flock to his house, and sit with him for hours together. To prevent his incurring any expense, one or other of his friends would bring him tobacco, and say, "Thakur Dada, this morning some tobacco was sent to me from Gaya. Do take it, and see how you like it."

Thakur Dada would take it, and say it was excellent. He would then, go on to tell of a certain exquisite tobacco which they once smoked in the old days at Nayanjore at the cost of a guinea an ounce.

"I wonder," he used to say, "I wonder if any one would like to try it now. I have some left, and can get it at once."

Everyone knew that, if they asked for it, then, somehow or other the key of the cupboard would be missing; or else Ganesh, his old family servant, had put it away somewhere.

"You never can be sure," he would add, "where things go to when servants are about. Now, this Ganesh of mine – I can't tell you what a fool he is, but I haven't the heart to dismiss him."

Ganesh, for the credit of the family, was quite ready to bear all the blame without a word.

One of the company usually said at this point, "Never mind, Thakur Dada. Please don't trouble to look for it. This tobacco we're smoking will do quite well. The other would be too strong."

Then, Thakur Dada would be relieved, and settle down again, and the talk would go on.

When his guests got up to go away, Thakur Dada would accompany them to the door, and say to them on the door-step, "Oh, by the way, when are you all coming to dine with me?"

One or other of us would answer, "Not just yet, Thakur Dada, not just yet. We'll fix a day later."

Quite right," he would answer. "Quite right. We had much better wait till the rains come. It's too hot now. And a grand rich dinner such as I should want to give you would upset us in weather like this."

But when the rains did come, Everyone was very careful not to remind him of his promise. If the subject was brought up, some friend would suggest gently that it was very inconvenient to get about when the rains were so severe, that it would be much better to wait till they were over. And so the game went on.

His poor lodging was much too small for his position, and we used to condole with him about it. His friends would assure him they quite understood his difficulties, it was next to impossible to get a decent house in Calcutta. Indeed, they had all been looking out for years for a house to suit him, but, I need hardly add, no friend had been foolish enough to find one. Thakur Dada used to say, after a long sigh of resignation, "Well, well, I suppose I shall have to put up with this house after all." Then, he would add with a genial smile, "But, you know, I could never bear to be away from my friends. I must be near you. That really compensates for everything."

Somehow I felt all this very deeply indeed. I suppose the real reason was, that when a man is young stupidity appears to him the worst of crimes. Kailas Babu was not really stupid. In ordinary business matters Everyone was ready to consult him. But with regard to Nayanjore his utterances were certainly void of common sense. Because, out of amused affection for him, no one contradicted his impossible statements, he refused to keep them in bounds. When people recounted in his hearing the glorious history of Nayanjore with absurd exaggerations he would accept all they said with the utmost gravity, and never doubted, even in his dreams, that any one could disbelieve it.

II

When I sit down and try to analyse the thoughts and feelings that I had towards Kailas Babu, I see that there was a still deeper reason for my dislike. I will now explain.

Though, I am the son of a rich man, and might have wasted time at college, my industry was such that I took my M.A. degree in Calcutta University when quite young. My moral character was flawless. In addition, my outward appearance was so handsome, that if I were to call myself beautiful, it might be thought a mark of self-estimation, but could not be considered an untruth.

There could be no question that among the young men of Bengal I was regarded by parents generally as a very eligible match. I was myself quite clear on the point, and had determined to obtain my full value in the marriage market. When I pictured my choice, I had before my mind's eye a wealthy father's only daughter, extremely beautiful and highly educated. Proposals came pouring in to me from far and near; large sums in cash were offered. I weighed these offers with rigid impartiality, in the delicate scales of my own estimation. But there was no one fit to be my partner. I became convinced, with the poet Bhabavuti, that

In this world's endless time and boundless space
One may be born at last to match my sovereign grace.

But in this puny modern age, and this contracted space of modern Bengal, it was doubtful if the peerless creature existed as yet.

Meanwhile my praises were sung in many tunes, and in different metres, by designing parents.

Whether I was pleased with their daughters or not, this worship which they offered was never unpleasing. I used to regard it as my proper due because I was so good. We are told that when the gods withhold their boons from mortals they still expect their worshippers to pay them fervent honour, and are angry if it is withheld. I had that divine expectance strongly developed in myself.

I have already mentioned that Thakur Dada had an only grand-daughter. I had seen her many times, but had never mistaken her for beautiful. No thought had ever entered my mind that she would be a possible partner for myself. All the same, it seemed quite certain to me that some day or other Kailas Babu would offer her, with all due worship, as an oblation at my shrine. Indeed – this was the secret of my dislike – I was thoroughly annoyed that he had not done it already.

I heard he had told his friends that the Babus of Nayanjore never craved a boon. Even if the girl remained unmarried, he would not break the family tradition. It was this arrogance of his that made me angry. My indignation smouldered for some time. But I remained perfectly silent, and bore it with the utmost patience, because I was so good.

As lightning accompanies thunder, so in my character a flash of humour was mingled with the mutterings of my wrath. It was, of course, impossible for me to punish the old man merely to give vent to my rage; and for a long time I did nothing at all. But suddenly one day such an amusing plan came into my head, that I could not resist the temptation of carrying it into effect.

I have already said that many of Kailas Babu's friends used to flatter the old man's vanity to the full. One, who was a retired Government servant, had told him that whenever he saw the Chhota Lord Saheb he always asked for the latest news about the Babus of Nayanjore, and the Chhota Lord had been heard to say that in all Bengal the only really respectable families were those of the Maharaja of Burdwan and the Babus of Nayanjore. When this monstrous falsehood was told to Kailas Babu he was extremely gratified, and often repeated the story. And wherever after that he met this Government servant in company he would ask, along with other questions,

"Oh, er – by the way, how is the Chhota Lord Saheb? Quite well, did you say? Ah, yes, I am so delighted to hear it! And the dear Mem Saheb, is she quite well too? Ah, yes! And the little children – are they quite well also? Ah, yes! That's very good news! Be sure and give them my compliments when you see them."

Kailas Babu would constantly express his intention of going some day and paying a visit to the Saheb. But it may be taken for granted that many Chhota Lords and Burra Lords also would come and go, and much water would pass down the Hoogly, before the family coach of Nayanjore would be furnished up to pay a visit to Government House.

One day, I took Kailas Babu aside, and told him in a whisper, "Thakur Dada, I was at the Levee yesterday, and the Chhota Lord happened to mention the Babus of Nayanjore. I told him that Kailas Babu had come to town. Do you know, he was terribly hurt because you hadn't called. He told me he was going to put etiquette on one side, and pay you a private visit himself this very afternoon."

Anybody else could have seen through this plot of mine in a moment. And, if it had been directed against another person, Kailas Babu would have understood the joke. But after all he had heard from his friend the government servant, and after all his own exaggerations, a visit from the Lieutenant-Governor seemed the most natural thing in the world. He became highly nervous and excited at my news. Each detail of the coming visit exercised him greatly – most of all his own ignorance of English. How on earth was that difficulty to be met? I told him there was no difficulty at all, it was aristocratic not to know English, and besides, the Lieutenant-Governor always brought an interpreter with him, and he had expressly mentioned that this visit was to be private.

About mid-day, when most of our neighbours are at work, and the rest are asleep, a carriage and pair stopped before the lodging of Kailas Babu. Two flunkeys in livery came up the stairs, and announced in a loud voice, "The Chhota Lord Saheb has arrived." Kailas Babu was ready, waiting for him, in his old-fashioned ceremonial robes and ancestral turban, and Ganesh was by his side, dressed in his master's best suit of clothes for the occasion. When the Chhota Lord Saheb was announced, Kailas Babu ran panting and puffing and trembling to the door, and led in a friend of mine, in disguise, with repeated salaams, bowing low at each step, and walking backward as best he could. He had his old family shawl spread over a hard wooden chair, and he asked the Lord Saheb to be seated. He then, made a high-flown speech in Urdu, the ancient Court language of the Sahebs, and presented on the golden salver a string of gold mohurs, the last relics of his broken fortune. The old family servant Ganesh, with an expression of awe bordering on terror, stood behind with the scent-sprinkler, drenching the Lord Saheb, touching him gingerly from time to time with the otto of roses from the filigree box.

Kailas Babu repeatedly expressed his regret at not being able to receive His Honour Bahadur with all the ancestral magnificence of his own family estate at Nayanjore. There he could have welcomed him properly with due ceremonial. But in Calcutta he was a mere stranger and sojourner – in fact a fish out of water.

My friend, with his tall silk hat on, very gravely nodded. I need hardly say that according to English custom the hat ought to have been removed inside the room. But my friend did not dare to take it off for fear of detection; and Kailas Babu and his old servant Ganesh were sublimely unconscious of the breach of etiquette.

After a ten minutes' interview, which consisted chiefly of nodding the head, my friend rose to his feet to depart. The two flunkeys in livery, as had been planned beforehand, carried off in state the string of gold mohurs, the gold salver, the old ancestral shawl, the silver scent-sprinkler, and the otto of roses filigree box; they placed them ceremoniously in the carriage. Kailas Babu regarded this as the usual habit of Chhota Lord Sahebs.

I was watching all the while from the next room. My sides were aching with suppressed laughter. When I could hold myself in no longer, I rushed into a further room, suddenly to discover, in a corner, a young girl sobbing as if her heart would break. When she saw my uproarious laughter she stood upright in passion, flashing the lightning of her big dark eyes in mine, and said with a tear-choked voice, "Tell me! What harm has my grandfather done to you? Why have you come to deceive him? Why have you come here? Why?"

She could say no more. She covered her face with her hands, and broke into sobs.

My laughter vanished in a moment. It had never occurred to me that there was anything but a supremely funny joke in this act of mine, and here I discovered that I had given the cruelest pain to this tenderest little heart. All the ugliness of my cruelty rose up to condemn me. I slunk out of the room in silence, like a kicked dog.

Hitherto I had only looked upon Kusum, the grand-daughter of Kailas Babu, as a somewhat worthless commodity in the marriage market, waiting in vain to attract a husband. But now I found, with a shock of surprise, that in the corner of that room a human heart was beating.

The whole night through, I had very little sleep. My mind was in a tumult. On the next day, very early in the morning, I took all those stolen goods back to Kailas Babu's lodgings, wishing to hand them over in secret to the servant Ganesh. I waited outside the door, and, not finding any one, went upstairs to Kailas Babu's room. I heard from the passage Kusum asking her grandfather in the most winning voice, "Dada, dearest, do tell me all that the Chhota Lord Saheb said to you yesterday. Don't leave out a single word. I am dying to hear it all over again."

And Dada needed no encouragement. His face beamed over with pride as he related all manner of praises, which the Lord Saheb had been good enough to utter concerning the ancient families of Nayanjore. The girl was seated before him, looking up into his face, and listening with rapt attention. She was determined, out of love for the old man, to play her part to the full.

My heart was deeply touched, and tears came to my eyes. I stood there in silence in the passage, while Thakur Dada finished all his embellishments of the Chhota Lord Saheb's wonderful visit. When he left the room at last, I took the stolen goods and laid them at the feet of the girl and came away without a word.

Later in the day, I called again to see Kailas Babu himself. According to our ugly modern custom, I had been in the habit of making no greeting at all to this old man when I came into the room. But on this day I made a low bow, and touched his feet. I am convinced the old man thought that the coming of the Chhota Lord Saheb to his house was the cause of my new politeness. He was highly gratified by it, and an air of benign severity shone from his eyes. His friends had flocked in, and he had already begun to tell again at full length the story of the Lieutenant-Governor's visit with still further adornments of a most fantastic kind. The interview was already becoming an epic, both in quality and in length.

When the other visitors had taken their leave, I made my proposal to the old man in a humble manner. I told him that, "Though I could never for a moment hope to be worthy of marriage connection with such an illustrious family, yet ... etc., etc."

When I made clear my proposal of marriage, the old man embraced me, and broke out in a tumult of joy, "I am a poor man, and could never have expected such great good fortune."

That was the first and last time in his life that Kailas Babu confessed to being poor. It was also the first and last time in his life that he forgot, if only for a single moment, the ancestral dignity that belongs to the Babus of Nayanjore.

10

Living or Dead?

I

The widow in the house of Saradasankar, the Ranihat zamindar, had no kinsmen of her father's family. One after another all had died. Nor had she in her husband's family any one she could call her own, neither husband nor son. The child of her brother-in-law Saradasankar was her darling. For a long time after his birth, his mother had been very ill, and the widow, his aunt Kadambini, had fostered him. If a woman fosters another's child, her love for him is all the stronger because she has no claim upon him – no claim of kinship, that is, but simply the claim of love. Love cannot prove its claim by any document which society accepts, and does not wish to prove it; it merely worships with double passion its life's uncertain treasure. Thus, all the widow's thwarted love went out towards this little child. One night in Sraban Kadambini died suddenly. For some reason her heart stopped beating. Everywhere else the world held on its course; only in this gentle little breast, suffering with love, the watch of time stood still for ever.

Lest they should be harassed by the police, four of the zamindar's Brahmin servants took away the body, without ceremony, to be burned. The burning-ground of Ranihat was very far from the village. There was a hut beside a tank, a huge banyan near it, and nothing more. Formerly a river, now completely dried up, ran through the ground, and a part of the watercourse had been dug out to make a tank for the performance of funeral rites. The people considered the tank as part of the river and reverenced it as such.

Taking the body into the hut, the four men sat down to wait for the wood. The time seemed so long that two of the four grew restless, and went to see why it did not come. Nitai and Gurucharan being gone, Bidhu and Banamali remained to watch over the body.

It was a dark night of Sraban. Heavy clouds hung in a starless sky. The two men sat silent in the dark room. Their matches and lamp were useless. The matches were damp, and would not light, for all their efforts, and the lantern went out. After a long silence, one said, "Brother, it would be good if we had a bowl of tobacco. In our hurry we brought none."

The other answered, "I can run and bring all we want."

Understanding why Banamali wanted to go, (from fear of ghosts, the burning-ground being considered haunted) Bidhu said, "I daresay! Meanwhile, I suppose I am to sit here alone!

Conversation ceased again. Five minutes seemed like an hour. In their minds they cursed the two, who had gone to fetch the wood, and they began to suspect that they sat gossiping in some pleasant nook. There was no sound anywhere, except the incessant noise of frogs and crickets from the tank. Then, suddenly they fancied that the bed shook slightly, as if the dead body had turned on its side. Bidhu and Banamali trembled, and began muttering, "Ram, Ram." A deep sigh was heard in the room. In a moment the watchers leapt out of the hut, and raced for the village. After running about three miles, they met their colleagues coming back with a lantern. As a matter of fact, they had gone to smoke, and knew nothing about the wood. But they declared that a tree had been cut down, and that, when it was split up, it would be brought along at once. Then, Bidhu and Banamali told them what had happened in the hut. Nitai and Gurucharan scoffed at the story, and abused Bidhu and Banamali angrily for leaving their duty.

Without delay all four returned to the hut. As they entered, they saw at once that the body was gone; nothing but an empty bed remained. They stared at one another. Could a jackal have taken it? But there was no scrap of clothing anywhere. Going outside, they saw that on the mud that had collected at the door of the hut there were a woman s tiny footprints, newly made. Saradasankar was no fool, and they could hardly persuade him to believe in this ghost story. So after much discussion the four decided that it would be best to say that the body had been burnt.

Towards dawn, when the men with the wood arrived they were told that, owing to their delay, the work had been done without them; there had been some wood in the hut after all. No one was likely to question this, since a dead body is not such a valuable property that any one would steal it.

II

Everyone knows that, even when there is no sign, life is often secretly present, and may begin again in an apparently dead body. Kadambini was not dead; only the machine of her life had for some reason suddenly stopped.

When consciousness returned, she saw dense darkness on all sides. It occurred to her that she was not lying in her usual place. She called out "Sister," but no answer came from the darkness. As she sat up, terror-stricken, she remembered her death-bed, the sudden pain at her breast, the beginning of a choking sensation. Her elder sister-in-law was warming some milk for the child, when Kadambini became faint, and fell on the bed, saying with a choking voice, "Sister, bring the child here. I am worried." After that everything was black, as when an ink-pot is upset over an exercise-book. Kadambini's memory and consciousness, all the letters of the world's book, in a moment became formless. The widow could not remember whether the child, in the sweet voice of love, called her "Auntie," as if for the last time, or not; she could not remember whether, as she left the world she knew for death's endless unknown journey, she had received a parting gift of affection, love's passage-money for the silent land. At first, I fancy, she thought the lonely dark place was the House of Yama, where there is nothing to see, nothing to hear, nothing to do, only an eternal watch. But when a cold damp wind drove through the open door, and she heard the croaking of frogs, she remembered vividly and in a moment all the rains of her short life, and could feel her kinship with the earth. Then, came a flash of lightning, and she saw the tank, the banyan, the great plain, the far-off trees. She remembered how at full moon she had sometimes come to bathe in this tank, and how dreadful death had seemed when she saw a corpse on the burning-ground.

Her first thought was to return home. But then, she reflected, "I am dead. How can I return home? That would bring disaster on them. I have left the kingdom of the living; I am my own ghost!" If this were not so, she reasoned, how could she have got out of Saradasankar's well-guarded zenana, and come to this distant burning-ground at midnight? Also, if her funeral rites had not been finished, where had the men gone who should burn her? Recalling her death-moment in Saradasankar's brightly-lit house, she now found herself alone in a distant, deserted, dark burning-ground. Surely she was no member of earthly society! Surely, she was a creature of horror, of ill-omen, her own ghost!

At this thought, all the bonds were snapped which bound her to the world. She felt that she had marvellous strength, endless freedom. She could do what she liked, go where she pleased. Mad with the inspiration of this new idea, she rushed from the hut like a gust of wind, and stood upon the burning-ground. All trace of shame or fear had left her.

But as she walked on and on, her feet grew tired, her body weak. The plain stretched on endlessly; here and there were paddy-fields; sometimes she found herself standing knee-deep in water.

At the first glimmer of dawn she heard one or two birds cry from the bamboo-clumps by the distant houses. Then, terror seized her. She could not tell in what new relation she stood to the earth and to living folk. So long as she had been on the plain, on the burning-ground, covered by the dark night of Sraban, so long she had been fearless, a denizen of her own kingdom. By daylight the homes of men filled her with fear. Men and ghosts dread each other, for their tribes inhabit different banks of the river of death.

III

Her clothes were clotted in the mud; strange thoughts and walking by night had given her the aspect of a madwoman; truly, her apparition was such that folk might have been afraid of her, and children might have stoned her or run away. Luckily, the first to catch sight of her was a traveller. He came up, and said, "Mother, you look a respectable woman. Wherever are you going, alone and in this guise?"

Kadambini, unable to collect her thoughts, stared at him in silence. She could not think that she was still in touch with the world, that she looked like a respectable woman, that a traveller was asking her questions.

Again the man said, "Come, mother, I will see you home. Tell me where you live."

Kadambini thought. To return to her father-in-law's house would be absurd, and she had no father's house. Then, she remembered the friend of her childhood. She had not seen Jogmaya since the days of her youth, but from time to time they had exchanged letters. Occasionally, there had been quarrels between them, as was only right, since Kadambini wished to make it clear that her love for Jogmaya was unbounded, while her friend complained that Kadambini did not return a love equal to her own. They were both sure that, if they once met, they would be inseparable.

Kadambini said to the traveller, "I will go to Sripati's house at Nisindapur."

As he was going to Calcutta, Nisindapur, though not near, was on his way. So he took Kadambini to Sripati's house, and the friends met again. At first they did not recognise one another, but gradually each recognised the features of the other's childhood.

"What luck!" said Jogmaya. "I never dreamt that I should see you again. But how have you come here, sister? Your father-in-law's folk surely didn't let you go!"

Kadambini remained silent, and at last said, "Sister, do not ask about my father-in-law. Give me a corner, and treat me as a servant, I will do your work."

"What?" cried Jogmaya. "Keep you like a servant! Why, you are my closest friend, you are my so on and so on."

Just then, Sripati came in. Kadambini stared at him for some time, and then, went out very slowly. She kept her head uncovered, and showed not the slightest modesty or respect. Jogmaya, fearing that Sripati would be prejudiced against her friend, began an elaborate explanation. But Sripati, who readily agreed to anything Jogmaya said, cut short her story, and left his wife uneasy in her mind.

Kadambini had come, but she was not at one with her friend, death was between them. She could feel no intimacy for others so long as her existence perplexed her and consciousness remained. Kadambini would look at Jogmaya, and brood. She would think, "She has her husband and her work, she lives in a world far away from mine. She shares affection and duty with the people of the world; I am an empty shadow. She is among the living; I am in eternity."

Jogmaya also was uneasy, but could not explain why. Women do not love mystery because though uncertainty may be transmuted into poetry, into heroism, into scholarship, it cannot be turned to account in household work. So when a woman cannot understand a thing, she either destroys and forgets it, or she shapes it anew for her own use; if she fails to deal with it in one of these ways, she loses her temper with it. The greater Kadambini's abstraction became, the more impatient was Jogmaya with her, wondering what trouble weighed upon her mind.

Then, a new danger arose. Kadambini was afraid of herself; yet she could not flee from herself. Those who fear ghosts fear those who are behind them; wherever they cannot see there is fear. But Kadambini's chief terror lay in herself, for she dreaded nothing external. At the dead of night, when alone in her room, she screamed; in the evening, when she saw her shadow in the lamp-light, her whole body shook. Watching her fearfulness, the rest of the house fell into a sort of terror. The servants and Jogmaya herself began to see ghosts.

One midnight, Kadambini came out from her bedroom weeping, and wailed at Jogmaya's door, "Sister, sister, let me lie at your feet! Do not put me by myself!"

Jogmaya's anger was no less than her fear. She would have liked to drive Kadambini from the house that very second. The good-natured Sripati, after much effort, succeeded in quieting their guest, and put her in the next room.

Next day Sripati was unexpectedly summoned to his wife's apartments. She began to upbraid him, "You, do you call yourself a man? A woman runs away from her father-in-law, and enters your house; a month passes, and you haven't hinted that she should go away, nor have I heard the slightest protest from you. I should take it as a favour if you would explain yourself. You men are all alike."

Men, as a race, have a natural partiality for womankind in general, for which women themselves hold them accountable. Although Sripati was prepared to touch Jogmaya's body, and swear that his kind feeling towards the helpless but beautiful Kadambini was no whit greater than it should be, he could not prove it by his behaviour. He thought that her father-in-law's people must have treated this forlorn widow abominably, if she could bear it no longer, and was driven to take refuge with him. As she had neither father nor mother, how could he desert her? So saying, he let the matter drop, for he had no mind to distress Kadambini by asking her unpleasant questions.

His wife, then, tried other means of attack upon her sluggish lord, until at last he saw that for the sake of peace he must send word to Kadambini's father-in-law. The result of a letter, he thought, might not be satisfactory; so he resolved to go to Ranihat, and act on what he learnt.

So Sripati went, and Jogmaya on her part said to Kadambini, "Friend, it hardly seems proper for you to stop here any longer. What will people say?"

Kadambini stared solemnly at Jogmaya, and said, "What have I to do with people?"

Jogmaya was astounded. Then, she said sharply, "If you have nothing to do with people, we have. How can we explain the detention of a woman belonging to another house?"

Kadambini said, "Where is my father-in-law's house?"

"Confound it!" thought Jogmaya. "What will the wretched woman say next?"

Very slowly Kadambini said, "What have I to do with you? Am I of the earth? You laugh, weep, love; each grips and holds his own; I merely look. You are human, I a shadow. I cannot understand why God has kept me in this world of yours."

So strange were her look and speech that Jogmaya understood something of her drift, though not all. Unable either to dismiss her, or to ask her any more questions, she went away, oppressed with thought.

IV

It was nearly ten o'clock at night when Sripati returned from Ranihat. The earth was drowned in torrents of rain. It seemed that the downpour would never stop, that the night would never end.

Jogmaya asked, "Well?"

"I've lots to say, presently."

So saying, Sripati changed his clothes, and sat down to supper; then, he lay down for a smoke. His mind was perplexed.

His wife stifled her curiosity for a long time; then, she came to his couch and demanded, "What did you hear?

"That you have certainly made a mistake."

Jogmaya was nettled. Women never make mistakes, or, if they do, a sensible man never mentions them; it is better to take them on his own shoulders. Jogmaya snapped, "May I be permitted to hear how?"

Sripati replied, "The woman you have taken into your house is not your Kadambini."

Hearing this, she was greatly annoyed, especially since it was her husband who said it. "What! I don't know my own friend? I must come to you to recognise her! You are clever, indeed!"

Sripati explained that there was no need to quarrel about his cleverness. He could prove what he said. There was no doubt that Jogmaya's Kadambini was dead.

Jogmaya replied, "Listen! You've certainly made some huge mistake. You've been to the wrong house, or are confused as to what you have heard. Who told you to go yourself? Write a letter, and everything will be cleared up."

Sripati was hurt by his wife's lack of faith in his executive ability; he produced all sorts of proof, without result. Midnight found them still asserting and contradicting. Although they were both agreed now that Kadambini should be got out of the house, although Sripati believed that their guest had deceived his wife all the time by a pretended acquaintance, and Jogmaya that she was a prostitute, yet in the present discussion neither would acknowledge defeat. By degrees their voices became so loud that they forgot that Kadambini was sleeping in the next room.

The one said, "We're in a nice fix! I tell you, I heard it with my own ears!" And the other answered angrily, "What do I care about that? I can see with my own eyes, surely."

At length Jogmaya said, "Very well. Tell me when Kadambini died." She thought that if she could find a discrepancy between the day of death and the date of some letter from Kadambini, she could prove that Sripati erred.

He told her the date of Kadambini's death, and they both saw that it fell on the very day before she came to their house. Jogmaya's heart trembled, and even Sripati was not unmoved.

Just then, the door flew open; a damp wind swept in and blew the lamp out. The darkness rushed after it, and filled the whole house. Kadambini stood in the room. It was nearly one o'clock, and the rain was pelting outside.

Kadambini spoke, "Friend, I am your Kadambini, but I am no longer living. I am dead."

Jogmaya screamed with terror; Sripati could not speak.

"But, save in being dead, I have done you no wrong. If I have no place among the living, I have none among the dead. Oh! Whither shall I go?" Crying as if to wake the sleeping Creator in the dense night of rain, she asked again, "Oh! Whither shall I go?"

So saying Kadambini left her friend fainting in the dark house, and went out into the world, seeking her own place.

V

It is hard to say how Kadambini reached Ranihat. At first she showed herself to no one, but spent the whole day in a ruined temple, starving. When the untimely afternoon of the rains was pitch-black, and people huddled into their houses for fear of the impending storm, then, Kadambini came forth. Her heart trembled as she reached her father-in-law's house; and when, drawing a thick veil over her face, she entered, none of the doorkeepers objected, since they took her for a servant. And the rain was pouring down, and the wind howled.

The mistress, Saradasankar's wife, was playing cards with her widowed sister. A servant was in the kitchen, the sick child was sleeping in the bedroom. Kadambini, escaping everyone's notice, entered this room. I do not know why she had come to her father-in-law's house; she herself did not know; she felt only that she wanted to see her child again. She had no thought where to go next, or what to do.

In the lighted room she saw the child sleeping, his fists clenched, his body wasted with fever. At sight of him, her heart became parched and thirsty. If only she could press that tortured body to her breast! Immediately the thought followed, "I do not exist. Who would see it? His mother loves company, loves gossip and cards. All the time that she left me in charge, she was herself free from anxiety, nor was she troubled about him in the least. Who will look after him now as I did?"

The child turned on his side, and cried, half-asleep, "Auntie, give me water." Her darling had not yet forgotten his auntie! In a fever of excitement, she poured out some water, and, taking him to her breast, she gave it him.

As long as he was asleep, the child felt no strangeness in taking water from the accustomed hand. But when Kadambini satisfied her long-starved longing, and kissed him and began rocking him asleep again, he awoke and embraced her. "Did you die, Auntie?" he asked.

"Yes, darling."

"And you have come back? Do not die again."

Before she could answer disaster overtook her. One of the maidservants coming in with a cup of sago dropped it, and fell down. At the crash the mistress left her cards, and entered the room. She stood like a pillar of wood, unable to flee or speak. Seeing all this, the child, too, became terrified, and burst out weeping, "Go away, auntie," he said, "go away!"

Now at last Kadambini understood that she had not died. The old room, the old things, the same child, the same love, all returned to their living state, without change or difference between her and them. In her friend's house she had felt that her childhood's companion was dead. In her child's room she knew that the boy's "auntie" was not dead at all. In anguished tones she said, "Sister, why do you dread me? See, I am as you knew me."

Her sister-in-law could endure no longer, and fell into a faint. Saradasankar himself entered the zenana. With folded hands, he said piteously, "Is this right? Satish is my only son. Why do you show yourself to him? Are we not your own kin since you went, he has wasted away daily; his fever has been incessant; day and night he cries, "Auntie, Auntie, you have left the world; break these bonds of maya. We will perform all funeral honours."

Kadambini could bear no more. She said, "Oh, I am not dead, I am not dead. Oh, how can I persuade you that I am not dead? I am living, living!" She lifted a brass pot from the ground and dashed it against her forehead. The blood ran from her brow. "Look!" she cried, "I am living!" Saradasankar stood like an image; the child screamed with fear, the two fainting women lay still.

Then, Kadambini, shouting "I am not dead, I am not dead," went down the steps to the zenana well, and plunged in. From the upper storey Saradasankar heard the splash.

All night the rain poured; it poured next day at dawn, was pouring still at noon. By dying, Kadambini had given proof that she was not dead.

11

"We Crown Thee King"

When Nabendu Shekhar was wedded to Arunlekha, the God of marriage smiled from behind the sacrificial fire. Alas! What is sport for the gods is not always a joke to us poor mortals.

Purnendu Shekhar, the father of Nabendu, was a man well known amongst the English Officials of the Government. In the voyage of life he had arrived at the desert shores of Rai Bahadurship by diligently plying his oars of salaams. He held in reserve enough for further advancement, but at the age of fifty-five, his tender gaze still fixed on the misty peak of Raja-hood, he suddenly found himself transported to a region where earthly honours and decorations are naught, and his salaam-wearied neck found everlasting repose on the funeral pyre.

According to modern science, force is not destroyed, but is merely converted to another form, and applied to another point. So Purnendu's salaam-force, constant handmaid of the fickle Goddess of Fortune, descended from the shoulder of the father to that of his worthy son; and the youthful head of Nabendu Shekhar began to move up and down, at the doors of high-placed Englishmen, like a pumpkin swayed by the wind.

The traditions of the family into which he had married were entirely different. Its eldest son, Pramathanath, had won for himself the love of his kinsfolk and the regard of all who knew him. His kinsmen and his neighbours looked up to him as their ideal in all things.

Pramathanath was a Bachelor of Arts, and in addition was gifted with common sense. But he held no high official position; he had no handsome salary; nor did he exert any influence with his pen. There was no one in power to lend him a helping hand, because he desired to keep away from Englishmen, as much as they desired to keep away from him. So it happened that he shone only within the sphere of his family and his friends, and excited no admiration beyond it.

Yet this Pramathanath had once sojourned in England for some three years. The kindly treatment he received during his stay there overpowered him so much that he forgot the sorrow and the humiliation of his own country, and came back dressed in European clothes. This rather grieved his brothers and his sisters at first, but after a few days they began to think that European clothes suited nobody better, and gradually they came to share his pride and dignity.

On his return from England, Pramathanath resolved that he would show the world how to associate with Anglo-Indians on terms of equality. Those of our countrymen who think that no such association is possible, unless we bend our knees to them, showed their utter lack of self-respect, and were also unjust to the English – so thought Pramathanath.

He brought with him letters of introduction from many distinguished Englishmen at home, and these gave him some recognition in Anglo-Indian society. He and his wife occasionally enjoyed English hospitality at tea, dinner, sports and other entertainments. Such good luck intoxicated him, and began to produce a tingling sensation in every vein of his body.

About this time, at the opening of a new railway line, many of the town, proud recipients of official favour, were invited by the Lieutenant-Governor to take the first trip. Pramathanath was among them. On the return journey, a European Sergeant of the Police expelled some Indian gentlemen from a railway-carriage with great insolence. Pramathanath, dressed in his European clothes, was there. He, too, was getting out, when the Sergeant said,

"You needn't move, Sir. Keep your seat, please." At first Pramathanath felt flattered at the special respect thus, shown to him. When, however, the train went on, the dull rays of the setting sun, at the west of the fields, now ploughed up and stripped of green, seemed in his eyes to spread a glow of shame over the whole country. Sitting near the window of his lonely compartment, he seemed to catch a glimpse of the down-cast eyes of his Motherland, hidden behind the trees. As Pramathanath sat there, lost in reverie, burning tears flowed down his cheeks, and his heart burst with indignation.

He now remembered the story of a donkey who was drawing the chariot of an idol along the street. The wayfarers bowed down to the idol, and touched the dusty ground with their foreheads. The foolish donkey imagined that all this reverence was being shown to him. "The only difference," said Pramathanath to himself, "Between the donkey and myself is this, I understand to-day that the respect I receive is not given to me but to the burden on my back."

Arriving home, Pramathanath called together all the children of the household, and lighting a big bonfire, threw all his European clothes into it one by one. The children danced round and round it, and the higher the flames shot up, the greater was their merriment. After that, Pramathanath gave up his sip of tea and bits of toast in Anglo-Indian houses, and once again sat inaccessible within the castle of his house, while his insulted friends went about from the door of one Englishman to that of another, bending their turbaned heads as before.

By an irony of fate, poor Nabendu Shekhar married the second daughter of this house. His sisters-in-law were well educated and handsome. Nabendu considered he had made a lucky bargain. But he lost no time in trying to impress on the family that it was a rare bargain on their side also. As if by mistake, he would often hand to his sisters-in-law sundry letters that his late father had received from Europeans. And when the cherry lips of those young ladies smiled sarcastically, and the point of a shining dagger peeped out of its sheath of red velvet, the unfortunate man saw his folly, and regretted it.

Labanyalekha, the eldest sister, surpassed the rest in beauty and cleverness. Finding an auspicious day, she put on the mantel-shelf of Nabendu's bedroom two pairs of English boots, daubed with vermilion, and arranged flowers, sandal-paste, incense and a couple of burning candles before them in true ceremonial fashion. When Nabendu came in, the two sisters-in-law stood on either side of him, and said with mock solemnity, "Bow down to your gods, and may you prosper through their blessings."

The third sister, Kiranlekha, spent many days in embroidering with red silk one hundred common English names such as Jones, Smith, Brown, Thomson, etc., on a chadar. When it was ready, she presented this namavali to Nabendu Shekhar with great ceremony.

The fourth, Sasankalekha, of tender age and therefore, of no account, said, "I will make you a string of beads, brother, with which to tell the names of your gods – the Sahebs." Her sisters reproved her, saying, "Run away, you saucy girl."

Feelings of shame and irritation assailed by turns the mind of Nabendu Shekhar. Still he could not forego the company of his sisters-in-law, especially as the eldest one was beautiful. Her honey was no less than her gall, and Nabendu's mind tasted at once the sweetness of the one and the bitterness of the other. The butterfly, with its bruised wings, buzzes round the flower in blind fury, unable to depart.

The society of his sisters-in-law so much infatuated him that at last Nabendu began to disavow his craving for European favours. When he went to salaam the Burra Saheb, he used to pretend that he was going to listen to a speech by Mr. Surendranath Banerjea. When he went to the railway station to pay respects to the Chhota Saheb, returning from Darjeeling, he would tell his sisters-in-law that he expected his youngest uncle.

It was a sore trial to the unhappy man placed between the cross-fires of his Sahebs and his sisters-in-law. The sisters-in-law, however, secretly vowed that they would not rest till the Sahebs had been put to rout.

About this time, it was rumoured that Nabendu's name would be included in the forthcoming list of Birthday honours, and that he would mount the first step of the ladder to Paradise by becoming a Rai Bahadur. The poor fellow had not the courage to break the joyful news to his sisters-in-law. One evening, however, when the autumn moon was flooding the earth with its mischievous beams, Nabendu's heart was so full that he could not contain himself any longer, and he told his wife. The next day, Mrs. Nabendu betook herself to her eldest sister's house in a palanquin, and in a voice choked with tears bewailed her lot.

"He isn't going to grow a tail," said Labanya, "By becoming a Rai Bahadur, is he? Why should you feel so very humiliated?"

"Oh, no, Sister dear," replied Arunlekha, "I am prepared to be anything – but not a Rai-Bahadurni." The fact was that in her circle of acquaintances there was one Bhutnath Babu, who was a Rai Bahadur, and that explained her intense aversion to that title.

Labanya said to her sister in soothing tones,

"Don't be upset about it, dear; I will see what I can do to prevent it."

Babu Nilratan, the husband of Labanya, was a pleader at Buxar. When the autumn was over, Nabendu received an invitation from Labanya to pay them a visit, and he started for Buxar greatly pleased.

The early winter of the western province endowed Labanyalekha with new health and beauty, and brought a glowing colour to her pale cheeks. She looked like the flower-laden kasa reeds on a clear autumn day, growing by the lonely bank of a rivulet. To Nabendu's enchanted eyes she appeared like a malati plant in full blossom, showering dew-drops brilliant with the morning light.

Nabendu had never felt better in his life. The exhilaration of his own health and the genial company of his pretty sister-in-law made him think himself light enough to tread on air. The Ganges in front of the garden seemed to him to be flowing ceaselessly to regions unknown, as though it gave shape to his own wild fantasies.

As he returned in the early morning from his walk on the bank of the river, the mellow rays of the winter sun gave his whole frame that pleasing sensation of warmth which lovers feel in each other's arms. Coming home, he would now and then, find his sister-in-law amusing herself by cooking some dishes. He would offer his help, and display his want of skill and ignorance at every step. But Nabendu did not appear to be at all anxious to improve himself by practice and attention. On the contrary he thoroughly enjoyed the rebukes he received from his sister-in-law. He was at great pains to prove every day that he was inefficient and helpless as a new-born babe in mixing spices, handling the saucepan, and regulating the heat so as to prevent things getting burnt and he was duly rewarded with pitiful smiles and scoldings.

In the middle of the day he ate a great deal of the good food set before him, incited by his keen appetite and the coaxing of his sister-in-law. Later on, he would sit down to a game of cards – at which he betrayed the same lack of ability. He would cheat, pry into his adversary's hand, quarrel – but never did he win a single rubber, and worse still, he would not acknowledge defeat. This brought him abuse every day, and still he remained incorrigible.

There was, however, one matter in which his reform was complete. For the time at least, he had forgotten that to win the smiles of Sahebs was the final goal of life. He was beginning to understand how happy and worthy we might feel by winning the affection and esteem of those near and dear to us.

Besides, Nabendu was now moving in a new atmosphere. Labanya's husband, Babu Nilratan, a leader of the bar, was reproached by many, because he refused to pay his respects to European officials. To all such reproaches Nilratan would reply, "No, thank you – if they are not polite enough to return my call – then, the politeness I offer them is a loss that can never be made up for. The sands of the desert may be very white and shiny, but I would much rather sow my seeds in black soil, where I can expect a return."

And Nabendu began to adopt similar ideas, all regardless of the future. His chance of Rai Bahadurship throve on the soil carefully prepared by his late father and also by himself in days gone by, nor was any fresh watering required. Had he not at great expense laid out a splendid race-course in a town, which was a fashionable resort of Europeans?

When the time of Congress drew near, Nilratan received a request from head-quarters to collect subscriptions. Nabendu, free from anxiety, was merrily engaged in a game of cards with his sister-in-law, when Nilratan Babu came upon him with a subscription-book in his hand, and said, "Your signature, please."

From old habit, Nabendu looked horrified. Labanya, assuming an air of great concern and anxiety said, "Never do that. It would ruin your race-course beyond repair."

Nabendu blurted out, "Do you suppose I pass sleepless nights through fear of that?"

"We won't publish your name in the papers," said Nilratan reassuringly.

Labanya, looking grave and anxious said,

"Still, it wouldn't be safe. Things spread so, from mouth to mouth."

Nabendu replied with vehemence, "My name wouldn't suffer by appearing in the newspapers." So saying, he snatched the subscription list from Nilratan's hand, and signed away a thousand rupees. Secretly, he hoped that the papers would not publish the news.

Labanya struck her forehead with her palm and gasped out, "What – have you – done?"

"Nothing wrong," said Nabendu boastfully.

"But – but –," drawled Labanya, "the Guard Saheb of Sealdah Station, the shop-assistant at Whiteaway's, the Syce Saheb of Hart Bros – these gentlemen might be angry with you, and decline to come to your Poojah dinner to drink your champagne, you know. Just think, they mightn't pat you on the back, when you meet them again!"

"It wouldn't break my heart," Nabendu snapped out.

A few days passed. One morning, Nabendu was sipping his tea, and glancing at a newspaper. Suddenly a letter signed "X" caught his eye. The writer thanked him profusely for his donation, and declared that the increase of strength the Congress had acquired by having such a man within its fold, was inestimable.

Alas, father Purnendu Shekhar! Was it to increase the strength of the Congress, that you brought this wretch into the world?

But the cloud of misfortune had its silver lining. That he was not a mere cypher was clear from the fact that the Anglo-Indian community on the one side and the Congress on the other were each waiting patiently, eager to hook him, and land him on their own side. So Nabendu, beaming with pleasure, took the paper to his sister-in-law, and showed her the letter. Looking as though she knew nothing about it, Labanya exclaimed in surprise, "Oh, what a pity! Everything has come out! Who bore you such ill-will? Oh, how cruel of him, how wicked of him!"

Nabendu laughed out, saying, "Now – now – don't call him names, Labanya. I forgive him with all my heart, and bless him too."

A couple of days after this, an anti-Congress Anglo-Indian paper reached Nabendu through the post. There was a letter in it, signed – "One who knows," and contradicting the above report. "Those who have the pleasure of Babu Nabendu Shekhar's personal acquaintance," the writer went on, "cannot for a moment believe this absurd libel to be true. For him to turn a Congresswalla is as impossible as it is for the leopard to change his spots. He is a man of genuine worth, and neither a disappointed candidate for Government employ nor a briefless barrister. He is not one of those who, after a brief sojourn in England, return aping our dress and manners, audaciously try to thrust themselves on Anglo-Indian society, and finally go back in dejection. So there is absolutely no reason why Babu Nabendu Shekhar, etc, etc"

Ah, father Purnendu Shekhar! What a reputation you had made with the Europeans before you died!

This letter also was paraded before his sister-in-law, for did it not assert that he was no mean, contemptible scallywag, but a man of real worth?

Labanya exclaimed again in feigned surprise, "Which of your friends wrote it now? Oh, come – is it the Ticket Collector, or the hide merchant, or is it the drum-major of the Fort?"

"You ought to send in a contradiction, I think," said Nilratan.

"Is it necessary?" said Nabendu loftily. "Must I contradict every little thing they choose to say against me?"

Labanya filled the room with a deluge of laughter. Nabendu felt a little disconcerted at this, and said, "Why? What's the matter?" She went on laughing, unable to check herself, and her youthful slender form waved to and fro. This torrent of merriment had the effect of overthrowing Nabendu completely, and he said in pitiable accents, "Do you imagine that I am afraid to contradict it?"

"Oh, dear, no," said Labanya, "I was thinking that you haven't yet ceased trying to save that race-course of yours, so full of promise. While there is life, there is hope, you know."

"That's what I am afraid of, you think, do you? Very well, you shall see," said Nabendu desperately, and forthwith sat down to write his contradiction. When he had finished, Labanya and Nilratan read it through, and said, "It isn't strong enough. We must give it them pretty hot, mustn't we?" And they kindly undertook to revise the composition. Thus, it ran, "When one connected to us by ties of blood turns our enemy he becomes far more dangerous than any outsider. To the Government of India, the haughty Anglo-Indians are worse enemies than the Russians or the frontier Pathans themselves – they are the impenetrable barrier – forever hindering the growth of any bond of friendship between the Government and people of the country. It is the Congress which has opened up the royal road to a better understanding between the rulers and the ruled, and the Anglo-Indian papers have planted themselves like thorns across the whole breadth of that road, etc., etc."

Nabendu had an inward fear as to the mischief this letter might do, but at the same time he felt elated at the excellence of its composition, which he fondly imagined to be his own. It was duly published, and for some days comments, replies, and rejoinders went on in various newspapers, and the air was full of trumpet-notes, proclaiming the fact that Nabendu had joined the Congress, and the amount of his subscription.

Nabendu, now grown desperate, talked as though he was a patriot of the fiercest type. Labanya laughed inwardly, and said to herself, "Well – well – you have to pass through the ordeal of fire yet."

One morning, when Nabendu, before his bath, had finished rubbing oil over his chest, and was trying various devices to reach the inaccessible portions of his back, the bearer brought in a card inscribed with the name of the District Magistrate himself! Good heavens! What would he do? He could not possibly go, and receive the Magistrate Saheb, thus, oil-besmeared. He shook and twitched like a koi-fish, ready dressed for the frying pan. He finished his bath in a great hurry, tugged on his clothes somehow, and ran breathlessly to the outer apartments. The bearer said that the Saheb had just left after waiting for a long time. How much of the blame for concocting this drama of invented incidents may be set down to Labanya, and how much to the bearer is a nice problem for ethical mathematics to solve.

Nabendu's heart was convulsed with pain within his breast, like the tail of a lizard just cut off. He moped like an owl all day long.

Labanya banished all traces of inward merriment from her face, and kept on enquiring in anxious tones, "What has happened to you? You are not ill, I hope?"

Nabendu made great efforts to smile, and find a humorous reply. "How can there be," he managed to say, "any illness within your jurisdiction, since you yourself are the Goddess of Health?"

But the smile soon flickered out. His thoughts were, "I subscribed to the Congress fund to begin with, published a nasty letter in a newspaper, and on the top of that, when the Magistrate Saheb himself did me the honour to call on me, I kept him waiting. I wonder what he is thinking of me."

Alas, father Purnendu Shekhar, by an irony of Fate I am made to appear what I am not.

The next morning, Nabendu decked himself in his best clothes, wore his watch and chain, and put a big turban on his head.

"Where are you off to?" enquired his sister-in-law.

"Urgent business," Nabendu replied. Labanya kept quiet.

Arriving at the Magistrate's gate, he took out his card-case.

"You cannot see him now," said the orderly peon icily.

Nabendu took out a couple of rupees from his pocket. The peon at once salaamed him and said, "There are five of us, Sir." Immediately Nabendu pulled out a ten-rupee note, and handed it to him.

He was sent for by the Magistrate, who was writing in his dressing-gown and bedroom slippers. Nabendu salaamed him. The Magistrate pointed to a chair with his finger, and without raising his eyes from the paper before him said, "What can I do for you, Babu?" Fingering his watch-chain nervously, Nabendu said in shaky tones, "Yesterday you were good enough to call at my place, Sir." The Saheb knitted his brows, and, lifting just one eye from his paper, said, "I called at your place! Babu, what nonsense are you talking?"

"Beg your pardon, Sir," faltered out Nabendu. "There has been a mistake, some confusion," and wet with perspiration, he tumbled out of the room somehow. And that night, as he lay tossing on his bed, a distant dream-like voice came into his ear with a recurring persistency, "Babu, you are a howling idiot."

On his way home, Nabendu came to the conclusion that the Magistrate denied having called, simply because he was highly offended.

So he explained to Labanya that he had been out purchasing rose-water. No sooner had he uttered the words than half-a-dozen chaprassis wearing the Collectorate badge made their appearance, and after salaaming Nabendu, stood there grinning.

"Have they come to arrest you because you subscribed to the Congress fund?" whispered Labanya with a smile.

The six peons displayed a dozen rows of teeth and said, "Bakshish – Babu Saheb."

From a side room Nilratan came out, and said in an irritated manner, "Bakshish? What for?"

The peons, grinning as before, answered, "The Babu Saheb went to see the Magistrate – so we have come for bakshish."

"I didn't know," laughed out Labanya, "That the Magistrate was selling rose-water nowadays. Coolness wasn't the special feature of his trade before."

Nabendu in trying to reconcile the story of his purchase with his visit to the Magistrate, uttered some incoherent words, which nobody could make sense of.

Nilratan spoke to the peons, "There has been no occasion for bakshish; you shan't have it."

Nabendu said, feeling very small, "Oh, they are poor men – what's the harm of giving them something?" And he took out a currency note. Nilratan snatched it way from Nabendu's hand, remarking, "There are poorer men in the world – I will give it to them for you."

Nabendu felt greatly distressed that he was not able to appease these ghostly retainers of the angry Siva. When the peons were leaving, with thunder in their eyes, he looked at them languishingly, as much as to say, "You know everything, gentlemen, it is not my fault."

The Congress was to be held at Calcutta this year. Nilratan went down thither with his wife to attend the sittings. Nabendu accompanied them.

As soon as they arrived at Calcutta, the Congress party surrounded Nabendu, and their delight and enthusiasm knew no bounds. They cheered him, honoured him, and extolled him up to the skies. Everybody said that, unless leading men like Nabendu devoted themselves to the Cause, there was no hope for the country. Nabendu was disposed to agree with them, and emerged out of the chaos of mistake and confusion as a leader of the country. When he entered the Congress Pavilion on the first day, everybody stood up, and shouted, "Hip, hip, hurrah," in a loud outlandish voice, hearing which our Motherland reddened with shame to the root of her ears.

In due time the Queen's birthday came, and Nabendu's name was not found in the list of Rai Bahadurs.

He received an invitation from Labanya for that evening. When he arrived there, Labanya with great pomp and ceremony presented him with a robe of honour, and with her own hand put a mark of red sandal paste on the middle of his forehead. Each of the other sisters threw round his neck a garland of flowers woven by herself. Decked in a pink Sari and dazzling jewels, his wife

Arunlekha was waiting in a side room, her face lit up with smiles and blushes. Her sisters rushed to her, and, placing another garland in her hand, insisted that she also should come, and do her part in the ceremony, but she would not listen to it; and that principal garland, cherishing a desire for Nabendu's neck, waited patiently for the still secrecy of midnight.

The sisters said to Nabendu, "To-day we crown thee King. Such honour will not be done to anybody else in Hindoostan."

Whether Nabendu derived any consolation from this, he alone can tell; but we greatly doubt it. We believe, in fact, that he will become a Rai Bahadur before he has done, and the Englishman and the Pioneer will write heart-rending articles lamenting his demise at the proper time. So, in the meanwhile, Three Cheers for Babu Purnendu Shekhar! Hip, hip, hurrah – Hip, hip, hurrah – Hip, hip, hurrah.

12

The Renunciation

I

It was a night of full moon early in the month of Phalgun. The youthful spring was everywhere sending forth its breeze laden with the fragrance of mango-blossoms. The melodious notes of an untiring papiya, (one of the sweetest songsters in Bengal. Anglo-Indian writers have nicknamed it the "brain-fever bird," which is a sheer libel) concealed within the thick foliage of an old lichi tree by the side of a tank, penetrated a sleepless bedroom of the Mukerji family. There Hemanta now restlessly twisted a lock of his wife's hair round his finger, now beat her churi against her wristlet until it tinkled, now pulled at the chaplet of flowers about her head, and left it hanging over her face. His mood was that of an evening breeze which played about a favourite flowering shrub, gently shaking her now this side, now that, in the hope of rousing her to animation.

But Kusum sat motionless, looking out of the open window, with eyes immersed in the moonlit depth of never-ending space beyond. Her husband's caresses were lost on her.

At last Hemanta clasped both the hands of his wife, and, shaking them gently, said, "Kusum, where are you? A patient search through a big telescope would reveal you only as a small speck – you seem to have receded so far away. O, do come closer to me, dear. See how beautiful the night is."

Kusum turned her eyes from the void of space towards her husband, and said slowly, "I know a mantra, which could in one moment shatter this spring night and the moon into pieces."

"If you do," laughed Hemanta, "Pray don't utter it. If any mantra of yours could bring three or four Saturdays during the week, and prolong the nights till P. M. the next day, say it by all means."

Saying this, he tried to draw his wife a little closer to him. Kusum, freeing herself from the embrace, said, "Do you know, tonight I feel a longing to tell you what I promised to reveal only on my death-bed. Tonight I feel that I could endure whatever punishment you might inflict on me."

Hemanta was on the point of making a jest about punishments by reciting a verse from Jayadeva, when the sound of an angry pair of slippers was heard approaching rapidly. They were the familiar footsteps of his father, Harihar Mukerji, and Hemanta, not knowing what it meant, was in a flutter of excitement.

Standing outside the door Harihar roared out, "Hemanta, turn your wife out of the house immediately."

Hemanta looked at his wife, and detected no trace of surprise in her features. She merely buried her face within the palms of her hands, and, with all the strength and intensity of her soul, wished that she could then, and there melt into nothingness. It was the same papiya whose song floated into the room with the south breeze, and no one heard it. Endless are the beauties of the earth – but alas, how easily everything is twisted out of shape.

II

Returning from without, Hemanta asked his wife, "Is it true?"

"It is," replied Kusum.

"Why didn't you tell me long ago?"

"I did try many a time, and I always failed. I am a wretched woman."

"Then, tell me everything now."

Kusum gravely told her story in a firm unshaken voice. She waded barefooted through fire, as it were, with slow unflinching steps, and nobody knew how much she was scorched. Having heard her to the end, Hemanta rose and walked out.

Kusum thought that her husband had gone, never to return to her again. It did not strike her as strange. She took it as naturally as any other incident of everyday life – so dry and apathetic had her mind become during the last few moments. Only the world and love seemed to her as a void and make-believe from beginning to end. Even the memory of the protestations of love, which her husband had made to her in days past, brought to her lips a dry, hard, joyless smile, like a sharp cruel knife which had cut through her heart. She was thinking, perhaps, that the love which seemed to fill so much of one's life, which brought in its train such fondness and depth of feeling, which made even the briefest separation so exquisitely painful and a moment's union so intensely sweet, which seemed boundless in its extent and eternal in its duration, the cessation of which could not be imagined even in births to come – that this was that love! So feeble was its support! No sooner does the priesthood touch it than your "eternal" love crumbles into a handful of dust! Only a short while ago Hemanta had whispered to her, "What a beautiful night!" The same night was not yet at an end, the same papiya was still warbling, the same south breeze still blew into the room, making the bed-curtain shiver; the same moonlight lay on the bed next the open window, sleeping like a beautiful heroine exhausted with gaiety. All this was unreal! Love was more falsely dissembling than she herself!

III

The next morning Hemanta, fagged after a sleepless night, and looking like one distracted, called at the house of Peari Shankar Ghosal. "What news, my son?" Peari Shankar greeted him.

Hemanta, flaring up like a big fire, said in a trembling voice, "You have defiled our caste. You have brought destruction upon us. And you will have to pay for it." He could say no more; he felt choked.

"And you have preserved my caste, prevented my ostracism from the community, and patted me on the back affectionately!" said Peari Shankar with a slight sarcastic smile.

Hemanta wished that his Brahmin-fury could reduce Peari Shankar to ashes in a moment, but his rage burnt only himself. Peari Shankar sat before him unscathed, and in the best of health.

"Did I ever do you any harm?" demanded Hemanta in a broken voice.

"Let me ask you one question," said Peari Sankar. "My daughter – my only child – what harm had she done your father? You were very young then, and probably never heard. Listen, then. Now, don't you excite yourself. There is much humour in what I am going to relate.

"You were quite small when my son-in-law, Nabakanta, ran away to England after stealing my daughter's jewels. You might truly remember the commotion in the village when he returned as a barrister five years later. Or, perhaps, you were unaware of it, as you were at school in Calcutta at the time. Your father, arrogating to himself the headship of the community, declared that if I sent my daughter to her husband's home, I must renounce her for good, and never again allow her to cross my threshold. I fell at your father's feet, and implored him, saying, 'Brother, save me this once. I will make the boy swallow cow-dung, and go through the prayaschitta ceremony. Do take him back into caste.' But your father remained obdurate. For my part, I could not disown my only child, and, bidding good-bye to my village and my kinsmen, I betook myself to Calcutta. There, too, my troubles followed me. When I had made every arrangement for my nephew's marriage, your father stirred up the girl's people, and they broke the match off. Then, I took a solemn vow that, if there was a drop of Brahmin blood flowing in my veins, I would avenge myself. You understand the business to some extent now, don't you? But wait a little longer. You will enjoy it, when I tell you the whole story; it is interesting.

"When you were attending college, one Bipradas Chatterji used to live next door to your lodgings. The poor fellow is dead now. In his house lived a child-widow called Kusum, the destitute orphan of a Kayestha gentleman. The girl was very pretty, and the old Brahmin desired to shield her from the hungry gaze of college students. But for a young girl to throw dust in the eyes of her old guardian was not at all a difficult task. She often went to the top of the roof, to hang her washing out to dry, and, I believe, you found your own roof best suited for your studies. Whether you two spoke to each other, when on your respective roofs, I cannot tell, but the girl's behaviour excited suspicion in the old man's mind. She made frequent mistakes in her household duties, and, like Parbati, (the wife of Shiva the Destroyer) engaged in her devotions, began gradually to renounce food and sleep. Some evenings she would burst into tears in the presence of the old gentleman, without any apparent reason.

"At last he discovered that you two saw each other from the roofs pretty frequently, and that you even went the length of absenting yourself from college to sit on the roof at mid-day with a book in your hand, so fond had you grown suddenly of solitary study. Bipradas came to me for advice, and told me everything. 'Uncle,' said I to him, 'For a long while you have cherished a desire to go on a pilgrimage to Benares. You had better do it now, and leave the girl in my charge. I will take care of her.'

"So he went. I lodged the girl in the house of Sripati Chatterji, passing him off as her father. What happened next is known to you. I feel a great relief today, having told you everything from the beginning. It sounds like a romance, doesn't it? I think of turning it into a book, and getting it printed. But I am not a writing-man myself. They say my nephew has some aptitude that way – I will get him to write it for me. But the best thing would be, if you would collaborate with him, because the conclusion of the story is not known to me so well."

Without paying much attention to the concluding remarks of Peari Shankar, Hemanta asked, "Did not Kusum object to this marriage?"

"Well," said Peari Shankar, "It is very difficult to guess. You know, my boy, how women's minds are constituted. When they say 'no,' they mean 'yes.' During the first few days after her removal to the new home, she went almost crazy at not seeing you. You, too, seemed to have discovered her new address somehow, as you used to lose your way after starting for college, and loiter about in front of Sripati's house. Your eyes did not appear to be exactly in search of the Presidency College, as they were directed towards the barred windows of a private house, through which nothing but insects and the hearts of moon-struck young men could obtain access. I felt very sorry for you both. I could see that your studies were being seriously interrupted, and that the plight of the girl was pitiable also.

"One day, I called Kusum to me, and said, 'Listen to me, my daughter. I am an old man, and you need feel no delicacy in my presence. I know whom you desire at heart. The young man's condition is hopeless too. I wish I could bring about your union.' At this Kusum suddenly melted into tears, and ran away. On several evenings after that, I visited Sripati's house, and, calling Kusum to me, discussed with her matters relating to you, and so I succeeded in gradually overcoming her shyness. At last, when I said that I would try to bring about a marriage, she asked me, 'How can it be?' 'Never mind,' I said, 'I would pass you off as a Brahmin maiden.' After a good deal of argument, she begged me to find out whether you would approve of it. 'What nonsense,' replied I, 'The boy is well-nigh mad as it were, what's the use of disclosing all these complications to him? Let the ceremony be over smoothly and then – all's well that ends well. Especially, as there is not the slightest risk of its ever leaking out, why go out of the way to make a fellow miserable for life?'

"I do not know whether the plan had Kusum's assent or not. At times she wept, and at other times she remained silent. If I said, 'Let us drop it then,' she would become very restless. When things were in this state, I sent Sripati to you with the proposal of marriage; you consented without a moment's hesitation. Everything was settled.

"Shortly before the day fixed, Kusum became so obstinate that I had the greatest difficulty in bringing her round again. 'Do let it drop, uncle,' she said to me constantly. 'What do you mean, you silly child,' I rebuked her, 'How can we back out now, when everything has been settled?'

"'Spread a rumour that I am dead,' she implored. 'Send me away somewhere.'

"'What would happen to the young man then?' said I. 'He is now in the seventh heaven of delight, expecting that his long cherished desire would be fulfilled tomorrow; and today you want me to send him the news of your death. The result would be that tomorrow I should have to bear the news of his death to you, and the same evening your death would be reported to me. Do you imagine, child, that I am capable of committing a girl-murder and a Brahmin-murder at my age?'

"Eventually the happy marriage was celebrated at the auspicious moment, and I felt relieved of a burdensome duty which I owed to myself. What happened afterwards you know best."

"Couldn't you stop after having done us an irreparable injury?" burst out Hemanta after a short silence. "Why have you told the secret now?"

With the utmost composure, Peari Shankar replied, "When I saw that all arrangements had been made for the wedding of your sister, I said to myself, 'Well, I have fouled the caste of one Brahmin, but that was only from a sense of duty. Here, another Brahmin's caste is imperilled, and this time it is my plain duty to prevent it.' So I wrote to them saying that I was in a position to prove that you had taken the daughter of a Shudra to wife."

Controlling himself with a gigantic effort, Hemanta said, "What will become of this girl whom I shall abandon now? Would you give her food and shelter?

"I have done what was mine to do," replied Peari Shankar calmly. "It is no part of my duty to look after the discarded wives of other people. Anybody there? Get a glass of coconut milk for Hemanta Babu with ice in it. And some pan too." Hemanta rose, and took his departure without waiting for this luxurious hospitality.

IV

It was the fifth night of the waning of the moon – and the night was dark. No birds were singing. The lichi tree by the tank looked like a smudge of ink on a background a shade less deep. The south wind was blindly roaming about in the darkness like a sleep-walker. The stars in the sky with vigilant unblinking eyes were trying to penetrate the darkness, in their effort to fathom some profound mystery.

No light shone in the bedroom. Hemanta was sitting on the side of the bed next the open window, gazing at the darkness in front of him. Kusum lay on the floor, clasping her husband's feet with both her arms, and her face resting on them. Time stood like an ocean hushed into stillness. On the background of eternal night, Fate seemed to have painted this one single picture for all time – annihilation on every side, the judge in the centre of it, and the guilty one at his feet.

The sound of slippers was heard again. Approaching the door, Harihar Mukerji said, "You have had enough time – I can't allow you more. Turn the girl out of the house."

Kusum, as she heard this, embraced her husband's feet with all the ardour of a lifetime, covered them with kisses, and touching her forehead to them reverentially, withdrew herself.

Hemanta rose, and walking to the door, said,

"Father, I won't forsake my wife."

"What!" roared out Harihar, "Would you lose your caste, Sir?"

"I don't care for caste," was Hemanta's calm reply.

"Then, you too I renounce."

13

Kabuliwala

(THE FRUITSELLER FROM KABUL)

My five years' old daughter Mini cannot live without chattering. I really believe that in all her life she has not wasted a minute in silence. Her mother is often vexed at this, and would stop her prattle, but I would not. To see Mini quiet is unnatural, and I cannot bear it long. And so my own talk with her is always lively.

One morning, for instance, when I was in the midst of the seventeenth chapter of my new novel, my little Mini stole into the room, and putting her hand into mine, said, "Father! Ramdayal the door-keeper calls a crow a krow! He doesn't know anything, does he?"

Before I could explain to her the differences of language in this world, she was embarked on the full tide of another subject. "'What do you think, Father? Bhola says there is an elephant in the clouds, blowing water out of his trunk, and that is why it rains!"

And then, darting off anew, while I sat still making ready some reply to this last saying, "Father! What relation is Mother to you?"

"My dear little sister in the law!" I murmured involuntarily to myself, but with a grave face contrived to answer, "Go and play with Bhola, Mini! I am busy!"

The window of my room overlooks the road. The child had seated herself at my feet near my table, and was playing softly, drumming on her knees. I was hard at work on my seventeenth chapter, where Protap Singh, the hero, had just caught Kanchanlata, the heroine, in his arms, and was about to escape with her by the third story window of the castle, when all of a sudden Mini left her play, and ran to the window, crying, "A Kabuliwala! A Kabuliwala!" Sure enough in the street below was a Kabuliwala, passing slowly along. He wore the loose soiled clothing of his people, with a tall turban; there was a bag on his back, and he carried boxes of grapes in his hand.

I cannot tell what were my daughter's feelings at the sight of this man, but she began to call him loudly. "Ah!" I thought, "he will come in, and my seventeenth chapter will never be finished!" At which exact moment the Kabuliwala turned, and looked up at the child. When she saw this, overcome by terror, she fled to her mother's protection, and disappeared. She had a blind belief that inside the bag, which the big man carried, there were perhaps two or three other children like herself. The pedlar meanwhile entered my doorway, and greeted me with a smiling face.

So precarious was the position of my hero and my heroine, that my first impulse was to stop and buy something, since the man had been called. I made some small purchases, and a conversation began about Abdur Rahman, the Russians, the English, and the Frontier Policy.

As he was about to leave, he asked, "And where is the little girl, Sir?"

And I, thinking that Mini must get rid of her false fear, had her brought out.

She stood by my chair, and looked at the Kabuliwala and his bag. He offered her nuts and raisins, but she would not be tempted, and only clung the closer to me, with all her doubts increased.

This was their first meeting.

One morning, however, not many days later, as I was leaving the house, I was startled to find Mini, seated on a bench near the door, laughing and talking, with the great Kabuliwala at her feet. In all her life, it appeared, my small daughter had never found so patient a listener, save her father, And already the corner of her little sari was stuffed with almonds and raisins, the gift of her visitor. "Why did you give her those?" I said, and taking out an eight-anna bit, I handed it to him. The man accepted the money without demur, and slipped it into his pocket.

Alas, on my return an hour later, I found the unfortunate coin had made twice its own worth of trouble! For the Kabuliwala had given it to Mini, and her mother catching sight of the bright round object, had pounced on the child with, "Where did you get that eight-anna bit?"

"The Kabuliwala gave it me," said Mini cheerfully.

"The Kabuliwala gave it you!" cried her mother much shocked. "Oh, Mini! How could you take it from him?"

I, entering at the moment, saved her from impending disaster, and proceeded to make my own inquiries.

It was not the first or second time, I found, that the two had met. The Kabuliwala had overcome the child's first terror by a judicious bribery of nuts and almonds, and the two were now great friends.

They had many quaint jokes, which afforded them much amusement. Seated in front of him, looking down on his gigantic frame in all her tiny dignity, Mini would ripple her face with laughter, and begin, "O Kabuliwala, Kabuliwala, what have you got in your bag?"

And he would reply, in the nasal accents of the mountaineer, "An elephant!" Not much cause for merriment, perhaps; but how they both enjoyed the witticism! And for me, this child's talk with a grown-up man had always in it something strangely fascinating.

Then, the Kabuliwala, not to be behindhand, would take his turn, "Well, little one, and when are you going to the father-in-law's house?"

Now most small Bengali maidens have heard long ago about the father-in-law's house; but we, being a little new-fangled, had kept these things from our child, and Mini at this question must have been a trifle bewildered. But she would not show it, and with ready tact replied, "Are you going there?"

Amongst men of the Kabuliwala's class, however, it is well known that the words father-in-law's house have a double meaning. It is a euphemism for jail, the place where we are well cared for, at no expense to ourselves. In this sense would the sturdy pedlar take my daughter's question. "Ah," he would say, shaking his fist at an invisible policeman, "I will thrash my father-in-law!" Hearing this, and picturing the poor discomfited relative, Mini would go off into peals of laughter, in which her formidable friend would join.

These were autumn mornings, the very time of year when kings of old went forth to conquest; and I, never stirring from my little corner in Calcutta, would let my mind wander over the whole world. At the very name of another country, my heart would go out to it, and at the sight of a foreigner in the streets, I would fall to weaving a network of dreams, – the mountains, the glens, and the forests of his distant home, with his cottage in its setting, and the free and independent life of far-away wilds. Perhaps the scenes of travel conjure themselves up before me, and pass and repass in my imagination all the more vividly, because I lead such a vegetable existence, that a call to travel would fall upon me like a thunderbolt. In the presence of this Kabuliwala, I was immediately transported to the foot of arid mountain peaks, with narrow little defiles twisting in and out amongst their towering heights. I could see the string of camels bearing the merchandise, and the company of turbaned merchants, carrying some of their queer old firearms, and some of their spears, journeying downward towards the plains. I could see – but at some such point. Mini's mother would intervene, imploring me to "beware of that man."

Mini's mother is unfortunately a very timid lady. Whenever she hears a noise in the street, or sees people coming towards the house, she always jumps to the conclusion that they are either thieves, or drunkards, or snakes, or tigers, or malaria or cockroaches, or caterpillars, or an English sailor. Even after all these years of experience, she is not able to overcome her terror. So she was full of doubts about the Kabuliwala, and used to beg me to keep a watchful eye on him.

I tried to laugh her fear gently away, but then, she would turn round on me seriously, and ask me solemn questions.

Were children never kidnapped?

Was it, then, not true that there was slavery in Kabul?

Was it so very absurd that this big man should be able to carry off a tiny child?

I urged that, though not impossible, it was highly improbable. But this was not enough, and her dread persisted. As it was indefinite, however, it did not seem right to forbid the man the house, and the intimacy went on unchecked.

Once a year in the middle of January, Rahamat, the Kabuliwala, was in the habit of returning to his country, and as the time approached he would be very busy, going from house to house collecting his debts. This year, however, he could always find time to come and see Mini. It would have seemed to an outsider that there was some conspiracy between the two, for when he could not come in the morning, he would appear in the evening.

Even to me it was a little startling now and then, in the corner of a dark room, suddenly to surprise this tall, loose-garmented, much bebagged man; but when Mini would run in smiling, with her, "O! Kabuliwala! Kabuliwala!" and the two friends, so far apart in age, would subside into their old laughter and their old jokes, I felt reassured.

One morning, a few days before he had made up his mind to go, I was correcting my proof sheets in my study. It was chilly weather. Through the window the rays of the sun touched my feet, and the slight warmth was very welcome. It was almost eight o'clock, and the early pedestrians were returning home, with their heads covered. All at once, I heard an uproar in the street, and, looking out, saw Rahamat being led away bound between two policemen, and behind them a crowd of curious boys. There were blood-stains on the clothes of the Kabuliwala, and one of the policemen carried a knife. Hurrying out, I stopped them, and enquired what it all meant. Partly from one, partly from another, I gathered that a certain neighbour had owed the pedlar something for a Rampuri shawl, but had falsely denied having bought it, and that in the course of the quarrel, Rahamat had struck him. Now in the heat of his excitement, the prisoner began calling his enemy all sorts of names, when suddenly in a verandah of my house appeared my little Mini, with her usual exclamation, "O Kabuliwala! Kabuliwala!" Rahamat's face lighted up as he turned to her. He had no bag under his arm today, so she could not discuss the elephant with him. She at once, therefore, proceeded to the next question, "Are you going to the father-in-law's house?" Rahamat laughed and said, "Just where I am going, little one!" Then, seeing that the reply did not amuse the child, he held up his fettered hands. "Ah," he said, "I would have thrashed that old father-in-law, but my hands are bound!"

On a charge of murderous assault, Rahamat was sentenced to some years' imprisonment.

Time passed away, and he was not remembered. The accustomed work in the accustomed place was ours, and the thought of the once-free mountaineer spending his years in prison seldom or never occurred to us. Even my light-hearted Mini, I am ashamed to say, forgot her old friend. New companions filled her life. As she grew older, she spent more of her time with girls. So much time indeed did she spend with them that she came no more, as she used to do, to her father's room. I was scarcely on speaking terms with her.

Years had passed away. It was once more autumn and we had made arrangements for our Mini's marriage. It was to take place during the Puja holidays. With Durga returning to Kailas, the light of our home also was to depart to her husband's house, and leave her father's in the shadow.

The morning was bright. After the rains, there was a sense of ablution in the air, and the sun-rays looked like pure gold. So bright were they that they gave a beautiful radiance even to the sordid brick walls of our Calcutta lanes. Since early dawn today the wedding-pipes had been sounding, and at each beat my own heart throbbed. The wail of the tune, Bhairavi, seemed to intensify my pain at the approaching separation. My Mini was to be married tonight.

From early morning noise and bustle had pervaded the house. In the courtyard the canopy had to be slung on its bamboo poles; the chandeliers with their tinkling sound must be hung in each room and verandah. There was no end of hurry and excitement. I was sitting in my study, looking through the accounts, when some one entered, saluting respectfully, and stood before me. It was Rahamat the Kabuliwala. At first I did not recognise him. He had no bag, nor the long hair, nor the same vigour that he used to have. But he smiled, and I knew him again.

"When did you come, Rahamat?" I asked him.

"Last evening," he said, "I was released from jail."

The words struck harsh upon my ears. I had never before talked with one who had wounded his fellow, and my heart shrank within itself, when I realised this, for I felt that the day would have been better-omened had he not turned up.

"There are ceremonies going on," I said, "and I am busy. Could you perhaps come another day?"

At once he turned to go; but as he reached the door he hesitated, and said, "May I not see the little one, Sir, for a moment?" It was his belief that Mini was still the same. He had pictured her running to him as she used, calling "O Kabuliwala! Kabuliwala!" He had imagined too that they would laugh and talk together, just as of old. In fact, in memory of former days he had brought, carefully wrapped up in paper, a few almonds and raisins and grapes, obtained somehow from a countryman, for his own little fund was dispersed.

I said again, "There is a ceremony in the house, and you will not be able to see any one today."

The man's face fell. He looked wistfully at me for a moment, said "Good morning," and went out. I felt a little sorry, and would have called him back, but I found he was returning of his own accord. He came close up to me holding out his offerings and said, "I brought these few things, Sir, for the little one. Will you give them to her?"

I took them and was going to pay him, but he caught my hand and said, "You are very kind, Sir! Keep me in your recollection. Do not offer me money! – You have a little girl, I too have one like her in my own home. I think of her, and bring fruits to your child, not to make a profit for myself."

Saying this, he put his hand inside his big loose robe, and brought out a small and dirty piece of paper. With great care he unfolded this, and smoothed it out with both hands on my table. It bore the impression of a little hand. Not a photograph. Not a drawing. The impression of an ink-smeared hand laid flat on the paper. This touch of his own little daughter had been always on his heart, as he had come year after year to Calcutta, to sell his wares in the streets.

Tears came to my eyes. I forgot that he was a poor Kabuli fruit-seller, while I was – but no, what was I more than he? He also was a father. That impression of the hand of his little Parbati in her distant mountain home reminded me of my own little Mini.

I sent for Mini immediately from the inner apartment. Many difficulties were raised, but I would not listen. Clad in the red silk of her wedding-day, with the sandal paste on her forehead, and adorned as a young bride, Mini came, and stood bashfully before me.

The Kabuliwala looked a little staggered at the apparition. He could not revive their old friendship. At last he smiled and said, "Little one, are you going to your father-in-law's house?"

But Mini now understood the meaning of the word "father-in-law," and she could not reply to him as of old. She flushed up at the question, and stood before him with her bride-like face turned down.

I remembered the day when the Kabuliwala and my Mini had first met, and I felt sad. When she had gone, Rahamat heaved a deep sigh, and sat down on the floor. The idea had suddenly come to him that his daughter too must have grown in this long time, and that he would have to make friends with her anew. Assuredly he would not find her, as he used to know her. And besides, what might not have happened to her in these eight years?

The marriage-pipes sounded, and the mild autumn sun streamed round us. But Rahamat sat in the little Calcutta lane, and saw before him the barren mountains of Afghanistan.

I took out a bank-note, and gave it to him, saying, "Go back to your own daughter, Rahamat, in your own country, and may the happiness of your meeting bring good fortune to my child!"

Having made this present, I had to curtail some of the festivities. I could not have the electric lights I had intended, nor the military band, and the ladies of the house were despondent at it. But to me the wedding feast was all the brighter for the thought that in a distant land a long-lost father met again with his only child.

14

Mashi

I

"Mashi!"

"Try to sleep, Jotin; it is getting late."

"Never mind if it is. I have not many days left. I was thinking that Mani should go to her father's house. – I forget where he is now."

"Sitarampur."

"Oh, yes! Sitarampur. Send her there. She should not remain any longer near a sick man. She herself is not strong."

"Just listen to him! How can she bear to leave you in this state?"

"Does she know what the doctors – ?"

"But she can see for herself! The other day she cried her eyes out at the merest hint of having to go to her father's house."

We must explain that in this statement there was a slight distortion of truth, to say the least of it. The actual talk with Mani was as follows, –

"I suppose, my child, you have got some news from your father? I thought I saw your cousin Anath here."

"Yes! Next Friday will be my little sister's annaprashan ceremony. So I'm thinking – "

"All right, my dear. Send her a gold necklace. It will please your mother."

"I'm thinking of going myself. I've never seen my little sister, and I want to ever so much."

"Whatever do you mean? You surely don't think of leaving Jotin alone? Haven't you heard what the doctor says about him?"

"But he said that just now there's no special cause for – "

"Even if he did, you can see his state."

"This is the first girl after three brothers, and she's a great favourite – I have heard that it's going to be a grand affair. If I don't go, mother will be very – "

"Yes, yes! I don't understand your mother. But I know very well that your father will be angry enough if you leave Jotin just now."

"You'll have to write a line to him saying that there is no special cause for anxiety, and that even if I go, there will be no – "

"You're right there; it will certainly be no great loss if you do go. But remember, if I write to your father, I'll tell him plainly what is in my mind."

"Then, you needn't write. I shall ask my husband, and he will surely – "

"Look here, child, I've home a good deal from you, but if you do that, I won't stand it for a moment. Your father knows you too well for you to deceive him."

When Mashi had left her, Mani lay down on her bed in a bad temper.

Her neighbour and friend came and asked what was the matter.

"Look here! What a shame it is! Here's my only sister's annaprashan coming, and they don't want to let me go to it!"

"Why! Surely you're never thinking of going, are you, with your husband so ill?"

"I don't do anything for him, and I couldn't if I tried. It's so deadly dull in this house, that I tell you frankly I can't bear it."

"You are a strange woman!"

"But I can't pretend, as you people do, and look glum lest any one should think ill of me."

"Well, tell me your plan."

"I must go. Nobody can prevent me."

"Ishhh! What an imperious young woman you are!"

II

Hearing that Mani had wept at the mere thought of going to her father's house, Jotin was so excited that he sat up in bed. Pulling his pillow towards him, he leaned back, and said, "Mashi, open this window a little, and take that lamp away."

The still night stood silently at the window like a pilgrim of eternity; and the stars gazed in, witnesses through untold ages of countless death-scenes.

Jotin saw his Mani's face traced on the background of the dark night, and saw those two big dark eyes brimming over with tears, as it were for all eternity.

Mashi felt relieved when she saw him so quiet, thinking he was asleep.

Suddenly he started up, and said, "Mashi, you all thought that Mani was too frivolous ever to be happy in our house. But you see now – "

"Yes, I see now, my baba, I was mistaken – but trial tests a person."

"Mashi!"

"Do try to sleep, dear!"

"Let me think a little, let me talk. Don't be vexed, Mashi!"

"Very well."

"Once, when I used to think I could not win Mani's heart, I bore it silently. But you – "

"No, dear, I won't allow you to say that; I also bore it."

"Our minds, you know, are not clods of earth which you can possess by merely picking up. I felt that Mani did not know her own mind, and that one day at some great shock – "

"Yes, Jotin, you are right."

"Therefore, I never took much notice of her waywardness."

Mashi remained silent, suppressing a sigh. Not once, but often she had seen Jotin spending the night on the verandah wet with the splashing rain, yet not caring to go into his bedroom. Many a day he lay with a throbbing head, longing, she knew, that Mani would come and soothe his brow, while Mani was getting ready to go to the theatre. Yet when Mashi went to fan him, he sent her away petulantly. She alone knew what pain lay hidden in that distress. Again and again she had wanted to say to Jotin, "Don't pay so much attention to that silly child, my dear; let her learn to want – to cry for things." But these things cannot be said, and are apt to be misunderstood. Jotin had in his heart a shrine set up to the goddess Woman, and there Mani had her throne. It was hard for him to imagine that his own fate was to be denied his share of the wine of love poured out by that divinity. Therefore, the worship went on, the sacrifice was offered, and the hope of a boon never ceased.

Mashi imagined once more that Jotin was sleeping, when he cried out suddenly,

"I know you thought that I was not happy with Mani, and therefore, you were angry with her. But, Mashi, happiness is like those stars. They don't cover all the darkness; there are gaps between. We make mistakes in life and we misunderstand, and yet there remain gaps through which truth shines. I do not know whence comes this gladness that fills my heart tonight."

Mashi began gently to soothe Jotin's brow, her tears unseen in the dark.

"I was thinking, Mashi, she's so young! What will she do when I am – ?"

"Young, Jotin? She's old enough. I too was young when I lost the idol of my life, only to find him in my heart for ever. Was that any loss, do you think? Besides, is happiness absolutely necessary?"

"Mashi, it seems as if just when Mani's heart shows signs of awakening I have to – "

"Don't you worry about that, Jotin. Isn't it enough if her heart awakes?"

Suddenly Jotin recollected the words of a village minstrel's song which he had heard long before,

O my heart! You woke not when the man of my heart came to my door.

At the sound of his departing steps you woke up.

Oh, you woke up in the dark!

"Mashi, what is the time now?"

"About nine."

"So early as that! Why, I thought it must be at least two or three o'clock. My midnight, you know, begins at sundown. But why did you want me to sleep, then?"

"Why, you know how late last night you kept awake talking; so today you must get to sleep early."

"Is Mani asleep?"

"Oh, no, she's busy making some soup for you."

"You don't mean to say so, Mashi? Does she – ?"

"Certainly! Why, she prepares all your food, the busy little woman."

"I thought perhaps Mani could not – "

"It doesn't take long for a woman to learn such things. With the need it comes of itself."

"The fish soup, that I had in the morning, had such a delicate flavour, I thought you had made it."

"Dear me, no! Surely you don't think Mani would let me do anything for you? Why, she does all your washing herself. She knows you can't bear anything dirty about you. If only you could see your sitting-room, how spick and span she keeps it! If I were to let her haunt your sick-room, she would wear herself out. But that's what she really wants to do."

"Is Mani's health, then – ?"

"The doctors think she should not be allowed to visit the sick-room too often. She's too tender-hearted."

"But, Mashi, how do you prevent her from coming?"

"Because she obeys me implicitly. But still I have constantly to be giving her news of you."

The stars glistened in the sky like tear-drops. Jotin bowed his head in gratitude to his life that was about to depart, and when Death stretched out his right hand towards him through the darkness, he took it in perfect trust.

Jotin sighed, and, with a slight gesture of impatience, said, "Mashi, if Mani is still awake, then, could I – if only for a – ?"

"Very well! I'll go and call her."

"I won't keep her long, only for five minutes. I have something particular to tell her."

Mashi, sighing, went out to call Mani. Meanwhile Jotin's pulse began to beat fast. He knew too well that he had never been able to have an intimate talk with Mani. The two instruments were tuned differently and it was not easy to play them in unison. Again and again, Jotin had felt pangs of jealousy on hearing Mani chattering and laughing merrily with her girl companions. Jotin blamed only himself – why couldn't he talk irrelevant trifles as they did? Not that he could not, for with his men friends he often chatted on all sorts of trivialities. But the small talk that suits men is not suitable for women. You can hold a philosophical discourse in monologue, ignoring your inattentive audience altogether, but small talk requires the co-operation of at least two. The bagpipes can be played singly, but there must be a pair of cymbals. How often in the evenings had Jotin, when sitting on the open verandah with Mani, made some strained attempts at conversation, only to feel the thread snap. And the very silence of the evening felt ashamed. Jotin was certain that Mani longed to get away. He had even wished earnestly that a third person would come. For talking is easy with three, when it is hard for two.

He began to think what he should say when Mani came. But such manufactured talk would not satisfy him. Jotin felt afraid that this five minutes of tonight would be wasted. Yet, for him, there were but few moments left for intimate talk.

III

"What's this, child, you're not going anywhere, are you?"

"Of course, I'm going to Sitarampur."

"What do you mean? Who is going to take you?"

"Anath."

"Not today, my child; some other day."

"But the compartment has already been reserved."

"What does that matter? That loss can easily be borne. Go tomorrow, early in the morning."

"Mashi, I don't hold by your inauspicious days. What harm if I do go today?"

"Jotin wants to have a talk with you."

"All right! There's still some time. I'll just go and see him."

"But you mustn't say that you are going."

"Very well, I won't tell him, but I shan't be able to stay long. Tomorrow is my sister's annaprashan, and I must go today."

"Oh, my child! I beg you to listen to me this once. Quiet your mind for a while and sit by him. Don't let him see your hurry."

"What can I do? The train won't Wait for me. Anath will be back in ten minutes. I can sit by him till then."

"No, that won't do. I shall never let you go to him in that frame of mind... Oh, you wretch! The man you are torturing is soon to leave this world; but I warn you, you will remember this day till the end of your days! That there is a God! That there is a God! You will some day understand!"

"Mashi, you mustn't curse me like that."

"Oh, my darling boy! My darling! Why do you go on living longer? There is no end to this sin, yet I cannot check it!"

Mashi after delaying a little returned to the sick-room, hoping by that time Jotin would be asleep. But Jotin moved in his bed when she entered. Mashi exclaimed,

"Just look what she has done!"

"What's happened? Hasn't Mani come? Why have you been so long, Mashi?"

"I found her weeping bitterly because she had allowed the milk for your soup to get burnt! I tried to console her, saying, 'Why, there's more milk to be had!' But that she could be so careless about the preparation of your soup made her wild. With great trouble I managed to pacify her and put her to bed. So I haven't brought her today. Let her sleep it off."

Though Jotin was pained when Mani didn't come, yet he felt a certain amount of relief. He had half feared that Mani's bodily presence would do violence to his heart's image of her. Such things had happened before in his life. And the gladness of the idea that Mani was miserable at burning his milk filled his heart to overflowing.

"Mashi!"

"What is it, Baba?"

"I feel quite certain that my days are drawing to a close. But I have no regrets. Don't grieve for me."

"No, dear, I won't grieve. I don't believe that only life is good and not death."

"Mashi, I tell you truly that death seems sweet."

Jotin, gazing at the dark sky, felt that it was Mani herself who was coming to him in Death's guise. She had immortal youth and the stars were flowers of blessing, showered upon her dark tresses by the hand of the World-Mother. It seemed as if once more he had his first sight of his bride under the veil of darkness. The immense night became filled with the loving gaze of Mani's dark eyes. Mani, the bride of this house, the little girl, became transformed into a world-image, – her throne on the altar of the stars at the confluence of life and death. Jotin said to himself with clasped hands, "At last the veil is raised, the covering is rent in this deep darkness. Ah, beautiful one! How often have you wrung my heart, but no longer shall you forsake me!"

IV

"I'm suffering, Mashi, but nothing like you imagine. It seems to me as if my pain were gradually separating itself from my life. Like a laden boat, it was so long being towed behind, but the rope has snapped, and now it floats away with all my burdens. Still I can see it, but it is no longer mine... But, Mashi, I've not seen Mani even once for the last two days!"

"Jotin, let me give you another pillow."

"It almost seems to me, Mashi, that Mani also has left me like that laden boat of sorrow which drifts away."

"Just sip some pomegranate juice, dear! Your throat must be getting dry."

"I wrote my will yesterday; did I show it to you? I can't recollect."

"There's no need to show it to me, Jotin."

"When mother died, I had nothing of my own. You fed me and brought me up. Therefore, I was saying – "

"Nonsense, child! I had only this house and a little property. You earned the rest."

"But this house – ?"

"That's nothing. Why, you've added to it so much that it's difficult to find out where my house was!"

"I'm sure Mani's love for you is really – "

"Yes, yes! I know that, Jotin. Now you try to sleep."

"Though I have bequeathed all my property to Mani, it is practically yours, Mashi. She will never disobey you."

"Why are you worrying so much about that, dear?"

"All I have I owe to you. When you see my will don't think for a moment that – "

"What do you mean, Jotin? Do you think I shall mind for a moment because you give to Mani what belongs to you? Surely I'm not so mean as that?"

"But you also will have – "

"Look here, Jotin, I shall get angry with you. You want to console me with money!"

"Oh, Mashi, how I wish I could give you something better than money!"

"That you have done, Jotin! More than enough. Haven't I had you to fill my lonely house? I must have won that great good-fortune in many previous births! You have given me so much that now, if my destiny's due is exhausted, I shall not complain. Yes, yes! Give away everything in Mani's name – your house, your money, your carriage, and your land – such burdens are too heavy for me!"

"Of course I know you have lost your taste for the enjoyments of life, but Mani is so young that – "

"No! You mustn't say that. If you want to leave her your property, it is all right, but as for enjoyment – "

"What harm if she does enjoy herself, Mashi?"

"No, no, it will be impossible. Her throat will become parched, and it will be dust and ashes to her."

Jotin remained silent. He could not decide whether it was true or not, and whether it was a matter of regret or otherwise, that the world would become distasteful to Mani for want of him. The stars seemed to whisper in his heart,

"Indeed it is true. We have been watching for thousands of years, and know that all these great preparations for enjoyment are but vanity."

Jotin sighed and said, "We cannot leave behind us what is really worth giving."

"It's no trifle you are giving, dearest. I only pray she may have the power to know the value of what is given her."

"Give me a little more of that pomegranate juice, Mashi; I'm thirsty. Did Mani come to me yesterday, I wonder?"

"Yes, she came, but you were asleep. She sat by your head, fanning you for a long time, and then, went away to get your clothes washed."

"How wonderful! I believe I was dreaming that very moment that Mani was trying to enter my room. The door was slightly open, and she was pushing against it, but it wouldn't open. But, Mashi, you're going too far, – you ought to let her see that I am dying; otherwise my death will be a terrible shock to her."

"Baba, let me put this shawl over your feet; they are getting cold."

"No, Mashi, I can't bear anything over me like that."

"Do you know, Jotin, Mani made this shawl for you? When she ought to have been asleep, she was busy at it. It was finished only yesterday."

Jotin took the shawl, and touched it tenderly with his hands. It seemed to him that the softness of the wool was Mani's own. Her loving thoughts had been woven night after night with its threads. It was not made merely of wool, but also of her touch. Therefore, when Mashi drew that shawl over his feet, it seemed as if, night after night, Mani had been caressing his tired limbs.

"But, Mashi, I thought Mani didn't know how to knit, – at any rate she never liked it."

"It doesn't take long to learn a thing. Of course I had to teach her. Then, there are a good many mistakes in it."

"Let there be mistakes; we're not going to send it to the Paris Exhibition. It will keep my feet warm in spite of its mistakes."

Jotin's mind began to picture Mani at her task, blundering and struggling, and yet patiently going on night after night. How sweetly pathetic it was! And again he went over the shawl with his caressing fingers.

"Mashi, is the doctor downstairs?"

"Yes, he will stay here tonight."

"But tell him it is useless for him to give me a sleeping draught. It doesn't bring me real rest and only adds to my pain. Let me remain properly awake. Do you know, Mashi, that my wedding took place on the night of the full moon in the month of Baisakh? Tomorrow will be that day, and the stars of that very night will be shining in the sky. Mani perhaps has forgotten. I want to remind her of it today; just call her to me for a minute or two… Why do you keep silent? I suppose the doctor has told you I am so weak that any excitement will – but I tell you truly, Mashi, tonight, if I can have only a few minutes' talk with her, there will be no need for any sleeping draughts. Mashi, don't cry like that! I am quite well. Today my heart is full as it has never been in my life before. That's why I want to see Mani. No, no, Mashi, I can't bear to see you crying! You have been so quiet all these last days. Why are you so troubled tonight?"

"Oh, Jotin, I thought that I had exhausted all my tears, but I find there are plenty left. I can't bear it any longer."

"Call Mani. I'll remind her of our wedding night, so that tomorrow she may –"

"I'm going, dear. Shombhu will wait at the door. If you want anything, call him."

Mashi went to Mani's bedroom and sat down on the floor crying – "Oh, come, come once, you heartless wretch! Keep his last request who has given you his all! Don't kill him who is already dying!"

Jotin hearing the sound of footsteps started up, saying, "Mani!"

"I am Shombhu. Did you call me?"

"Ask your mistress to come?"

"Ask whom?"

"Your mistress."

"She has not yet returned."

"Returned? From where?"

"From Sitarampur."

"When did she go?"

"Three days ago."

For a moment Jotin felt numb all over, and his head began to swim. He slipped down from the pillows, on which he was reclining, and kicked off the woollen shawl that was over his feet.

When Mashi came back after a long time, Jotin did not mention Mani's name, and Mashi thought he had forgotten all about her.

Suddenly Jotin cried out, "Mashi, did I tell you about the dream I had the other night?"

"Which dream?"

"That in which Mani was pushing the door, and the door wouldn't open more than an inch. She stood outside unable to enter. Now I know that Mani has to stand outside my door till the last."

Mashi kept silent. She realised that the heaven she had been building for Jotin out of falsehood had toppled down at last. If sorrow comes, it is best to acknowledge it – when God strikes, we cannot avoid the blow.

"Mashi, the love I have got from you will last through all my births. I have filled this life with it to carry it with me. In the next birth, I am sure you will be born as my daughter, and I shall tend you with all my love."

"What are you saying, Jotin? Do you mean to say I shall be born again as a woman? Why can't you pray that I should come to your arms as a son?"

"No, no, not a son! You will come to my house in that wonderful beauty which you had when you were young. I can even imagine how I shall dress you."

"Don't talk so much, Jotin, but try to sleep."

"I shall name you 'Lakshmi.'"

"But that is an old-fashioned name, Jotin!"

"Yes, but you are my old-fashioned Mashi. Come to my house again with those beautiful old-fashioned manners."

"I can't wish that I should come and burden your home with the misfortune of a girl-child!"

"Mashi, you think me weak, and are wanting to save me all trouble."

"My child, I am a woman, so I have my weakness. Therefore, I have tried all my life to save you from all sorts of trouble – only to fail."

"Mashi, I have not had time in this life to apply the lessons I have learnt. But they will keep for my next birth. I shall show then, what a man is able to do. I have learnt how false it is always to be looking after oneself."

"Whatever you may say, darling, you have never grasped anything for yourself, but given everything to others."

"Mashi, I can boast of one thing at any rate. I have never been a tyrant in my happiness, or tried to enforce my claims by violence. Because lies could not content me, I have had to wait long. Perhaps truth will be kind to me at last. – Who is that, Mashi; who is that?"

"Where? There's no one there, Jotin!"

"Mashi, just go and see in the other room. I thought I – "

"No, dear! I don't see anybody."

"But it seemed quite clear to me that – "

"No, Jotin, it's nothing. So keep quiet! The doctor is coming now."

When the doctor entered, he said,

"Look here, you mustn't stay near the patient so much; you excite him. You go to bed, and my assistant will remain with him."

"No, Mashi, I can't let you go."

"All right, Baba! I will sit quietly in that corner."

"No, no! You must sit by my side. I can't let go your hand, not till the very end. I have been made by your hand, and only from your hand shall God take me."

"All right," said the doctor, "you can remain there. But, Jotin Babu, you must not talk to her. It's time for you to take your medicine."

"Time for my medicine? Nonsense! The time for that is over. To give medicine now is merely to deceive; besides I am not afraid to die. Mashi, Death is busy with his physic; why do you add another nuisance in the shape of a doctor? Send him away, send him away! It is you alone I need now! No one else, none whatever! No more falsehood!"

"I protest, as a doctor; this excitement is doing you harm."

"Then, go, doctor; don't excite me any more! – Mashi, has he gone? ... That's good! Now come and take my head in your lap."

"All right, dear! Now, Baba, try to sleep!"

"No, Mashi, don't ask me to sleep. If I sleep, I shall never wake, I still need to keep awake a little longer. Don't you hear a sound? Somebody is coming."

V

"Jotin dear, just open your eyes a little. She has come. Look once and see!"

"Who has come? A dream?"

"Not a dream, darling! Mani has come with her father."

"Who are you?"

"Can't you see? This is your Mani!"

"Mani? Has that door opened?"

"Yes, Baba, it is wide open."

"No, Mashi, not that shawl; not that shawl! That shawl is a fraud!"

"It is not a shawl, Jotin! It is our Mani, who has flung herself on your feet. Put your hand on her head and bless her. Don't cry like that, Mani! There will be time enough for that. Keep quiet now for a little."

15

The Skeleton

In the room next to the one in which we boys used to sleep, there hung a human skeleton. In the night it would rattle in the breeze which played about its bones. In the day these bones were rattled by us. We were taking lessons in osteology from a student in the Campbell Medical School, for our guardians were determined to make us masters of all the sciences. How far they succeeded we need not tell those who know us; and it is better hidden from those who do not.

Many years have passed since then. In the meantime the skeleton has vanished from the room, and the science of osteology from our brains, leaving no trace behind.

The other day, our house was crowded with guests, and I had to pass the night in the same old room. In these now unfamiliar surroundings, sleep refused to come, and, as I tossed from side to side, I heard all the hours of the night chimed, one after another, by the church clock near by. At length the lamp in the corner of the room, after some minutes of choking and spluttering, went out altogether. One or two bereavements had recently happened in the family, so the going out of the lamp naturally led me to thoughts of death. In the great arena of nature, I thought, the light of a lamp losing itself in eternal darkness, and the going out of the light of our little human lives, by day or by night, were much the same thing.

My train of thought recalled to my mind the skeleton. While I was trying to imagine what the body which had clothed it could have been like, it suddenly seemed to me that something was walking round and round my bed, groping along the walls of the room. I could hear its rapid breathing. It seemed as if it was searching for something which it could not find, and pacing round the room with ever-hastier steps. I felt quite sure that this was a mere fancy of my sleepless, excited brain; and that the throbbing of the veins in my temples was really the sound which seemed like running footsteps. Nevertheless, a cold shiver ran all over me. To help to get rid of this hallucination, I called out aloud, "Who is there?" The footsteps seemed to stop at my bedside, and the reply came, "It is I. I have come to look for that skeleton of mine."

It seemed absurd to show any fear before the creature of my own imagination; so, clutching my pillow a little more tightly, I said in a casual sort of way, "A nice business for this time of night! Of what use will that skeleton be to you now?"

The reply seemed to come almost from my mosquito-curtain itself. "What a question! In that skeleton were the bones that encircled my heart; the youthful charm of my six-and-twenty years bloomed about it. Should I not desire to see it once more?"

"Of course," said I, "a perfectly reasonable desire. Well, go on with your search, while I try to get a little sleep."

Said the voice, "But I fancy you are lonely. All right; I'll sit down a while, and we will have a little chat. Years ago I used to sit by men and talk to them. But during the last thirty-five years I have only moaned in the wind in the burning-places of the dead. I would talk once more with a man as in the old times."

I felt that some one sat down just near my curtain. Resigning myself to the situation, I replied with as much cordiality as I could summon, "That will be very nice indeed. Let us talk of something cheerful."

"The funniest thing I can think of is my own life-story. Let me tell you that."

The church clock chimed the hour of two.

"When I was in the land of the living, and young, I feared one thing like death itself, and that was my husband. My feelings can be likened only to those of a fish caught with a hook. For it was as if a stranger had snatched me away with the sharpest of hooks from the peaceful calm of my childhood's home – and from him I had no means of escape. My husband died two months after my marriage, and my friends and relations moaned pathetically on my behalf. My husband's father, after scrutinizing my face with great care, said to my mother-in-law, 'Do you not see, she has the evil eye?' – Well, are you listening? I hope you are enjoying the story?"

"Very much indeed!" said I. "The beginning is extremely humorous."

"Let me proceed then. I came back to my father's house in great glee. People tried to conceal it from me, but I knew well that I was endowed with a rare and radiant beauty. What is your opinion?"

"Very likely," I murmured. "But you must remember that I never saw you."

"What! Not seen me? What about that skeleton of mine? Ha! Ha! Ha! Never mind. I was only joking. How can I ever make you believe that those two cavernous hollows contained the brightest of dark, languishing eyes? And that the smile which was revealed by those ruby lips had no resemblance whatever to the grinning teeth which you used to see? The mere attempt to convey to you some idea of the grace, the charm, the soft, firm, dimpled curves, which in the fulness of youth were growing and blossoming over those dry old bones makes me smile; it also makes me angry. The most eminent doctors of my time could not have dreamed of the bones of that body of mine as materials for teaching osteology. Do you know, one young doctor that I knew of actually compared me to a golden champak blossom. It meant that to him the rest of humankind was fit only to illustrate the science of physiology, that I was a flower of beauty. Does any one think of the skeleton of a champak flower?

"When I walked, I felt that, like a diamond scattering splendour, my every movement set waves of beauty radiating on every side. I used to spend hours gazing on my hands – hands which could gracefully have reined the liveliest of male creatures.

"But that stark and staring old skeleton of mine has borne false-witness to you against me, while I was unable to refute the shameless libel. That is why of all men I hate you most! I feel I would like once for all to banish sleep from your eyes with a vision of that warm rosy loveliness of mine, to sweep out with it all the wretched osteological stuff of which your brain is full."

"I could have sworn by your body," cried I, "if you had it still, that no vestige of osteology has remained in my head, and that the only thing that it is now full of is a radiant vision of perfect loveliness, glowing against the black background of night. I cannot say more than that."

"I had no girl-companions," went on the voice. "My only brother had made up his mind not to marry. In the zenana I was alone. Alone I used to sit in the garden under the shade of the trees, and dream that the whole world was in love with me; that the stars with sleepless gaze were drinking in my beauty; that the wind was languishing in sighs as on some pretext or other it brushed past me; and that the lawn on which my feet rested, had it been conscious, would have lost consciousness again at their touch. It seemed to me that all the young men in the world were as blades of grass at my feet; and my heart, I know not why, used to grow sad.

"When my brother's friend, Shekhar, had passed out of the Medical College, he became our family doctor. I had already often seen him from behind a curtain. My brother was a strange man, and did not care to look on the world with open eyes. It was not empty enough for his taste; so he gradually moved away from it, until he was quite lost in an obscure corner. Shekhar was his one friend, so he was the only young man I could ever get to see. And when I held my evening court in my garden, then, the host of imaginary young men whom I had at my feet were each one a Shekhar – are you listening? What are you thinking of?"

I sighed as I replied. "I was wishing I was Shekhar!"

"Wait a bit. Hear the whole story first. One day, in the rains, I was feverish. The doctor came to see me. That was our first meeting. I was reclining opposite the window, so that the blush of the evening sky might temper the pallor of my complexion. When the doctor, coming in, looked up into my face, I put myself into his place, and gazed at myself in imagination. I saw in the glorious evening light that delicate wan face laid like a drooping flower against the soft white pillow, with the unrestrained curls playing over the forehead, and the bashfully lowered eyelids casting a pathetic shade over the whole countenance.

"The doctor, in a tone bashfully low, asked my brother, 'Might I feel her pulse?'

"I put out a tired, well-rounded wrist from beneath the coverlet. 'Ah!' thought I, as I looked on it, 'if only there had been a sapphire bracelet.' I have never before seen a doctor so awkward about feeling a patient's pulse. His fingers trembled as they felt my wrist. He measured the heat of my fever, I gauged the pulse of his heart. – Don't you believe me?"

"Very easily," said I; "the human heart-beat tells its tale."

"After I had been taken ill and restored to health several times, I found that the number of the courtiers who attended my imaginary evening reception began to dwindle till they were reduced to only one! And at last in my little world there remained only one doctor and one patient.

"In these evenings I used to dress myself secretly in a canary-coloured sari; twine about the braided knot into which I did my hair a garland of white jasmine blossoms; and with a little mirror in my hand betake myself to my usual seat under the trees.

"Well! Are you perhaps thinking that the sight of one's own beauty would soon grow wearisome? Ah no! for I did not see myself with my own eyes. I was then, one and also two. I used to see myself as though I were the doctor; I gazed, I was charmed, I fell madly in love. But, in spite of all the caresses I lavished on myself, a sigh would wander about my heart, moaning like the evening breeze.

"Anyhow, from that time I was never alone. When I walked I watched with downcast eyes the play of my dainty little toes on the earth, and wondered what the doctor would have felt had he been there to see. At mid-day the sky would be filled with the glare of the sun, without a sound, save now and then, the distant cry of a passing kite. Outside our garden-walls the hawker would pass with his musical cry of 'Bangles for sale, crystal bangles.' And I, spreading a snow-white sheet on the lawn, would lie on it with my head on my arm. With studied carelessness the other arm would rest lightly on the soft sheet, and I would imagine to myself that some one had caught sight of the wonderful pose of my hand, that some one had clasped it in both of his and imprinted a kiss on its rosy palm, and was slowly walking away – what if I ended the story here? How would it do?"

"Not half a bad ending," I replied thoughtfully. "It would no doubt remain a little incomplete, but I could easily spend the rest of the night putting in the finishing touches."

"But that would make the story too serious. Where would the laugh come in? Where would be the skeleton with its grinning teeth?

"So let me go on. As soon as the doctor had got a little practice, he took a room on the ground-floor of our house for a consulting-chamber. I used then, sometimes to ask him jokingly about medicines and poisons, and how much of this drug or that would kill a man. The subject was congenial and he would wax eloquent. These talks familiarised me with the idea of death; and so love and death were the only two things that filled my little world. My story is now nearly ended – there is not much left."

"Not much of the night is left either," I muttered.

"After a time I noticed that the doctor had grown strangely absent-minded, and it seemed as if he were ashamed of something which he was trying to keep from me. One day he came in, somewhat smartly dressed, and borrowed my brother's carriage for the evening.

"My curiosity became too much for me, and I went up to my brother for information. After some talk beside the point, I at last asked him, 'By the way, Dada, where is the doctor going this evening in your carriage?'

"My brother briefly replied, 'To his death.'

"'Oh, do tell me,' I importuned. 'Where is he really going?'

"'To be married,' he said, a little more explicitly.

"'Oh, indeed!' said I, as I laughed long and loudly.

"I gradually learnt that the bride was an heiress, who would bring the doctor a large sum of money. But why did he insult me by hiding all this from me? Had I ever begged and prayed him not to marry, because it would break my heart? Men are not to be trusted. I have known only one man in all my life, and in a moment I made this discovery.

"When the doctor came in after his work and was ready to start, I said to him, rippling with laughter the while, 'Well, doctor, so you are to be married tonight?'

"My gaiety not only made the doctor lose countenance; it thoroughly irritated him.

"'How is it,' I went on, 'that there is no illumination, no band of music?'

"With a sigh he replied, 'Is marriage then, such a joyful occasion?'

"I burst out into renewed laughter. 'No, no,' said I, 'this will never do. Who ever heard of a wedding without lights and music?'

"I bothered my brother about it so much that he at once ordered all the trappings of a gay wedding.

"All the time I kept on gaily talking of the bride, of what would happen, of what I would do when the bride came home. 'And, doctor,' I asked, 'will you still go on feeling pulses?' Ha! Ha! Ha! Though the inner workings of people's, especially men's, minds are not visible, still I can take my oath that these words were piercing the doctor's bosom like deadly darts.

"The marriage was to be celebrated late at night. Before starting, the doctor and my brother were having a glass of wine together on the terrace, as was their daily habit. The moon had just risen.

"I went up smiling, and said, 'Have you forgotten your wedding, doctor? It is time to start.'

"I must here tell you one little thing. I had meanwhile gone down to the dispensary and got a little powder, which at a convenient opportunity I had dropped unobserved into the doctor's glass.

"The doctor, draining his glass at a gulp, in a voice thick with emotion, and with a look that pierced me to the heart, said, 'Then, I must go.'

"The music struck up. I went into my room and dressed myself in my bridal-robes of silk and gold. I took out my jewellery and ornaments from the safe and put them all on; I put the red mark of wifehood on the parting in my hair. And then, under the tree in the garden I prepared my bed.

"It was a beautiful night. The gentle south wind was kissing away the weariness of the world. The scent of jasmine and bela filled the garden with rejoicing.

"When the sound of the music began to grow fainter and fainter; the light of the moon to get dimmer and dimmer; the world with its lifelong associations of home and kin to fade away from my perceptions like some illusion – then, I closed my eyes, and smiled.

"I fancied that when people came and found me they would see that smile of mine lingering on my lips like a trace of rose-coloured wine, that when I thus, slowly entered my eternal bridal-chamber I should carry with me this smile, illuminating my face. But alas for the bridal-chamber! Alas for the bridal-robes of silk and gold! When I woke at the sound of a rattling within me, I found three urchins learning osteology from my skeleton. Where in my bosom my joys and griefs used to throb, and the petals of youth to open one by one, there the master with his pointer was busy naming my bones. And as to that last smile, which I had so carefully rehearsed, did you see any sign of that?

"Well, well, how did you like the story?"

"It has been delightful," said I.

At this point the first crow began to caw. "Are you there?" I asked. There was no reply.

The morning light entered the room.

16

The Auspicious Vision

Kantichandra was young; yet after his wife's death he sought no second partner, and gave his mind to the hunting of beasts and birds. His body was long and slender, hard and agile; his sight keen; his aim unerring. He dressed like a countryman, and took with him Hira Singh the wrestler, Chakkanlal, Khan Saheb the musician, Mian Saheb, and many others. He had no lack of idle followers.

In the month of Agrahayan Kanti had gone out shooting near the swamp of Nydighi with a few sporting companions. They were in boats, and an army of servants, in boats also, filled the bathing-ghats. The village women found it well-nigh impossible to bathe or to draw water. All day long, land and water trembled to the firing of the guns; and every evening musicians killed the chance of sleep.

One morning as Kanti was seated in his boat cleaning a favourite gun, he suddenly started at what he thought was the cry of wild duck. Looking up, he saw a village maiden, coming to the water's edge, with two white ducklings clasped to her breast. The little stream was almost stagnant. Many weeds choked the current. The girl put the birds into the water, and watched them anxiously. Evidently the presence of the sportsmen was the cause of her care and not the wildness of the ducks.

The girl's beauty had a rare freshness – as if she had just come from Vishwakarma's workshop. It was difficult to guess her age. Her figure was almost a woman's, but her face was so childish that clearly the world had left no impression there. She seemed not to know herself that she had reached the threshold of youth.

Kanti's gun-cleaning stopped for a while. He was fascinated. He had not expected to see such a face in such a spot. And yet its beauty suited its surroundings better than it would have suited a palace. A bud is lovelier on the bough than in a golden vase. That day the blossoming reeds glittered in the autumn dew and morning sun, and the fresh, simple face set in the midst was like a picture of festival to Kanti's enchanted mind. Kalidas has forgotten to sing how Siva's Mountain-Queen herself sometimes has come to the young Ganges, with just such ducklings in her breast. As he gazed, the maiden started in terror, and hurriedly took back the ducks into her bosom with a half-articulate cry of pain. In another moment, she had left the river-bank and disappeared into the bamboo thicket hard by. Looking round, Kanti saw one of his men pointing an unloaded gun at the ducks. He at once went up to him, wrenched away his gun, and bestowed on his cheek a prodigious slap. The astonished humourist finished his joke on the floor Kanti went on cleaning his gun.

But curiosity drove Kanti to the thicket wherein he had seen the girl disappear. Pushing his way through, he found himself in the yard of a well-to-do householder. On one side was a row of conical thatched barns, on the other a clean cow-shed, at the end of which grew a zizyph bush. Under the bush was seated the girl he had seen that morning, sobbing over a wounded dove, into whose yellow beak she was trying to wring a little water from the moist corner of her garment. A grey cat, its fore-paws on her knee, was looking eagerly at the bird, and every now and then, when it got too forward, she kept it in its place by a warning tap on the nose.

This little picture, set in the peaceful mid-day surroundings of the householder's yard, instantly impressed itself on Kanti's sensitive heart. The checkered light and shade, flickering beneath the delicate foliage of the zizyph, played on the girl's lap. Not far off a cow was chewing the cud, and lazily keeping off the flies with slow movements of its head and tail. The north wind whispered softly in the rustling bamboo thickets. And she who at dawn on the river-bank had looked like the Forest Queen, now in the silence of noon showed the eager pity of the Divine Housewife. Kanti, coming in upon her with his gun, had a sense of intrusion. He felt like a thief caught red-handed. He longed to explain that it was not he who had hurt the dove. As he wondered how he should begin, there came a call of "Sudha!" from the house. The girl jumped up. "Sudha!" came the voice again. She took up her dove, and ran within. "Sudha," thought Kanti, "what an appropriate name!"

Kanti returned to the boat, handed his gun to his men, and went over to the front door of the house. He found a middle-aged Brahmin, with a peaceful, clean-shaven face, seated on a bench outside, and reading a devotional book. Kanti saw in his kindly, thoughtful face something of the tenderness which shone in the face of the maiden.

Kanti saluted him, and said, "May I ask for some water, Sir? I am very thirsty." The elder man welcomed him with eager hospitality, and, offering him a seat on the bench, went inside and fetched with his own hands a little brass plate of sugar wafers and a bell-metal vessel full of water.

After Kanti had eaten and drunk, the Brahmin begged him to introduce himself. Kanti gave his own name, his father's name, and the address of his home, and then, said in the usual way, "If I can be of any service, Sir, I shall deem myself fortunate."

"I require no service, my son," said Nabin Banerji; "I have only one care at present."

"What is that, Sir?" said Kanti.

"It is my daughter, Sudha, who is growing up" (Kanti smiled as he thought of her babyish face) "and for whom I have not yet been able to find a worthy bridegroom. If I could only see her well married, all my debt to this world would be paid. But there is no suitable bridegroom here, and I cannot leave my charge of Gopinath here to search for a husband elsewhere."

"If you would see me in my boat, Sir, we would have a talk about the marriage of your daughter." So saying, Kanti repeated his salute and went back. He then, sent some of his men into the village to inquire, and in answer heard nothing but praise of the beauty and virtues of the Brahmin's daughter.

When next day the old man came to the boat on his promised visit, Kanti bent low in salutation, and begged the hand of his daughter for himself. The Brahmin was so much overcome by this undreamed-of piece of good fortune – for Kanti not only belonged to a well-known Brahmin family, but was also a landed proprietor of wealth and position – that at first he could hardly utter a word in reply. He thought there must have been some mistake, and at length mechanically repeated, "You desire to marry my daughter?"

"If you will deign to give her to me," said Kanti.

"You mean Sudha?" he asked again.

"Yes," was the reply.

"But will you not first see and speak to her – ?"

Kanti, pretending he had not seen her already, said, "Oh, that we shall do at the moment of the Auspicious Vision."

In a voice husky with emotion the old man said, "My Sudha is indeed a good girl, well skilled in all the household arts. As you are so generously taking her on trust, may she never cause you a moment's regret. This is my blessing!"

The brick-built mansion of the Mazumdars had been borrowed for the wedding ceremony, which was fixed for next Magh, as Kanti did not wish to delay. In due time the bridegroom arrived on his elephant, with drums and music and with a torch-light procession, and the ceremony began.

When the bridal couple were covered with the scarlet screen for the rite of the Auspicious Vision, Kanti looked up at his bride. In that bashful, downcast face, crowned with the wedding coronet and bedecked with sandal paste, he could scarcely recognise the village maiden of his fancy, and in the fulness of his emotion a mist seemed to becloud his eyes.

At the gathering of women in the bridal chamber, after the wedding ceremony was over, an old village dame insisted that

Kanti himself should take off his wife's bridal veil. As he did so he started back. It was not the same girl.

Something rose from within his breast and pierced into his brain. The light of the lamps seemed to grow dim, and darkness to tarnish the face of the bride herself.

At first he felt angry with his father-in-law. The old scoundrel had shown him one girl, and married him to another. But on calmer reflection he remembered that the old man had not shown him any daughter at all – that it was all his own fault. He thought it best not to show his arrant folly to the world, and took his place again with apparent calmness.

He could swallow the powder; he could not get rid of its taste. He could not bear the merry-makings of the festive throng. He was in a blaze of anger with himself as well as with everybody else.

Suddenly he felt the bride, seated by his side, give a little start and a suppressed scream; a leveret, scampering into the room, had brushed across her feet. Close upon it followed the girl he had seen before. She caught up the leveret in her arms, and began to caress it with an affectionate murmuring. "Oh, the mad girl!" cried the women as they made signs to her to leave the room. She heeded them not, however, but came and unconcernedly sat in front of the wedded pair, looking into their faces with a childish curiosity. When a maidservant came and took her by the arm to lead her away, Kanti hurriedly interposed, saying, "Let her be."

"What is your name?" he then, went on to ask her.

The girl swayed backwards and forwards but gave no reply. All the women in the room began to titter.

Kanti put another question, "Have those ducklings of yours grown up?"

The girl stared at him as unconcernedly as before.

The bewildered Kanti screwed up courage for another effort, and asked tenderly after the wounded dove, but with no avail. The increasing laughter in the room betokened an amusing joke.

At last Kanti learned that the girl was deaf and dumb, the companion of all the animals and birds of the locality. It was but by chance that she rose the other day when the name of Sudha was called.

Kanti now received a second shock. A black screen lifted from before his eyes. With a sigh of intense relief, as of escape from calamity, he looked once more into the face of his bride. Then, came the true Auspicious Vision. The light from his heart and from the smokeless lamps fell on her gracious face; and he saw it in its true radiance, knowing that Nabin's blessing would find fulfilment.

17

Raja And Rani

Bipin Kisore was born "with a golden spoon in his mouth"; hence he knew how to squander money twice as well as how to earn it. The natural result was that he could not live long in the house where he was born.

He was a delicate young man of comely appearance, an adept in music, a fool in business, and unfit for life's handicap. He rolled along life's road like the wheel of Jagannath's car. He could not long command his wonted style of magnificent living.

Luckily, however, Raja Chittaranjan, having got back his property from the Court of Wards, was intent upon organizing an Amateur Theatre Party. Captivated by the prepossessing looks of Bipin Kisore and his musical endowments, the Raja gladly "admitted him of his crew."

Chittaranjan was a B.A. He was not given to any excesses. Though the son of a rich man, he used to dine and sleep at appointed hours and even at appointed places. And he suddenly became enamoured of Bipin like one unto drink. Often did meals cool and nights grow old while he listened to Bipin and discussed with him the merits of operatic compositions. The Dewan remarked that the only blemish in the otherwise perfect character of his master was his inordinate fondness for Bipin Kisore.

Rani Basanta Kumari raved at her husband, and said that he was wasting himself on a luckless baboon. The sooner she could do away with him, the easier she would feel.

The Raja was much pleased in his heart at this seeming jealousy of his youthful wife. He smiled, and thought that women-folk know only one man upon the earth – him they love; and never think of other men's deserts. That there may be many whose merits deserve regard, is not recorded in the scriptures of women. The only good man and the only object of a woman's favours is he who has blabbered into her ears the matrimonial incantations. A little moment behind the usual hour of her husband's meals is a world of anxiety to her, but she never cares a brass button if her husband's dependents have a mouthful or not. This inconsiderate partiality of the softer sex might be cavilled at, but to Chittaranjan it did not seem unpleasant. Thus, he would often indulge in hyperbolic laudations of Bipin in his wife's presence, just to provoke a display of her delightful fulminations.

But what was sport to the "royal" couple, was death to poor Bipin. The servants of the house, as is their wont, took their cue from the Rani's apathetic and wilful neglect of the wretched hanger-on, and grew more apathetic and wilful still. They contrived to forget to look after his comforts, to Bipin's infinite chagrin and untold sufferings.

Once the Rani rebuked the servant Puté, and said, "You are always shirking work; what do you do all through the day?" "Pray, madam, the whole day is taken up in serving Bipin Babu under the Maharaja's orders," stammered the poor valet.

The Rani retorted, "Your Bipin Babu is a great Nawab, eh?" This was enough for Puté. He took the hint. From the very next day he left Bipin Babu's orts as they were, and at times forgot to cover the food for him. With unpractised hands Bipin often scoured his own dishes and not unfrequently went without meals. But it was not in him to whine and report to the Raja. It was not in him to lower himself by petty squabblings with menials. He did not mind it; he took everything in good part. And thus, while the

Raja's favours grew, the Rani's disfavour intensified, and at last knew no bounds.

Now the opera of Subhadraharan was ready after due rehearsal. The stage was fitted up in the palace court-yard. The Raja acted the part of "Krishna," and Bipin that of "Arjuna." Oh, how sweetly he sang! How beautiful he looked! The audience applauded in transports of joy.

The play over, the Raja came to the Rani and asked her how she liked it. The Rani replied, "Indeed, Bipin acted the part of 'Arjuna' gloriously! He does look like the scion of a noble family. His voice is rare!" The Raja said jocosely, "And how do I look? Am I not fair? Have I not a sweet voice?" "Oh, yours is a different case!" added the Rani, and again fell to dilating on the histrionic abilities of Bipin Kisore.

The tables were now turned. He who used to praise, now began to deprecate. The Raja, who was never weary of indulging in high-sounding panegyrics of Bipin before his consort, now suddenly fell reflecting that, after all, unthinking people made too much of Bipin's actual merits. What was extraordinary about his appearance or voice? A short while before he himself was one of those unthinking men, but in a sudden and mysterious way he developed symptoms of thoughtfulness!

From the day following, every good arrangement was made for Bipin's meals. The Rani told the Raja, "It is undoubtedly wrong to lodge Bipin Babu with the petty officers of the Raj in the Kachari; for all he now is, he was once a man of means." The Raja ejaculated curtly, "Ha!" and turned the subject. The Rani proposed that there might be another performance on the occasion of the first-rice ceremony of the "royal" weanling. The Raja heard and heard her not.

Once on being reprimanded by the Raja for not properly laying his cloth, the servant Puté replied, "What can I do? According to the Rani's behests I have to look after Bipin Babu and wait on him the livelong day." This angered the Raja, and he exclaimed, highly nettled, "Pshaw! Bipin Babu is a veritable Nawab, I see! Can't he cleanse his own dishes himself?" The servant, as before, took his cue, and Bipin lapsed back into his former wretchedness.

The Rani liked Bipin's songs – they were sweet – there was no gainsaying it. When her husband sat with Bipin to the wanted discourses of sweet music of an evening, she would listen from behind the screen in an adjoining room. Not long afterwards, the Raja began again his old habit of dining and sleeping at regular hours. The music came to an end. Bipin's evening services were no more needed.

Raja Chittaranjan used to look after his zamindari affairs at noon. One day he came earlier to the zenana, and found his consort reading something. On his asking her what she read, the Rani was a little taken aback, but promptly replied, "I am conning over a few songs from Bipin Babu's song-book. We have not had any music since you tired abruptly of your musical hobby." Poor woman! it was she who had herself made no end of efforts to eradicate the hobby from her husband's mind.

On the morrow the Raja dismissed Bipin – without a thought as to how and where the poor fellow would get a morsel henceforth!

Nor was this the only matter of regret to Bipin. He had been bound to the Raja by the dearest and most sincere tie of attachment. He served him more for affection than for pay. He was fonder of his friend than of the wages he received. Even after deep cogitation, Bipin could not ascertain the cause of the Raja's sudden estrangement. "'Tis Fate! All is Fate!" Bipin said to himself. And then, silently and bravely, he heaved a deep sigh, picked up his old guitar, put it up in the case, paid the last two coins in his pocket as a farewell bakshish to Puté, and walked out into the wide wide world where he had not a soul to call his friend.

18

The Trust Property

I

Brindaban Kundu came to his father in a rage and said, "I am off this moment."

"Ungrateful wretch!" sneered the father, Jagannath Kundu. "When you have paid me back all that I have spent on your food and clothing, it will be time enough to give yourself these airs."

Such food and clothing as was customary in Jagannath's household could not have cost very much. Our rishis of old managed to feed and clothe themselves on an incredibly small outlay. Jagannath's behaviour showed that his ideal in these respects was equally high. That he could not fully live up to it was due partly to the bad influence of the degenerate society around him, and partly to certain unreasonable demands of Nature in her attempt to keep body and soul together.

So long as Brindaban was single, things went smoothly enough, but after his marriage he began to depart from the high and rarefied standard cherished by his sire. It was clear that the son's ideas of comfort were moving away from the spiritual to the material, and imitating the ways of the world. He was unwilling to put up with the discomforts of heat and cold, thirst and hunger. His minimum of food and clothing rose apace.

Frequent were the quarrels between the father and the son. At last Brindaban's wife became seriously ill and a kabiraj was called in. But when the doctor prescribed a costly medicine for his patient, Jagannath took it as a proof of sheer incompetence, and turned him out immediately. At first Brindaban besought his father to allow the treatment to continue; then, he quarrelled with him about it, but to no purpose. When his wife died, he abused his father and called him a murderer.

"Nonsense!" said the father. "Don't people die even after swallowing all kinds of drugs? If costly medicines could save life, how is it that kings and emperors are not immortal? You don't expect your wife to die with more pomp and ceremony than did your mother and your grandmother before her, do you?"

Brindaban might really have derived a great consolation from these words, had he not been overwhelmed with grief and incapable of proper thinking. Neither his mother nor his grandmother had taken any medicine before making their exit from this world, and this was the time-honoured custom of the family. But, alas, the younger generation was unwilling to die according to ancient custom. The English had newly come to the country at the time we speak of. Even in those remote days, the good old folks were horrified at the unorthodox ways of the new generation, and sat speechless, trying to draw comfort from their hookahs.

Be that as it may, the modern Brindaban said to his old fogy of a father, "I am off."

The father instantly agreed, and wished publicly that, should he ever give his son one single pice in future, the gods might reckon his act as shedding the holy blood of cows. Brindaban in his turn similarly wished that, should he ever accept anything from his father, his act might be held as bad as matricide.

The people of the village looked upon this small revolution as a great relief after a long period of monotony. And when Jagannath disinherited his only son, Everyone did his best to console him. All were unanimous in the opinion that to quarrel with a father for the sake of a wife was possible only in these degenerate days. And the reason they gave was sound too. "When your wife dies," they said, "you can find a second one without delay. But when your father dies, you can't get another to replace him for love or money." Their logic no doubt was perfect, but we suspect that the utter hopelessness of getting another father did not trouble the misguided son very much. On the contrary, he looked upon it as a mercy.

Nor did separation from Brindaban weigh heavily on the mind of his father. In the first place, his absence from home reduced the household expenses. Then, again, the father was freed from a great anxiety. The fear of being poisoned by his son and heir had always haunted him. When he ate his scanty fare, he could never banish the thought of poison from his mind. This fear had abated somewhat after the death of his daughter-in-law, and, now that the son was gone, it disappeared altogether.

But there was one tender spot in the old man's heart. Brindaban had taken away with him his four-year-old son, Gokul Chandra. Now, the expense of keeping the child was comparatively small, and so Jagannath's affection for him was without a drawback. Still, when Brindaban took him away, his grief, sincere as it was, was mingled at first with calculation as to how much he would save a month by the absence of the two, how much the sum would come to in a year, and what would be the capital to bring it in as interest.

But the empty house, without Gokul Chandra in it to make mischief, became more and more difficult for the old man to live in. There was no one now to play tricks upon him when he was engaged in his puja, no one to snatch away his food and eat it, no one to run away with his ink-pot, when he was writing up his accounts. His daily routine of life, now uninterrupted, became an intolerable burden to him. He bethought him that this unworried peace was endurable only in the world to come. When he caught sight of the holes made in his quilt by his grandchild, and the pen-and-ink sketches executed by the same artist on his rush-mat, his heart was heavy with grief. Once upon a time he had reproached the boy bitterly because he had torn his dhoti into pieces within the short space of two years; now tears stood in Jagannath's eyes as he gazed upon the dirty remnants lying in the bedroom. He carefully put them away in his safe, and registered a vow that, should Gokul ever come back again, he should not be reprimanded even if he destroyed one dhoti a year.

But Gokul did not return, and poor Jagannath aged rapidly. His empty home seemed emptier every day.

No longer could the old man stay peacefully at home. Even in the middle of the day, when all respectable folks in the village enjoyed their after-dinner siesta, Jagannath might be seen roaming over the village, hookah in hand. The boys, at sight of him, would give up their play, and, retiring in a body to a safe distance, chant verses composed by a local poet, praising the old gentleman's economical habits. No one ventured to say his real name, lest he should have to go without his meal that day – and so people gave him names after their own fancy. Elderly people called him Jagannash, but the reason why the younger generation preferred to call him a vampire was hard to guess. It may be that the bloodless, dried-up skin of the old man had some physical resemblance to the vampire's.

II

One afternoon, when Jagannath was rambling as usual through the village lanes shaded by mango trees, he saw a boy, apparently a stranger, assuming the captaincy of the village boys and explaining to them the scheme of some new prank. Won by the force of his character and the startling novelty of his ideas, the boys had all sworn allegiance to him. Unlike the others, he did not run away from the old man as he approached, but came quite close to him and began to shake his own chadar. The result was that a live lizard sprang out of it on to the old man's body, ran down his back and off towards the jungle. Sudden fright made the poor man shiver from head to foot, to the great amusement of the other boys, who shouted with glee. Before Jagannath had gone far, cursing and swearing, the gamcha on his shoulder suddenly disappeared, and the next moment it was seen on the head of the new boy, transformed into a turban.

The novel attentions of this manikin came as a great relief to Jagannath. It was long since any boy had taken such freedom with him. After a good deal of coaxing and many fair promises, he at last persuaded the boy to come to him, and this was the conversation which followed,

"What's your name, my boy?"

"Nitai Pal."

"Where's your home?"

"Won't tell."

"Who's your father?"

"Won't tell."

"Why won't you?"

"Because I have run away from home."

"What made you do it?"

"My father wanted to send me to school."

It occurred to Jagannath that it would be useless extravagance to send such a boy to school, and his father must have been an unpractical fool not to have thought so.

"Well, well," said Jagannath, "how would you like to come and stay with me?"

"Don't mind," said the boy, and forthwith he installed himself in Jagannath's house. He felt as little hesitation as though it were the shadow of a tree by the wayside. And not only that. He began to proclaim his wishes as regards his food and clothing with such coolness that you would have thought he had paid his reckoning in full beforehand; and, when anything went wrong, he did not scruple to quarrel with the old man. It had been easy enough for Jagannath to get the better of his own child; but, now, where another man's child was concerned, he had to acknowledge defeat.

III

The people of the village marvelled when Nitai Pal was unexpectedly made so much of by Jagannath. They felt sure that the old man's end was near, and the prospect of his bequeathing all his property to this unknown brat made their hearts sore. Furious with envy, they determined to do the boy an injury, but the old man took care of him as though he was a rib in his breast.

At times, the boy threatened that he would go away, and the old man used to say to him temptingly, "I will leave you all the property I possess." Young as he was, the boy fully understood the grandeur of this promise.

The village people then, began to make inquiries after the father of the boy. Their hearts melted with compassion for the agonised parents, and they declared that the son must be a rascal to cause them so much suffering. They heaped abuses on his head, but the heat with which they did it betrayed envy rather than a sense of justice.

One day the old man learned from a wayfarer that one Damodar Pal was seeking his lost son, and was even now coming towards the village. Nitai, when he heard this, became very restless and was ready to run away, leaving his future wealth to take care of itself. Jagannath reassured him, saying, "I mean to hide you where nobody can find you – not even the village people themselves."

This whetted the curiosity of the boy and he said, "Oh, where? Do show me."

"People will know, if I show you now. Wait till it is night," said Jagannath.

The hope of discovering the mysterious hiding-place delighted Nitai. He planned to himself how, as soon as his father had gone away without him, he would have a bet with his comrades, and play hide-and-seek. Nobody would be able to find him. Wouldn't it be fun? His father, too, would ransack the whole village, and not find him – that would be rare fun also.

At noon, Jagannath shut the boy up in his house, and disappeared for some time. When he came home again, Nitai worried him with questions.

No sooner was it dark than Nitai said, "Grandfather, shall we go now?"

"It isn't night yet," replied Jagannath.

A little while later the boy exclaimed, "It is night now, grandfather; come let's go."

"The village people haven't gone to bed yet," whispered Jagannath.

Nitai waited but a moment, and said, "They have gone to bed now, grandfather; I am sure they have. Let's start now."

The night advanced. Sleep began to weigh heavily on the eyelids of the poor boy, and it was a hard struggle for him to keep awake. At midnight, Jagannath caught hold of the boy's arm, and left the house, groping through the dark lanes of the sleeping village. Not a sound disturbed the stillness, except the occasional howl of a dog, when all the other dogs far and near would join in chorus, or perhaps the flapping of a night-bird, scared by the sound of human footsteps at that unusual hour. Nitai trembled with fear, and held Jagannath fast by the arm.

Across many a field they went, and at last came to a jungle, where stood a dilapidated temple without a god in it. "What, here!" exclaimed Nitai in a tone of disappointment. It was nothing like what he had imagined. There was not much mystery about it. Often, since running away from home, he had passed nights in deserted temples like this. It was not a bad place for playing hide-and-seek; still it was quite possible that his comrades might track him there.

From the middle of the floor inside, Jagannath removed a slab of stone, and an underground room with a lamp burning in it was revealed to the astonished eyes of the boy. Fear and curiosity assailed his little heart. Jagannath descended by a ladder and Nitai followed him.

Looking around, the boy saw that there were brass ghurras on all sides of him. In the middle lay spread an assan, and in front of it were arranged vermilion, sandal paste, flowers, and other articles of puja. To satisfy his curiosity the boy dipped his hand into some of the ghurras, and drew out their contents. They were rupees and gold mohurs.

Jagannath, addressing the boy, said, "I told you, Nitai, that I would give you all my money. I have not got much – these ghurras are all that I possess. These I will make over to you today."

The boy jumped with delight, "All?" he exclaimed; "you won't take back a rupee, will you?"

"If I do," said the old man in solemn tones, "may my hand be attacked with leprosy. But there is one condition. If ever my grandson, Gokul Chandra, or his son, or his grandson, or his great-grandson or any of his progeny should happen to pass this way, then, you must make over to him, or to them, every rupee and every mohur here."

The boy thought that the old man was raving. "Very well," he replied.

"Then, sit on this assan," said Jagannath.

"What for?"

"Because puja will be done to you."

"But why?" said the boy, taken aback.

"This is the rule."

The boy squatted on the assan as he was told. Jagannath smeared his forehead with sandal paste, put a mark of vermilion between his eyebrows, flung a garland of flowers round his neck, and began to recite mantras.

To sit there like a god, and hear mantras recited made poor Nitai feel very uneasy. "Grandfather," he whispered.

But Jagannath did not reply, and went on muttering his incantations.

Finally, with great difficulty he dragged each ghurra before the boy and made him repeat the following vow after him,

"I do solemnly promise that I will make over all this treasure to Gokul Chandra Kundu, the son of Brindaban Kundu, the grandson of Jagannath Kundu, or to the son or to the grandson or to the great-grandson of the said Gokul Chandra Kundu, or any other progeny of his who may be the rightful heir."

The boy repeated this over and over again, until he felt stupefied, and his tongue began to grow still in his mouth. When the ceremony was over, the air of the cave was laden with the smoke of the ear then lamp and the breath-poison of the two. The boy felt that the roof of his mouth had become dry as dust, and his hands and feet were burning. He was nearly suffocated.

The lamp became dimmer and dimmer, and then, went out altogether. In the total darkness that followed, Nitai could hear the old man climbing up the ladder. "Grandfather, where are you going to?" said he, greatly distressed.

"I am going now," replied Jagannath; "you remain here. No one will be able to find you. Remember the name Gokul Chandra, the son of Brindaban, and the grandson of Jagannath."

He then, withdrew the ladder. In a stifled, agonised voice the boy implored, "I want to go back to father."

Jagannath replaced the slab. He then, knelt down and placed his ear on the stone. Nitai's voice was heard once more – "Father" – and then, came a sound of some heavy object falling with a bump – and then – everything was still.

Having thus, placed his wealth in the hands of a yak, Jagannath began to cover up the stone with earth. Then, he piled broken bricks and loose mortar over it. On the top of all he planted turfs of grass and jungle weeds. The night was almost spent, but he could not tear himself away from the spot. Now and again he placed his ear to the ground, and tried to listen. It seemed to him that from far far below – from the abysmal depth of the earth's interior – came a wailing. It seemed to him that the night-sky was flooded with that one sound, that the sleeping humanity of all the world was awake, and was sitting on its beds, trying to listen.

The old man in his frenzy kept on heaping earth higher and higher. He wanted somehow to stifle that sound, but still he fancied he could hear "Father."

He struck the spot with all his might and said, "Be quiet – people might hear you." But still he imagined he heard "Father."

The sun lighted up the eastern horizon. Jagannath then, left the temple, and came into the open fields.

There, too, somebody called out "Father." Startled at the sound, he turned back and saw his son at his heels.

"Father," said Brindaban, "I hear my boy is hiding himself in your house. I must have him back."

His eyes dilated and distorted mouth, the old man leaned forward and exclaimed, "Your boy?"

"Yes, my boy Gokul. He is Nitai Pal now, and I myself go by the name of Damodar Pal. Your fame has spread so widely in the neighbourhood, that we were obliged to cover up our origin, lest people should have refused to pronounce our names."

Slowly the old man lifted both his arms above his head. His fingers began to twitch convulsively, as though he was trying to catch hold of some imaginary object in the air. He then, fell on the ground.

When he came to his senses again, he dragged his son towards the ruined temple. When they were both inside it, he said, "Do you hear any wailing sound?"

"No, I don't," said Brindaban.

"Just listen very carefully. Do you hear anybody calling out 'Father'?"

"No."

This seemed to relieve him greatly.

From that day forward, he used to go about asking people, "Do you hear any wailing sound?" They laughed at the raving dotard.

About four years later, Jagannath lay on his death-bed. When the light of this world was gradually fading away from his eyes, and his breathing became more and more difficult, he suddenly sat up in a state of delirium. Throwing both his hands in the air he seemed to grope about for something, muttering, "Nitai, who has removed my ladder?"

Unable to find the ladder to climb out of his terrible dungeon, where there was no light to see and no air to breathe, he fell on his bed once more, and disappeared into that region where no one has ever been found out in the world's eternal game of hide-and-seek.

19

The Riddle Solved

I

Krishna Gopal Sircar, Zamindar of Jhikrakota, made over his estates to his eldest son, and retired to Kashi, as befits a good Hindu, to spend the evening of his life in religious devotion. All the poor and the destitute of the neighbourhood were in tears at the parting. Everyone declared that such piety and benevolence were rare in these degenerate days.

His son, Bipin Bihari, was a young man well educated after the modern fashion, and had taken the degree of Bachelor of Arts. He sported a pair of spectacles, wore a beard, and seldom mixed with others. His private life was unsullied. He did not smoke, and never touched cards. He was a man of stern disposition, though he looked soft and pliable. This trait of his character soon came home to his tenantry in diverse ways. Unlike his father, he would on no account allow the remission of one single pice out of the rents justly due to him. In no circumstances would he grant any tenant one single day's grace in paying up.

On taking over the management of the property, Bipin Bihari discovered that his father had allowed a large number of

Brahmins to hold land entirely rent-free, and a larger number at rents much below the prevailing rates. His father was incapable of resisting the importunate solicitation of others – such was the weakness of his character.

Bipin Bihari said this could never be. He could not abandon the income of half his property – and he reasoned with himself thus, firstly, the persons who were in actual enjoyment of the concessions and getting fat at his expense were a lot of worthless people, and wholly undeserving of charity. Charity bestowed on such objects only encouraged idleness. Secondly, living nowadays had become much costlier than in the days of his ancestors. Wants had increased apace. For a gentleman to keep up his position had become four times as expensive as in days past. So he could not afford to scatter gifts right and left as his father had done. On the contrary, it was his bounden duty to call back as many of them as he possibly could.

So Bipin Bihari lost no time in carrying into effect what he considered to be his duty. He was a man of strict principles.

What had gone out of his grasp, returned to him little by little. Only a very small portion of his father's grants did he allow to remain undisturbed, and he took good care to arrange that even those should not be deemed permanent.

The wails of the tenants reached Krishna Gopal at Benares through the post. Some even made a journey to that place to represent their grievances to him in person. Krishna Gopal wrote to his son intimating his displeasure. Bipin Bihari replied, pointing out that the times had changed. In former days, he said, the zamindar was compensated for the gifts he made by the many customary presents he received from his tenantry. Recent statutes had made all such impositions illegal. The zamindar had now to rest content with just the stipulated rent, and nothing more. "Unless," he continued, "we keep a strict watch over the payment of our just dues, what will be left to us? Since the tenants won't give us anything extra now, how can we allow them concessions? Our relations must henceforth be strictly commercial. We shall be ruined if we go on making gifts and endowments, and the preservation of our property and the keeping up of our position will be rendered very difficult."

Krishna Gopal became uneasy at finding that times should have changed so much. "Well, well," he murmured to himself, "the younger generation knows best, I suppose. Our old-fashioned methods won't do now. If I interfere, my son might refuse to manage the property, and insist on my going back. No, thank you – I would rather not. I prefer to devote the few days that are left me to the service of my god."

II

So things went on. Bipin Bihari put his affairs in order after much litigation in the Courts, and by less constitutional methods outside. Most of the tenants submitted to his will out of fear. Only a fellow called Asimuddin, son of Mirza Bibi, remained refractory.

Bipin's displeasure was keenest against this man. He could quite understand his father having granted rent-free lands to Brahmins, but why this Mohammedan should be holding so much land, some free and some at rents lower than the prevailing rates, was a riddle to him. And what was he? The son of a low Mohammedan widow, giving himself airs and defying the whole world, simply because he had learnt to read and write a little at the village school. To Bipin it was intolerable.

He made inquiries of his clerks about Asimuddin's holdings. All that they could tell him was that Babu Krishna Gopal himself had made these grants to the family many years back, but they had no idea as to what his motive might have been. They imagined, however, that perhaps the widow won the compassion of the kind-hearted zamindar, by representing to him her woe and misery.

To Bipin these favours seemed to be utterly undeserved. He had not seen the pitiable condition of these people in days gone by. Their comparative ease at the present day and their arrogance drove him to the conclusion that they had impudently swindled his tender-hearted father out of a part of his lawful income.

Asimuddin was a stiff-necked sort of a fellow, too. He vowed that he would lay down his life sooner than give up an inch of his land. Then, came open hostilities.

The poor old widow tried her best to pacify her son. "It is no good fighting with the zamindar," she would often say to him. "His kindness has kept us alive so long; let us depend upon him still, though he may curtail his favours. Surrender to him part of the lands as he desires."

"Oh, mother!" protested Asimuddin. "What do you know of these matters, pray?"

One by one, Asimuddin lost the cases instituted against him. The more he lost, the more his obstinacy increased. For the sake of his all, he staked all that was his.

One afternoon, Mirza Bibi collected some fruits and vegetables from her little garden, and unknown to her son went and sought an interview with Bipin Babu. She looked at him with a tenderness maternal in its intensity, and spoke, "May Allah bless you, my son. Do not destroy Asim – it wouldn't be right of you. To your charge I commit him. Take him as though he were one whom it is your duty to support – as though he were a ne'er-do-well younger brother of yours. Vast is your wealth – don't grudge him a small particle of it, my son."

This assumption of familiarity on the part of the garrulous old woman annoyed Bipin not a little. "What do you know of these things, my good woman?" he condescended to say. "If you have any representations to make, send your son to me."

Being assured for the second time that she knew nothing about these affairs, Mirza Bibi returned home, wiping her eyes with her apron all the way, and offering her silent prayers to Allah.

III

The litigation dragged its weary length from the Criminal to the Civil Courts, and thence to the High Court, where at last Asimuddin met with a partial success. Eighteen months passed in this way. But he was a ruined man now – plunged in debts up to his very ears. His creditors took this opportunity to execute the decrees they had obtained against him. A date was fixed for putting up to auction every stick and stone that he had left.

It was Monday. The village market had assembled by the side of a tiny river, now swollen by the rains. Buying and selling were going on, partly on the bank and partly in the boats moored there. The hubbub was great. Among the commodities for sale jack-fruits preponderated, it being the month of Asadh. Hilsa-fish were seen in large quantities also. The sky was cloudy. Many of the stall-holders, apprehending a downpour, had stretched a piece of cloth overhead, across bamboo poles put up for the purpose.

Asimuddin had come too – but he had not a copper with him. No shopkeepers allowed him credit nowadays. He therefore, had brought a brass thali and a dao with him. These he would pawn, and then, buy what he needed.

Towards evening, Bipin Babu was out for a walk attended by two or three retainers armed with lathis. Attracted by the noise, he directed his steps towards the market. On his arrival, he stopped awhile before the stall of Dwari, the oil-man, and made kindly inquiries about his business. All on a sudden, Asimuddin raised his dao and ran towards Bipin Babu, roaring like a tiger. The market people caught hold of him half-way, and quickly disarmed him. He was forthwith given in custody to the police. Business in the market then, went on as usual.

We cannot say that Bipin Babu was not inwardly pleased at this incident. It is intolerable that the creature we are hunting down should turn and show fight. "The badmash," Bipin chuckled; "I have got him at last."

The ladies of Bipin Babu's house, when they heard the news, exclaimed with horror, "Oh, the ruffian! What a mercy they seized him in time!" They found consolation in the prospect of the man being punished as he richly deserved.

In another part of the village the same evening the widow's humble cottage, devoid of bread and bereft of her son, became darker than death. Others dismissed the incident of the afternoon from their minds, sat down to their meals, retired to bed and went to sleep, but to the widow the event loomed larger than anything else in this wide world. But, alas, who was there to combat it?

Only a bundle of wearied bones and a helpless mother's heart trembling with fear.

IV

Three days have passed in the meanwhile. Tomorrow the case would come up for trial before a Deputy Magistrate. Bipin Babu would have to be examined as a witness. Never before this did a zamindar of Jhikrakota appear in the witness-box, but Bipin did not mind.

The next day at the appointed hour, Bipin Babu arrived at the Court in a palanquin in great state. He wore a turban on his head, and a watch-chain dangled on his breast. The Deputy Magistrate invited him to a seat on the dais, beside his own. The Court-room was crowded to suffocation. So great a sensation had not been witnessed in this Court for many years.

When the time for the case to be called drew near, a chaprassi came and whispered something in Bipin Babu's ear. He got up very agitated and walked out, begging the Deputy Magistrate to excuse him for a few minutes.

Outside he saw his old father a little way off, standing under a banyan tree, barefooted and wrapped in a piece of namabali. A string of beads was in his hand. His slender form shone with a gentle lustre, and tranquil compassion seemed to radiate from his forehead.

Bipin, hampered by his close-fitting trousers and his flowing chapkan, touched his father's feet with his forehead. As he did this his turban came off and kissed his nose, and his watch, popping out of his pocket, swung to and fro in the air. Bipin hurriedly straightened his turban, and begged his father to come to his pleader's house close by.

"No, thank you," Krishna Gopal replied, "I will tell you here what I have got to say."

A curious crowd had gathered by this time. Bipin's attendants pushed them back.

Then, Krishna Gopal said, "You must do what you can to get Asim acquitted, and restore him the lands that you have taken away from him."

"Is it for this, father," said Bipin, very much surprised, "that you have come all the way from Benares? Would you tell me why you have made these people the objects of your special favour?"

"What would you gain by knowing it, my boy?"

But Bipin persisted. "It is only this, father," he went on; "I have revoked many a grant because I thought the tenants were not deserving. There were many Brahmins among them, but of them you never said a word. Why are you so keen about these Mohammedans now? After all that has happened, if I drop this case against Asim, and give him back his lands, what shall I say to people?"

Krishna Gopal kept silence for some moments. Then, passing the beads through his shaky fingers with rapidity, he spoke with a tremendous voice, "Should it be necessary to explain your conduct to people, you may tell them that Asimuddin is my son – and your brother."

"What?" exclaimed Bipin in painful surprise. "From a Musalman's womb?"

"Even so, my son," was the calm reply.

Bipin stood there for some time in mute astonishment. Then, he found words to say, "Come home, father; we will talk about it afterwards."

"No, my son," replied the old man, "having once relinquished the world to serve my god, I cannot go home again. I return hence. Now I leave you to do what your sense of duty may suggest." He then blessed his son, and, checking his tears with difficulty, walked off with tottering steps.

Bipin was dumbfounded, not knowing what to say nor what to do. "So, such was the piety of the older generation," he said to himself. He reflected with pride how much better he was than his father in point of education and morality. This was the result, he concluded, of not having a principle to guide one's actions.

Returning to the Court, he saw Asimuddin outside between two constables, awaiting his trial. He looked emaciated and worn out. His lips were pale and dry, and his eyes unnaturally bright. A dirty piece of cloth worn to shreds covered him. "This my brother!" Bipin shuddered at the thought.

The Deputy Magistrate and Bipin were friends, and the case ended in a fiasco. In a few days Asimuddin was restored to his former condition. Why all this happened, he could not understand. The village people were greatly surprised also.

However, the news of Krishna Gopal's arrival just before the trial soon got abroad. People began to exchange meaning glances. The pleaders in their shrewdness guessed the whole affair. One of them, Ram Taran Babu, was beholden to Krishna Gopal for his education and his start in life. Somehow or other he had always suspected that the virtue and piety of his benefactor were shams. Now he was fully convinced that, if a searching inquiry were made, all "pious" men might be found out. "Let them tell their beads as much as they like," he thought with glee, "everybody in this world is just as bad as myself. The only difference between a good and a bad man is that the good practise dissimulation while the bad don't." The revelation that Krishna Gopal's far-famed piety, benevolence, and magnanimity were nothing but a cloak of hypocrisy, settled a difficulty that had oppressed Ram Taran Babu for many years. By what process of reasoning, we do not know, the burden of gratitude was greatly lifted off his mind. It was a vast relief to him!

20

SUBHA

When the girl was given the name of Subhashini, who could have guessed that she would prove dumb? Her two elder sisters were Sukeshini and Suhashini, and for the sake of uniformity her father named his youngest girl Subhashini. She was called Subha for short.

Her two elder sisters had been married with the usual cost and difficulty, and now the youngest daughter lay like a silent weight upon the heart of her parents. All the world seemed to think that, because she did not speak, therefore, she did not feel; it discussed her future and its own anxiety freely in her presence. She had understood from her earliest childhood that God had sent her like a curse to her father's house, so she withdrew herself from ordinary people, and tried to live apart. If only they would all forget her she felt she could endure it. But who can forget pain? Night and day her parents' minds were aching on her account. Especially, her mother looked upon her as a deformity in herself. To a mother a daughter is a more closely intimate part of herself than a son can be; and a fault in her is a source of personal shame. Banikantha, Subha's father, loved her rather better than his other daughters; her mother regarded her with aversion as a stain upon her own body.

If Subha lacked speech, she did not lack a pair of large dark eyes, shaded with long lashes; and her lips trembled like a leaf in response to any thought that rose in her mind.

When we express our thought in words, the medium is not found easily. There must be a process of translation, which is often inexact, and then, we fall into error. But black eyes need no translating; the mind itself throws a shadow upon them. In them thought opens or shuts, shines forth, or goes out in darkness, hangs steadfast like the setting moon, or, like the swift and restless lightning, illumines all quarters of the sky. They who from birth have had no other speech than the trembling of their lips learn a language of the eyes, endless in expression, deep as the sea, clear as the heavens, wherein play dawn and sunset, light and shadow. The dumb have a lonely grandeur like Nature's own. Wherefore the other children almost dreaded Subha, and never played with her. She was silent and companionless as noontide.

The hamlet where she lived was Chandipur. Its river, small for a river of Bengal, kept to its narrow bounds like a daughter of the middle class. This busy streak of water never overflowed its banks, but went about its duties as though it were a member of every family in the villages beside it. On either side were houses and banks shaded with trees. So stepping from her queenly throne, the river-goddess became a garden deity of each home; and forgetful of herself, performed her task of endless benediction with swift and cheerful foot.

Banikantha's house looked upon the stream. Every but and stack in the place could be seen by the passing boatmen. I know not if amid these signs of worldly wealth any one noticed the little girl who, when her work was done, stole away to the waterside, and sat there. But here Nature fulfilled her want of speech, and spoke for her. The murmur of the brook, the voice of the village folk, the songs of the boatmen, the crying of the birds and rustle of trees mingled, and were one with the trembling of her heart. They became one vast wave of sound, which beat upon her restless soul. This murmur and movement of Nature were the dumb girl's language; that speech of the dark eyes, which the long lashes shaded, was the language of the world about her. From the trees, where the cicalas chirped, to the quiet stars there was nothing but signs and gestures, weeping and sighing. And in the deep mid-noon, when the boatmen and fisher-folk had gone to their dinner, when the villagers slept, and birds were still, when the ferry-boats were idle, when the great busy world paused in its toil, and became suddenly a lonely, awful giant, then, beneath the vast impressive heavens there were only dumb Nature and a dumb girl, sitting very silent – one under the spreading sunlight, the other where a small tree cast its shadow.

But Subha was not altogether without friends. In the stall were two cows, Sharbbashi and Panguli. They had never heard their names from her lips, but they knew her footfall. Though she had no words, she murmured lovingly and they understood her gentle murmuring better than all speech. When she fondled them or scolded or coaxed them, they understood her better than men could do. Subha would come to the shed, and throw her arms round Sharbbashi's neck; she would rub her check against her friends, and Panguli would turn her great kind eyes and lick her face. The girl paid them three regular visits every day, and others that were irregular. Whenever she heard any words that hurt her, she would come to these dumb friends out of due time. It was as though they guessed her anguish of spirit from her quiet look of sadness. Coming close to her, they would rub their horns softly against her arms, and in dumb, puzzled fashion try to comfort her. Besides these two, there were goats and a kitten; but Subha had not the same equality of friendship with them, though they showed the same attachment. Every time it got a chance, night or day, the kitten would jump into her lap, and settle down to slumber, and show its appreciation of an aid to sleep as Subha drew her soft fingers over its neck and back.

Subha had a comrade also among the higher animals, and it is hard to say what were the girl's relations with him, for he could speak, and his gift of speech left them without any common language. He was the youngest boy of the Gosains, Pratap by name, an idle fellow. After long effort, his parents had abandoned the hope that he would ever make his living. Now losels have this advantage, that, though their own folk disapprove of them, they are generally popular with Everyone else. Having no work to chain them, they become public property. Just as every town needs an open space where all may breathe, so a village needs two or three gentlemen of leisure, who can give time to all; so that, if we are lazy and want a companion, one is to hand.

Pratap's chief ambition was to catch fish. He managed to waste a lot of time this way, and might be seen almost any afternoon so employed. It was thus, most often that he met Subha. Whatever he was about, he liked a companion; and, when one is catching fish, a silent companion is best of all. Pratap respected Subha for her taciturnity, and, as Everyone called her Subha, he showed his affection by calling her Su. Subha used to sit beneath a tamarind, and Pratap, a little distance off, would cast his line. Pratap took with him a small allowance of betel, and Subha prepared it for him. And I think that, sitting and gazing a long while, she desired ardently to bring some great help to Pratap, to be of real aid, to prove by any means that she was not a useless burden to the world. But there was nothing to do. Then, she turned to the Creator in prayer for some rare power, that by an astonishing miracle she might startle Pratap into exclaiming, "My! I never dreamt our Su could have done this!"

Only think! If Subha had been a water nymph, she might have risen slowly from the river, bringing the gem of a snake's crown to the landing-place. Then, Pratap, leaving his paltry fishing, might dive into the lower world, and see there, on a golden bed in a palace of silver, whom else but dumb little Su, Banikantha's child! Yes, our Su, the only daughter of the king of that shining city of jewels! But that might not be, it was impossible. Not that anything is really impossible, but Su had been born, not into the royal house of Patalpur, but into Banikantha's family, and she knew no means of astonishing the Gosains' boy.

Gradually she grew up. Gradually she began to find herself. A new inexpressible consciousness like a tide from the central places of the sea, when the moon is full, swept through her. She saw herself, questioned herself, but no answer came that she could understand.

Once upon a time, late on a night of full moon, she slowly opened her door, and peeped out timidly. Nature, herself at full moon, like lonely Subha, was looking down on the sleeping earth. Her strong young life beat within her; joy and sadness filled her being to its brim; she reached the limits even of her own illimitable loneliness, nay, passed beyond them. Her heart was heavy, and she could not speak! At the skirts of this silent, troubled Mother there stood a silent troubled girl.

The thought of her marriage filled her parents with an anxious care. People blamed them, and even talked of making them outcasts. Banikantha was well off; they had fish-curry twice daily; and consequently he did not lack enemies. Then, the women interfered, and Bani went away for a few days. Presently he returned, and said, "We must go to Calcutta."

They got ready to go to this strange country. Subha's heart was heavy with tears, like a mist-wrapt dawn. With a vague fear that had been gathering for days, she dogged her father and mother like a dumb animal. With her large eyes wide open, she scanned their faces as though she wished to learn something. But not a word did they vouchsafe. One afternoon in the midst of all this, as Pratap was fishing, he laughed, "So then, Su, they have caught your bridegroom and you are going to be married! Mind you don't forget me altogether!" Then, he turned his mind again to his fish. As a stricken doe looks in the hunter's face, asking in silent agony, "What have I done to you?" so Subha looked at Pratap. That day she sat no longer beneath her tree. Banikantha, having finished his nap, was smoking in his bedroom when Subha dropped down at his feet and burst out weeping as she gazed towards him. Banikantha tried to comfort her, and his cheek grew wet with tears.

It was settled that on the morrow they should go to Calcutta. Subha went to the cow-shed to bid farewell to her childhood's comrades. She fed them with her hand; she clasped their necks; she looked into their faces, and tears fell fast from the eyes which spoke for her. That night was the tenth of the moon. Subha left her room, and flung herself down on her grassy couch beside her dear river. It was as if she threw her arms about Earth, her strong, silent mother, and tried to say, "Do not let me leave you, mother. Put your arms about me, as I have put mine about you, and hold me fast."

One day in a house in Calcutta, Subha's mother dressed her up with great care. She imprisoned her hair, knotting it up in laces, she hung her about with ornaments and did her best to kill her natural beauty. Subha's eyes filled with tears. Her mother, fearing they would grow swollen with weeping, scolded her harshly, but the tears disregarded the scolding. The bridegroom came with a friend to inspect the bride. Her parents were dizzy with anxiety and fear when they saw the god arrive to select the beast for his sacrifice. Behind the stage, the mother called her instructions aloud, and increased her daughter's weeping twofold, before she sent her into the examiner's presence. The great man, after scanning her a long time, observed, "Not so bad."

He took special note of her tears, and thought she must have a tender heart. He put it to her credit in the account, arguing that the heart, which today was distressed at leaving her parents, would presently prove a useful possession. Like the oyster's pearls, the child's tears only increased her value, and he made no other comment.

The almanac was consulted, and the marriage took place on an auspicious day. Having delivered over their dumb girl into another's hands, Subha's parents returned home. Thank God! Their caste in this and their safety in the next world were assured! The bridegroom's work lay in the west, and shortly after their marriage he took his wife thither.

In less than ten days Everyone knew that the bride was dumb! At least, if any one did not, it was not her fault, for she deceived no one. Her eyes told them everything, though no one understood her. She looked on every hand; she found no speech; she missed the faces, familiar from birth, of those who had understood a dumb girl's language. In her silent heart there sounded an endless, voiceless weeping, which only the Searcher of Hearts could hear.

21

The Elder Sister

I

Having described at length the misdeeds of an unfortunate woman's wicked, tyrannical husband, Tara, the woman's neighbour in the village, very shortly declared her verdict, "Fire be to such a husband's mouth."

At this Joygopal Babu's wife felt much hurt; it did not become womankind to wish, in any circumstances whatever, a worse species of fire than that of a cigar in a husband's mouth.

When, therefore, she mildly disapproved the verdict, hard-hearted Tara cried with redoubled vehemence, "'Twere better to be a widow seven births over than the wife of such a husband," and saying this she broke up the meeting and left.

Shashi said within himself, "I can't imagine any offence in a husband that could so harden the heart against him." Even as she turned the matter over in her mind, all the tenderness of her loving soul gushed forth towards her own husband now abroad. Throwing herself with outstretched arms on that part of the bed whereon her husband was wont to lie, she kissed the empty pillow, caught the smell of her husband's head, and, shutting the door, brought out from a wooden box an old and almost faded photograph with some letters in his handwriting, and sat gazing upon them. Thus, she passed the hushed noontide alone in her room, musing of old memories and shedding tears of sadness.

It was no new yoke this between Shashikala and Joygopal. They had been married at an early age and had children. Their long companionship had made the days go by in an easy, commonplace sort of way. On neither side had there been any symptoms of excessive passion. They had lived together nearly sixteen years without a break, when her husband was suddenly called away from home on business, and then, a great impulse of love awoke in Shashi's soul. As separation strained the tie, love's knot grew tighter, and the passion, whose existence Shashi had not felt, now made her throb with pain.

So it happened that after so many long years, and at such an age, and being the mother of children, Shashi, on this spring noon, in her lonely chamber, lying on the bed of separation, began to dream the sweet dream of a bride in her budding youth. That love of which hitherto she had been unconscious suddenly aroused her with its murmuring music. She wandered a long way up the stream, and saw many a golden mansion and many a grove on either bank; but no foothold could she find now amid the vanished hopes of happiness. She began to say to herself that, when next she met her husband, life should not be insipid nor should the spring come in vain. How very often, in idle disputation or some petty quarrel, had she teased her husband! With all the singleness of a penitent heart she vowed that she would never show impatience again, never oppose her husband's wishes, bear all his commands, and with a tender heart submit to whatever he wished of good or ill; for the husband was all-in-all, the husband was the dearest object of love, the husband was divine.

Shashikala was the only and much-petted daughter of her parents. For this reason, though he had only a small property of his own, Joygopal had no anxieties about the future. His father-in-law had enough to support them in a village with royal state.

And then, in his old age a son was born untimely to Shashikala's father. To tell the truth, Shashi was very sore in her mind at this unlooked-for, improper, and unjust action of her parents; nor was Joygopal particularly pleased.

The parents' love centred in this son of their advanced years, and when the newly arrived, diminutive, sleepy brother-in-law seized with his two weak tiny fists all the hopes and expectations of Joygopal, Joygopal found a place in a tea-garden in Assam.

His friends urged him to look for employment hard-by, but whether out of a general feeling of resentment, or knowing the chances of rapid rise in a tea-garden, Joygopal would not pay heed to anybody. He sent his wife and children to his father-in-law's, and left for Assam. It was the first separation between husband and wife in their married life.

This incident made Shashikala very angry with her baby brother. The soreness which may not pass the lips is felt the more keenly within. When the little fellow sucked and slept at his ease, his big sister found a hundred reasons, such as the rice is cold, the boys are too late for school, to worry herself and others, day and night, with her petulant humours.

But in a short time the child's mother died. Before her death, she committed her infant son to her daughter's care.

Then, did the motherless child easily conquer his sister's heart. With loud whoops he would fling himself upon her, and with right good-will try to get her mouth, nose, eyes within his own tiny mouth; he would seize her hair within his little fists and refuse to give it up; awaking before the dawn, he would roll over to her side and thrill her with his soft touch, and babble like a noisy brook; later on, he would call her Jiji and Jijima, and in hours of work and rest, by doing forbidden things, eating forbidden food, going to forbidden places, would set up a regular tyranny over her; then, Shashi could resist no longer. She surrendered herself completely to this wayward little tyrant. Since the child had no mother, his influence over her became the greater.

II

The child was named Nilmani. When he was two years old his father fell seriously ill. A letter reached Joygopal asking him to come as quickly as possible. When after much trouble he got leave and arrived, Kaliprasanna's last hour had come.

Before he died Kaliprasanna entrusted Joygopal with the charge of his son, and left a quarter of his estate to his daughter.

So Joygopal gave up his appointment, and came home to look after his property.

After a long time husband and wife met again. When a material body breaks it may be put together again. But when two human beings are divided, after a long separation, they never re-unite at the same place, and to the same time; for the mind is a living thing, and moment by moment it grows and changes.

In Shashi reunion stirred a new emotion. The numbness of age-long habit in their old marriage was entirely removed by the longing born of separation, and she seemed to win her husband much more closely than before. Had she not vowed in her mind that whatever days might come, and how long soever they might be, she would never let the brightness of this glowing love for her husband be dimmed.

Of this reunion, however, Joygopal felt differently. When they were constantly together before he had been bound to his wife by his interests and idiosyncrasies. His wife was then, a living truth in his life, and there would have been a great rent in the web of his daily habit if she were left out. Consequently Joygopal found himself in deep waters at first when he went abroad. But in time this breach in habit was patched up by a new habit.

And this was not all. Formerly his days went by in the most indolent and careless fashion. For the last two years, the stimulus of bettering his condition had stirred so powerfully in his breast that he had nothing else in his thoughts. As compared with the intensity of this new passion, his old life seemed like an unsubstantial shadow. The greatest changes in a woman's nature are wrought by love; in a man's, by ambition.

Joygopal, when he returned after two years, found his wife not quite the same as of old. To her life his infant brother-in-law had added a new breadth. This part of her life was wholly unfamiliar to him – here he had no communion with his wife. His wife tried hard to share her love for the child with him, but it cannot be said that she succeeded. Shashi would come with the child in her arms, and hold him before her husband with a smiling face – Nilmani would clasp Shashi's neck, and hide his face on her shoulder, and admit no obligation of kindred. Shashi wished that her little brother might show Joygopal all the arts he had learnt to capture a man's mind. But Joygopal was not very keen about it. How could the child show any enthusiasm? Joygopal could not at all understand what there was in the heavy-pated, grave-faced, dusky child that so much love should be wasted on him.

Women quickly understand the ways of love. Shashi at once understood that Joygopal did not care for Nilmani. Henceforth, she used to screen her brother with the greatest care – to keep him away from the unloving, repelling look of her husband. Thus, the child came to be the treasure of her secret care, the object of her isolated love.

Joygopal was greatly annoyed when Nilmani cried; so Shashi would quickly press the child to her breast, and with her whole heart and soul try to soothe him. And when Nilmani's cry happened to disturb Joygopal's sleep at night, and Joygopal with an expression of displeasure, and in a tortured spirit, growled at the child, Shashi felt humbled and fluttered like a guilty thing. Then, she would take up the child in her lap, retire to a distance, and in a voice of pleading love, with such endearments as "my gold, my treasure, my jewel," lull him to sleep.

Children will fall out for a hundred things. Formerly in such cases, Shashi would punish her children, and side with her brother, for he was motherless. Now the law changed with the judge. Nilmani had often to bear heavy punishment without fault and without inquiry. This wrong went like a dagger to Shashi's heart; so she would take her punished brother into her room, and with sweets and toys, and by caressing and kissing him, solace as much as she could his stricken heart.

Thus, the more Shashi loved Nilmani, the more Joygopal was annoyed with him. On the other hand, the more Joygopal showed his contempt for Nilmani, the more would Shashi bathe the child with the nectar of her love.

And when the fellow Joygopal behaved harshly to his wife, Shashi would minister to him silently, meekly, and with loving-kindness. But inwardly they hurt each other, moment by moment, about Nilmani.

The hidden clash of a silent conflict like this is far harder to bear than an open quarrel.

III

Nilmani's head was the largest part of him. It seemed as if the Creator had blown through a slender stick a big bubble at its top. The doctors feared sometimes that the child might be as frail and as quickly evanescent as a bubble. For a long time he could neither speak nor walk. Looking at his sad grave face, you might think that his parents had unburdened all the sad weight of their advanced years upon the head of this little child.

With his sister's care and nursing, Nilmani passed the period of danger, and arrived at his sixth year.

In the month of Kartik, on the Bhaiphoto day, Shashi had dressed Nilmani up as a little Babu, in coat and chadar and red-bordered dhoti, and was giving him the "brother's mark," when her outspoken neighbour Tara came in and, for one reason or another, began a quarrel.

"'Tis no use," cried she, "giving the 'brother's mark' with so much show and ruining the brother in secret."

At this Shashi was thunderstruck with astonishment, rage, and pain. Tara repeated the rumour that Shashi and her husband had conspired together to put the minor Nilmani's property up for sale for arrears of rent, and to purchase it in the name of her husband's cousin. When Shashi heard this, she uttered a curse that those who could spread such a foul lie might be stricken with leprosy in the mouth. And then, she went weeping to her husband, and told him of the gossip. Joygopal said, "Nobody can be trusted in these days. Upen is my aunt's son, and I felt quite safe in leaving him in charge of the property. He could not have allowed the taluk Hasilpur to fall into arrears and purchase it himself in secret, if I had had the least inkling about it."

"Won't you sue then,?" asked Shashi in astonishment.

"Sue one's cousin!" said Joygopal. "Besides, it would be useless, a simple waste of money."

It was Shashi's supreme duty to trust her husband's word, but Shashi could not. At last her happy home, the domesticity of her love seemed hateful to her. That home life which had once seemed her supreme refuge was nothing more than a cruel snare of self-interest, which had surrounded them, brother and sister, on all sides. She was a woman, single-handed, and she knew not how she could save the helpless Nilmani. The more she thought, the more her heart filled with terror, loathing, and an infinite love for her imperilled little brother. She thought that, if she only knew how, she would appear before the Lat Saheb, nay, write to the Maharani herself, to save her brother's property. The Maharani would surely not allow Nilmani's taluk of Hasilpur, with an income of seven hundred and fifty-eight rupees a year, to be sold.

When Shashi was thus, thinking of bringing her husband's cousin to book by appealing to the Maharani herself, Nilmani was suddenly seized with fever and convulsions.

Joygopal called in the village doctor. When Shashi asked for a better doctor, Joygopal said, "Why, Matilal isn't a bad sort."

Shashi fell at his feet, and charged him with an oath on her own head; whereupon Joygopal said, "Well, I shall send for the doctor from town."

Shashi lay with Nilmani in her lap, nor would Nilmani let her out of his sight for a minute; he clung to her lest by some pretence she should escape; even while he slept he would not loosen his hold of her dress.

Thus, the whole day passed, and Joygopal came after nightfall to say that the doctor was not at home; he had gone to see a patient at a distance. He added that he himself had to leave that very day on account of a lawsuit, and that he had told Matilal, who would regularly call to see the patient.

At night Nilmani wandered in his sleep. As soon as the morning dawned, Shashi, without the least scruple, took a boat with her sick brother, and went straight to the doctor's house. The doctor was at home – he had not left the town. He quickly found lodgings for her, and having installed her under the care of an elderly widow, undertook the treatment of the boy.

The next day Joygopal arrived. Blazing with fury, he ordered his wife to return home with him at once.

"Even if you cut me to pieces, I won't return," replied his wife. "You all want to kill my Nilmani, who has no father, no mother, none other than me, but I will save him."

"Then, you remain here, and don't come back to my house," cried Joygopal indignantly.

Shashi at length fired up. "Your house! Why, 'tis my brother's!"

"All right, we'll see," said Joygopal. The neighbours made a great stir over this incident. "If you want to quarrel with your husband," said Tara, "do so at home. What is the good of leaving your house? After all, Joygopal is your husband."

By spending all the money she had with her, and selling her ornaments, Shashi saved her brother from the jaws of death. Then, she heard that the big property which they had in Dwarigram, where their dwelling-house stood, the income of which was more than Rs. 1500 a year, had been transferred by Joygopal into his own name with the help of the zamindar. And now the whole property belonged to them, not to her brother.

When he had recovered from his illness, Nilmani would cry plaintively, "Let us go home, sister." His heart was pining for his nephews and nieces, his companions. So he repeatedly said, "Let us go home, sister, to that old house of ours." At this Shashi wept. Where was their home?

But it was no good crying. Her brother had no one else besides herself in the world. Shashi thought of this, wiped her tears, and, entering the zenana of the Deputy Magistrate, Tarini Babu, appealed to his wife. The Deputy Magistrate knew Joygopal. That a woman should forsake her home, and engage in a dispute with her husband regarding matters of property, greatly incensed him against Shashi. However, Tarini Babu kept Shashi diverted, and instantly wrote to Joygopal. Joygopal put his wife and brother-in-law into a boat by force, and brought them home.

Husband and wife, after a second separation, met again for the second time! The decree of Prajapati!

Having got back his old companions after a long absence, Nilmani was perfectly happy. Seeing his unsuspecting joy, Shashi felt as if her heart would break.

IV

The Magistrate was touring in the Mofussil during the cold weather and pitched his tent within the village to shoot. The Saheb met Nilmani on the village maidan. The other boys gave him a wide berth, varying Chanakya's couplet a little, and adding the Saheb to the list of "the clawed, the toothed, and the horned beasts." But grave-natured Nilmani in imperturbable curiosity serenely gazed at the Saheb.

The Saheb was amused and came up and asked in Bengali, "You read at the pathsala?"

The boy silently nodded. "What pustaks do you read?" asked the Saheb.

As Nilmani did not understand the word pustak, he silently fixed his gaze on the Magistrate's face. Nilmani told his sister the story of his meeting the Magistrate with great enthusiasm.

At noon, Joygopal, dressed in trousers, chapkan and pagri, went to pay his salams to the Saheb. A crowd of suitors, chaprassies, and constables stood about him. Fearing the heat, the Saheb had seated himself at a court-table outside the tent, in the open shade, and placing Joygopal in a chair, questioned him about the state of the village. Having taken the seat of honour in open view of the community, Joygopal swelled inwardly, and thought it would be a good thing if any of the Chakrabartis or Nandis came and saw him there.

At this moment, a woman, closely veiled, and accompanied by Nilmani, came straight up to the Magistrate. She said, "Saheb, into your hands I resign my helpless brother. Save him." The Saheb, seeing the large-headed, solemn boy, whose acquaintance he had already made, and thinking that the woman must be of a respectable family, at once stood up and said, "Please enter the tent."

The woman said, "What I have to say I will say here."

Joygopal writhed and turned pale. The curious villagers thought it capital fun, and pressed closer. But the moment the Saheb lifted his cane they scampered off.

Holding her brother by the hand, Shashi narrated the history of the orphan from the beginning. As Joygopal tried to interrupt now and then, the Magistrate thundered with a flushed face, "Chup raho," and with the tip of his cane motioned to Joygopal to leave the chair and stand up.

Joygopal, inwardly raging against Shashi, stood speechless. Nilmani nestled up close to his sister, and listened awe-struck.

When Shashi had finished her story, the Magistrate put a few questions to Joygopal, and on hearing his answers, kept silence for a long while, and then, addressed Shashi thus, "My good woman, though this matter may not come up before me, still rest assured I will do all that is needful about it. You can return home with your brother without the least misgiving."

Shashi said, "Saheb, so long as he does not get back his own home, I dare not take him there. Unless you keep Nilmani with you, none else will be able to save him."

"And what would you do?" queried the Saheb.

"I will retire to my husband's house," said Shashi; "there is nothing to fear for me."

The Saheb smiled a little, and as there was nothing else to do, agreed to take charge of this lean, dusty, grave, sedate, gentle Bengali boy whose neck was ringed with amulets.

When Shashi was about to take her leave, the boy clutched her dress. "Don't be frightened, Baba – come," said the Saheb. With tears streaming behind her veil, Shashi said, "Do go, my brother, my darling brother – you will meet your sister again!"

Saying this she embraced him and stroked his head and back, and releasing her dress, hastily withdrew; and just then, the Saheb put his left arm round him. The child wailed out, "Sister, oh, my sister!" Shashi turned round at once, and with outstretched arm made a sign of speechless solace, and with a bursting heart withdrew.

Again in that old, ever-familiar house husband and wife met. The decree of Prajapati!

But this union did not last long. For soon after the villagers learnt one morning that Shashi had died of cholera in the night, and had been instantly cremated.

None uttered a word about it. Only neighbour Tara would sometimes be on the point of bursting out, but people would shut up her mouth, saying, "Hush!"

At parting, Shashi gave her word to her brother they would meet again. Where that word was kept none can tell.

22

THE POSTMASTER

The postmaster first took up his duties in the village of Ulapur. Though the village was a small one, there was an indigo factory near by, and the proprietor, an Englishman, had managed to get a post office established.

Our postmaster belonged to Calcutta. He felt like a fish out of water in this remote village. His office and living-room were in a dark thatched shed, not far from a green, slimy pond, surrounded on all sides by a dense growth.

The men employed in the indigo factory had no leisure; moreover, they were hardly desirable companions for decent folk. Nor is a Calcutta boy an adept in the art of associating with others. Among strangers he appears either proud or ill at ease. At any rate the postmaster had but little company; nor had he much to do.

At times he tried his hand at writing a verse or two. That the movement of the leaves and the clouds of the sky were enough to fill life with joy – such were the sentiments to which he sought to give expression. But God knows that the poor fellow would have felt it as the gift of a new life, if some genie of the Arabian Nights had in one night swept away the trees, leaves and all, and replaced them with a macadamised road, hiding the clouds from view with rows of tall houses.

The postmaster's salary was small. He had to cook his own meals, which he used to share with Ratan, an orphan girl of the village, who did odd jobs for him.

When in the evening the smoke began to curl up from the village cow-sheds, and the cicalas chirped in every bush; when the fakirs of the Baul sect sang their shrill songs in their daily meeting-place, when any poet, who had attempted to watch the movement of the leaves in the dense bamboo thickets, would have felt a ghostly shiver run down his back, the postmaster would light his little lamp, and call out "Ratan."

Ratan would sit outside waiting for this call, and, instead of coming in at once, would reply, "Did you call me, Sir?"

"What are you doing?" the postmaster would ask.

"I must be going to light the kitchen fire," would be the answer.

And the postmaster would say, "Oh, let the kitchen fire be for awhile; light me my pipe first."

At last Ratan would enter, with puffed-out cheeks, vigorously blowing into a flame a live coal to light the tobacco. This would give the postmaster an opportunity of conversing. "Well, Ratan," perhaps he would begin, "do you remember anything of your mother?" That was a fertile subject. Ratan partly remembered, and partly didn't. Her father had been fonder of her than her mother; him she recollected more vividly. He used to come home in the evening after his work, and one or two evenings stood out more clearly than others, like pictures in her memory. Ratan would squat on the floor near the postmaster's feet, as memories crowded in upon her. She called to mind a little brother that she had – and how on some bygone cloudy day she had played at fishing with him on the edge of the pond, with a twig for a make-believe fishing-rod. Such little incidents would drive out greater events from her mind. Thus, as they talked, it would often get very late, and the postmaster would feel too lazy to do any cooking at all. Ratan would then, hastily light the fire, and toast some unleavened bread, which, with the cold remnants of the morning meal, was enough for their supper.

On some evenings, seated at his desk in the corner of the big empty shed, the postmaster too would call up memories of his own home, of his mother and his sister, of those for whom in his exile his heart was sad – memories which were always haunting him, but which he could not talk about with the men of the factory, though he found himself naturally recalling them aloud in the presence of the simple little girl. And so it came about that the girl would allude to his people as mother, brother, and sister, as if she had known them all her life. In fact, she had a complete picture of each one of them painted in her little heart.

One noon, during a break in the rains, there was a cool soft breeze blowing; the smell of the damp grass and leaves in the hot sun felt like the warm breathing of the tired earth on one's body. A persistent bird went on all the afternoon repeating the burden of its one complaint in Nature's audience chamber.

The postmaster had nothing to do. The shimmer of the freshly washed leaves, and the banked-up remnants of the retreating rain-clouds were sights to see; and the postmaster was watching them, and thinking to himself, "Oh, if only some kindred soul were near – just one loving human being whom I could hold near my heart!" This was exactly, he went on to think, what that bird was trying to say, and it was the same feeling which the murmuring leaves were striving to express. But no one knows, or would believe, that such an idea might also take possession of an ill-paid village postmaster in the deep, silent mid-day interval of his work.

The postmaster sighed, and called out "Ratan." Ratan was then, sprawling beneath the guava-tree, busily engaged in eating unripe guavas. At the voice of her master, she ran up breathlessly, saying, "Were you calling me, Dada?" "I was thinking," said the postmaster, "of teaching you to read," and then, for the rest of the afternoon he taught her the alphabet.

Thus, in a very short time, Ratan had got as far as the double consonants.

It seemed as though the showers of the season would never end. Canals, ditches, and hollows were all overflowing with water. Day and night the patter of rain was heard, and the creaking of frogs. The village roads became impassable, and marketing had to be done in punts.

One heavily clouded morning, the postmaster's little pupil had been long waiting outside the door for her call, but, not hearing it as usual, she took up her dog-cared book, and slowly entered the room. She found her master stretched out on his pallet, and, thinking he was resting, she was about to retire on tip-toe, when she suddenly heard her name – "Ratan!" She turned at once and asked, "Were you sleeping, Dada?" The postmaster in a plaintive voice said, "I am not well. Feel my head; is it very hot?"

In the loneliness of his exile, and in the gloom of the rains, his ailing body needed a little tender nursing. He longed to remember the touch on the forehead of soft hands with tinkling bracelets, to imagine the presence of loving womanhood, the nearness of mother and sister. And the exile was not disappointed. Ratan ceased to be a little girl. She at once stepped into the post of mother, called in the village doctor, gave the patient his pills at the proper intervals, sat up all night by his pillow, cooked his gruel for him, and every now and then, asked, "Are you feeling a little better, Dada?"

It was some time before the postmaster, with weakened body, was able to leave his sick-bed. "No more of this," said he with decision. "I must get a transfer." He at once wrote off to Calcutta an application for a transfer, on the ground of the unhealthiness of the place.

Relieved of her duties as nurse, Ratan again took up her old-place outside the door. But she no longer heard the same old call. She would sometimes peep inside furtively to find the postmaster sitting on his chair, or stretched on his pallet, and staring absent-mindedly into the air. While Ratan was awaiting her call, the postmaster was awaiting a reply to his application. The girl read her old lessons over and over again – her great fear was lest, when the call came, she might be found wanting in the double consonants. At last, after a week, the call did come one evening. With an overflowing heart Ratan rushed into the room with her – "Were you calling me, Dada?"

The postmaster said, "I am going away tomorrow, Ratan."

"Where are you going, Dada?"

"I am going home."

"When will you come back?"

"I am not coming back."

Ratan asked no other question. The postmaster, of his own accord, went on to tell her that his application for a transfer had been rejected, so he had resigned his post, and was going home.

For a long time neither of them spoke another word. The lamp went on dimly burning, and from a leak in one corner of the thatch water dripped steadily into an earthen, vessel on the floor beneath it.

After a while Ratan rose, and went off to the kitchen to prepare the meal; but she was not so quick about it as on other days. Many new things to think of had entered her little brain. When the postmaster had finished his supper, the girl suddenly asked him, "Dada, will you take me to your home?"

The postmaster laughed. "What an idea!" said he; but he did not think it necessary to explain to the girl wherein lay the absurdity.

That whole night, in her waking and in her dreams, the postmaster's laughing reply haunted her – "What an idea!"

On getting up in the morning, the postmaster found his bath ready. He had stuck to his Calcutta habit of bathing in water drawn and kept in pitchers, instead of taking a plunge in the river as was the custom of the village. For some reason or other, the girl could not ask him about the time of his departure, so she had fetched the water from the river long before sunrise, that it should be ready as early as he might want it. After the bath came a call for Ratan. She entered noiselessly, and looked silently into her master's face for orders. The master said, "You need not be anxious about my going away, Ratan; I shall tell my successor to look after you." These words were kindly meant, no doubt, but inscrutable are the ways of a woman's heart!

Ratan had borne many a scolding from her master without complaint, but these kind words she could not bear. She burst out weeping, and said, "No, no, you need not tell anybody anything at all about me; I don't want to stay on here."

The postmaster was dumbfounded. He had never seen Ratan like this before.

The new incumbent duly arrived, and the postmaster, having given over charge, prepared to depart. Just before starting he called Ratan, and said, "Here is something for you; I hope it will keep you for some little time." He brought out from his pocket the whole of his month's salary, retaining only a trifle for his travelling expenses. Then, Ratan fell at his feet and cried, "Oh, Dada, I pray you, don't give me anything, don't in any way trouble about me," and then, she ran away out of sight.

The postmaster heaved a sigh, took up his carpet bag, put his umbrella over his shoulder, and, accompanied by a man carrying his many-coloured tin trunk, he slowly made for the boat.

When he got in and the boat was under way, and the rain-swollen river, like a stream of tears welling up from the earth, swirled and sobbed at her bows, then, he felt a sort of pain at heart; the grief-stricken face of a village girl seemed to represent for him the great unspoken pervading grief of Mother Earth herself. At one time he had an impulse to go back, and bring away along with him that lonesome waif, forsaken of the world. But the wind had just filled the sails, the boat had got well into the middle of the turbulent current, and already the village was left behind, and its outlying burning-ground came in sight.

So the traveller, borne on the breast of the swift-flowing river, consoled himself with philosophical reflections on the numberless meetings and partings going on in the world – on death, the great parting, from which none returns.

But Ratan had no philosophy. She was wandering about the post office in a flood of tears. It may be that she had still a lurking hope in some corner of her heart that her Dada would return, and that is why she could not tear herself away. Alas for the foolish human heart!

23

The Castaway

Towards evening the storm was at its height. From the terrific downpour of rain, the crash of thunder, and the repeated flashes of lightning, you might think that a battle of the gods and demons was raging in the skies. Black clouds waved like the Flags of Doom. The Ganges was lashed into a fury, and the trees of the gardens on either bank swayed from side to side with sighs and groans.

In a closed room of one of the riverside houses at Chandernagore, a husband and his wife were seated on a bed spread on the floor, intently discussing. An earthen, lamp burned beside them.

The husband, Sharat, was saying, "I wish you would stay on a few days more; you would then, be able to return home quite strong again."

The wife, Kiran, was saying, "I have quite recovered already. It will not, cannot possibly, do me any harm to go home now."

Every married person will at once understand that the conversation was not quite so brief as I have reported it. The matter was not difficult, but the arguments for and against did not advance it towards a solution. Like a rudderless boat, the discussion kept turning round and round the same point; and at last it threatened to be overwhelmed in a flood of tears.

Sharat said, "The doctor thinks you should stop here a few days longer."

Kiran replied, "Your doctor knows everything!"

"Well," said Sharat, "you know that just now all sorts of illness are abroad. You would do well to stop here a month or two more."

"And at this moment I suppose Everyone in this place is perfectly well!"

What had happened was this, Kiran was a universal favourite with her family and neighbours, so that, when she fell seriously ill, they were all anxious. The village wiseacres thought it shameless for her husband to make so much fuss about a mere wife and even to suggest a change of air, and asked if Sharat supposed that no woman had ever been ill before, or whether he had found out that the folk of the place to which he meant to take her were immortal. Did he imagine that the writ of Fate did not run there? But Sharat and his mother turned a deaf ear to them, thinking that the little life of their darling was of greater importance than the united wisdom of a village. People are wont to reason thus, when danger threatens their loved ones. So Sharat went to Chandernagore, and Kiran recovered, though she was still very weak. There was a pinched look on her face which filled the beholder with pity, and made his heart tremble, as he thought how narrowly she had escaped death.

Kiran was fond of society and amusement; the loneliness of her riverside villa did not suit her at all. There was nothing to do, there were no interesting neighbours, and she hated to be busy all day with medicine and dieting. There was no fun in measuring doses and making fomentations. Such was the subject discussed in their closed room on this stormy evening.

So long as Kiran deigned to argue, there was a chance of a fair fight. When she ceased to reply, and with a toss of her head disconsolately looked the other way, the poor man was disarmed. He was on the point of surrendering unconditionally when a servant shouted a message through the shut door.

Sharat got up, and, opening the door, learnt that a boat had been upset in the storm, and that one of the occupants, a young Brahmin boy, had succeeded in swimming ashore in their garden.

Kiran was at once her own sweet self, and set to work to get out some dry clothes for the boy. She then, warmed a cup of milk, and invited him to her room.

The boy had long curly hair, big expressive eyes, and no sign yet of hair on the face. Kiran, after getting him to drink some milk, asked him all about himself.

He told her that his name was Nilkanta, and that he belonged to a theatrical troupe. They were coming to play in a neighbouring villa when the boat suddenly foundered in the storm. He had no idea what had become of his companions. He was a good swimmer, and had just managed to reach the shore.

The boy stayed with them. His narrow escape from a terrible death made Kiran take a warm interest in him. Sharat thought the boy's appearance at this moment rather a good thing, as his wife would now have something to amuse her, and might be persuaded to stay on for some time longer. Her mother-in-law, too, was pleased at the prospect of profiting their Brahmin guest by her kindness. And Nilkanta himself was delighted at his double escape from his master and from the other world, as well as at finding a home in this wealthy family.

But in a short while Sharat and his mother changed their opinion, and longed for his departure. The boy found a secret pleasure in smoking Sharat's hookas; he would calmly go off in pouring rain with Sharat's best silk umbrella for a stroll through the village, and make friends with all whom he met. Moreover, he had got hold of a mongrel village dog which he petted so recklessly that it came indoors with muddy paws, and left tokens of its visit on Sharat's spotless bed. Then, he gathered about him a devoted band of boys of all sorts and sizes, and the result was that not a solitary mango in the neighbourhood had a chance of ripening that season.

There is no doubt that Kiran had a hand in spoiling the boy. Sharat often warned her about it, but she would not listen to him. She made a dandy of him with Sharat's cast-off clothes, and gave him new ones too. And because she felt drawn towards him, and also had a curiosity to know more about him, she was constantly calling him to her own room. After her bath and mid-day meal Kiran would be seated on the bedstead with her betel-leaf box by her side; and while her maid combed and dried her hair, Nilkanta would stand in front and recite pieces out of his repertory with appropriate gesture and song, his elf-locks waving wildly. Thus, the long afternoon hours passed merrily away. Kiran would often try to persuade Sharat to sit with her as one of the audience, but Sharat, who had taken a cordial dislike to the boy, refused, nor could Nilkanta do his part half so well when Sharat was there. His mother would sometimes be lured by the hope of hearing sacred names in the recitation; but love of her mid-day sleep speedily overcame devotion, and she lay lapped in dreams.

The boy often got his ears boxed and pulled by Sharat, but as this was nothing to what he had been used to as a member of the troupe, he did not mind it in the least. In his short experience of the world he had come to the conclusion that, as the earth consisted of land and water, so human life was made up of eatings and beatings, and that the beatings largely predominated.

It was hard to tell Nilkanta's age. If it was about fourteen or fifteen, then, his face was too old for his years; if seventeen or eighteen, then, it was too young. He was either a man too early or a boy too late. The fact was that, joining the theatrical band when very young, he had played the parts of Radhika, Damayanti, Sita, and Bidya's companion. A thoughtful Providence so arranged things that he grew to the exact stature that his manager required, and then, growth ceased. Since everyone saw how small he was, and he himself felt small, he did not receive due respect for his years. These causes, natural and artificial, combined to make him sometimes seem immature for seventeen years, and at other times a lad of fourteen but far too knowing for seventeen. And as no sign of hair appeared on his face, the confusion became greater. Either because he smoked or because he used language beyond his years, his lips puckered into lines that showed him to be old and hard; but innocence and youth shone in his large eyes. I fancy that his heart remained young, but the hot glare of publicity had been a forcing-house that ripened untimely his outward aspect.

In the quiet shelter of Sharat's house and garden at Chandernagore, Nature had leisure to work her way unimpeded. He had lingered in a kind of unnatural youth, but now he silently and swiftly overpassed that stage. His seventeen or eighteen years came to adequate revelation. No one observed the change, and its first sign was this, that when Kiran treated him like a boy, he felt ashamed. When the gay Kiran one day proposed that he should play the part of lady's companion, the idea of woman's dress hurt him, though he could not say why. So now, when she called for him to act over again his old characters, he disappeared. It never occurred to him that he was even now not much more than a lad-of-all-work in a strolling company. He even made up his mind to pick up a little education from Sharat's factor. But, because Nilkanta was the pet of his master's wife, the factor could not endure the sight of him. Also, his restless training made it impossible for him to keep his mind long engaged; presently, the alphabet did a misty dance before his eyes. He would sit long enough with an open book on his lap, leaning against a champak bush beside the Ganges. The waves sighed below, boats floated past, birds flitted and twittered restlessly above. What thoughts passed through his mind as he looked down on that book he alone knew, if indeed he did know. He never advanced from one word to another, but the glorious thought that he was actually reading a book filled his soul with exultation. Whenever a boat went by, he lifted his book, and pretended to be reading hard, shouting at the top of his voice. But his energy dropped as soon as the audience was gone.

Formerly he sang his songs automatically, but now their tunes stirred in his mind. Their words were of little import, and full of trifling alliteration. Even the little meaning they had was beyond his comprehension; yet when he sang –

Twice-born bird! Ah! Wherefore stirred
To wrong our royal lady?

Goose, ah! Say why wilt thou slay
Her in forest shady?

Then, he felt as if transported to another world, and to far other folk. This familiar earth and his own poor life became music, and he was transformed. That tale of goose and king's daughter flung upon the mirror of his mind a picture of surpassing beauty. It is impossible to say what he imagined he himself was, but the destitute little slave of the theatrical troupe faded from his memory.

When with evening the child of want lies down, dirty and hungry, in his squalid home, and hears of prince and princess and fabled gold, then, in the dark hovel with its dim flickering candle, his mind springs free from her bonds of poverty and misery, and walks in fresh beauty and glowing raiment, strong beyond all fear of hindrance, through that fairy realm where all is possible.

Even so, this drudge of wandering players fashioned himself and his world anew, as he moved in spirit amid his songs. The lapping water, rustling leaves, and calling birds; the goddess who had given shelter to him, the helpless, the God-forsaken; her gracious, lovely face, her exquisite arms with their shining bangles, her rosy feet as soft as flower-petals; all these by some magic became one with the music of his song. When the singing ended, the mirage faded, and Nilkanta of the stage appeared again, with his wild elf-locks. Fresh from the complaints of his neighbour, the owner of the despoiled mango-orchard, Sharat would come and box his ears and cuff him. The boy Nilkanta, the misleader of adoring youths went forth once more, to make ever new mischief by land and water and in the branches that are above the earth.

Shortly after the advent of Nilkanta, Sharat's younger brother Satish, came to spend his college vacation with them. Kiran was hugely pleased at finding a fresh occupation. She and Satish were of the same age, and the time passed pleasantly in games and quarrels and makings-up and laughter and even tears. Suddenly she would clasp him over the eyes, from behind, with vermilion-stained hands, she would write "monkey" on his back, and sometimes bolt the door on him from outside amidst peals of laughter. Satish in his turn did not take things lying down; he would take her keys and rings, he would put pepper among her betel; he would tie her to the bed when she was not looking.

Meanwhile, heaven only knows what possessed poor Nilkanta. He was suddenly filled with a bitterness which he must avenge on somebody or something. He thrashed his devoted boy-followers for no fault, and sent them away crying. He would kick his pet mongrel till it made the skies resound with its whinings. When he went out for a walk, he would litter his path with twigs and leaves beaten from the roadside shrubs with his cane.

Kiran liked to see people enjoying good fare. Nilkanta had an immense capacity for eating, and never refused a good thing, however, often it was offered. So Kiran liked to send for him to have his meals in her presence, and ply him with delicacies, happy in the bliss of seeing this Brahmin boy eat to satiety. After Satish's arrival she had much less spare time on her hands, and was seldom present when Nilkanta's meals were served. Before, her absence made no difference to the boy's appetite, and he would not rise till he had drained his cup of milk, and rinsed it thoroughly with water.

But now, if Kiran was not present to ask him to try this and that, he was miserable, and nothing tasted right. He would get up without eating much, and say to the serving-maid in a choking voice, "I am not hungry." He thought in imagination that the news of his repeated refusal, "I am not hungry," would reach Kiran; he pictured her concern, and hoped that she would send for him, and press him to eat. But nothing of the sort happened. Kiran never knew, and never sent for him; and the maid finished whatever he left. He would then, put out the lamp in his room, and throw himself on his bed in the darkness, burying his head in the pillow in a paroxysm of sobs. What was his grievance? Against whom? And from whom did he expect redress? At last, when none else came, Mother Sleep soothed with her soft caresses the wounded heart of the motherless lad.

Nilkanta came to the unshakable conviction that Satish was poisoning Kiran's mind against him. If Kiran was absent-minded, and had not her usual smile, he would jump at the conclusion that some trick of Satish had made her angry with him. He took to praying to the gods, with all the fervour of his hate, to make him at the next rebirth Satish, and Satish him. He had an idea that a Brahmin's wrath could never be in vain; and the more he tried to consume Satish with the fire of his curses, the more did his own heart burn within him. And upstairs he would hear Satish laughing and joking with his sister-in-law.

Nilkanta never dared openly to show his enmity to Satish. But he would contrive a hundred petty ways of causing him annoyance. When Satish went for a swim in the river, and left his soap on the steps of the bathing-place, on coming back for it he would find that it had disappeared. Once he found his favourite striped tunic floating past him on the water, and thought it had been blown away by the wind.

One day Kiran, desiring to entertain Satish, sent for Nilkanta to recite as usual, but he stood there in gloomy silence. Quite surprised, Kiran asked him what was the matter. But he remained silent. And when again pressed by her to repeat some particular favourite piece of hers, he answered, "I don't remember," and walked away.

At last the time came for their return home. Everybody was busy packing up. Satish was going with them. But to Nilkanta nobody said a word. The question whether he was to go or not seemed not to have occurred to anybody.

The question, as a matter of fact, had been raised by Kiran, who had proposed to take him along with them. But her husband and his mother and brother had all objected so strenuously that she let the matter drop. A couple of days before they were to start, she sent for the boy, and with kind words advised him to go back to his own home.

So many days had he felt neglected that this touch of kindness was too much for him; he burst into tears. Kiran's eyes were also brimming over. She was filled with remorse at the thought that she had created a tie of affection, which could not be permanent.

But Satish was much annoyed at the blubbering of this overgrown boy. "Why does the fool stand there howling instead of speaking?" said he. When Kiran scolded him for an unfeeling creature, he replied, "Sister mine, you do not understand. You are too good and trustful. This fellow turns up from the Lord knows where, and is treated like a king. Naturally the tiger has no wish to become a mouse again. And he has evidently discovered that there is nothing like a tear or two to soften your heart."

Nilkanta hurriedly left the spot. He felt he would like to be a knife to cut Satish to pieces; a needle to pierce him through and through; a fire to burn him to ashes. But Satish was not even scarred. It was only his own heart that bled and bled.

Satish had brought with him from Calcutta a grand inkstand. The ink-pot was set in a mother-of-pearl boat drawn by a German-silver goose supporting a penholder. It was a great favourite of his, and he cleaned it carefully every day with an old silk handkerchief. Kiran would laugh and, tapping the silver bird's beak, would say –

Twice-born bird, ah! wherefore stirred
To wrong our royal lady?

And the usual war of words would break out between her and her brother-in-law.

The day before they were to start, the inkstand was missing, and could nowhere be found. Kiran smiled, and said, "Brother-in-law, your goose has flown off to look for your Damayanti." But Satish was in a great rage. He was certain that Nilkanta had stolen it – for several people said they had seen him prowling about the room the night before. He had the accused brought before him. Kiran also was there. "You have stolen my inkstand, you thief!" he blurted out. "Bring it back at once." Nilkanta had always taken punishment from Sharat, deserved or undeserved, with perfect equanimity. But, when he was called a thief in Kiran's presence, his eyes blazed with a fierce anger, his breast swelled, and his throat choked. If Satish had said another word he would have flown at him like a wild cat, and used his nails like claws.

Kiran was greatly distressed at the scene, and taking the boy into another room said in her sweet, kind way, "Nilu, if you really have taken that ink-stand give it to me quietly, and I shall see that no one says another word to you about it." Big tears coursed down the boy's cheeks, till at last he hid his face in his hands, and wept bitterly. Kiran came back from the room, and said, "I am sure Nilkanta has not taken the inkstand." Sharat and Satish were equally positive that no other than Nilkanta could have done it.

But Kiran said determinedly, "Never."

Sharat wanted to cross-examine the boy, but his wife refused to allow it.

Then, Satish suggested that his room and box should be searched. And Kiran said, "If you dare do such a thing I will never, never forgive you. You shall not spy on the poor innocent boy." And as she spoke, her wonderful eyes filled with tears. That settled the matter, and effectually prevented any further molestation of Nilkanta!

Kiran's heart overflowed with pity at this attempted outrage on a homeless lad. She got two new suits of clothes and a pair of shoes, and with these and a banknote in her hand she quietly went into Nilkanta's room in the evening. She intended to put these parting presents into his box as a surprise. The box itself had been her gift.

From her bunch of keys she selected one that fitted, and noiselessly opened the box. It was so jumbled up with odds and ends that the new clothes would not go in. So she thought she had better take everything out and pack the box for him. At first knives, tops, kite-flying reels, bamboo twigs, polished shells for peeling green mangoes, bottoms of broken tumblers and such like things dear to a boy's heart were discovered. Then, there came a layer of linen, clean and otherwise. And from under the linen there emerged the missing inkstand, goose and all!

Kiran, with flushed face, sat down helplessly with the inkstand in her hand, puzzled and wondering.

In the meantime, Nilkanta had come into the room from behind without Kiran knowing it. He had seen the whole thing, and thought that Kiran had come like a thief to catch him in his thieving, – and that his deed was out. How could he ever hope to convince her that he was not a thief, and that only revenge had prompted him to take the inkstand, which he meant to throw into the river at the first chance? In a weak moment he had put it in his box instead. "He was not a thief," his heart cried out, "not a thief!" Then, what was he? What could he say? He had stolen, and yet he was not a thief! He could never explain to Kiran how grievously wrong she was in taking him for a thief; how could he bear the thought that she had tried to spy on him?

At last Kiran with a deep sigh replaced the ink-stand in the box, and, as if she were the thief herself, covered it up with the linen and the trinkets as they were before; and at the top she placed the presents together with the banknote which she had brought for him.

The next day the boy was nowhere to be found. The villagers had not seen him; the police could discover no trace of him. Said Sharat, "Now, as a matter of curiosity, let us have a look at his box." But Kiran was obstinate in her refusal to allow that to be done.

She had the box brought up to her own room; and taking out the inkstand alone, threw it into the river.

The whole family went home. In a day the garden became desolate. And only that starving mongrel of Nilkanta's remained prowling along the river-bank, whining and whining as if its heart would break.

24

My Fair Neighbour

My feelings towards the young widow who lived in the next house to mine were feelings of worship; at least, that is what I told my friends and myself. Even my nearest intimate, Nabin, knew nothing of the real state of my mind. And I had a sort of pride that I could keep my passion pure by thus, concealing it in the inmost recesses of my heart. She was like a dew-drenched sephali blossom, untimely fallen to earth. Too radiant and holy for the flower-decked marriage-bed, she had been dedicated to Heaven.

But passion is like the mountain stream, and refuses to be enclosed in the place of its birth; it must seek an outlet. That is why I tried to give expression to my emotions in poems; but my unwilling pen refused to desecrate the object of my worship.

It happened curiously that just at this time my friend Nabin was afflicted with a madness of verse. It came upon him like an earthquake. It was the poor fellow's first attack, and he was equally unprepared for rhyme and rhythm. Nevertheless he could not refrain, for he succumbed to the fascination, as a widower to his second wife.

So Nabin sought help from me. The subject of his poems was the old, old one, which is ever new, his poems were all addressed to the beloved one. I slapped his back in jest, and asked him, "Well, old chap, who is she?"

Nabin laughed, as he replied, "That I have not yet discovered!"

I confess that I found considerable comfort in bringing help to my friend. Like a hen brooding on a duck's egg, I lavished all the warmth of my pent-up passion on Nabin's effusions. So vigorously did I revise and improve his crude productions, that the larger part of each poem became my own.

Then, Nabin would say in surprise, "That is just what I wanted to say, but could not. How on earth do you manage to get hold of all these fine sentiments?"

Poet-like, I would reply, "They come from my imagination; for, as you know, truth is silent, and it is imagination only which waxes eloquent. Reality represses the flow of feeling like a rock; imagination cuts out a path for itself."

And the poor puzzled Nabin would say, "Y-e-s, I see; yes, of course"; and then, after some thought would murmur again, "Yes, yes, you are right!"

As I have already said, in my own love there was a feeling of reverential delicacy which prevented me from putting it into words. But with Nabin as a screen, there was nothing to hinder the flow of my pen; and a true warmth of feeling gushed out into these vicarious poems.

Nabin in his lucid moment's would say, "But these are yours! Let me publish them over your name."

"Nonsense!" I would reply. "They are yours, my dear fellow; I have only added a touch or two here and there."

And Nabin gradually came to believe it.

I will not deny that, with a feeling akin to that of the astronomer gazing into the starry heavens, I did sometimes turn my eyes towards the window of the house next door. It is also true that now and again my furtive glances would be rewarded with a vision. And the least glimpse of the pure light of that countenance would at once still and clarify all that was turbulent and unworthy in my emotions.

But one day I was startled. Could I believe my eyes? It was a hot summer afternoon. One of the fierce and fitful nor'westers was threatening. Black clouds were massed in the north-west corner of the sky; and against the strange and fearful light of that background my fair neighbour stood, gazing out into empty space. And what a world of forlorn longing did I discover in the far-away look of those lustrous black eyes! Was there then, perchance, still some living volcano within the serene radiance of that moon of mine? Alas! That look of limitless yearning, which was winging its way through the clouds like an eager bird, surely sought – not heaven – but the nest of some human heart!

At the sight of the unutterable passion of that look I could hardly contain myself. I was no longer satisfied with correcting crude poems. My whole being longed to express itself in some worthy action. At last I thought I would devote myself to making widow-remarriage popular in my country. I was prepared not only to speak and write on the subject, but also to spend money on its cause.

Nabin began to argue with me. "Permanent widowhood," said he, "has in it a sense of immense purity and peace; a calm beauty like that of the silent places of the dead shimmering in the wan light of the eleventh moon. Would not the mere possibility of remarriage destroy its divine beauty?"

Now this sort of sentimentality always makes me furious. In time of famine, if a well-fed man speaks scornfully of food, and advises a starving man at point of death to glut his hunger on the fragrance of flowers and the song of birds, what are we to think of him? I said with some heat, "Look here, Nabin, to the artist a ruin may be a beautiful object; but houses are built not only for the contemplation of artists, but that people may live therein; so they have to be kept in repair in spite of artistic susceptibilities. It is all very well for you to idealise widowhood from your safe distance, but you should remember that within widowhood there is a sensitive human heart, throbbing with pain and desire."

I had an impression that the conversion of Nabin would be a difficult matter, so perhaps I was more impassioned that I need have been. I was somewhat surprised to find at the conclusion of my little speech that Nabin after a single thoughtful sigh completely agreed with me. The even more convincing peroration which I felt I might have delivered was not needed!

After about a week Nabin came to me, and said that if I would help him he was prepared to lead the way by marrying a widow himself.

I was overjoyed. I embraced him effusively, and promised him any money that might be required for the purpose. Then, Nabin told me his story.

I learned that Nabin's loved one was not an imaginary being. It appeared that Nabin, too, had for some time adored a widow from a distance, but had not spoken of his feelings to any living soul. Then, the magazines in which Nabin's poems, or rather my poems, used to appear had reached the fair one's hands; and the poems had not been ineffective.

Not that Nabin had deliberately intended, as he was careful to explain, to conduct love-making in that way. In fact, said he, he had no idea that the widow knew how to read. He used to post the magazine, without disclosing the sender's name, addressed to the widow's brother. It was only a sort of fancy of his, a concession to his hopeless passion. It was flinging garlands before a deity; it is not the worshipper's affair whether the god knows or not, whether he accepts or ignores the offering.

And Nabin particularly wanted me to understand that he had no definite end in view when on diverse pretexts he sought and made the acquaintance of the widow's brother. Any near relation of the loved one needs must have a special interest for the lover.

Then, followed a long story about how an illness of the brother at last brought them together. The presence of the poet himself naturally led to much discussion of the poems; nor was the discussion necessarily restricted to the subject out of which it arose.

After his recent defeat in argument at my hands, Nabin had mustered up courage to propose marriage to the widow. At first he could not gain her consent. But when he had made full use of my eloquent words, supplemented by a tear or two of his own, the fair one capitulated unconditionally. Some money was now wanted by her guardian to make arrangements.

"Take it at once," said I.

"But," Nabin went on, "you know it will be some months before I can appease my father sufficiently for him to continue my allowance. How are we to live in the meantime?" I wrote out the necessary cheque without a word, and then, I said, "Now tell me who she is. You need not look on me as a possible rival, for I swear I will not write poems to her; and even if I do I will not send them to her brother, but to you!"

"Don't be absurd," said Nabin; "I have not kept back her name because I feared your rivalry! The fact is, she was very much perturbed at taking this unusual step, and had asked me not to talk about the matter to my friends. But it no longer matters, now that everything has been satisfactorily settled. She lives at No. 19, the house next to yours."

If my heart had been an iron boiler it would have burst. "So she has no objection to remarriage?" I simply asked.

"Not at the present moment," replied Nabin with a smile.

"And was it the poems alone which wrought the magic change?"

"Well, my poems were not so bad, you know," said Nabin, "were they?"

I swore mentally.

But at whom was I to swear? At him? At myself? At Providence? All the same, I swore.

25

Giribala

I

Giribala is overflowing with the exuberance of her youth that seems spilling over all around her, in the folds of her dress, the turning of her neck, the motion of her hands, in the rhythm of her steps, now quick, now languid, in her tinkling anklets and ringing laughter, in her voice and her swift glances. Often she is seen, wrapt in a blue silk, walking on her terrace, in an impulse of unmeaning restlessness. Her limbs seem eager to dance to the time of an inner music unceasing and unheard. She takes pleasure in merely moving her body, causing ripples to break out in the flood of her young life. Suddenly she will pluck a leaf from a plant in the flower-pot, and throw it up in the sky, and her bangles give a sudden tinkle and the careless grace of her hand, like a bird freed from its cage, flies unseen in the air. With her swift fingers she brushes away from her dress a mere nothing; standing on tiptoe she peeps over her terrace walls for no cause whatever, and then, with a rapid motion turns round to go to another direction, swinging her bunch of keys tied to a corner of her garment. She loosens her hair in an untimely caprice, sitting before her mirror to do it up again, and then, in a fit of laziness flings herself upon her bed like a line of stray moonlight, slipping through some opening of the leaves, idling in the shadow.

She has no children and, having been married into a wealthy family, has very little work to do. Thus, she seems daily accumulating her own self without expenditure till the vessel is brimming over with the seething surplus. She has her husband, but not under her control. She has grown up from a girl into a woman, and yet through familiarity escaping her husband's notice.

When she was newly married, and her husband, Gopinath, was attending his college, he would often play the truant and, under cover of the mid-day siesta of his elders, secretly come to make love to Giribala. Though they lived under the same roof he would create occasions to send her letters on tinted notepaper perfumed with rosewater, and even would gloat upon exaggerated grievances over some imaginary neglect of love.

Just then, his father died, and he became the sole owner of his property. Like an unseasoned piece of timber, the immature youth of Gopinath attracted parasites that began to bore into his substance. From now his movements took the course which led him in a contrary direction from his wife.

There is a dangerous fascination in being a leader of men, to which has succumbed many a strong soul. To be accepted as the leader of a small circle of sycophants in his own parlour has the same fearful attraction for a man who suffers from a scarcity of brains and character. Gopinath assumed the part of a hero among his friends and acquaintances, and tried daily to invent new wonders in all manner of extravagance. He won a reputation among his followers for his audacity of excesses, which goaded him not only to keep up his fame but to surpass himself at all costs.

In the meanwhile, Giribala in the seclusion of her lonely youth felt like a queen who had her throne but no subjects. She knew she had the power in her hand which could make the world of men her captive, only that world itself was missing. Giribala has a maid-servant whose name is Sudha. She can sing and dance and improvise verses, and she freely gives expression to her regret that such a beauty as that of her mistress should be dedicated to a fool who forgets to enjoy that which he has in his possession. Giribala is never tired of hearing from her the details of her charms of beauty, while at the same time contradicting her, calling her a liar and flatterer, exciting her to swear by all that is sacred that she is earnest in her admiration – which statement, even without the accompaniment of a solemn oath, is not difficult for Giribala to believe.

Sudha used to sing to her a song beginning with the line, "Let me write myself a slave upon the soles of thy feet," and Giribala in her imagination could feel that her beautiful feet were fully worthy of bearing inscriptions of everlasting slavery from conquered hearts, if only they could be free in their career of conquest.

But the woman to whom her husband Gopinath has surrendered himself as a slave is Lavanga, the actress, who has the reputation of playing to perfection the part of a maiden languishing in hopeless love, and swooning on the stage with an exquisite naturalness. Before her husband had altogether vanished from her sphere of influence, Giribala had often heard from him about the wonderful histrionic powers of this woman, and in her jealous curiosity had greatly desired to see Lavanga on the stage. But she could not secure her husband's consent, because Gopinath was firm in his opinion that the theatre was a place not fit for any decent woman to visit.

At last she paid for a seat, and sent Sudha to see this famous actress in one of her best parts. The account that she received from her on her return was far from flattering to Lavanga, either as to her personal appearance or as to her stage accomplishments. Since, for obvious reasons, she had great faith in Sudha's power of appreciation where it was due, she did not hesitate to believe in her description of Lavanga which was accompanied by mimicry of a ludicrous mannerism.

When at last her husband deserted her in his infatuation for this woman, she began to feel qualms of doubt. But as Sudha repeatedly asserted her former opinion with a greater vehemence, comparing Lavanga to a piece of burnt log dressed up in a woman's clothes, Giribala determined secretly to go to the theatre herself and settle this question for good. And she did go there one night with all the excitement of a forbidden entry. Her very trepidation of heart lent a special charm to what she saw there. She gazed at the faces of the spectators, lit up with an unnatural shine of lamplight; and, with the magic of its music and the painted canvas of its scenery, the theatre seemed to her like a world where society was suddenly freed from its law of gravitation.

Coming from her walled-up terrace and joyless home, she had entered a region where dreams and reality had clasped their hands in friendship, over the wine-cup of art.

The bell rang, the orchestra music stopped, the audience sat still in their seats, the stage lights shone brighter, and the curtain was drawn up. Suddenly appeared in the light from the mystery of the unseen the shepherd girls of the Vrinda Forest, and with the accompaniment of songs commenced their dance, punctuated with the uproarious applause of the audience. The blood began to throb all over Giribala's body, and she forgot for the moment that her life was limited to her circumstances, and that she had not been set free in a world where all laws had melted in music.

Sudha came occasionally to interrupt her with anxious whispers, urging her to hasten back home for fear of being detected. But she paid no heed to the warning, for her sense of fear had gone.

The play goes on. Krishna has given offence to his beloved Radha, and she in her wounded pride refuses to recognise him. He is entreating her, abasing himself at her feet, but in vain. Giribala's heart seems to swell. She imagines herself as the offended Radha; and feels that she also has in her this woman's power to vindicate her pride. She had heard what a force was woman's beauty in the world, but tonight it became to her palpable.

At last the curtain dropped, the light became dim, the audience got ready to leave the theatre, but Giribala sat still like one in a dream. The thought that she would have to go home had vanished from her mind. She waited for the curtain to rise again and the eternal theme of Krishna's humiliation at the feet of Radha to continue. But Sudha came to remind her that the play had ended, and the lamps would soon be put out.

It was late when Giribala came back home. A kerosene lamp was dimly burning in the melancholy solitude and silence of her room. Near her window upon her lonely bed a mosquito curtain was slightly moving in a gentle breeze. Her world seemed to her distasteful and mean, like a rotten fruit swept into the dustbin.

From now she regularly visited the theatre every Saturday. The fascination of her first sight of it lost much of its glamour. The painted vulgarity of the actresses and the falseness of their affectation became more and more evident, yet the habit grew upon her. Every time the curtain rose the window of her life's prison-house seemed to open before her, and the stage, bordered off from the world of reality by its gilded frame and scenic display, by its array of lights and even its flimsiness of conventionalism, appeared to her like a fairyland, where it was not impossible for herself to occupy the throne of the fairy queen.

When for the first time she saw her husband among the audience shouting his drunken admiration for a certain actress, she felt an intense disgust, and prayed in her mind that a day might come when she might have an opportunity to spurn him away with her contempt. But the opportunity seemed remoter every day, for Gopinath was hardly ever to be seen at his home now, being carried away, one knew not where, in the centre of a dust-storm of dissipation.

One evening in the month of March, in the light of the full moon, Giribala was sitting on her terrace dressed in her cream-coloured robe. It was her habit daily to deck herself with jewelry, as if for some festive occasion. For these costly gems were like wine to her – they sent heightened consciousness of beauty to her limbs; she felt like a plant in spring tingling with the impulse of flowers in all its branches. She wore a pair of diamond bracelets on her arms, a necklace of rubies and pearls on her neck, and a ring with a big sapphire on the little finger of her left hand. Sudha was sitting near her bare feet, admiringly touching them with her hand, and expressing her wish that she were a man privileged to offer his life as homage to such a pair of feet.

Sudha gently hummed a love-song to her, and the evening wore on to night. Everybody in the household had finished the evening meal, and gone to sleep. Then, suddenly Gopinath appeared reeking with scent and liquor, and Sudha, drawing her sari over her face, hastily ran away from the terrace.

Giribala thought for a moment that her day had come at last. She turned away her face, and sat silent.

But the curtain in her stage did not rise, and no song of entreaty came from her hero with the words,

Listen to the pleading of the moonlight, my love, and hide not thy face.

In his dry unmusical voice Gopinath said, "Give me your keys."

A gust of south wind like a sigh of the insulted romance of the poetic world scattered all over the terrace the smell of the night-blooming jasmines, and loosened some wisp of hair on Giribala's cheek. She let go her pride, and got up and said, "You shall have your keys if you listen to what I have to say."

Gopinath said, "I cannot delay. Give me your keys."

Giribala said, "I will give you the keys and everything that is in the safe, but you must not leave me."

Gopinath said, "That cannot be. I have urgent business."

"Then, you shan't have the keys," said Giribala.

Gopinath began to search for them. He opened the drawers of the dressing-table, broke open the lid of the box that contained Giribala's toilet requisites, smashed the glass panes of her almirah, groped under the pillows and mattress of the bed, but the keys he could not find. Giribala stood near the door stiff and silent, like a marble image gazing at vacancy. Trembling with rage, Gopinath came to her, and said with an angry growl, "Give me your keys or you will repent it."

Giribala did not answer, and Gopinath, pinning her to the wall, snatched away by force her bracelets, necklace and ring, and, giving her a parting kick, went away.

Nobody in the house woke up from his sleep, none in the neighbourhood knew of this outrage, the moonlight remained placid, and the peace of the night undisturbed. Hearts can be rent never to heal again amidst such serene silence.

The next morning Giribala said she was going to see her father, and left home. As Gopinath's present destination was not known, and she was not responsible to anybody else in the house, her absence was not noticed.

II

The new play of Manorama was on rehearsal in the theatre where Gopinath was a constant visitor. Lavanga was practising for the part of the heroine Manorama, and Gopinath, sitting in the front seat with his rabble of followers, would vociferously encourage his favourite actress with his approbation. This greatly disturbed the rehearsal, but the proprietors of the theatre did not dare to annoy a patron of whose vindictiveness they were afraid. But one day he went so far as to molest an actress in the green-room, and he had to be turned away with the aid of the police.

Gopinath determined to take his revenge, and when, after a great deal of preparation and shrieking advertisements, the new play Manorama was about to be produced, Gopinath took away the principal actress Lavanga with him, and disappeared. It was a great shock to the manager, who had to postpone the opening night, get hold of a new actress, and teach her the part, bringing out the play before the public with considerable misgivings in his mind.

But the success was as unexpected as it was unprecedented. When the news reached Gopinath, he could not resist the curiosity to come and see the performance.

The play opens with Manorama living in her husband's house neglected and hardly noticed. Near the end of the drama her husband deserts her, and, concealing his first marriage, manages to marry a millionaire's daughter. When the wedding ceremony is over, and the bridal veil is raised from her face, she is discovered to be the same Manorama, only no longer the former drudge, but queenly in her beauty and splendour of dress and ornaments. In her infancy she had been brought up in a poor home, having been kidnapped from the house of her rich father. He, having traced her to her husband's home, brings her back to him, and celebrates her marriage once again in a fitting manner.

In the concluding scene, when the husband is going through his period of penitence and humiliation, as is fit in a play which has a moral, a sudden disturbance arose among the audience. So long as Manorama appeared obscured in her position of drudgery Gopinath showed no sign of perturbation; but when after the wedding ceremony she came out dressed in her red bridal robe, and took her veil off, when with majestic pride of her overwhelming beauty she turned her face towards the audience and, slightly bending her neck, shot a fiery glance of exultation at Gopinath, applause broke out in wave after wave, and the enthusiasm of the spectators became unbounded.

Suddenly Gopinath cried out in a thick voice, "Giribala," and like a madman tried to rush upon the stage. The audience shouted, "Turn him out," the police came to drag him away, and he struggled and screamed, "I will kill her," while the curtain dropped.

26

The Son Of Rashmani

I

Kalipada's mother was Rashmani, but she had to do the duty of the father as well, because when both of the parents are "mother" then, it is bad for the child. Bhavani, her husband, was wholly incapable of keeping his children under discipline. To know why he was bent on spoiling his son, you must hear something of the former history of the family.

Bhavani was born in the famous house of Saniari. His father, Abhaya Charan, had a son, Shyama Charan, by his first wife. When he married again after her death he had himself passed the marriageable age, and his new father-in-law took advantage of the weakness of his position to have a special portion of his estate settled on his daughter. In this way he was satisfied that proper provision had been made, if his daughter should become a widow early in life. She would be independent of the charity of Shyama Charan.

The first part of his anticipation came true. For very soon after the birth of a son, whom she called Bhavani, Abhaya Charan died. It gave the father-in-law great peace and consolation, as he looked forward to his own death, to know that his daughter was properly looked after.

Shyama Charan was quite grown up. In fact his own eldest boy was a year older than Bhavani. He brought up the latter with his own son. In doing this he never took a farthing from the property allotted to his step-mother, and every year he got a receipt from her after submitting detailed accounts. His honesty in this affair surprised the neighbourhood. In fact they thought that such honesty was another name for foolishness. They did not like the idea of a division being made in the undivided ancestral property. If Shyama Charan in some underhand manner had been able to annul the dowry, his neighbours would have admired his sagacity; and there were good advisers ready to hand who could have rendered him material aid in the attainment of such an object. But Shyama Charan, in spite of the risk of crippling his patrimony, strictly set aside the dowry which came to the share of his step-mother; and the widow, Vraja Sundari, being naturally affectionate and trustful, had every confidence in Shyama Charan whom she trusted as her own son. More than once she had chided him for being so particular about her portion of the property. She would tell him that, as she was not going to take her property with her when she died, and as it would in any case revert to the family, it was not necessary to be so very strict about rendering accounts. But he never listened to her.

Shyama Charan was a severe disciplinarian by habit and his children were perfectly aware of the fact. But Bhavani had every possible freedom, and this gave rise to the impression that he was more partial to his step-brother than to his own sons. But Bhavani's education was sadly neglected and he completely relied on Shyama Charan for the management of his share of the property. He merely had to sign documents occasionally without ever spending a thought on their contents. On the other hand, Tarapada, the eldest son of Shyama Charan, was quite an expert in the management of the estate, having to act as an assistant to his father.

After the death of Shyama Charan, Tarapada said to Bhavani, "Uncle, we must not live together as we have done for so long, because some trifling misunderstanding may come at any moment and cause utter disruption."

Bhavani never imagined, even in his dream, that a day might come when he would have to manage his own affairs. The world in which he had been born and bred ever appeared to him complete and entire in itself. It was an incomprehensible calamity to him that there could be a dividing line somewhere and that this world of his could be split into two. When he found that Tarapada was immovable and indifferent to the grief and dishonour that such a step would bring to the family, he began to rack his brain to find out how the property could be divided with the least possible strain.

Tarapada showed surprise at his uncle's anxiety and said that there was no need to trouble about this, because the division had already been made in the life-time of his grandfather. Bhavani said in amazement, "But I know nothing of this!" Tarapada said in answer, "Then, you must be the only one in the whole neighbourhood who does not. For, lest there should be ruinous litigation after he had gone, my grandfather had already given a portion of the property to your mother." Bhavani thought this not unlikely and asked, "What about the house?" Tarapada said, "If you wish, you can keep this house to yourself and we shall be contented with the other house in the district town."

As Bhavani had never been to this town-house, he had neither knowledge of it, nor affection for it. He was astounded at the magnanimity of Tarapada for so easily relinquishing his right to the house in the village where they had been brought up. But when Bhavani told everything to his mother, she struck her forehead with her hand and said, "This is preposterous! What I got from my husband was my own dowry and its income is very small. I do not see why you should be deprived of your share in your father's property."

Bhavani said, "Tarapada is quite positive that his grandfather never gave us any thing except this land."

Vraja Sundari was astonished and informed her son that her husband had made two copies of his will, one of which was still lying in her own box. The box was opened and it was found that there was only the deed of gift for the property belonging to the mother and nothing else. The copy of the will had been taken out.

The help of advisers was sought. The man who came to their rescue was Bagala, the son of their family guru. It was the profession of the father to look after the spiritual needs of the village; the material side was left to the son. The two of them had divided between themselves the other world and this. Whatever might be the result for others, they themselves had nothing to suffer from this division. Bagala said that, even if the will was missing, the shares in the ancestral property must be equal, as between the brothers.

Just at this time, a copy of a will made its appearance supporting the claims of the other side. In this document there was no mention of Bhavani and the whole property was given to the grandsons at the time when no son was born to Bhavani. With Bagala as his captain Bhavani set out on his voyage across the perilous sea of litigation. When his vessel at last reached harbour his funds were nearly exhausted and the ancestral property was in the hands of the other party. The land which was given to his mother had dwindled to such an extent, that it could barely give them shelter, or keep up the family dignity. Then, Tarapada went away to the district town and they never met again.

II

Shyama Charan's treachery pierced the heart of the widow like an assassin's knife. To the end of her life, almost every day she would heave a sigh and say that God would never suffer such an injustice to be done. She was quite firm in her faith when she said to Bhavani, "I do not know your law or your law courts, but I am certain that my husband's true will and testament will someday be recovered. You will find it again."

Because Bhavani was helpless in worldly matters such assurances as these gave him great consolation. He settled down in his inactivity, certain in his own mind that his pious mother's prophecy could never remain unfulfilled. After his mother's death his faith became all the stronger, since the memory of her piety acquired greater radiance through death's mystery. He felt quite unconcerned about the stress of their poverty which became more and more formidable as the years went by. The necessities of life and the maintenance of family traditions, – these seemed to him like play acting on a temporary stage, not real things. When his former expensive clothing was outworn and he had to buy cheap materials in the shop, this amused him almost like a joke. He smiled and said to himself – "These people do not know that this is only a passing phase of my fortune. Their surprise will be all the greater, when some day I shall celebrate the Puja festival with unwonted magnificence."

This certainty of future prodigality was so clear to his mind's eye that present penury escaped his attention. His servant, Noto, was the principal companion with whom he had discussions about these things. They used to have animated conversations, in which sometimes his opinion differed from his master's, as to the propriety of bringing down a theatrical troupe from Calcutta for these future occasions. Noto used to get reprimands from Bhavani for his natural miserliness in these items of future expenditure.

While Bhavani's one anxiety was about the absence of an heir, who could inherit his vast possible wealth, a son was born to him. The horoscope plainly indicated that the lost property would come back to this boy.

From the time of the birth of his son, Bhavani's attitude was changed. It became cruelly difficult for him now to bear his poverty with his old amused equanimity, because he felt that he had a duty towards this new representative of the illustrious house of Saniari, who had such a glorious future before him. That the traditional extravagance could not be maintained on the occasion of the birth of his child gave him the keenest sorrow. He felt as if he were cheating his own son. So he compensated his boy with an inordinate amount of spoiling.

Bhavani's wife, Rashmani, had a different temperament from her husband. She never felt any anxiety about the family traditions of the Chaudhuris of Saniari. Bhavani was quite aware of the fact and indulgently smiled to himself, as though nothing better could be expected from a woman who came from a Vaishnava family of very humble lineage. Rashmani frankly acknowledged that she could not share the family sentiments, what concerned her most was the welfare of her own child.

There was hardly an acquaintance in the neighbourhood with whom Bhavani did not discuss the question of the lost will; but he never spoke a word about it to his wife. Once or twice he had tried, but her perfect unconcern had made him drop the subject. She neither paid attention to the past greatness of the family, nor to its future glories – she kept her mind busy with the actual necessities of the present, and those necessities were not small in number or quality.

When the Goddess of Fortune deserts a house, she usually leaves some of her burdens behind, and this ancient family was still encumbered with its host of dependents, though its own shelter was nearly crumbling to dust. These parasites take it to be an insult if they are asked to do any service. They get head-aches at the least touch of the kitchen smoke. They are visited with sudden rheumatism the moment they are asked to run errands. Therefore, all the responsibilities of maintaining the family were laid upon Rashmani herself. Women lose their delicacy of refinement, when they are compelled night and day to haggle with their destiny over things which are pitifully small, and for this they are blamed by those for whom they toil.

Besides her household affairs Rashmani had to keep all the accounts of the little landed property which remained and also to make arrangements for collecting rents. Never before was the estate managed with such strictness. Bhavani had been quite incapable of collecting his dues, Rashmani never made any remission of the least fraction of rent. The tenants, and even her own agents, reviled her behind her back for the meanness of the family from which she came. Even her husband occasionally used to enter his protest against the harsh economy which went against the grain of the world-famed house of Saniari.

Rashmani quite ungrudgingly took the blame of all this upon herself and openly confessed the poverty of her parents. Tying the end of her sari tightly round her waist she went on with her household duties in her own vigorous fashion and made herself thoroughly disagreeable both to the inmates of the house and to her neighbours. But nobody ever had the courage to interfere. Only one thing she carefully avoided. She never asked her husband to help her in any work and she was nervously afraid of his taking up any responsibilities. Indeed she was always furiously engaged in keeping her husband idle; and because he had received the best possible training in this direction she was wholly successful in her mission.

Rashmani had attained middle age before her son came. Up to this time all the pent-up tenderness of the mother in her and all the love of the wife had their centre of devotion in this simple-hearted good-for-nothing husband. Bhavani was a child grown up by mistake beyond its natural age. This was the reason why, after the death of her husband's mother, she had to assume the position of mother and mistress in one.

In order to protect her husband from invasions of Bagala, the son of the guru, and other calamities, Rashmani adopted such a stern demeanour, that the companions of her husband used to be terribly afraid of her. She never had the opportunity, which a woman usually has, of keeping her fierceness hidden and of softening the keen edge of her words – maintaining a dignified reserve towards men such as is proper for a woman.

Bhavani meekly accepted his wife's authority with regard to himself, but it became extremely hard for him to obey her when it related to Kalipada, his son. The reason was, that Rashmani never regarded Bhavani's son from the point of view of Bhavani himself. In her heart she pitied her husband and said, "Poor man, it was no fault of his, but his misfortune, to be born into a rich family." That is why she never could expect her husband to be deprived of any comfort to which he had been accustomed. Whatever might be the condition of the household finance, she tried hard to keep him in his habitual ease and luxury. Under her regime all expense was strictly limited except in the case of

Bhavani. She would never allow him to notice if some inevitable gap occurred in the preparation of his meals or his apparel. She would blame some imaginary dog for spoiling dishes that were never made and would blame herself for her carelessness. She would attack Noto for letting some fictitious article of dress be stolen or lost. This had the usual effect of rousing Bhavani's sympathy on behalf of his favourite servant and he would take up his defence. Indeed it had often happened that Bhavani had confessed with bare-faced shamelessness that he had used the dress which had never been bought, and for whose loss Noto was blamed; but what happened afterwards, he had not the power to invent and was obliged to rely upon the fertile imagination of his wife who was also the accuser!

Thus, Rashmani treated her husband, but she never put her son in the same category. For he was her own child and why should he be allowed to give himself airs? Kalipada had to be content for his breakfast with a few handfuls of puffed rice and some treacle. During the cold weather he had to wrap his body as well as his head with a thick rough cotton chadar. She would call his teacher before her and warn him never to spare her boy, if he was the least neglectful with his lessons. This treatment of his own son was the hardest blow that Bhavani Charan suffered since the days of his destitution. But as he had always acknowledged defeat at the hands of the powerful, he had not the spirit to stand up against his wife in her method of dealing with the boy.

The dress which Rashmani provided for her son, during the Puja festivities, was made of such poor material that in former days the very servants of the house would have rebelled if it had been offered to them. But Rashmani more than once tried her best to explain to her husband that Kalipada, being the most recent addition to the Chowdhuri family, had never known their former splendour and so was quite glad to get what was given to him. But this pathetic innocence of the boy about his own destiny hurt Bhavani more than anything else, and he could not forgive himself for deceiving the child. When Kalipada would dance for joy and rush to him to show him some present from his mother, which was ridiculously trivial, Bhavani's heart would suffer torture.

Bagala, the guru's son, was now in an affluent condition owing to his agency in the law suit which had brought about the ruin of Bhavani. With the money which he had in hand he used to buy cheap tinsel wares from Calcutta before the Puja holidays. Invisible ink, – absurd combinations of stick, fishing-rod and umbrella – letter-paper with pictures in the corner – silk fabrics bought at auctions, and other things of this kind, attractive to the simple villagers – these were his stock in trade. All the forward young men of the village vied with one another in rising above their rusticity by purchasing these sweepings of the Calcutta market which, they were told, were absolutely necessary for the city gentry.

Once Bagala had bought a wonderful toy – a doll in the form of a foreign woman – which, when wound up, would rise from her chair and begin to fan herself with sudden alacrity. Kalipada was fascinated by it. He had a very good reason to avoid asking his mother about the toy; so he went straight to his father and begged him to purchase it for him. Bhavani answered "yes" at once, but when he heard the price his face fell. Rashmani kept all the money and he went to her as a timid beggar. He began with all sorts of irrelevant remarks and then, took a desperate plunge into the subject with startling incoherence.

Rashmani briefly remarked, "Are you mad?" Bhavani Charan sat silent revolving in his mind what to say next.

"Look here," he exclaimed, "I don't think I need milk pudding daily with my dinner."

"Who told you?" said Rashmani sharply.

"The doctor says it's very bad for biliousness."

"The doctor's a fool!"

"But I'm sure that rice agrees with me better than your luchis. They are too indigestible."

"I've never seen the least sign of indigestion in you. You have been accustomed to them all your life!"

Bhavani Charan was ready enough to make sacrifices, but there his passage was barred. Butter might rise in price, but the number of his luchis never diminished. Milk was quite enough for him at his midday meal, but curds also had to be supplied because that was the family tradition. Rashmani could not have borne seeing him sit down to his meal, if curds were not supplied. Therefore, all his attempts to make a breach in his daily provisions, through which the fanning foreign woman might enter, were an utter failure.

Then, Bhavani paid a visit to Bagala for no reason whatever, and after a great deal of round about talk asked concerning the foreign doll. Of course his straightened circumstances had long been known to Bagala, yet it was a perfect misery to Bhavani to have to hesitate to buy this doll for his son owing to want of ready money. Swallowing his pride, he brought out from under his arm an expensive old Kashmir shawl, and said in a husky voice, "My circumstances are bad just at present and I haven't got much cash. So I have determined to mortgage this shawl and buy that doll for Kalipada."

If the object offered had been less expensive than this Kashmir shawl, Bagala would at once have closed the bargain. But knowing that it would not be possible for him to take possession of this shawl in face of the village opinion, and still more in face of Rashmani's watchfulness, he refused to accept it; and Bhavani had to go back home disappointed with the Kashmir shawl hidden under his arm.

Kalipada asked every day for that foreign fanning toy, and Bhavani smiled every day and said – "Wait, a bit, my boy, till the seventh day of the moon comes round." But every new day it became more and more difficult to keep up that smile.

On the fourth day of the moon Bhavani made a sudden inroad upon his wife and said,

"I've noticed that there's something wrong with Kalipada – something the matter with his health."

"Nonsense," said Rashmani, "he's in the best of health."

"Haven't you noticed him sitting silent for hours together?"

"I should be very greatly relieved if he could sit still for as many minutes."

When all his arrows had missed their mark, and no impression had been made, Bhavani Charan heaved a deep sigh and passing his fingers through his hair went away and sat down on the verandah and began to smoke with fearful assiduity.

On the fifth day, at his morning meal, Bhavani passed by the curds and the milk pudding without touching them. In the evening he simply took one single piece of sandesh. The luchis were left unheeded. He complained of want of appetite. This time a considerable breach was made in the fortifications.

On the sixth day, Rashmani took Kalipada into the room and sweetly calling him by his pet name said, "Betu, you are old enough to know that it is the halfway house to stealing to desire that which you can't have."

Kalipada whimpered and said, "What do I know about it? Father promised to give me that doll."

Rashmani sat down to explain to him how much lay behind his father's promise – how much pain, how much affection, how much loss and privation. Rashmani had never in her life before talked thus, to Kalipada, because it was her habit to give short and sharp commands. It filled the boy with amazement when he found his mother coaxing him and explaining things at such a length, and mere child though he was, he could fathom something of the deep suffering of his mother's heart. Yet at the same time it will be easily understood, that it was hard for this boy to turn his mind away altogether from that captivating foreign fanning woman. He pulled a long face and began to scratch the ground.

This made Rashmani's heart at once hard, and she said in her severe tone, "Yes, you may weep and cry, or become angry, but you shall never get that which is not for you to have." And she hastened away without another word.

Kalipada went out. Bhavani Charan was still smoking his hookah. Noticing Kalipada from a distance he got up and walked in the opposite direction as if he had some urgent business. Kalipada ran to him and said – "But that doll?" Bhavani could not raise a smile that day. He put his arm round Kalipada's neck and said,

"Baba, wait a little. I have some pressing business to get through. Let me finish it first, and then, we will talk about it." Saying this, he went out of his house.

Kalipada saw him brush a tear from his eyes. He stood at the door and watched his father, and it was quite evident, even to this boy, that he was going nowhere in particular, and that he was dragging the weight of a despair which could not be relieved.

Kalipada at once went back to his mother and said,

"Mother, I don't want that foreign doll."

That morning Bhavani Charan returned late. When he sat down to his meal, after his bath, it was quite evident, by the look on his face, that the curds and the milk pudding would fare no better with him than on the day before, and that the best part of the fish would go to the cat.

Just at this critical juncture Rashmani brought in a card-board box, bound round with twine, and set it before her husband. Her intention had been to reveal the mystery of this packet to her husband when he went to take his nap after his meal. But in order to remove the undeserved neglect of the curds and the milk and the fish, she had to disclose its contents before the time. So the foreign doll came out of the box and without more ado began to fan itself vigorously.

After this, the cat had to go away disappointed. Bhavani remarked to his wife that the cooking was the best he had ever tasted. The fish soup was incomparable, the curds had set themselves with an exactness that was rarely attained, and the milk pudding was superb.

On the seventh day of the moon, Kalipada got the toy for which he had been pining. During the whole of that day he allowed the foreigner to go on fanning herself and thereby made his boy companions jealous. In any other case this performance would have seemed to him monotonously tiresome, but knowing that on the following day he would have to give the toy back, his constancy to it on that single occasion remained unabated. At the rental of two rupees per diem Rashmani had hired it from Bagala.

On the eighth day of the moon, Kalipada heaved a deep sigh and returned the toy, along with the box and twine, to Bagala with his own hands. From that day forward Kalipada began to share the confidences of his mother, and it became so absurdly easy for Bhavani to give expensive presents every year, that it surprised even himself.

When, with the help of his mother, Kalipada came to know that nothing in this world could be gained without paying for it with the inevitable price of suffering, he rapidly grew up in his mind and became a valued assistant to his mother in her daily tasks. It come to be a natural rule of life with him that no one should add to the burden of the world, but that each should try to lighten it.

When Kalipada won a scholarship at the Vernacular examination, Bhavani proposed that he should give up his studies and take in hand the supervision of the estate. Kalipada went to his mother and said, – "I shall never be a man, if I do not complete my education."

The mother said – "You are right, Baba, you must go to Calcutta."

Kalipada explained to her that it would not be necessary to spend a single pice on him; his scholarship would be sufficient, and he would try to get some work to supplement it.

But it was necessary to convince Bhavani of the wisdom of the course. Rashmani did not wish to employ the argument that there was very little of the estate remaining to require supervision; for she knew how it would hurt him. She said that Kalipada must become a man whom everyone could respect. But all the members of the Chowdhuri family had attained their respectability without ever going a step outside the limits of Saniari. The outer world was as unknown to them as the world beyond the grave. Bhavani, therefore, could not conceive how anybody could think of a boy like Kalipada going to Calcutta. But the cleverest man in the village, Bagala, fortunately agreed with Rashmani.

"It is perfectly clear," he said, "that, one day, Kalipada will become a lawyer; and then, he will set matters right concerning the property of which the family has been deprived."

This was a great consolation to Bhavani Charan and he brought out the file of records about the theft of the will and tried to explain the whole thing to Kalipada by dint of daily discussion.

But his son was lacking in proper enthusiasm and merely echoed his father's sentiment about this solemn wrong.

The day before Kalipada's departure for Calcutta Rashmani hung round his neck an amulet containing some mantras to protect him from evils. She gave him at the same time a fifty-rupee currency note, advising him to keep it for any special emergency. This note, which was the symbol of his mother's numberless daily acts of self-denial, was the truest amulet of all for Kalipada. He determined to keep it by him and never to spend it, whatever might happen.

III

From this time onward the old interminable discussions about the theft of the will became less frequent on the part of Bhavani. His one topic of conversation was the marvellous adventure of Kalipada in search of his education. Kalipada was actually engaged in his studies in the city of Calcutta! Kalipada knew Calcutta as well as the palm of his hand! Kalipada had been the first to hear the great news that another bridge was going to be built over the Ganges near Hughli! The day on which the father received his son's letter, he would go to every house in the village to read it to his neighbours and he would hardly find time even to take his spectacles from his nose. On arriving at a fresh house he would remove them from their case with the utmost deliberation; then, he would wipe them carefully with the end of his dhoti; then, word by word, he would slowly read the letter through to one neighbour after another, with something like the following comment –

"Brother, just listen! What is the world coming to? Even the dogs and the jackals are to cross the holy Ganges without washing the dust from their feet! Who could imagine such a sacrilege?"

No doubt it was very deplorable; but all the same it gave Bhavani Charan a peculiar pleasure to communicate at first hand such important news from his own son's letter, and this more than compensated for the spiritual disaster which must surely overtake the numberless creatures of this present age. To everyone he met he solemnly nodded his head and prophesied that the days were soon coming when Mother Ganges would disappear altogether; all the while cherishing the hope that the news of such a momentous event would come to him by letter from his own son in the proper time.

Kalipada, with very great difficulty, scraped together just enough money to pay his expenses till he passed his Matriculation and again won a scholarship. Bhavani at once made up his mind to invite all the village to a feast, for he imagined that his son's good ship of fortune had now reached its haven and there would be no more occasion for economy. But he received no encouragement from Rashmani.

Kalipada was fortunate enough to secure a place of study in a students' lodging house near his college. The proprietor allowed him to occupy a small room on the ground floor which was absolutely useless for other lodgers. In exchange for this and his board, he had to coach the son of the owner of the house. The one great advantage was that there would be no chance of any fellow lodger ever sharing his quarters. So, although ventilation was lacking, his studies were uninterrupted.

Those of the students who paid their rent and lived in the upper story had no concern with Kalipada; but soon it became painfully evident that those who are up above have the power to hurl missiles at those below with all the more deadly force because of their distance. The leader of those above was Sailen.

Sailen was the scion of a rich family. It was unnecessary for him to live in a students' mess, but he successfully convinced his guardians that this would be best for his studies. The real reason was that Sailen was naturally fond of company, and the students' lodging house was an ideal place where he could have all the pleasure of companionship without any of its responsibilities. It was the firm conviction of Sailen that he was a good fellow and a man of feeling. The advantage of harbouring such a conviction was that it needed no proof in practise. Vanity is not like a horse or an elephant requiring expensive fodder.

Nevertheless, as Sailen had plenty of money he did not allow his vanity merely to graze at large; he took special pride in keeping it stall-fed. It must be said to his credit that he had a genuine desire to help people in their need, but the desire in him was of such a character, that if a man in difficulty refused to come to him for help, he would turn round on him and do his best to add to his trouble. His mess mates had their tickets for the theatre bought for them by Sailen, and it cost them nothing to have occasional feasts. They could borrow money from him without meaning to pay it back. When a newly married youth was in doubt about the choice of some gift for his wife, he could fully rely on Sailen's good taste in the matter. On these occasions the love-lorn youth would take Sailen to the shop and pretend to select the cheapest and least suitable presents, then, Sailen, with a contemptuous laugh would intervene and select the right thing. At the mention of the price the young husband would pull a long face, but Sailen would always be ready to abide by his own superior choice and to pay the cost.

In this manner Sailen became the acknowledged patron of the students upstairs. It made him intolerant of the insolence of any one who refused to accept his help. Indeed, to help others in this way had become his hobby.

Kalipada, in his tattered jersey, used to sit on a dirty mat in his damp room below and recite his lessons, swinging himself from side to side to the rhythm of the sentence. It was a sheer necessity for him to get that scholarship next year.

Kalipada's mother had made him promise, before he left home for Calcutta that he would avoid the company of rich young men. Therefore, he bore the burden of his indigence alone, strictly keeping himself from those who had been more favoured by fortune. But to Sailen, it seemed a sheer impertinence that a student as poor as Kalipada should yet have the pride to keep away from his patronage. Besides this, in his food and dress and everything, Kalipada's poverty was so blatantly exposed, it hurt Sailen's sense of decency. Every time he looked down into Kalipada's room, he was offended by the sight of the cheap clothing, the dingy mosquito net and the tattered bedding. Whenever he passed on his way to his own room in the upper story the sight of these things was unavoidable. To crown it all there was that absurd amulet which Kalipada always had hanging round his neck, and those daily rites of devotion which were so ridiculously out of fashion!

One day Sailen and his followers condescended to invite Kalipada to a feast, thinking that his gratitude would know no bounds. But Kalipada sent an answer saying that his habits were different and it would not be wholesome for him to accept the invitation. Sailen was unaccustomed to such a refusal, and it roused up in him all the ferocity of his insulted benevolence. For some days after this, the noise on the upper story became so loudly insistent that it was impossible for Kalipada to go on with his studies. He was compelled to spend the greater part of his days studying in the Park, and to get up very early and sit down to his work long before it was light.

Owing to his half-starved condition, his mental overwork, and badly-ventilated room, Kalipada began to suffer from continual attacks of headache. There were times when he was obliged to lie down on his bed for three or four days together. But he made no mention of his illness in his letters to his father. Bhavani himself was certain that, just as vegetation grew rank in his village surroundings, so comforts of all kinds sprang up of themselves from the soil of Calcutta. Kalipada never for a moment disabused his mind of that misconception. He did not fail to write to his father, even when suffering from one of these paroxysms of pain. The deliberate rowdiness of the students in the upper story added at such times to his distress.

Kalipada tried to make himself as scarce and small as possible, in order to avoid notice; but this did not bring him relief. One day, he found that a cheap shoe of his own had been taken away and replaced by an expensive foreign one. It was impossible for him to go to college with such an incongruous pair. He made no complaint, however, but bought some old second-hand shoes from the cobbler. One day, a student from the upper story came into his room and asked him,

"Have you, by any mistake, brought away my silver cigarette case with you?"

Kalipada got annoyed and answered,

"I have never been inside your room in my life."

The student stooped down. "Hullo!" he said, "here it is!" And the valuable cigarette case was picked up from the corner of the room.

Kalipada determined to leave this lodging house as soon as ever he had passed his Intermediate Examination, provided only he could get a scholarship to enable him to do so.

Every year the students of the house used to have their annual Saraswati Puja. Though the greater part of the expenses fell to the share of Sailen, Everyone else contributed according to his means. The year before, they had contemptuously left out Kalipada from the list of contributors; but this year, merely to tease him, they came with their subscription book. Kalipada instantly paid five rupees to the fund, though he had no intention of participating in the feast. His penury had long brought on him the contempt of his fellow lodgers, but this unexpected gift of five rupees became to them insufferable. The Saraswati Puja was performed with great éclat and the five rupees could easily have been spared. It had been hard indeed for Kalipada to part with it. While he took the food given him in his landlord's house he had no control over the time at which it was served. Besides this, since the servants brought him the food, he did not like to criticise the dishes. He preferred to provide himself with some extra things; and after the forced extravagance of his five-rupee subscription he had to forgo all this and suffered in consequence. His paroxysms of headache became more frequent, and though he passed his examination, he failed to obtain the scholarship that he desired.

The loss of the scholarship drove Kalipada to do extra work as a private tutor and to stick to the same unhealthy room in the lodging house. The students overhead had hoped that they would be relieved of his presence. But punctually to the day the room was unlocked on the lower floor. Kalipada entered, clad in the same old dirty check Parsee coat. A coolie from Sealdah Station took down from his head a steel trunk and other miscellaneous packages and laid them on the floor of the room; and a long wrangle ensued as to the proper amount of pice that were due.

In the depths of those packages there were mango chutneys and other condiments which his mother had specially prepared. Kalipada was aware that, in his absence, the upper-story students, in search of a jest, did not scruple to come into his room by stealth.

He was especially anxious to keep these home gifts from their cruel scrutiny. As tokens of home affection they were supremely precious to him; but to the town students, they denoted merely the boorishness of poverty-stricken villagers. The vessels were crude and earthen, fastened up by an earthen, lid fixed on with paste of flour. They were neither glass nor porcelain, and therefore, sure to be regarded with insolent disdain by rich town-bred people.

Formerly Kalipada used to keep these stores hidden under his bed, covering them up with old newspapers. But this time he took the precaution of always locking up his door, even if he went out for a few minutes. This still further roused the spleen of Sailen and his party. It seemed to them preposterous that the room which was poor enough to draw tears from the eyes of the most hardened burglar should be as carefully guarded as if it were a second Bank of Bengal.

"Does he actually believe," they said among themselves, "that the temptation will be irresistible for us to steal that Parsi coat?"

Sailen had never visited this dark and mildewed room from which the plaster was dropping. The glimpses that he had taken, while going up-stairs – especially when, in the evening, Kalipada, the upper part of his body bare, would sit poring over his books with a smoky lamp beside him, – were enough to give him a sense of suffocation. Sailen asked his boon companions to explore the room below and find out the treasure which Kalipada had hidden. Everybody felt intensely amused at the proposal.

The lock on Kalipada's door was a cheap one, which had the magnanimity to lend itself to any key. One evening when Kalipada had gone out to his private tuition, two or three of the students with an exuberant sense of humour took a lantern and unlocked the room and entered. It did not need a moment to discover the pots of chutney under the bed, but these hardly seemed valuable enough to demand such watchful care on the part of Kalipada. A further search disclosed a key on a ring under the pillow. They opened the steel trunk with the key and found a few soiled clothes, books and writing material. They were about to shut the box in disgust when they saw, at the very bottom, a packet covered by a dirty handkerchief. On uncovering three or four wrappers they found a currency note of fifty rupees. This made them burst out into peals of laughter. They felt certain that Kalipada was harbouring suspicion against the whole world in his mind because of this fifty rupees!

The meanness of this suspicious precaution deepened the intensity of their contempt for Kalipada. Just then, they heard a foot-step outside. They hastily shut the box, locked the door, and ran upstairs with the note in their possession.

Sailen was vastly amused. Though fifty rupees was a mere trifle, he could never have believed that Kalipada had so much money in his trunk. They all decided to watch the result of this loss upon that queer creature downstairs.

When Kalipada came home that night after his tuition was over, he was too tired to notice any disorder in his room. One of his worst attacks of nervous headache was coming on and he went straight to bed.

The next day, when he brought out his trunk from under the bed and took out his clothes, he found it open. He was naturally careful, but it was not unlikely, he thought, that he had forgotten to lock it on the day before. But when he lifted the lid he found all the contents topsy-turvy, and his heart gave a great thud when he discovered that the note, given to him by his mother, was missing. He searched the box over and over again in the vain hope of finding it, and when his loss was made certain, he flung himself upon his bed and lay like one dead.

Just then, he heard footsteps following one another on the stairs, and every now and then, an outburst of laughter from the upper room. It struck him, all of a sudden, that this was not a theft, Sailen and his party must have taken the note to amuse themselves and make laughter out of it. It would have given him less pain if a thief had stolen it. It seemed to him that these young men had laid their impious hands upon his mother herself.

This was the first time that Kalipada had ascended those stairs. He ran to the upper floor – the old jersey on his shoulders, – his face flushed with anger and the pain of his illness. As it was Sunday, Sailen and his company were seated in the verandah, laughing and talking. Without any warning, Kalipada burst upon them and shouted,

"Give me back my note!"

If he had begged it of them, they would have relented; but the sight of his anger made them furious. They started up from their chairs and exclaimed,

"What do you mean, Sir? What do you mean? What note?"

Kalipada shouted, "The note you have taken from my box!"

"How dare you?" they shouted back. "Do you take us to be thieves?"

If Kalipada had held any weapon in his hand at that moment he certainly would have killed some one among them. But when he was about to spring, they fell on him, and four or five of them dragged him down to his room and thrust him inside.

Sailen said to his companions, "Here, take this hundred-rupee note, and throw it to that dog!"

They all loudly exclaimed, "No! Let him climb down first and give us a written apology. Then, we shall consider it!"

Sailen's party all went to bed at the proper time and slept the sleep of the innocent. In the morning they had almost forgotten Kalipada. But some of them, while passing his room, heard the sound of talking and they thought that possibly he was busy consulting some lawyer. The door was shut from the inside. They tried to overhear, but what they heard had nothing legal about it. It was quite incoherent.

They informed Sailen. He came down and stood with his ear close to the door. The only thing that could be distinctly heard was the word 'Father.' This frightened Sailen. He thought that possibly Kalipada had gone mad on account of the grief of losing that fifty-rupee note. Sailen shouted "Kalipada Babu!" two or three times, but got no answer. Only that muttering sound continued. Sailen called – "Kalipada Babu – please open the door.

Your note has been found." But still the door was not opened and that muttering sound went on.

Sailen had never anticipated such a result as this. He did not express a word of repentance to his followers, but he felt the sting of it all the same. Some advised him to break open the door, others thought that the police should be called in – for Kalipada might be in a dangerous state of lunacy. Sailen at once sent for a doctor who lived close at hand. When they burst open the door they found the bedding hanging from the bed and Kalipada lying on the floor unconscious. He was tossing about and throwing up his arms and muttering, with his eyes red and open and his face all flushed. The doctor examined him and asked if there were any relative near at hand; for the case was serious.

Sailen answered that he knew nothing, but would make inquiries. The doctor then, advised the removal of the patient at once to an upstairs room and proper nursing arrangements day and night. Sailen took him up to his own room and dismissed his followers. He got some ice and put it on Kalipada's head and began to fan him with his own hand.

Kalipada, fearing that mocking references would be made, had concealed the names and address of his parents from these people with special care. So Sailen had no alternative but to open his box. He found two bundles of letters tied up with ribbon. One of them contained his mother's letters, the other contained his father's. His mother's letters were fewer in number than his father's. Sailen closed the door and began to read the letters. He was startled when he saw the address, – Saniari, the house of the Chaudhuries – and then, the name of the father, Bhavani. He folded up the letters and sat still, gazing at Kalipada's face. Some of his friends had casually mentioned, that there was a resemblance between Kalipada and himself. But he was offended at the remark and did not believe it. Today, he discovered the truth. He knew that his own grandfather, Shyama Charan, had a step-brother named Bhavani; but the later history to the family had remained a secret to him. He did not even know that Bhavani had a son named Kalipada; and he never suspected that Bhavani had come to such an abject state of poverty as this. He now felt not only relieved, but proud of his own relative, Kalipada, that he had refused to enter himself on the list of protégés.

IV

Knowing that his party had insulted Kalipada almost every day, Sailen felt reluctant to keep him in the lodging house with them. So he rented another suitable house and kept him there. Bhavani came down in haste to Calcutta the moment he received a letter from Sailen informing him of his son's illness. Rashmani parted with all her savings giving instructions to her husband to spare no expense upon her son. It was not considered proper for the daughters of the great Chaudhuri family to leave their home and go to Calcutta unless absolutely obliged, and therefore, she had to remain behind offering prayers to all the tutelary gods. When Bhavani Charan arrived he found Kalipada still unconscious and delirious. It nearly broke Bhavani's heart when he heard himself called 'Master Mashai.' Kalipada often called him in his delirium and he tried to make himself recognised by his son, but in vain.

The doctor came again and said the fever was getting less. He thought the case was taking a more favourable turn. For Bhavani, it was an impossibility to imagine that his son would not recover. He must live, it was his destiny to live. Bhavani was much struck with the behaviour of Sailen. It was difficult to believe that he was not of their own kith and kin. He supposed all this kindness to be due to the town training which Sailen had received. Bhavani spoke to Sailen disparagingly of the country habits which village people like himself got into.

Gradually the fever went down and Kalipada recovered consciousness. He was astonished beyond measure when he saw his father sitting in the room beside him. His first anxiety was lest he should discover the miserable state in which he had been living. But what would be harder still to bear was, if his father with his rustic manners became the butt of the people upstairs. He looked round him, but could not recognise his own room and wondered if he had been dreaming. But he found himself too weak to think.

He supposed that it had been his father who had removed him to this better lodging, but he had no power to calculate how he could possibly bear the expense. The only thing that concerned him at that moment was that he felt he must live, and for that he had a claim upon the world.

Once when his father was absent Sailen came in with a plate of grapes in his hand. Kalipada could not understand this at all and wondered if there was some practical joke behind it. He at once became excited and wondered how he could save his father from annoyance. Sailen set the plate down on the table and touched Kalipada's feet humbly and said, "My offence has been great, pray forgive me."

Kalipada started and sat up on his bed. He could see that Sailen's repentance was sincere and he was greatly moved.

When Kalipada had first come to the students' lodging house he had felt strongly drawn towards this handsome youth. He never missed a chance of looking at his face when Sailen passed by his room on his way upstairs. He would have given all the world to be friends with him, but the barrier was too great to overcome. Now to-day when Sailen brought him the grapes and asked his forgiveness, he silently looked at his face and silently accepted the grapes which spoke of his repentance.

It amused Kalipada greatly when he noticed the intimacy that had sprung up between his father and Sailen. Sailen used to call Bhavani Charan "grandfather" and exercised to the full the grandchild's privilege of joking with him. The principal object of the jokes was the absent "grandmother." Sailen made the confession that he had taken the opportunity of Kalipada's illness to steal all the delicious chutneys which his "grandmother" had made with her own hand. The news of his act of "thieving" gave Kalipada very great joy. He found it easy to deprive himself, if he could find any one who could appreciate the good things made by his mother. Thus, this time of his convalescence became the happiest period in the whole of Kalipada's life.

There was only one flaw in this unalloyed happiness. Kalipada had a fierce pride in his poverty which prevented him ever speaking about his family's better days. Therefore, when his father used to talk of his former prosperity Kalipada winced. Bhavani could not keep to himself the one great event of his life, – the theft of that will which he was absolutely certain that he would some day recover. Kalipada had always regarded this as a kind of mania of his father's, and in collusion with his mother he had often humoured his father concerning this amiable weakness. But he shrank in shame when his father talked about this to Sailen. He noticed particularly that Sailen did not relish such conversation and that he often tried to prove, with a certain amount of feeling, its absurdity. But Bhavani, who was ready to give in to others in matters much more serious, in this matter was adamant. Kalipada tried to pacify him by saying that there was no great need to worry about it, because those who were enjoying its benefit were almost the same as his own children, since they were his nephews.

Such talk Sailen could not bear for long and he used to leave the room. This pained Kalipada, because he thought that Sailen might get quite a wrong conception of his father and imagine him to be a grasping worldly old man. Sailen would have revealed his own relationship to Kalipada and his father long before, but this discussion about the theft of the will prevented him. It was hard for him to believe that his grandfather or father had stolen the will; on the other hand he could not but think that some cruel injustice had been done in depriving Bhavani of his share of the ancestral property. Therefore, he gave up arguing when the subject was brought forward and took some occasion to leave as soon as possible.

Though Kalipada still had headaches in the evening, with a slight rise in temperature, he did not take it at all seriously. He became anxious to resume his studies because he felt it would be a calamity to him if he again missed his scholarship. He secretly began to read once more, without taking any notice of the strict orders of the doctor. Kalipada asked his father to return home, assuring him that he was in the best of health. Bhavani had been all his life fed and nourished and cooked for by his wife; he was pining to get back. He did not, therefore, wait to be pressed.

On the morning of his intended departure, when he went to say good-bye to Kalipada, he found him very ill indeed, his face red with fever and his whole body burning. He had been committing to memory page after page of his text book of Logic half through the night, and for the remainder he could not sleep at all. The doctor took Sailen aside. "This relapse," he said, "is fatal." Sailen came to Bhavani and said, "The patient requires a mother's nursing, she must be brought to Calcutta."

It was evening when Rashmani came, and she only saw her son alive for a few hours. Not knowing how her husband could survive such a terrible shock she altogether suppressed her own sorrow. Her son was merged in her husband again, and she took up this burden of the dead and the living on her own aching heart. She said to her God – "It is too much for me to bear." But she did bear it.

V

It was midnight. With the very weariness of her sorrow Rashmani had fallen asleep soon after reaching her own home in the village. But Bhavani had no sleep that night. Tossing on his bed for hours he heaved a deep sigh saying – "Merciful God!" Then, he got up from his bed and went out. He entered the room where Kalipada had been wont to do his lessons in his childhood. The lamp shook as he held it in his hand. On the wooden settle there was still the torn, ink-stained quilt, made long ago by Rashmani herself. On the wall were figures of Euclid and Algebra drawn in charcoal. The remains of a Royal Reader No. III and a few exercise books were lying about; and the one odd slipper of his infancy, which had evaded notice so long, was keeping its place in the dusty obscurity of the corner of the room. To-day it had become so important that nothing in the world, however great, could keep it hidden any longer. Bhavani put the lamp in the niche on the wall and silently sat on the settle; his eyes were dry, but he felt choked as if with want of breath.

Bhavani opened the shutters on the eastern side and stood still, grasping the iron bars, gazing into the darkness. Through the drizzling rain he could see the outline of the clump of trees at the end of the outer wall. At this spot Kalipada had made his own garden. The passion flowers which he had planted with his own hand had grown densely thick. While he gazed at this Bhavani felt his heart come up into his throat with choking pain. There was nobody now to wait for and expect daily. The summer vacation had come, but no one would come back home to fill the vacant room and use its old familiar furniture.

"O Baba mine!" he cried, "O Baba! O Baba mine!"

He sat down. The rain came faster. A sound of footsteps was heard among the grass and withered leaves. Bhavani's heart stood still. He hoped it was ... that which was beyond all hope. He thought it was Kalipada himself come to see his own garden, – and in this downpour of rain how wet he would be! Anxiety about this made him restless. Then, somebody stood for a moment in front of the iron window bars. The cloak round his head made it impossible for Bhavani to see his face clearly, but his height was the same as that of Kalipada.

"Darling!" cried Bhavani, "You have come!" and he rushed to open the door.

But when he came outside to the spot where the figure had stood, there was no one to be seen. He walked up and down in the garden through the drenching rain, but no one was there. He stood still for a moment raising his voice and calling, – "Kalipada," but no answer came. The servant, Noto, who was sleeping in the cowshed, heard his cry and came out and coaxed him back to his room.

Next day, in the morning, Noto, while sweeping the room found a bundle just underneath the grated window. He brought it to Bhavani who opened it and found it was an old document. He put on his spectacles and after reading a few lines came rushing in to Rashmani and gave the paper into her hand.

Rashmani asked, "What is it?"

Bhavani replied, "It is the will!"

"Who gave it you?"

"He himself came last night to give it to me."

"What are you going to do with it?"

Bhavani said, "I have no need of it now." And he tore the will to pieces.

When the news reached the village Bagala proudly nodded his head and said, "Didn't I prophesy that the will would be recovered through Kalipada?"

But the grocer Ramcharan replied, "Last night when the ten o'clock train reached the Station a handsome looking young man came to my shop and asked the way to the Chaudhuri's house and I thought he had some kind of bundle in his hand."

"Absurd," said Bagala.

27

The Patriot

I am sure that Chitragupta, who keeps strict record at the gate of Death, must have noted down in big letters accusations against me, which had escaped my attention altogether. On the other hand many of my sins, that have passed unnoticed by others, loom large in my own memory. The story of my transgression, that I am going to relate, belongs to the latter kind, and I hope that a frank confession of it, before it is finally entered in the Book of Doom, may lessen its culpability.

It all happened yesterday afternoon, on a day of festival for the Jains in our neighbourhood. I was going out with my wife, Kalika, to tea at the house of my friend Nayanmohan.

My wife's name means literally a 'bud.' It was given by my father-in-law, who is thus, solely responsible for any discrepancy between its implication and the reality to which it is attached. There is not the least tremor of hesitancy in my wife's nature; her opinions on most subjects have reached their terminus. Once, when she had been vigorously engaged in picketing against British cloth in Burrabazar, the awe-struck members of her party in a fit of excessive admiration gave her the name, Dhruva-vrata, the woman of unwavering vows.

My name is Girindra, the Lord of the Rocks, so common among my countrymen, whose character generally fails to act up to it. Kalika's admirers simply know me as the husband of my wife and pay no heed to my name. By good luck inherited from my ancestors I have, however, some kind of significance, which is considered to be convenient by her followers at the time of collecting subscriptions.

There is a greater chance of harmony between husband and wife, when they are different in character, like the shower of rain and the dry earth, than when they are of a uniform constitution. I am somewhat slipshod by nature, having no grip over things, while my wife has a tenacity of mind which never allows her to let go the thing which it has in its clutches. This very dissimilarity helps to preserve peace in our household.

But there is one point of difference between us, regarding which no adjustment has yet become possible. Kalika believes that I am unpatriotic.

This is very disconcerting, because according to her, truth is what she proclaims to be true. She has numerous internal evidences of my love for my country; but as it disdains to don the livery of the brand of nationalism, professed by her own party, she fiercely refuses to acknowledge it.

From my younger days, I have continued to be a confirmed book-lover, indeed, I am hopelessly addicted to buying books. Even my enemies would not dare to deny that I read them; and my friends know only too well how fond I am of discussing their contents. This had the effect of eliminating most of my friends, till I have left to me Banbihari, the sole companion of my lonely debates. We have just passed through a period, when our police authorities, on the one hand, have associated the worst form of sedition with the presence of the *Gita* in our possession; and our patriots, on their side, have found it impossible to reconcile appreciation of foreign literature with devotion to one's Motherland. Our traditional Goddess of Culture, Saraswati, because of her white complexion, has come to be regarded with-suspicion by our young nationalists. It was openly declared, when the students shunned their College lectures, that the water of the divine lake, on which Saraswati had her white lotus seat, had no efficacy in extinguishing the fire of ill-fortune that has been raging for centuries round the throne of our Mother, Bharat-Lakshmi. In any case, intellectual culture was considered to be a superfluity in the proper growth of our political life.

In spite of my wife's excellent example and powerful urgings I do not wear khaddar – not because there is anything wrong in it, nor because I am too fastidious in the choice of my wardrobe. On the contrary, among those of my traits, which are not in perfect consonance with our own national habits, I cannot include a scrupulous care as to how I dress. Once upon a time, before Kalika had her modern transformation, I used to wear broad-toed shoes from Chinese shops and forgot to have them polished. I had a dread of putting on socks, I preferred punjabis to English shirts, and overlooked their accidental deficiency in buttons. These habits of mine constantly produced domestic cataclysms, threatening our permanent separation. Kalika declared that she felt ashamed to appear before the public in my company. I readily absolved her from the wifely duty of accompanying me to those parties where my presence would be discordant.

The times have changed, but my evil fortune persists. Kalika still has the habit of repeating, 'I am ashamed to go out with you.' Formerly, I hesitated to adopt the uniform of her set, when she belonged to the pre-nationalist age; and I still feel reluctant to adopt the uniform of the present regime, to which she owns her allegiance.

The fault lies deep in my own nature. I shrink from all conscious display of sectarian marks about my person. This shyness on my part leads to incessant verbal explosions in our domestic world, because of the inherent incapacity of Kalika to accept as final any natural difference, which her partner in life may possess. Her mind is like a mountain stream, that boisterously goes round and round a rock, pushing against it in a vain effort to make it flow with its own current. Her contact with a different point of view from her own seems to exercise an irresistible reflex action upon her nerves, throwing her into involuntary convulsions.

While getting ready to go out yesterday, the tone with which Kalika protested against my non-khaddar dress was anything but sweet. Unfortunately, I had my inveterate pride of intellect, that forced me into a discussion with my wife. It was unpleasant, and what more, futile.

'Women find it convenient,' I said to her, 'to veil their eyes and walk tied to the leading strings of authority. They feel safe when they deprive their thoughts of all freedom, and confine them in the strict zenana of conformity. Our ladies today have easily developed their devotion to khaddar, because it has added to the over-burdened list of our outward criterion's of propriety, which seem to comfort them.'

Kalika replied with almost fanatical fury, 'It will be a great day for my country, when the sanctity of wearing khaddar is as blindly believed in as a dip in the holy water of the Ganges. Reason crystallised becomes custom. Free thoughts are like ghosts, which find their bodies in convention. Then, alone they have their solid work, and no longer float about in a thin atmosphere of vacillation.'

I could see that these were the wise sayings of Nayanmohan, with the quotation marks worn out; Kalika found no difficulty in imagining that they were her own.

The man who invented the proverb, 'The silent silence all antagonist', must have been unmarried. It made my wife all the more furious, when I offered her no answer. 'Your protest against caste', she explained, 'is only confined to your mouth. We, on the contrary, carry it out in practice by imposing a uniformly white cover over all colour distinctions.'

I was about to reply, that my protest against caste did truly have its origin in my mouth, whenever I accepted with relish the excellent food cooked by a Muhammadan. It was certainly oral, but not verbal; and its movements were truly inward. An external cover hides distinctions, but does not remove them.

I am sure my argument deserved utterance, but being a helpless male, I timidly sought safety in a speechless neutrality; for, I knew, from repeated experience, that such discussions, started in our domestic seclusion, are invariably carried by my wife, like soiled linen, to her friendly circle to be ruthlessly beaten and mangled. She has the unpleasant habit of collecting counter-arguments from the mouth of Professor Nayanmohan, exultantly flinging them in my face, and then, rushing away from the arena without waiting for my answer.

I was perfectly certain about what was in store for me at the Professor's tea-table. There would be some abstruse dissertation on the relative position in Hindu culture of tradition and free thought, the inherited experience of ages and reason which is volatile, inconclusive, and colourlessly universal. In the meanwhile, the vision floated before my mind's eye of the newly-brought books, redolent of Morocco leather, mysteriously veiled in a brown paper cover, waiting for me by my cushions, with their shy virginity of uncut pages.

All the same, I was compelled to keep my engagement by the dread of words, uttered and unuttered, and gestures suggestive of trouble.

We had travelled only a short distance from our house. Passing by the street-hydrant, we had reached the tiled hut occupied by an up-country shopkeeper, who was giving various forms to indigestibility in his cauldron of boiling mustard oil, when we were obstructed by a fearful uproar.

The Marwaris, proceeding to their temple, carrying their costly paraphernalia of worship, had suddenly stopped at this place. There were angry shouts, mingled with the sound of thrashing, and I thought that the crowd were dealing with some pickpocket, enjoying the vigour of their own indignation, which gave them-the delightful freedom to be merciless towards one of their own fellow beings. When, by dint of impatient footing of horn, our motor car reached the centre of the excited crowd, we found that the old municipal sweeper of our district was being beaten. He had just taken his afternoon bath and was carrying a bucket of clean water in his right hand with a broom under his arm. Dressed in a check-patterned vest, with carefully combed hair still wet, he was walking home, holding his seven-year-old grandson by his left hand, when accidentally he came in contact with somebody, or something, which gave rise to this violent outburst. The boy was piteously imploring everybody not to hurt his grandfather; and the old man himself with joined hands uplifted, was asking forgiveness for his unintentional offence. Tears were streaming from his frightened eyes, and blood was smeared across his grey beard.

The sight was intolerable to me. I decided at once to take up the sweeper into my car and thereby demonstrate to the pious party, that I was not of their cult.

Noticing my restlessness, Kalika guessed what was in my mind. Griping my arm, she whispered, 'What are you doing? Don't you see he is a sweeper?'

'He maybe a sweeper,' said I, 'but those people have no right to beat him in this brutal manner.'

'It's his own fault.' Kalika answered, 'Would it have hurt his dignity, if he had avoided the middle of the road?'

'I don't know', I said impatiently. 'Anyhow, I am going to take him into my car.'

'Then, I leave your car this moment,' said Kalika angrily. 'I refuse to travel with a sweeper.'

'Can't you see,' I argued, 'that he was just bathed, and his clothes are clean, – in fact, much cleaner than those of the people who are beating him?'

"He's a sweeper!" She said decisively. Then, she called to the chauffeur, 'Gangadin, drive on'.

I was defeated. It was my cowardice.

Nayanmohan, I am told, brought out some very profound sociological arguments, at the tea-table, specially dealing with the inevitable inequality imposed upon men by their profession and the natural humiliation which is inherent in the scheme of things. But his words did not reach my ears, and I sat silent all through the evening.

28

The Hidden Treasure

I

It was a moonless night, and Mrityunjaya was seated before the ancestral image of the goddess Kali. As he finished his devotions the cawing of an early morning crow was heard from a neighbouring mango grove.

First, seeing that the door of the temple was shut, he bowed once more before the image and, shifting its pedestal, took from under it a strong wooden box. This he opened with a key which hung on his sacred thread, but the moment he had looked inside he started in dismay. He took up the box and shook it several times. It had not been broken open, for the lock was uninjured. He groped all round the image a dozen times, but could find nothing.

Mrityunjaya's little temple stood on one side of his inner garden which was surrounded by a wall. It was sheltered by the shade of some tall trees. Inside there was nothing but the image of Kali, and it had only one entrance. Like a mad man Mrityunjaya threw open the door, and began to roam round on all sides in search of a clue, but in vain. By this time daylight had come.

In despair he sat on some steps and with his head buried in his hands began to think. He was just beginning to feel sleepy after his long sleepless night when suddenly he heard someone say, "Greeting, my son!" Looking up he saw in the courtyard before him a long-haired sannyasi. Mrityunjaya made a deep obeisance to him and the ascetic placed his hand on his head, saying, "My son, your sorrow is vain."

Mrityunjaya, in astonishment, replied, "Can you read people's thoughts? How do you know about my sorrow? I have spoken of it to no one."

The sannyasi answered, "My son, instead of sorrowing over what you have lost, you ought to rejoice."

Clasping his feet Mrityunjaya exclaimed, "Then, you know everything? Tell me how it got lost and where I can recover it."

The sannyasi replied, "If I wanted you to suffer misfortune Then, I would tell you. But you must not grieve over that which the goddess has taken from you out of pity."

But Mrityunjaya was not satisfied and in the hope of pleasing his visitor he spent the whole of that day serving him in different ways. But when early next morning he was bringing him a bowl of fresh milk from his own cow he found that the sannyasi had disappeared.

II

When Mrityunjaya had been a child his grandfather, Harihar, was sitting one day on those same steps of the temple, smoking his hookah, when a sannyasi came into the courtyard and greeted him. Harihar invited him into his home and for several days treated him as an honoured guest.

When about to go the sannyasi said to him, "My son, you are poor, are you not?" to which Harihar replied, "Father, I am indeed. Only hear what my condition is. Once our family was the most prosperous in the village but now our condition is so miserable that we can hardly hold up our heads. I beg you to tell me how we can restore ourselves to prosperity again."

The sannyasi laughing slightly said, "My son, why not be satisfied with your present position? What's the use of trying to become wealthy?"

But Harihar persisted and declared that he was ready to undertake anything that would restore his family to their proper rank in society.

Thereupon the sannyasi took out a roll of cloth in which an old and stained piece of paper was wrapped. It looked like a horoscope. The sannyasi unrolled it and Harihar saw that it had some signs in cypher written within circles, and below these was a lot of doggerel verse which commenced thus,

For attainment of your goal
Find a word that rhymes with soul.
From the 'radha' take its 'dha',
After that at last put 'ra'.
From the tamarind-banyan's mouth
Turn your face towards the south.
When the light is in the East
There shall be of wealth a feast.

There was much more of the same kind of rigmarole.

Harihar said, "Father, I can't understand a single word of it."

To this the sannyasi replied, "Keep it by you. Make your puja to the goddess Kali and by her grace you, or some descendant of yours, will gain the untold wealth of which this writing tells the secret hiding place."

Harihar entreated him to explain the writing, but the sannyasi said that only by the practice of austerity could its meaning be discovered.

Just at this moment Harihar's youngest brother, Shankar, arrived on the scene and Harihar tried to snatch the paper away before it could be observed. But the sannyasi, laughing, said, "Already, I see, you have started on the painful road to greatness. But you need not be afraid. The secret can only be discovered by one person. If anyone else tries a thousand times he will never be able to solve it. It will be a member of your family, so you can show this paper to anyone without fear."

The sannyasi having left them, Harihar could not rest until he had hidden the paper. Fearful lest anyone else should profit by it, and above all lest his young brother Shankar should enjoy this hidden wealth, he locked the paper in a strong wooden box and hid it under the seat of the household goddess Kali. Every month, at the time of the new moon, he would go in the dead of night to the temple and there he would offer prayers to the goddess in the hope that she would give him the power to decipher the secret writing.

Some time after this Shankar came to his brother and begged him to show him the paper.

"Go away, you idiot!" shouted Harihar, "that paper was nothing. That rascal of a sannyasi wrote a lot of nonsense on it simply to deceive me. I burnt it long ago."

Shankar remained silent, but some weeks afterwards he disappeared from the house and was never seen again.

From that time Harihar gave up all other occupations, and spent all his waking moments in thinking about the hidden treasure.

When he died he left this mysterious paper to his eldest son, Shyamapada, who, as soon as he got possession of it, gave up his business and spent his whole time in studying the secret cypher and in worshipping the goddess in the hope of good luck coming to him.

Mrityunjaya was Shyamapada's eldest child, so he became the owner of this precious heirloom on his father's death. The worse his condition became the greater the eagerness he showed in trying to solve the secret. It was about this time that the loss of the paper occurred. The visit of the long-haired sannyasi coinciding with its disappearance, Mrityunjaya determined that he would try to find him, feeling sure he could discover everything from him. So he left his home on the quest.

III

After spending a year in going from place to place Mrityunjaya one day arrived at a village named Dharagole. There he stayed at a grocer's shop, and as he was sitting absent-mindedly smoking and thinking, a sannyasi passed along the edge of a neighbouring field. At first Mrityunjaya did not pay much attention, but after a few minutes he came to himself and it flashed across his mind that that was the very sannyasi for whom he had been searching. Hurriedly laying aside his hookah he rushed past the startled storekeeper and dashed from the shop into the street. But the sannyasi was nowhere to be seen.

As it was dark and the place was strange to him he gave up the idea of searching further and returned to the shop. There he asked the storekeeper what lay beyond the village in the great forest near by. The man replied,

"Once a great city was there, but owing to the curse of the sage Agastya, its king and all his subjects died of some dreadful pestilence. People say that enormous wealth and piles of jewels are still hidden there, but no one dares to enter that forest even at midday. Those who have done so have never returned."

Mrityunjaya's mind became restless, and all night long he lay on his mat tormented by mosquitoes and by thoughts of the forest, the sannyasi, and his lost secret. He had read the verses so often that he could almost repeat them by heart, and hour after hour the opening lines kept ringing through his mind, until his brain reeled,

For attainment of your goal
Find a word that rhymes with soul.
From the 'radha' take its 'dha'
After that at last put 'ra'.

He could not get the words out of his head. At last when dawn came he fell asleep and in a dream the meaning of the verse became as clear as day-light. Taking the 'dha' from 'radha' and at the end of that putting 'ra' you get 'dhara', and 'gole' rhymes with soul! The name of the village in which he was staying was 'Dharagole'! He jumped up from his mat sure that he was at last near the end of his search.

IV

The whole of that day Mrityunjaya spent roaming about the forest in the hope of finding a path. He returned to the village at night half dead with hunger and fatigue, but next day he took a bundle of parched rice and started off again. At midday he arrived at the side of a lake round which there were traces of a path. The water was clear in the middle but near the banks it was a tangle of weeds and water-lilies. Having soaked his rice in the water by some broken stone steps on the bank he finished eating it and began to walk slowly round the lake looking carefully everywhere for signs of buildings. Suddenly when he had reached the west side of the lake he stood stock still, for there before him was a tamarind tree growing right in the centre of a gigantic banyan. He immediately recalled the lines,

From the tamarind-banyan's mouth
Turn your face towards the south.

After walking some distance towards the south he found himself in the middle of a thick jungle through which it was impossible to force a way. He however determined not to lose sight of the tamarind tree.

Turning back he noticed in the distance through the branches of the tree the pinnacles of a building. Making his way in that direction he came upon a ruined temple, by the side of which were the ashes of a recent fire. With great caution Mrityunjaya made his way to a broken door and peeped in. There was no one there, not even an image, only a blanket, and a water pot with a sannyasi's scarf lying beside it.

Evening was approaching, the village was far off, and it would be difficult to find a path back by night, so Mrityunjaya was pleased at seeing signs of a human being. By the door lay a large piece of stone which had fallen from the ruin. On this he seated himself and was deep in thought when he suddenly noticed what appeared to be written characters on the surface of the stone. Looking closely he saw a circular symbol which was familiar to him. It was partly obliterated, it is true, but it was sufficiently distinct for him to recognise the design as that which had appeared at the top of his lost piece of paper. He had studied it so often that it was clearly printed on his brain. How many times had he begged the goddess to reveal to him the meaning of that mystic sign as he sat at midnight in the dimly lit temple of his home with the fragrance of incense filling the night air. Tonight the fulfilment of his long cherished desire seemed so near that his whole body trembled. Fearing that by some slight blunder he might frustrate all his hopes, and above all dreading lest the sannyasi had been beforehand in discovering his treasure he shook with terror. He could not decide what to do. The thought came to him that he might even at that very moment be sitting above untold wealth without knowing it.

As he sat repeating the name of Kali, evening fell and the sombre darkness of the forest resounded with the continual chirping of crickets.

V

Just as he was wondering what to do he saw through the thick foliage the distant gleam of a fire. Getting up from the stone on which he was seated he carefully marked the spot he was leaving and went off in the direction of the light.

Having progressed with great difficulty a short way he saw from behind the trunk of a tree the very sannyasi he had been seeking with the well-known paper in his hand. He had opened it and, by the light of the flames, he was working out its meaning in the ashes with a stick.

There was the very paper which belonged to Mrityunjaya and which had belonged to his father and his grandfather before him, in the hands of a thief and a cheat! It was for this then, that this rogue of a sannyasi had bidden Mrityunjaya not to sorrow over his loss!

The sannyasi was calculating the meaning of the signs, and every now and then, would measure certain distances on the ground with a stick. Sometimes he would stop and shake his head with a disappointed air, and then, he would go back and make fresh calculations.

In this way the night was nearly spent and it was not until the cool breeze of daybreak began to rustle in the leafy branches of the trees that the sannyasi folded up the paper and went away.

Mrityunjaya was perplexed. He was quite sure that without the sannyasi's help it would be impossible for him to decipher the mystery of the paper. But he was equally certain that the covetous rascal would not knowingly assist him. Therefore, to watch the sannyasi secretly was his only hope; but as he could not get any food without going back to the village, Mrityunjaya decided he would return to his lodgings that morning.

When it became light enough he left the tree behind which he had been hiding and made his way to the place where the sannyasi had been making his calculations in the ashes. But he could make nothing of the marks. Nor, after wandering all round, could he see that the forest there differed in any way from other parts of the jungle.

As the sunlight began to penetrate the thick shade of the trees Mrityunjaya made his way towards the village, looking carefully on every side as he went. His chief fear was lest the sannyasi should catch sight of him.

That morning a feast was given to Brahmins at the shop where Mrityunjaya had taken shelter, so he came in for a sumptuous meal. Having fasted so long he could not resist eating heavily, and after the feast he soon rolled over on his mat and fell sound asleep.

Although he had not slept all night, Mrityunjaya had made up his mind that he would that day take his meals in good time and start off early in the afternoon. What happened was exactly the opposite, for when he woke the sun had already set. But although it was getting dark, he could not refrain from entering the forest.

Night fell suddenly and so dense was the darkness that it was impossible for him to see his way through the deep shadows of the thick jungle. He could not make out which way he was going and when day broke he found that he had been going round and round in one part of the forest quite near the village.

The raucous cawing of some crows from near by sounded to Mrityunjaya like mockery.

VI

After many miscalculations and corrections the sannyasi had at length discovered the path to the entrance of a subterranean tunnel. Lighting a torch he entered. The brick walls were mouldy with moss and slime, and water oozed out from the many cracks. In some places sleeping toads could be seen piled up in heaps. After proceeding over slippery stones for some distance the sannyasi came to a wall. The passage was blocked! He struck the wall in several places with a heavy iron bar but there was not the least suspicion of a hollow sound. There was not a crack anywhere; without a doubt the tunnel ended there.

He spent the whole of that night studying the paper again, and next morning having finished his calculations, he entered the underground passage once more. This time, carefully following the secret directions, he loosened a stone from a certain place and discovered a branch turning. This he followed, but once more he came to a stop where another wall blocked all further progress.

But finally, on the fifth night, the sannyasi as he entered exclaimed, "Tonight I shall find the way without the shadow of a doubt!"

The passage was like a labyrinth. There seemed no end to its branches and turnings. In some places it was so low and narrow that he had to crawl on hands and knees. Carefully holding the torch he arrived at length at a large circular room, in the middle of which was a wide well of solid masonry. By the light of his torch the sannyasi was unable to see how deep it was, but he saw that from the roof there descended into it a thick heavy iron chain. He pulled with all his strength at this chain and it shook very slightly. But there rose from the depth of the well a metallic clang which reverberated through that dark dismal chamber. The sannyasi called out in excitement, "At last I have found it!"

Next moment a huge stone rolled through the hole in the broken wall through which he had entered and someone fell on the floor with a loud cry. Startled by this sudden sound the sannyasi let his torch fall to the ground and the room was plunged in darkness.

VII

He called out "Who is there?" but there was no answer. Putting out his hand he touched a man's body. Shaking it. he asked, "Who are you?" Still he got no reply. The man was unconscious.

Striking a flint he at last found his torch and lighted it. In the meantime the man had regained consciousness and was trying to sit up though he was groaning with pain.

On seeing him the sannyasi exclaimed, "Why, it is Mrityunjaya! What are you doing here?"

Mrityunjaya replied, "Father, pardon me. God has punished me enough. I was trying to roll that stone on you when my foot slipped and I fell. My leg must be broken."

To this the sannyasi answered, "But what good would it have done you to kill me?"

Mrityunjaya exclaimed, "What good indeed! Why did you steal into my temple and rob me of that secret paper? And what are you doing in this underground place yourself? You are a thief, and a cheat! The sannyasi who gave that paper to my grandfather told him that one of his family was to discover the secret of the writing. The secret is mine by rights and it is for this reason that I have been following you day and night like your shadow, going without food and sleep all these days. Then, today when you exclaimed At last I have found it!' I could restrain myself no longer. I had followed you and was hiding behind the wall where you had made the hole, and I tried to kill you. I failed because I am weak and the ground was slippery and I fell. Kill me if you wish, then, I can become a guardian spirit to watch over this treasure of mine. But if I live, you will never be able to take it. Never! Never! Never! If you try, I will bring the curse of a Brahmin on you by jumping into this well and committing suicide. Never will you be able to enjoy this treasure. My father, and his father before him, thought of nothing but this treasure and they died thinking of it. We have become poor for its sake. In search of it I have left wife and children, and without food or sleep have wandered from place to place like a maniac. Never shall you take this treasure from me while I have eyes to see!"

VIII

The sannyasi said quietly, "Mrityunjaya, listen to me. I will tell you everything. You remember that your grandfather's youngest brother was called Shankar?"

"Yes," replied Mrityunjaya, "he left home and was never heard of again."

"Well," said the sannyasi, "I am that Shankar!" Mrityunjaya gave a gasp of despair. He had so long regarded himself as the sole owner of this hidden wealth that, now that this relative had turned up and proved his equal right, he felt as if his claim were destroyed.

Shankar continued, "From the moment that my brother got that paper from the sannyasi he tried every means in his power to keep it hidden from me. But the harder he tried the greater became my curiosity, and I soon found that he had hidden it in a wooden box under the seat of the goddess. I got hold of a duplicate key, and by degrees, whenever the opportunity occurred, I copied out the whole of the writing and the signs. The very day I had finished copying it I left home in quest of the treasure. I even left my wife and only child neither of whom is now living. There is no need to describe all the places I visited in my wanderings. I felt sure that as the paper had been given to my brother by a sannyasi I would be able to find out its meaning from one, so I began to serve sannyasis whenever I had the chance. Many of them were impostors and tried to steal the writing from me. In this way many years passed, but not for a single moment did I have any peace or happiness.

"At last in my search, by virtue of some right action in a previous birth, I had the good fortune to meet in the mountains Swami Rupananda. He said to me, 'My child, give up desire, and the imperishable wealth of the whole universe will be yours.'

"He cooled the fever of my mind. By his grace the light of the sky and the green verdure of the earth seemed to me equal to the wealth of kings. One winter day at the foot of the mountain I lit a fire in the brazier of my revered Guru and offered up the paper in its flames. The Swami laughed slightly as I did it. At the time I did not understand that laugh. But now I do. Doubtless he thought it is easy enough to burn a piece of paper, but to burn to ashes our desires is not so simple!

"When not a vestige of the paper remained it seemed as if my heart had suddenly filled with the rare joy of freedom. My mind at last realised the meaning of detachment. I said to myself, 'Now I have no more fear, I desire nothing in the world.'

"Shortly after this I parted from the Swami and although I have often sought for him since, I have never seen him again.

"I then, wandered as a sannyasi with my mind detached from worldly things. Many years passed and I had almost forgotten the existence of the paper, when one day I came to the forest near Dharagole and took shelter in a ruined temple. After a day or two I noticed that there were inscriptions on the walls, some of which I recognised. There could be no doubt that here was a clue to what I had spent so many years of my life in trying to discover. I said to myself, 'I must not stay here. I must leave this forest.'

"But I did not go. I thought there was no harm in staying to see what I could find out, just to satisfy my curiosity. I examined the signs carefully, but without result. I kept thinking of the paper I had burnt. Why had I destroyed it? What harm would there have been in keeping it?

"At last I went back to the village of my birth. On seeing the miserable condition of my ancestral home I thought to myself, 'I am a sannyasi, I have no need of wealth for myself, but these poor people have a home to keep up. There can be no sin in recovering the hidden treasure for their benefit.'

"I knew where the paper was, so it was not difficult for me to steal it.

"For a whole year since then, I have been living in this lonely forest searching for the clue. I could think of nothing else. The oftener I was thwarted the greater did my eagerness become. I had the unflagging energy of a mad man as I sat night after night concentrating on the attempt to solve my problem.

"When it was that you discovered me I do not know. If I had been in an ordinary frame of mind you would never have remained concealed, but I was so absorbed in my task that I never noticed what was going on around me.

"It was not until today that I discovered at last what I had been so long searching for. The treasure hidden here is greater than that of the richest king in the world, and to find it the meaning of only one more sign had to be deciphered.

"This secret is the most difficult of all, but in my mind I had come even to its solution. That was why I cried out in my delight, 'At last I have found it!' If I wish I can in a moment enter that hidden storehouse of gold and jewels." Mrityunjaya fell at Shankar's feet and exclaimed,

"You are a sannyasi, you have no use for wealth – but take me to that treasure. Do not cheat me again!"

Shankar replied, "Today the last link of my fetters is broken! That stone which you intended should kill me did not indeed strike my body but it has shattered forever the folly of my infatuation. Today I have seen how monstrous is the image of desire. That calm and incomprehensible smile of my saintly Guru has at last kindled the inextinguishable lamp of my soul." Mrityunjaya again begged pitifully, "You are free, but I am not. I do not even want freedom. You must not cheat me of this wealth."

The sannyasi answered, "Very well, my son, take this paper of yours, and if you can find this treasure, keep it." Saying this the sannyasi handed the paper and his staff to Mrityunjaya and left him alone. Mrityunjaya called out in despair, "Have pity on me. Do not leave me. Show me the treasure!" But there was no answer.

Mrityunjaya dragged himself up and with the help of the stick tried to find his way out of the tunnels, but they were such a maze that he was again and again completely puzzled. At last worn out he lay down and fell asleep.

When he awoke there was no means of telling whether it was night or day. As he felt hungry he ate some parched rice, and again began to grope for the way out. At length in despair he stopped and called out, "Oh! Sannyasi, where are you?" His cry echoed and re-echoed through the tangled labyrinth of those underground tunnels, and when the sound of his own voice had died away, he heard from close by a reply, "I am near you – what is it you want?"

Mrityunjaya answered, "Have pity on me and show me where the treasure is."

There was no answer, and although he called again and again all was silent.

After a time Mrityunjaya fell asleep again in this underground realm of perpetual darkness where there was neither night nor day. When he woke up and found it still dark he called out beseechingly, "Oh! Sannyasi, tell me where you are."

The answer came from near at hand, "I am here. What do you want?"

Mrityunjaya answered, "I want nothing now but that you should rescue me from this dungeon."

The sannyasi asked, "Don't you want the treasure?" Mrityunjaya replied, "No."

There was the sound of a flint being struck and the next moment there was a light. The sannyasi said, "Well Mrityunjaya, let us go."

Mrityunjaya, "Then, Father, is all my trouble to be in vain? Shall I never obtain that wealth?"

Immediately the torch went out. Mrityunjaya exclaimed "How cruel!', and sat down in the silence to think. There was no means of measuring time and the darkness was without end. How he wished that he could with all the strength of his mind and body shatter that gloom to atoms. His heart began to feel restless for the light, for the open sky, and for all the varied beauty of the world, and he called out, "Oh! Sannyasi, cruel Sannyasi, I do not want the treasure. I want you to rescue me."

The answer came, "You no longer want the treasure? Then, take my hand, and come with me."

This time no torch was lighted. Mrityunjaya holding his stick in one hand and clinging to the sannyasi with the other slowly began to move. After twisting and turning many times through the maze of tunnels they came to a place where the sannyasi said, "Now stand still."

Standing still Mrityunjaya heard the sound of an iron door opening. The next moment the sannyasi seized his hand, and said, "Come!"

Mrityunjaya advanced into what appeared to be a vast hall. He heard the sound of a flint being struck and then, the blaze of the torch revealed to his astonished eyes the most amazing sight that he had ever dreamed of. On every side thick plates of gold were arranged in piles. They stood against the walls glittering like heaped rays of solid sunlight stored in the bowels of the earth. Mrityunjaya's eyes began to gleam. Like a mad man he cried, "All this gold is mine – I will never part with it!"

"Very well," replied the sannyasi, "here is my torch, some barley and parched rice, and this large pitcher of water for you. Farewell."

And as he spoke the sannyasi went out, clanging the heavy iron door behind him.

Mrityunjaya began to go round and round the hall touching the piles of gold again and again. Seizing some small pieces he threw them down on the floor, he lifted them into his lap, striking them one against another he made them ring, he even stroked his body all over with the precious metal. At length, tired out, he spread a large flat plate of gold on the floor, lay down on it, and fell asleep.

When he woke he saw the gold glittering on every side. There was nothing but gold. He began to wonder whether day had dawned and whether the birds were awake and revelling in the morning sunlight. It seemed as though in imagination he could smell the fragrant breeze of daybreak coming from the garden by the little lake near his home. It was as if he could actually see the ducks floating on the water, and hear their contented cackle as the maidservant came from the house to the steps of the ghat, with the brass vessels in her hand to be cleaned.

Striking the door Mrityunjaya called out, "Oh, Sannyasi, listen to me!"

The door opened and the sannyasi entered. "What do you want?" he asked.

"I want to go out," replied Mrityunjaya, "but can't I take away a little of this gold?"

Without giving any answer the sannyasi lighted a fresh torch, and placing a full water pot and a few handfuls of rice on the floor went out closing the door behind him.

Mrityunjaya took up a thin plate of gold, bent it and broke it into small fragments. These he scattered about the room like lumps of dirt. On some of them he made marks with his teeth. Then, he threw a plate of gold on the floor and trampled on it. He asked himself, 'How many men in the world are rich enough to be able to throw gold about as I am doing!' Then, he became oppressed with a fever for destruction. He was seized with a longing to crush all these heaps of gold into dust and sweep them away with a broom. In this way he could show his contempt for the covetous greed of all the kings and maharajahs in the world.

At last he became tired of throwing the gold about in this way and fell asleep. Again he saw on awakening those heaps of gold, and rushing to the door he struck at it with all his strength and called out, "Oh Sannyasi, I do not want this gold. I do not want it!"

But the door remained closed. Mrityunjaya shouted till his throat was hoarse and still the door did not open. He threw lump after lump of gold against it, but with no effect. He was in despair. Would the sannyasi leave him there to shrivel up and die, inch by inch, in that golden prison?

As Mrityunjaya watched the gold fear gripped him. Those piles of glittering metal surrounded him on all sides with a terrifying smile, hard, silent, without tremor or change, until his body began to tremble, his mind to quake. What connection had he with these heaps of gold? They could not share his feelings – they had no sympathy with him in his sorrows. They had no need of the light, or the sky. They did not long for the cool breezes, they did not even want life. They had no desire for freedom. In this eternal darkness they remained hard and bright for ever.

On earth perhaps sunset had come with its golden gift of limpid light – that golden-light which cools the eyes as it bids farewell to the fading day, falling like tears on the face of darkness. Now the evening star would be gazing serenely down on the courtyard of his home where his young wife had tended the cows in the meadow and lit the lamp in the corner of the house, while the tinkling of the temple bell spoke of the closing ceremony of the day.

Today, the most trifling events of his home and his village shone in Mrityunjaya's imagination with overpowering lustre. Even the thought of his old dog lying curled up asleep in front of the stove caused him pain. He thought of the grocer in whose shop he had stayed while he was at Dharagole and imagined him putting out his lamp, shutting up his shop and walking leisurely to some house in the village to take his evening meal, and as he thought of him he envied him his happiness. He did not know what day it was, but if it were Sunday he could picture to himself the villagers returning to their homes after market, calling their friends from over the fields and crossing the river together in the ferry boat. He could see a peasant, with a couple of fish dangling in his hand and a basket on his head, walking through the meadow paths, or making his way along the dikes of the paddy fields, past the bamboo fences of the little hamlets, returning to his village after the day's work in the dim light of the star-strewn sky.

The call came to him from the world of men. But layers of earth separated him from the most insignificant occurrences of life's varied and unceasing pilgrimage. That life, that sky, and that light appeared to him now as more priceless than all the treasures of the universe. He felt that if only he could for one moment again lie in the dusty lap of mother earth in her green clad beauty, beneath the free open spaces of the sky, filling his lungs with the fragrant breeze laden with the scents of mown grass and of blossoms, he could die feeling that his life was complete.

As these thoughts came to him the door opened, and the sannyasi entering asked, "Mrityunjaya, what do you want now?"

He answered, "I want nothing further. I want only to go out from this maze of darkness. I want to leave this delusive gold. I want light, and the sky; I want freedom!"

The sannyasi said, "There is another storehouse full of rarest gems of incalculable value, tenfold more precious than all this gold. Do you not wish to go there?"

Mrityunjaya answered, "No."

"Haven't you the curiosity just to see it once?"

"No, I don't want even to see it. If I have to beg in rags for the rest of my life I would not spend another moment here."

"Then, come," said the sannyasi, and taking Mrityunjaya's hand he led him in front of the deep well. Stopping here he took out the paper and asked, "And what will you do with this?"

Taking it Mrityunjaya tore it into fragments and threw them down the well.

29

The Cloud and the Sun

I

It had rained the previous day. But this morning there was no sign of rain and the pale sunlight and scattered clouds between them were painting the nearly-ripe autumnal corn-fields alternately with their long brushes; the broad green landscape was now being touched with light to a glittering whiteness, and again smeared over the next moment with the deep coolness of shadow.

While these two actors, sun and cloud, were playing their own parts by themselves with the whole sky for a stage, innumerable plays were being enacted down below in various places on the stage of the world.

In the particular place on which we are about to raise the curtain on one of life's little plays, a house can be seen by the side of a village lane. Only one of the outer rooms is brick-built, and on either side of it a dilapidated brick wall runs to encircle a few mud huts. From the lane one can discover through the grated window a young man with the upper half of his body uncovered, sitting on a plank bed, trying every now and then, to drive away both heat and mosquitoes with a palm-leaf fan held in his left hand and reading attentively a book held in his right. Out in the village lane, a girl wearing a striped sari with some black plums tied in a corner thereof, which she was engaged in demolishing one by one, kept passing again and again in front of the said grated window. From the expression of her face it could be clearly perceived that the young girl was on terms of intimacy with the person sitting and reading on the bed inside and that she was bent on attracting his attention somehow or other and letting him know by her silent contempt, 'Just now I am busily engaged in eating black plums and don't care a fig for you.'

Unfortunately, the man engaged in reading inside the room was short-sighted and the silent scorn of the girl could not touch him from afar. The girl herself knew this, so that after many fruitless journeyings to and fro, she was obliged to use pellets of plum stones in lieu of silent scorn. So difficult is it to preserve the purity of disdain when one has to deal with the blind.

When three or four stones thrown at random, as it were, every now and again rapped against the wooden door, the reader raised his head and looked out. When the designing young person came to know this, she began to choose succulent black plums from her sun'-knot with redoubled attention. The man, puckering his brows and straining his eyes, recognised the girl at last and putting down his book came up to the window and smilingly called out "Giribala!"

Giribala, while keeping her attention fixed steadily and wholly upon the task of examining the black plums tied in her sari-end, proceeded to walk on slowly step by step.

Upon this it was brought home to the myopic young man that he was being punished for some unknown misdeed. Hurriedly coming outside he asked, "I say, how is it you haven't given me any plums today?" Turning a deaf ear to this question Giribala chose a plum after much searching and deliberation, and proceeded to eat it with the utmost composure.

These plums came from Giribala's home-garden, and were the daily perquisite of the young man. But for some reason or other

Giribala seemed to have forgotten this fact, and her behaviour went to indicate that she had gathered them for herself alone. However, it was not clear what the idea was of plucking fruit from one's own garden and coming and eating it ostentatiously in front of another's door. Hence the youth came out and caught hold of her hand. At first Giribala turned and twisted and tried to wriggle out of his grasp, but suddenly she burst into a flood of tears and scattering the plums from her sari on to the ground, rushed away.

The restless sunlight and shadows of the morning had become tired and tranquil in the afternoon. White swollen clouds lay massed in a corner of the sky and the fading evening light glimmered upon the leaves of the trees, the water in the ponds, and every nook and corner of the rain-washed landscape. Again we see the girl in front of the grated window, and the young man sitting inside the room, the only difference being that there are no plums now in the girl's sari-end, neither does the youth hold any book in his hand. There may have been certain other deeper and more serious differences also.

It is difficult to say what particular need has brought the girl again this afternoon to this particular spot. Whatever other grounds she may have had, it is quite apparent from her behaviour that talking to the man inside the room is not one of them. Rather it would appear as if she has come to see whether the plums she had scattered upon the ground this morning had sprouted in the afternoon.

But one of the principal reasons for their not sprouting was that the fruits were lying heaped up at present in front of the young man on the wooden bed; and whilst the girl was occupied in bending low every now and then, in search of some imaginary object, the youth, suppressing his inward laughter, was gravely eating the plums one after another, after carefully selecting them. At length, when one or two stones came and fell by chance near the girl's feet or even upon them, she realised that the young man was paying her back for her fit of pique. But was this fair! When she had thrown overboard all the pride of her little heart and was seeking for some means of surrendering herself, wasn't it cruel of him to place an obstacle in her very difficult path? As the girl came to realise with a blush that she had been caught in the attempt of giving herself up, and began to seek some means of escape, the youth came out and caught hold of her hand.

This time too the girl turned and twisted and made several attempts to shake off his grasp and run away as she had done this morning; but she did not cry. On the other hand she flushed and, turning her head aside, hid her face on her tormentor's back and laughed profusely and, as if compelled by outward force alone, entered the iron-barred cell like a conquered captive.

Like the light play of sun and cloud in the sky, the play of these two human beings in a corner of the earth was equally trivial and equally transient. Again as the play of sun and cloud in the sky is not really unimportant and not really a game but only looks like it, so the humble history of an idle-rainy day spent by these ordinary folk may seem to be of no account amidst the hundreds of events happening in this world; but as a matter of fact it was not so. The ancient and stupendous Fate that eternally weaves one age into another with unchanging sternness of countenance, that same Ancient was causing the seeds of grief and joy throughout the girl's whole life to sprout amidst the trivial tears and laughter of this morning and evening. And yet the uncalled-for grievance of the girl seemed altogether incomprehensible, not only to the onlookers, but also to the young man – the hero of this little play. Why the girl should get annoyed one day and lavish unbounded affection on another, why she should increase the rations one day and on another stop them altogether, was not easy to understand. Some day it was as if all her powers of imagination and thought and skill were concentrated on giving pleasure to the young man; again on another day she would muster all her limited stock of energy and hardness to try and hurt him. When she failed to wound him her hardness was redoubled; when she succeeded, it was dissolved in profuse showers of repentant tears and flowed in a thousand streams of affection.

The first part of the trivial history of this trivial play of sun and shadow is briefly narrated in the following chapter.

II

All the other people in the village were occupied with factions, plotting against one another, sugarcane planting, false lawsuits and trade in jute; the only ones interested in ideas and literature were Sashibhushan and Giribala.

There was no call for anybody to be curious or anxious on this account. Because Giribala was ten years old and Sashibhushan was a newly-fledged M.A., b.l. They were neighbours only.

Giribala's father Harakumar was at one time the sublandlord of his village. Falling on evil days, he had sold everything and accepted the post of manager of their absentee landlord. He had to superintend the same pargana in which he lived, so that he was not obliged to move from his home.

Sashibhushan had taken his M.A. degree and also passed his examination in law, but he did not take up any work for a living. He could not bring himself to mix with people or speak even a few words at a meeting. Because of his short sight he could not recognise his acquaintances, hence he had to resort to frowning, which people considered a sign of arrogance.

It is all very well to keep oneself to oneself in the sea of humanity of a city like Calcutta; but in a village such behaviour is looked upon as haughtiness. When after many unsuccessful efforts, Sashibhushan's father at length sent his good-for-nothing son to look after their small village estate, Sashibhushan had to put up with a lot of ill-treatment, harassment and ridicule from his village neighbours. There was another reason for this persecution; peace-loving Sashibhushan was unwilling to marry – hence the worried parents of marriageable girls looked upon this unwillingness of his as intolerable pride and could not find it in their hearts to forgive him.

The more Sashibhushan was persecuted the more he hid himself in his den. He used to sit on a plank bed in a corner room with some bound English volumes before him and read whichever one he liked. This was all the work he did, and how the property managed to exist, the property alone knew.

We have already seen that Gitibala was the only human being with whom he had any contact.

Giribala's brothers used to go to school and on their return would ask their silly little sister some day what the shape of the earth was; another day they would want to know which was bigger, the sun or the earth. And when she made mistakes, they corrected her with infinite contempt. If in the absence of proof to the contrary, Giribala considered the belief that the sun was bigger than the earth to be groundless, and if she had the boldness to express her doubts, then, her brothers would declare with redoubled scorn, "Indeed! it is written in our books, and you – ".

When Giribala heard that this fact was recorded in printed books, she was completely silenced and did not think any other proof necessary.

But she felt a great desire to be able to read books like her brothers. Some days she would sit in her own room with an open book before her, and go on muttering to herself as if she were reading, and keep turning over the pages quickly one after another. The small black unknown letters seemed to be keeping guard at the lion's gate of some great hall of mystery in endless serried rows, with bayonets of vowels raised aloft on their shoulders, and gave no reply to the questions put by Giribala. The Book of Fables revealed not a single word of its tigers, foxes, horses and donkeys to the curiosity-tormented girl, and the Book of Tales with all its tales remained gazing dumbly as if under a vow of silence.

Giribala had suggested taking lessons from her brothers, but they had not paid the slightest heed to her request. Sashibhushan was her sole ally.

Like the Fables and The Book of Tales, Sashibhushan also at first seemed to Giribala to be full of inscrutable mystery. The young man used to sit alone in the small sitting-room with iron-grated windows by the roadside, on a plank bed surrounded by books. Standing outside and catching hold of the bars Giribala would fix a wondering gaze upon this strange figure with bent back, absorbed in reading; and comparing the number of books, would decide in her own mind that Sashibhushan was much more learned than her brothers. She could conceive of nothing more wonderful than this.

She had not the slightest doubt that Sashibhushan had read through all the world's greatest books, such as the Book of Fables, etc. Hence when Sashibhushan turned over the pages, she stood stock-still, unable to measure the depths of his learning.

At length this wonderstruck girl came to attract the attention even of the short-sighted Sashibhushan. One day he opened a glittering bound volume and said, "Giribala, come and look at the pictures." Giribala immediately ran away.

This is how their acquaintance started, and it would require some historical research to determine the exact date on which it ripened into intimacy and the girl, entering Sashibhushan's room from outside the grating, obtained a seat amongst the bound books on the plank bed.

Giribala began taking lessons from Sashibhushan. My readers will laugh when they hear that this teacher taught his little pupil not only her letters, spelling and grammar, but translated and read out many great poems to her and asked her opinion of them. God alone knows what the girl understood but that she liked it, there is no doubt. She drew many imaginary and wonderful pictures in her child-mind made up of a mixture of understanding and non-understanding, and she listened intently and silently with wide-open eyes, asked one or two altogether foolish questions now and then, and sometimes veered off suddenly to an irrelevant subject. Sashibhushan never objected to this, but derived a particular pleasure from hearing this tiny little critic praise and blame and comment on famous poems. Giribala was his only discerning friend in the whole neighbourhood.

When Sashibhushan first came to know her, Giri was eight years old; now she was ten. In these two years, she had learnt the English and Bengali alphabet, and finished reading three or four easy books. At the same time Sashibhushan also had not felt these two years of village life to be altogether lonely and uninteresting.

III

But Sashibhushan had not been able to get on well with Giribala's father Harakumar. Harakumar used to come and ask this M.A., b.l. to advise him about his lawsuits. The said M.A., b.l., however, did not show much interest, nor did he hesitate to confess his ignorance of law to the Manager Babu, who considered this to be pure evasion. In this way two years passed.

At about this time, it had become imperative to punish a recalcitrant tenant. The Manager Babu earnestly entreated Sashibhushan to advise him with regard to his intention of prosecuting the said tenant in different districts on different charges and claims. But far from advising him, Sashibhushan said certain things to him quietly yet firmly, which did not strike him as being at all pleasant.

On the other hand Harakumar was unable to win a single case against this tenant, so he became firmly convinced that Sashibhushan had been helping the unfortunate man and vowed that the village should be rid of such a person without delay.

Sashibhushan found that cows kept straying into his fields, his pulse-stores were catching fire, his boundaries were being disputed, his tenants were making difficulties about paying their rents and not only that, were trying to bring false cases against him. There were even rumours that he would get a beating if he went out in the evenings, and his house would be set on fire some night.

At last the harmless peace-loving Sashibhushan prepared to leave the village and escape to Calcutta.

Whilst he was making his preparations, the Joint Magistrate Saheb's tents were pitched in the village, which thereupon became astir with constables, khansamas, dogs, horses, syces and sweepers. Batches of small boys began to wander about the outskirts of the Saheb's camp with fearful curiosity, like packs of jackals on a tiger's trail.

The Manager Babu proceeded to supply fowls, eggs, ghee and milk to the Saheb under the heading of hospitality, according to custom. He freely and unquestioningly supplied a much larger quantity of food than was actually required by the Joint Saheb; but when the Saheb's sweeper came one morning and demanded four seers of ghee at once for the Saheb's dog, then, as ill-luck would have it, Harakumar felt this was the limit and explained to the sweeper that though the Saheb's dog could doubtlessly digest much more ghee than a country dog without fear of consequences, still such a large quantity of fat was not good for its health; and he refused to supply the ghee.

The sweeper went and told the Saheb that he had gone to enquire from the Manager Babu where dog's meat could be had, but because he belonged to the sweeper caste the Manager had driven him away with contempt before everybody, and had not even hesitated to show disrespect to the Saheb.

As a rule Sahebs are easily offended by the Brahmin's pride of caste, moreover, they had dared to insult his sweeper; so that he found it impossible to control his temper, and immediately ordered his chaprassi to send for the Manager Babu.

The trembling Manager came and stood before the Saheb's tent, inwardly muttering the name of the goddess Durga. Coming out of the tent with loud creaking of boots, the Saheb shouted at the Manager in Bengali with a foreign accent, "Why have you driven away my sweeper?"

The flurried Harakumar hastened to assure the Saheb with folded hands that he could never dare to be so insolent as to drive away the Saheb's sweeper, but since the latter had asked for four seers of ghee at once for the dog, he (the Manager) had at first entered a mild protest in the interests of the said quadruped, and then, sent out messengers to various places for procuring the ghee.

The Saheb enquired who had been sent out and where.

Harakumar promptly mentioned some names haphazard as they occurred to him.

The Saheb despatched messengers at once to enquire whether the aforesaid persons had been sent to the aforesaid villages to procure ghee and meanwhile kept the Manager Babu waiting in his tent.

The messengers came back in the afternoon and informed the Saheb that nobody had been sent anywhere for the ghee. This left no doubt in his mind that everything the Manager had said was false and his sweeper had spoken the truth. Whereupon, roaring with rage, the Joint Saheb called the sweeper and said, "Catch hold of this swine by the ear and race him round the tent", which command the sweeper executed in front of the crowd of spectators, without waste of time.

The report of this event spread like wild fire through the village and Harakumar came home and lay down like one half dead, without touching a morsel of food.

The Manager had made many enemies in connection with his zamindari work. They were overjoyed at the news, but when the departing Sashibhushan heard it, his blood boiled within him, and he could not sleep the whole night.

Next morning he went to Harakumar's house; the latter caught hold of his hand and began to weep bitterly. Sashibhushan said, "A case for libel must be brought against the Saheb, and I will fight it as your counsel."

At first Harakumar was frightened to hear that a suit must be filed against the Magistrate Saheb himself, but Sashibhushan strongly insisted upon it.

Harakumar asked for time to think it over. But when he found that the rumour had spread throughout the village and his enemies were openly expressing their jubilation, he hesitated no longer, and appealed to Sashibhushan, saying "My boy, I hear you are preparing to go to Calcutta for no ostensible reason – but you can't possibly do so. It is such a tower of strength for us to have a person like you in the village! Anyhow you must deliver me from this terrible indignity."

IV

That Sashibhushan who had hitherto always tried to lead a guarded and secluded life screened from the public eye, it was that same Sashibhushan who now presented himself in court. On hearing his case, the Magistrate took him into his private chamber, and treated him with the utmost courtesy, saying "Sashi Babu, wouldn't it be better to compromise this case privately?"

Keeping his short-sighted frowning gaze fixed very steadily upon the cover of a law-book lying on the table Sashi Babu replied, "I cannot advise my client to do so. How can he make a compromise privately when he has been insulted publicly?" After exchanging a few words, the Saheb realised that this myopic and laconic young man was not to be easily moved and said, "All right Babu, let's see how it turns out in the end." Saying which, the Magistrate adjourned the case and went on tour to the moffussil.

On the other hand, the Joint Saheb wrote as follows to the zamindar, "Your Manager has insulted my servants and shown disrespect to me. I trust you will take necessary action." The zamindar was thoroughly upset and sent for Harakumar at once. The Manager recounted the whole affair in detail, from beginning to end. The zamindar got extremely annoyed and said, "When the Saheb's sweeper asked for four seers of ghee, why didn't you give it to him at once without any question? Would it have cost you your father's money?" Harakumar couldn't deny that his paternal property would not have suffered any loss thereby. Admitting he was to blame, he said, "It was my bad luck that made me act so foolishly." "Then, again, who told you to prosecute the Saheb", asked the zamindar.

"O Incarnation of Righteousness", replied Harakumar, "I had no wish to prosecute, it was that young fellow Sashi of our village, who never gets a single brief – who got me into this mess by insisting upon it, almost without my permission."

Whereupon the zamindar became highly incensed with Sashibhushan. He gathered that the aforesaid youth was a worthless new pleader, who was trying to attract the public eye by creating a sensation. He ordered the Manager to withdraw the case, and appease the pair of magistrates, elder and younger, immediately.

The Manager presented himself at the Joint Magistrate's quarters with a peace-offering of fruits and sweets calculated to cool the atmosphere. He informed the Saheb that it was altogether foreign to his nature to bring a case against him; it was only that green young duffer of a pleader known as Sashibhushan of their village who had the impudence to act thus, practically without his knowledge. The Saheb was exceedingly annoyed with Sashibhushan and extremely pleased with the Manager, whom he was dukkhito to have given dandobidhan in a fit of temper. The Saheb had recently won a prize in a Bengali examination, hence he was given to speaking in high-flown book language with all and sundry.

The Manager averred that parents sometimes punished their children in anger, at others drew them into their affectionate embrace, so that there was no occasion for either the parents or the children to feel sorry.

Whereupon, after distributing adequate largesse to all the Joint Saheb's servants, Harakumar went to the moffussil to see the Magistrate Saheb. After hearing all about Sashibhushan's arrogant behaviour from him, the Magistrate remarked, "It struck me also as very strange that the Manager Babu whom I had always thought to be such a nice person, instead of informing me first and arranging for private compromise, should rush to bring a suit. The whole thing seemed so preposterous! Now I understand everything."

Finally, he asked the Manager whether Sashibhushan had joined the Congress. Without turning a hair the latter calmly replied, "Yes".

The Saheb's normal ruling-race complex led him to perceive clearly that this was all the Congress' doing. The myrmidons of the Congress were secretly going about everywhere seeking for opportunities to engineer trouble and write articles in the Amrit Bazar picking a quarrel with the Government. The Saheb inwardly cursed the Government of India's weakness in not giving more summary powers to the Magistrates to crush these puny thorns underfoot forthwith. But the name of Sashibhushan the Congressman remained in the Magistrate's memory.

V

When the big things of life raise their powerful heads, the small things also are not deterred from spreading their hungry little network of roots and putting forward their claim in the affairs of the world.

When Sashibhushan was particularly busy with the Magistrate's annoying case, when he was collecting notes on law from various volumes, sharpening in his mind the points he would make in his speech, cross-examining imaginary witnesses, and trembling and perspiring every now and again at the mental picture of the crowded court-room and the future sequence of cantos in his war-epic – then, his little pupil used to come regularly to his door, shabby reader and ink-stained exercise-book in hand, sometimes with flowers and fruit, sometimes with pickles, coconut-sweets and spiced homemade catechu with the fragrance of the ketaki from her mother's store-room.

The first few days she noticed that Sashibhushan was absent-mindedly turning over the pages of a huge forbidding-looking volume without pictures, but it did not seem as if he was reading it very attentively either. Sashibhushan used to try and explain to Giribala some portion at least of the books he read on other occasions – were there then, not even a few words in that heavy black-bound volume which he could read out to her? And in any case, was that book so very important and Giribala so very insignificant?

At first, in order to attract her preceptor's attention Giribala began to spell and read her lessons out aloud in a sing-song tone, swaying the upper half of her body including her plait, violently to and fro. But she found this plan did not work very well. She became intensely annoyed in her own mind with that heavy black book, which she began to look upon as an ugly, hard, cruel human being. Every unintelligible page of that book took on the form of a wicked man's face and silently expressed its utter contempt of Giribala, because she was a little girl. If some thief could have stolen that book, she would have rewarded him with all the spiced catechu in her mother's store-room. The gods did not listen to all the unreasonable and impossible prayers she mentally said to them for the destruction of that book, nor do I think it necessary for my readers to hear them either.

Then, the dejected girl gave up going to her tutor's home, lesson-book in hand, for a day or two. On coming to the path in front of Sashibhushan's room to see the result of these two days of separation, and glancing inside, she found that Sashibhushan, putting aside the black book, was standing alone and addressing the iron bars in some foreign language with gesticulations.

Probably he was experimenting on those irons how to melt the heart of the judge.

Sashibhushan the bookworm, ignorant of the ways of the world, thought it not altogether impossible even in these mercenary days to perform the wonderful feats of orators like

Demosthenes, Cicero, Burke, Sheridan, etc., who by the piercing arrows of their winged words had torn injustice to shreds, cowed down the tyrant, and humbled pride to the dust in the olden days. Standing in the small dilapidated house of Tilkuchi village, Sashibhushan was practising how to put to shame the arrogant English race flushed with the wine of victory, and make them repent for their misdeeds before the whole world. Whether the gods in heaven laughed to hear him or whether their divine eyes moistened with tears, nobody knows.

So he failed to notice Giribala. On that day the girl had no plums in her sari-end. Having been caught once in the act of throwing plum-stones, she had become very sensitive with regard to that fruit, so much so that if Sashibhushan innocently asked some day – "Giri, are there no plums for me today?" she took it to be a veiled taunt and prepared to run away with the reproving exclamation "jah" on her lips.

In the absence of plum-stones, she had to take recourse to a trick today. Suddenly looking at a distant point, she cried, "Swarna, dear, don't go, I shall be coming in a minute."

My masculine readers may think that these words were addressed to some distant companion, but my feminine readers will easily surmise that there was nobody in the distance and that the object aimed at was close at hand. But alas! the shot missed the blind man. Not that Sashibhushan had not heard, but he failed to perceive the purport of the call. He thought that-the girl was really anxious to go and play and he had not the energy that day to draw her away from play to study, because he also was trying to aim his sharp arrows at somebody's heart. Just as the trifling aim of the girl's small hand missed the mark, so did the high aim of his practised hand, as my readers already know.

Plum-stones have this advantage that they can be thrown several times and if four miss the mark, then, the fifth has a chance of hitting it. But however imaginary a person Swarna may be, she cannot be kept standing for long after one has told her "I am coming." If one treats her so, then, people may naturally begin to entertain doubts as to her existence. So when this means failed, Giribala had to go without further delay. Still one did not notice in her steps that celerity which a sincere desire to join a distant companion would have warranted. It was as if she were trying to feel with her back whether anyone was following her or not; when she knew for certain that nobody was coming, then, with a last feeble fraction of hope she looked round once, and not seeing anyone tore to pieces both that tiny hope and her loose-leaved lesson-book and scattered them on the road. If she could have found some possible means of returning the little knowledge that Sashibhushan had imparted to her, then, probably she would have thrown it all down with a bang at Sashibhushan's door like the unwanted plum-stones, and come away. The girl vowed that before she met Sashibhushan next, she would forget all her lessons and not be able to answer any question he put to her – not one, not one, not even a single one! And then! Then, Sashibhushan would be served right.

Giribala's eyes filled with tears. She derived some small comfort in her aching heart from thinking how deeply repentant Sashibhushan would feel if she forgot all her lessons, and a spring of pity welled up in her imagination for that future wretched Giribala, who would forget everything she had learnt, simply for Sashibhushan's fault.

Clouds gathered in the sky, as they do every day in the rainy season. Giribala stood behind a roadside tree sobbing for wounded pride. Such idle tears are shed every day by many a girl; it was nothing worthy of note.

VI

My readers are aware of the reasons why Sashibhushan's researches into the law and his essays in oratory proved fruitless. The case against the Magistrate was suddenly withdrawn. Harakumar was appointed an Honorary Magistrate on the District bench and he used to go often to the district town in a soiled chapkan and greasy turban, to pay his respects to the Sahebs.

At long last Giribala's curses on that fat black book began to bear fruit – and it lay neglected, forgotten and exiled in a dark corner, collecting dust. But where was Giribala the girl who would have taken delight in this neglect?

The day when Sashibhushan closed his law-book and sat alone, he suddenly realised that Giribala had not come. Then, he began to recollect the daily history of those few days, little by little. He remembered how one bright morning Giribala had brought a heap of bakul flowers wet with the new rains, tied in a corner of her sari. When he did not raise his eyes from his book even on seeing her, her ardour became suddenly damped. Taking a needle-and-thread stuck in her sari-end, she began to weave a garland of bakul flowers one by one, with bent head. She wove it very slowly, and it took a long time to finish; the day began to wear on, it was time for Giribala to go home, and yet Sashibhushan had not finished reading. Giribala left the garland on the plank bed, and sorrowfully went away. He remembered how her wounded feelings gradually gained in depth every day; how the time came when she gave up entering his room, and would appear now and again on the footpath in front and go away; and how at last the girl had even given up coming to the path – that too was now some days ago. Giribala's fit of pique never used to last so long. Sashibhushan sighed and remained sitting with his back against the wall like one bewildered and with nothing to do. In the absence of his little pupil, his books became distasteful to him.

He kept pulling one or two books towards him, then, pushing them away again after reading two or three pages. If he began to write, his expectant eyes would throw an eager glance every now and again towards the lane and the house opposite, and his writing would be interrupted.

Sashibhushan was afraid Giribala had fallen ill. On making discreet enquiries, however, he learnt that his fears were groundless. Giribala did not go out of the house nowadays. A bridegroom had been settled for her.

On the morning following the day on which Giribala had strewn the muddy village lane with the torn leaves of her lesson-book, she was leaving the house early with quick steps, bearing various presents tied in her little sari-end. Having passed a sleepless night owing to the intense heat, Harakumar was sitting outside with bared body, pulling at his hookah, since early morning. "Where are you going?" he asked Giri. "To Sashidada's house", she replied. "You needn't go to Sashibhushan's house", scolded Harakumar, "go back home." Saying which he spoke long and sternly to her anent the shameless behaviour of a grown-up girl about to enter her father-in-law's house. Since that day she had been forbidden to leave the house. This time she found no opportunity of humbling her pride and making it up with Sashibhushan. Mango-preserves, spiced catechu and pickled limes were relegated to their proper place on the store-room shelf. It went on raining, the bakul flowers went on falling, the guava-trees became laden with ripe fruit, and the ground beneath the plum trees became littered every day with succulent black plums dropped from the branches by pecking birds. Alas! Even the loose-leaved lesson-book was no longer there.

VII

On the day when the sanai was playing in the village for Giribala's wedding, the uninvited Sashibhushan was going to Calcutta by boat.

Since the withdrawal of the lawsuit the very sight of Sashibhushan had become a curse to Harakumar, for he was certain in his own mind that Sashibhushan looked down upon him with contempt. He began to discover a thousand imaginary proofs of this in Sashibhushan's looks and behaviour. All the other village-folk were gradually forgetting the history of his past indignity, only Sashibhushan was keeping alive its memory, he thought; hence he could not bear him. Whenever he met him, he used to feel a kind of shrinking shame, accompanied by a strong resentment. He vowed to himself that he would drive Sashibhushan out of the village.

It was not a very difficult task to constrain a person like Sashibhushan to leave the village. So the Manager Babu's desire was soon fulfilled. One morning Sashibhushan got into a boat with a load of books and a few tin boxes. The one happy tie that had bound him to the village, even that was being snapped today with great éclat. He had not fully realised before how firmly that delicate bond had entwined itself around his heart. Today when the boat set off, when the tops of the village trees and the sound of the wedding-music became gradually more and more indistinct, then, suddenly a mist of tears spread over his heart and choked his voice, a rush of blood caused the veins in his forehead to throb with pain, and the whole panorama of the world seemed exceedingly hazy as if composed of shadowy illusion.

A strong wind was blowing from the opposite direction; hence the boat advanced slowly, though the current was favourable. At this juncture something happened on the river, which hindered Sashibhushan's journey.

A new steamer line had recently been opened from the station landing-place to the district town. Their steamer came noisily puffing along against the current, with its propellers working like wings and setting up waves on either side. The young Manager Saheb of the new line and a few passengers were on board, among whom were some inhabitants of Sashibhushan's village.

A money-lender's country-boat was trying to race the steamer from a little way off; at times it seemed about to catch up with her, and again kept falling behind. The boatman's spirit of rivalry was awakened. He put out a second sail on top of the first one, and even a third small sail atop of that. The tall mast bent low before the blast, and the parted waves danced madly with a loud splashing noise, on either side of the boat. The boat plunged forward like a horse with its reins snapped.

At a certain point the path of the steamer took a slight bend, and here the boat outstripped it by taking a shorter cut. The Manager Saheb was leaning over the railing, eagerly watching this race. When the boat was flying along at top speed and had outstripped the steamer by about a yard, just then, the Saheb raised his revolver and fired a shot at the swollen sail. In a moment the sail burst, the boat sank, and the steamer was hidden from sight round the bend.

Why the Manager acted thus, it is difficult to say. We Bengalis cannot always understand the workings of the Saheb's mind. Perhaps he felt the rivalry of an Indian sail to be intolerable; perhaps there is a fierce pleasure in putting a bullet through something broad and swollen in the twinkling of an eye; perhaps there is a certain ferocious and fiendish humour in putting the proud boat hors de combat in a second by making a few holes in its cloth. What the reason was I do not know exactly. But this I know for certain that the Englishman believed he would not be liable to be punished for this little joke, and he had an idea that the people whose boat was lost and who were in danger of losing their lives also could not be counted as human beings.

When the Saheb fired and the boat sank, Sashibhushan's boat had approached the place of occurrence. Sashibhushan was an eye-witness of the last scene. He hastened to the spot with his boat and rescued the boatmen. Only the man who was grinding spices for cooking in the kitchen could not be traced. The rain-swollen river flowed on swiftly.

The hot blood boiled in Sashibhushan's veins. The law was very dilatory – like a huge complex iron machine; it accepted proofs after weighing them, and apportioned punishment calmly – it did not possess the warmth of the human heart. But to separate food from hunger, desire from enjoyment, and anger from punishment appeared to Sashibhushan to be equally unnatural. There are many crimes which as soon as witnessed demand an immediate retribution from the witness' own hand, otherwise the god in him seems to sear the witness from within. At such a moment one feels inwardly ashamed to find comfort in the idea of the law. But the machine-made law and the machine-made steamer took the Manager further away from Sashibhushan. Whether the world was benefited in other ways, I cannot say, but this much is certain that Sashibhushan's Indian spleen was saved at this juncture.

Sashibhushan returned to the village with the boatmen who had survived. The boat had been laden with jute, which he appointed men to salvage, and tried to persuade the boatman to bring a police-case against the Manager.

But the boatman was unwilling to do so. He said the boat was sunk for good, but he was not prepared to sink with it. First of all, he would have to grease the palms, of the police; then, he would have to give up all work and food and rest and wander about the law-courts; then, God alone knows what trouble was in store for him and what the result would be if he prosecuted the Saheb. At last when he heard that Sashibhushan was himself a pleader, that he himself would pay all the costs of the suit and that there was every chance of his getting damages, he agreed. But the people of Sashibhushan's village who were present on board the steamer flatly refused to bear witness. "We didn't see anything, Sir", they said to Sashibhushan, "we were at the back of the steamer, it was impossible to hear a gunshot for the throbbing of the machine and the lapping of the water."

Inwardly cursing his countrymen, Sashibhushan continued to conduct the case before the Magistrate.

No witnesses were required. The Manager admitted he had fired a shot. He said it was aimed at a flock of cranes flying in the sky. The steamer was then, going at full speed and had just turned round the bend. So he could not possibly know whether a crow died or a crane died or the boat sank. Earth and sky contained so many things to aim at that no man in his senses would knowingly waste a pice-worth of shot on a dirty rag.

Acquitted on all charges, the Manager Saheb, puffing at a cigar, went to play whist at his club. The dead body of the man who was grinding spices in the boat was washed up on land nine miles farther off, and Sashibhushan returned to his village with frustration raging in his breast.

The day he returned, they were taking Giribala to her husband's home in a decorated boat. Though nobody had asked him, yet Sashibhushan came slowly to the riverside. The landing-place was crowded, so instead of going there he stood a little way off. When the boat left the landing-steps and passed in front of him, he caught a fleeting glimpse of the new bride, sitting with her sari drawn down over her bowed head. Giribala had long been hoping to see Sashibhushan somehow or other before leaving the village, but today she did not even know that her preceptor was standing there not very far away. She did not even raise her head once to look; only the tears coursed down both her cheeks in silent weeping.

The boat gradually receded and passed out of sight. The morning light glittered on the river; from the branch of a mango-tree nearby, a papiya burst into rapturous song every now and then, seeking in vain to unburden the passion of its heart; the ferry-boat, laden with passengers, kept plying from one side of the river to the other; the women coming to the landing-steps to draw water, began discussing Giri's departure for her father-in-law's house in a loud babel of voices; and Sashibhushan, taking off his glasses and wiping his eyes, turned back and entered the small iron-grated room by the roadside. Suddenly it seemed as if he heard Giribala's voice calling "Sashidada!"

–Where, oh where?

Nowhere! Not in the room, not in the lane, not in the village – but in the midst of his own heart.

VIII

Sashibhushan again packed up his things and started for Calcutta. He had nothing to do in Calcutta, there was no particular object in going there; so instead of going by rail, he decided to travel all the way by boat.

At the height of the rainy season, a network of big and small zig-zag waterways had spread over the whole of Bengal. The veins and arteries of this green land seemed to be overflowing with sap on all sides into trees and plants, bushes and grass, corn and jute and sugarcane, in a mad exuberance of riotous youth.

Sashibhushan's boat proceeded to thread its way through all these narrow serpentine alleys of water, which had by then, become level with the bank. The white-tufted grass and reeds and in some places the cornfields were under water. The bamboo-groves and mango-groves and fencing of the village had reached the very edge of the river, as if the daughters of the gods had filled with water to the brink the circular grooves around the tree-roots.

When he set out the woods were bright and smiling and glistening after their bath; but it soon clouded over and began to rain; whichever way one turned, it looked dismal and dingy. Just as during a flood, the cattle huddle together in their dirty, slushy, narrow byre and get drenched in the incessant showers of July, standing patiently with pathetic eyes; so was the harassed countryside of Bengal, dumb and sorrowful, being soaked continuously in its dense swamped and slippery jungles. The peasants were going about with their palm-leaf umbrellas; the women were going from one hut to another in the course of their daily household duties, getting drenched and shrinking from the cold wet wind and treading the slippery landing-stairs very cautiously to draw water from the river in their wet clothes. The men were sitting in their verandahs smoking, or if absolutely necessary, going out with chadar wound round the waist, umbrellas over their heads and shoes in their hands. It is not one of our ancient and sacred customs to provide our long-suffering womenfolk with umbrellas in this sun-burnt and rain-swept land of Bengal.

When the rain showed no signs of stopping, Sashibhushan began to get tired of the closed boat, and again decided to travel by rail. Arriving at a wide confluence of the river, he moored the boat and began to prepare for his midday meal.

It is the lame man's foot that falls into the ditch, as the saying goes. It is not the fault of the ditch alone, but the lame man's foot also has a special bent for falling into the ditch. On that day Sashibhushan furnished a good proof of this.

The fishermen had fixed bamboo-poles on either side of the confluence of two rivers and spread a huge net over them, keeping only room on one side for boats to pass. They had been doing this since a long time, and also paying rent for it. As ill luck would have it, this year the august District Superintendent of Police had suddenly deigned to come this way. Seeing his boat draw near, the fishermen warned his boatman beforehand in a loud voice and pointed out the passage at the side. But the Saheb's boatman was not in the habit of showing deference to any man-made barrier by taking a roundabout route, so he steered the boat clean through the net. The net stooped and made way for the boat, but its rudder became enmeshed and it took some time and trouble to disentangle it.

The Police Saheb got extremely red and angry, and had the boat moored. The four fishermen, seeing his threatening attitude, promptly decamped. The Saheb ordered his oarsmen to cut up the net, and the huge net, made at a cost of seven or eight hundred rupees, was cut to pieces.

After venting his wrath on the net, the Saheb finally sent for the fishermen. Unable to find the four runaway men, the constable caught hold of whichever four fishermen came to hand. They pleaded their innocence with folded hands supplicatingly. As the Police Bahadur was giving orders to his men to take the prisoners along with them, the bespectacled Sashibhushan with an unbuttoned shirt hastily thrown over his shoulders and his slippers pattering on the ground came in breathless haste to the police boat. In a quivering voice he said, "Sir, you have no right to cut up the net of these fishermen, and to harass these four men."

As soon as the Burra Saheb of the Police uttered a particularly offensive invective in Hindi, Sashibhushan sprang into the boat from the slightly raised river-bank, and throwing himself at once upon the Saheb, began to pummel him right and left like a child, like a madman.

After that he did not know what happened. When he awoke in the police-station, we are constrained to say that the treatment he received was conducive neither to his sense of dignity nor to his physical comfort.

IX

Sashibhushan's father, with the assistance of pleaders and barristers, first got his son released on bail. Then, preparations were set afoot for conducting the. case.

The fishermen whose net had been destroyed belonged to the same holding and were under the same zamindar as Sashibhushan. When in difficulty, they used to come to him sometimes for legal advice. The men who had been seized and brought to the boat by the Saheb were also not unknown to him.

Sashibhushan sent for them in order to cite them as witnesses, but they were frightened out of their wits. If those who had to pass their daily lives with wife and children were to quarrel with the police, then, where would their troubles end? How many lives were there in one man's body? The loss they had suffered was over and done with, now why this further trouble of a subpoena for bearing witness! "Sir, you have landed us in a great mess!" they all declared.

After much persuasion, they agreed to tell the truth.

In the meantime, when Harakumar took the opportunity of sitting on the bench to go and salaam the Sahebs, the Police Saheb said with a smile, "Manager Babu, I hear your tenants are ready to bear false witness against the police."

"Indeed! is such a thing possible?" said the startled manager, "that the sons of swine should have it in their bones to dare to do a thing like that!"

Readers of newspapers know that Sashibhushan's case had no legs to stand on.

One by one the fishermen came and deposed that the Saheb had not cut up their net, but had sent for them to the boat and taken down their names and addresses.

Not only that, but three or four of his village acquaintances stated that they were present at the place and time of occurrence, as members of a wedding-party, and had seen with their own eyes how Sashibhushan without any provocation had come forward and harassed the police constables.

Sashibhushan admitted that on being abused he had jumped into the boat and struck the Saheb; but the real reason for that was the destruction of the net and the ill-treatment of the fishermen.

Under the circumstances, that Sashibhushan should be punished could not be called unjust. But the sentence was somewhat severe. There were three or four charges – assault, trespass, interfering with police officers on duty, etc. – all of which were fully proved against him.

Leaving his beloved books in that small room, Sashibhushan went to jail for five years. When his father wanted to appeal, Sashibhushan repeatedly forbade him to do so. "Jail is welcome" he said, "iron bonds don't lie, but the freedom we have outside deceives us and gets us into trouble. And if you talk of good company, then, the liars and cowards in jail are comparatively fewer, because there is less room – outside their number is much larger."

X

Soon after Sashibhushan went to jail, his father died. He had hardly any relatives to speak of. A brother of his had been holding a post in the Central Provinces since a long time, and could not make it convenient to come home very often; he had built a house for himself and settled there with his family. Whatever property he had in his village home was mostly appropriated by the manager Harakumar on various pretexts.

Fate so willed it that Sashibhushan had to undergo much more suffering in jail than usually fell to the lot of prisoners. Still the five long years passed.

Again one rainy day Sashibhushan came and stood outside the prison walls with ruined health and vacant mind. He had gained his freedom, and that was all he had, he had no one and nothing to call his own. With no home, no relatives and no friends, he felt that the vast world was too big and loose for his solitary self.

While he was deliberating where to begin to pick up the broken threads of his life, a big carriage and pair came and stood in front of him. A servant alighted and asked him, "Is your name Sashibhushan Babu?" "Yes", he replied.

The man immediately held open the carriage-door and waited for Sashibhushan to get in. "Where am I to go?" he asked in surprise.

"My master has sent for you", replied the servant.

As the curious looks of the passers-by were getting intolerable, Sashibhushan jumped into the carriage without more ado. Surely there must be some mistake, he thought to himself. But he had to go somewhere in any case, and a mistake might just as well serve as the prelude to a new life.

On that day also sunshine and clouds were chasing each other all over the sky; and the rain-washed dark green cornfields skirting the road were chequered with the lively play of sun and shadow. There was a huge chariot lying near the market-place, and from a grocer's shop nearby some Vaishnava mendicants were singing to the accompaniment of string instruments, drums and cymbals,

Come back, come back! O lord of my heart, Beloved, come back to this hungry,
parched and fevered breast.

As the carriage advanced, the lines of the song could be heard growing fainter and still more faint in the distance,

O cruel one, come back! O soft and loving come!
Come back, O thou of the tender hue
of the rain cloud!

The words of the song became gradually blurred and indistinct and could no longer be followed. But its rhythm had set up a turmoil in Sashibhushan's breast; he began humming to himself and adding line after line to the song, and seemed unable to stop,

O my joy, forever and forever my grief,
come back!
O treasure churned from all my grief and joy,
come to my heart.

O ever-desired, and ever-cherished one,
O thou fleeting, O thou everlasting,
come to my arms.
Come to my bosom, to my eyes, in my sleep,
in my dreams, in the clothes and jewels I wear,
to my whole world.
Come in the laughter of my lips, in the
tears of my eyes,
My caresses, my wiles, my wounded pride,
In every remembrance and in forgetfulness.
In my faith and my work, my love's
ardour and shyness,
In my life and my death, O come!

Sashibhushan's singing came to an end when the carriage entered a walled garden and stopped in front of a two-storeyed house.

Without asking any questions he followed the servant's directions and entered the house.

The room in which he came and sat was lined on all sides with big glass book cases filled with rows upon rows of books of various colours and various bindings. At this sight his former life was set free from prison at once for the second time. These gilted and multi-coloured books seemed to him like familiar jewelled lion-gates at the entrance of the kingdom of joy.

There were some things lying on the table also. The shortsighted Sashibhushan bent forward and saw a cracked slate upon which were some old exercise books, a much torn arithmetic book, the Book of Fables and a Kashiram Das Mahabharata.

Upon the wooden frame of the slate was written in bold characters in Sashibhushan's hand – Giribala Devi. Upon the books and exercise books the same name was written in the same hand.

Now Sashibhushan knew where he had come. The blood coursed wildly in his veins. He looked out of the open window, and what did he see there? The small iron-barred room, the uneven village lane, the little girl in a striped sari, – and his own carefree, quiet and peaceful daily life.

The happy life of those days was nothing wonderful nor extraordinary; day after day used to pass by unconsciously in trivial tasks and trivial joys, and the teaching of a little girl pupil was only one amongst those trifling things but that secluded life in a village corner, that circumscribed peace, those small joys, the face of that little girl – everything seemed to exist in a land of desire and shadowy imagination – in a heaven outside time and space and beyond his grasp.

All the scenes and memories of those bygone days, mingled with the soft light of this rainy morning and the kirtan song softly ringing in his ears, seemed to take on a new beauty of melodious sound and radiant light. The memory of the sad and hurt look on the face of the little neglected girl as he had last seen her in the jungle-girt muddy village lane was transformed on the canvas of his mind into a unique and wonderful picture full of deep pathos and a divine beauty. The sad tune of the kirtan blended with that picture, and it seemed to him that the ineffable sorrow at the heart of the universe had cast its shadow upon the face of that village maiden. Placing both arms on the slate and books upon the table, and hiding his face in them, Sashibhushan began after many years to dream dreams of long ago.

After a long time, hearing a slight noise Sashibhushan started and raised his head. He saw before him fruits and sweets on a silver salver, and at a little distance, Giribala standing and silently waiting. As soon as he looked up, Giribala, clad all in white in widow's garb, without a single ornament on her person, came and knelt before him, and took the dust of his feet.

She rose and looked at him – so emaciated and pale and broken in health – with her eyes full of sweet sympathy; and tears coursed down her cheeks.

Sashibhushan made an effort to ask her how she was, but could not find words to do so; stifled tears choked his utterance. The kirtan singers came and stood in front of the house in the course of their begging round and began to sing over and over again –

Come back, Beloved, come back!

30

Mahamaya

I

They met together in a ruined temple on the river bank, Mahamaya and Rajib.

In silence she cast her naturally grave look at Rajib with a tinge of reproach. It meant to say, "How durst you call me here at this unusual hour today? You have ventured to do it only because I have so long obeyed you in all things!"

Rajib had a little awe of Mahamaya at all times, and now this look of hers thoroughly upset him, he at once gave up his fondly conceived plan of making a set speech to her. And yet he had to give quickly some reason for this interview. So, he hurriedly blurted out, "I say, let us run away from this place and marry." True, Rajib thus, delivered himself of what he had had in his mind; but the preface he had silently composed was lost. His speech sounded very dry and bald – even absurd. He himself felt confused after saying it, and had no power left in him to add some words to modify its effect. The fool! After calling Mahamaya to that ruined temple by the riverside at midday, he could only tell her, "Come, let us marry!"

Mahamaya was a kulin's daughter, twenty-four years old – in the full bloom of her youth and beauty, like an image of pure gold, of the hue of the early autumn sunlight; radiant and still as that sunshine, with a gaze free and fearless as daylight itself.

She was an orphan. Her elder brother, Bhavanicharan Chattopadhyay, looked after her. The two were of the same mould – taciturn, but possessing a force of character which burnt silently like the midday sun. People feared Bhavanicharan without knowing why.

Rajib had come there from afar with the Burra Saheb of the silk factory of the place. His father had served this Saheb, and when he died, the Saheb undertook to bring up his orphan boy and took him with himself to this Bamanhati factory. In those early days such instances of sympathy were frequent among the Sahebs. The boy was accompanied by his loving aunt, and they lived in Bhavanicharan's neighbourhood. Mahamaya was Rajib's playmate in childhood, and was dearly loved by his aunt.

Rajib grew up to be sixteen, seventeen, eighteen, and even nineteen; and yet, in spite of his aunt's constant urging, he refused to marry. The Saheb was highly pleased to hear of this uncommon instance of good sense in a Bengali youth, and imagined that Rajib had taken him as his ideal in life. I may here add that the Saheb was a bachelor. The aunt died soon after.

For Mahamaya, too, no bridegroom of an equal grade of blue blood could be secured except for an impossible dowry. She steadily grew up in maidenhood.

The reader hardly needs to be told that though the god who ties the marriage knot had so long been ignoring this young couple, the god who forms the bond of love had not been idle all this time. While old Prajapati was dozing, young Kandarpa was very much awake.

Kandarpa's influence shows itself differently in different persons. Under his inspiration Rajib constantly sought for a chance of whispering his heart's longings, but Mahamaya never gave him such an opportunity; her silent and grave look sent a chill of fear through the wild heart of Rajib.

Today he had, by a hundred solemn entreaties and conjurations, at last succeeded in bringing her to this ruined temple. He had planned that he would today freely tell her all that he had to say and thereafter there would be for him either lifelong happiness or death in life. Yet at this crisis of his fate Rajib could only say, "Come, let us go and marry", and then, he stood confused and silent like a boy who had forgotten his lesson.

For a long while she did not reply, as if she had never expected such a proposal from Rajib.

The noontide has many undefined plaintive notes of its own; these began to make themselves heard in the midst of that stillness. The broken door of the temple, half detached from its hinge, began at times to open and to close in the wind with a low wailing creak. The pigeon, perched on the temple window, began its deep booming. The wood-pecker kept up its monotonous noise as it sat working on the shimul branch outside. The lizard darted through the heaps of dry leaves with a rustling sound. A sudden gust of warm wind blowing from the fields passed through the trees, making all their foliage whistle. Of a sudden the river waters woke into ripple and lapped on the broken steps of the ghat. Amidst these stray, languid sounds came the rustic notes of a cow-boy's flute from a far-off tree-shade. Rajib stood reclining against the ruinous plinth of the temple like a tired dreamer, gazing at the river; he had not the spirit to look Mahamaya in the face.

After a while he turned his head and again cast a supplicating glance at Mahamaya's face. She shook her head and replied, "No, it can't be."

At once the whole fabric of his hopes was dashed to the ground; for he knew that when Mahamaya shook her head it was through her own convictions, and nobody else in the world could bend her to his own will. The high pride of pedigree had run in the blood of Mahamaya's family for untold generations – could she ever consent to marry a Brahmin of low pedigree like Rajib? To love is one thing, and to marry quite another. She, however, now realised that her own thoughtless conduct in the past had encouraged Rajib to hope so audaciously; and at once she prepared to leave the temple.

Rajib understood her, and quickly broke in with "I am leaving these parts tomorrow."

At first she thought of appearing indifferent to the news; but she could not. Her feet did not move when she wanted to depart. Calmly she asked, "Why?" Rajib replied, "My Saheb has been transferred from here to the Sonapur factory, and he is taking me with him." Again she stood in long silence, musing thus, 'Our lives are moving in two contrary directions. I cannot hope to keep a man a prisoner of my eyes for ever.' So she opened her compressed lips a little and said, "Very well." It sounded rather like a deep sigh.

With this word only she was again about to leave, when Rajib started up with the whisper, "your brother!"

She looked out and saw her brother coming towards the temple, and she knew that he had found out their assignation. Rajib, fearing to place Mahamaya in a false position, tried to escape by jumping out of the hole in the temple wall; but Mahamaya seized his arm and kept him back by main force. Bhavanicharan entered the temple, and only cast one silent and placid glance at the pair.

Mahamaya looked at Rajib and said with an unruffled voice, "Yes, I will go to your house, Rajib. Do you wait for me."

Silently Bhavanicharan left the temple, and Mahamaya followed him as silently. And Rajib? He stood in a maze as if he had been doomed to death.

II

That very night Bhavanicharan gave a crimson silk sari to Mahamaya and told her to put it on at once. Then, he said, "Follow me". Nobody had ever disobeyed Bhavanicharan's bidding or even his hint; Mahamaya herself was no exception to it.

That night the two walked to the burning-place on the river-bank, not far from their home. There in the hut for sheltering dying men brought to the holy river's side, an old Brahmin was lying in expectation of death. The two went up to his bedside. A Brahmin priest was present in one corner of the room; Bhavanicharan beckoned to him. The priest quickly got his things ready for the happy ceremony. Mahamaya realised that she was to be married to this dying man, but she did not make the least objection. In the dim room, faintly lit up by the glare of two funeral pyres hard by, the muttered sacred texts mingled with the groans of the dying as Mahamaya's marriage was celebrated.

The day following her marriage she became a widow. But she did not feel excessively grieved at the bereavement. And Rajib, too, was not so crushed by the news of her widowhood as he had been by the unexpected tidings of her marriage. Nay, he felt rather cheered. But this feeling did not last long. A second terrible blow laid him utterly in the dust; he heard that there was a grand ceremony at the burning ghat that day as Mahamaya was going to burn herself with her husband's corpse.

At first he thought of informing his Saheb and forcibly stopping the cruel sacrifice with his help. But then, he recollected that the Saheb had made over charge and left for Sonapur that very day; he had wanted to take Rajib with him, but the youth had stayed behind on a month's leave.

Mahamaya had told him "Wait for me". This request he must by no means disregard. He had at first taken a month's leave, but if need were he would take two months', then, three months' leave and finally throw up the Saheb's service and live by begging, yet he would wait for her to his life's close.

Just when Rajib was going to rush out madly and commit suicide or some other terrible deed, a deluge of rain came down with a desolating storm at sunset. The tempest threatened to tumble his house down on his head. He gained some composure when he found that the convulsion in outer nature was harmonizing with the storm within his soul. It seemed to him that all Nature had taken up his cause and was going to bring him some sort of remedy. The force he wished to apply in his own person but could not was now being applied by Nature herself over earth and sky.

At such a time some one pushed the door hard from outside. Rajib hastened to open it. A woman entered the room, clad in a wet garment, with a long veil covering her entire face. Rajib at once knew her for Mahamaya.

In a voice full of emotion he asked, "Mahamaya, have you come away from the funeral pyre?"

She replied, "Yes, I had promised you to come to your house. Here I am, to keep my word. But, Rajib, I am not exactly the same person; I am changed altogether. I am the Mahamaya of old in my mind only. Speak now, I can yet go back to the funeral pyre. But if you swear never to draw my veil aside, never to look on my face, then, I shall live in your house."

It was enough to get her back from the hand of Death; all other considerations vanished before it. Rajib promptly replied, "Live here in any fashion you like; if you leave me I shall die."

Mahamaya said, "Then, come away at once. Let us go where your Saheb has gone on transfer."

Abandoning all his property in that house, Rajib went forth into the midst of the storm with Mahamaya. The force of the wind made it hard for them to stand erect; the gravel driven by the wind pricked their limbs like buck shot. The two took to the open fields, lest the trees by the roadside should crash down on their heads. The violence of the wind struck them from behind, as if the tempest had torn the couple asunder from human habitations and was blowing them away on to destruction.

III

The reader must not discredit my tale as false or supernatural. There are traditions of a few such occurrences having taken place in the days when the burning of widows was customary.

Mahamaya had been bound hand and foot and placed on the funeral pyre, to which fire was applied at the appointed time. The flames had shot up from the pile, when a violent storm and rain-shower began. Those who had come to conduct the cremation quickly fled for refuge to the hut for dying men and shut the door. The rain put the funeral fire out in no time. Meantime the bands on Mahamaya's wrists had been burnt to ashes, setting her hands free. Without uttering a groan amidst the intolerable pain of burning, she sat up and untied her feet. Then, wrapping round herself her partly burnt cloth, she rose half-naked from the pyre, and first came to her own house. There was no one there; all had gone to the burning ghat. She lighted a lamp, put on a fresh cloth, and looked at her face in a glass. Dashing the mirror down on the ground, she mused for a while. Then, she drew a long veil over her face and went to Rajib's house which was hard by. The reader knows what happened next.

True, Mahamaya now lived in Rajib's house, but there was no joy in his life. It was not much, but only a simple veil that parted the one from the other. And yet that veil was eternal like death, but more agonizing than death itself; because despair in time deadens the pang of death's separation, while a living hope was being daily and hourly crushed by the separation which that veil caused.

For one thing there was a spirit of motionless silence in Mahamaya from of old; and now the hush from within the veil appeared doubly unbearable. She seemed to be living within a winding sheet of death. This silent death clasped the life of Rajib and daily seemed to shrivel it up. He lost the Mahamaya whom he had known of old, and at the same time this veiled figure ever sitting by his side silently prevented him from enshrining in his life the sweet memory of her as she was in her girlhood. He brooded, 'Nature has placed barrier enough between one human being and another. Mahamaya, in particular, has been born, like Karua of old, with a natural charm against all evil. There is an innate fence round her being. And now she seems to have been born a second time and come to me with a second line of fences round herself. Ever by my side, she yet has become so remote as to be no longer within my reach. I am sitting outside the inviolable circle of her magic and trying, with an unsatiated thirsty soul, to penetrate this thin but unfathomable mystery, as the stars wear out the hours night after night in the vain attempt to pierce the mystery of the 'dark Night with their sleepless winkless downcast gaze.'

Long did these two companionless lonely creatures thus, pass their days together.

One night, on the tenth day of the new moon, the clouds withdrew for the first time in that rainy season, and the moon showed herself. The motionless moonlit night seemed to be sitting in a vigil by the head of the sleeping world. That night Rajib too had quit his bed and sat gazing out of his window. From the heat-oppressed woodland a peculiar scent and the lazy hum of the cricket were entering into his room. As he gazed, the sleeping tank by the dark rows of trees glimmered like a polished silver plate. It is hard to say whether man at such a time thinks any clearly defined thought. Only his heart rushes in a particular direction – it sends forth an effusion of odour like the woodland, it utters a cricket hum like the night. What Rajib was thinking of I know not; but it seemed to him that that night all the old laws had been set aside; that day the rainy season's night had drawn aside her veil of clouds, and this night looked silent, beautiful and grave like the Mahamaya of those early days. All the currents of his being flowed impetuously together towards that Mahamaya.

Like one moving in a dream, Rajib entered Mahamaya's bedroom. She was asleep then.

He stood by her side and stooped down to gaze on her. The moonbeams had fallen on her face. But, Oh horror! Where was that face known of old? The flame of the funeral pyre, with its ruthless greedy tongue, had utterly licked away a part of the beauty from the left cheek of Mahamaya and left there only the ravages of its hunger.

Did Rajib start? Did a muffled cry escape from his lips? Probably so. Mahamaya woke up with a start – and saw Rajib before her. At once she replaced her veil and stood erect, leaving her bed. Rajib knew that the thunderbolt was uplifted. He fell down before her – he clasped her feet, crying, "forgive me!"

She answered not a word, she did not look back for a moment as she walked out of the room. She never came back. No trace of her was found anywhere. The parting left all the remaining days of Rajib's life branded with a long scar.

31

THE CONCLUSION

I

Apurba had got his B.A. degree and was coming back home to his village. The river, which flowed past it, was a small one. It became dried up during the hot weather, but now in the July monsoon the heavy rains had swollen its current and it was full to the brim.

The boat, which carried Apurba, reached the ghat whence the roof of his home could be seen through the dense foliage of the trees. Nobody knew that he was coming and therefore, there was no one to receive him at the landing. The boatman offered to carry his bag, but Apurba picked it up himself, and took a leap from the boat. The bank was slippery, and he fell flat upon the muddy stair, bag and all.

As he did so, peal after peal of very sweet laughter rose in the sky, and startled the birds in the neighbouring trees. Apurba got up and tried to regain his composure as best as he could. When he sought for the source of his discomfiture, he found, sitting upon a heap of bricks lately unloaded from some cargo boat, a girl shaking her sides with laughter. Apurba recognised her as Mrinmayi, the daughter of their neighbour. This family had built their former house some distance away, but the river shifted its course cutting away into the land; and they had been obliged to change their quarter and settle down in the village only about two years ago.

Mrinmayi was the talk of all the village. The men called her 'madcap', but the village matrons were in a state of perpetual anxiety because of her untractable wildness. All her games were with the boys of the place, and she had the utmost contempt for the girls of her own age. The favourite child of her father, she had got into these unmanageable ways. Her mother would often complain to her friends of her husband's spoiling the child. But, because she was well aware that the father would be cut to the quick if he saw his daughter in tears, the mother had not the heart to punish the girl herself.

Mrinmayi's face was more like that of a boy than a girl. Her short crop of curly hair reached down to her shoulders, and her big dark eyes showed no sign of fear or shyness. When the boat, carrying the absentee landlord of the village, was moored at the landing stage, she did not share the feeling of awe which possessed the neighbourhood, but shook her curly mane and took up a naked child in her arms and was the first to come and take her observation of the habits of this strange creature.

Apurba had come in touch with this girl on former occasions, and he had got into the habit of thinking about her from time to time during his leisure, and even while at work. Naturally, therefore, this laughter, with which she greeted his arrival, did not please him, in spite of its musical quality. He gave up his bag to the boatman and almost ran away towards his house. The whole setting of things was romantic – the river bank, the shade of the trees, the morning sunshine with birds' songs, and his youth of twenty years. The brick heaps hardly fitted in with the picture, but the girl who sat on the top of them made up for all deficiencies.

II

The widowed mother was beside herself with joy when her son returned unexpectedly. She at once sent her men to all parts of the village to search for milk and curds and fish. There was quite a stir among the neighbours. After the midday meal, the mother ventured to suggest to Apurba that he should turn his thoughts towards marriage. Apurba was prepared for this attack, as it had been tried before, and he had then, put it off on the plea of examinations. But now that he had got his degree, he could have no such excuse to delay the inevitable. So he told his mother that if a suitable bride could be discovered he could then, make up his mind.

The mother said that the discovery had been already made, and therefore, there was no further excuse for deliberation. But Apurba was of opinion that deliberation was necessary, and insisted on seeing the girl before consenting to marry her. The mother agreed to this, though the request seemed superfluous.

The next day Apurba went out on his marriage expedition. The intended bride lived in a house which was not far from their own. Apurba took special care about his dress before starting. He put on his new silk suit and a fashionable turban much affected by the Calcutta people. He did not forget to display his patent leather shoes and silk umbrella. His reception was loudly cordial in the house of his would-be father-in-law. The little victim – the intended bride – was scrubbed and painted, beribboned and bejewelled, and brought before Apurba. She sat in a corner of the room, veiled up to her chin, with her head nearly touching her knees, and her middle-aged maidservant at her back to encourage her when in trouble. Her young brother sat near closely observing Apurba – his turban, his watch-chain, his newly budding moustache.

Apurba solemnly asked the girl, "What text-books are you reading in your school?"

No answer came from this bundle of bashfulness wrapped in coloured silk. After repeated questionings and secret pushings in the back by the maidservant, she rapidly gave the names of all her lesson-books in one breath.

Just at this moment the sound of scampering feet was heard outside and Mrinmayi burst into the room very much out of breath. She did not give the least heed to Apurba, but at once caught hold of the hand of Rakhal, the young brother, and tried to drag him outside. But Rakhal was intently engaged in cultivating his faculty of observation and refused to stir. The maidservant tried to scold Mrinmayi, keeping the pitch of her voice within the proper limits of decorum. Apurba retained his composure and sat still and sullen, fondling the watch-chain with his fingers.

When Mrinmayi failed in her attempt to make Rakhal move, she gave the boy a sounding smack on the shoulder, then, she pulled up the veil from the face of the intended bride, and rushed out of the room like a miniature tornado. The maidservant growled and grumbled and Rakhal began to laugh immoderately at the sudden unveiling of his sister. He evidently did not take ill the blow he had received, because they had with each other a running account of such amenities. There was once a time when Mrinmayi had her hair long enough to reach her waist, and it was Rakhal who had ploughed his scissors through it one day till the girl in disgust had snatched them from the boy's hand and completed the destruction herself, leaving a mass of curls lying upon the dust like a bunch of black grapes.

After this cataclysm, the business of the examination came to a sudden stop. The girl-bride rose from her seat and changed from a circle of misery into a straight line, and then, disappeared into the inner apartment. Apurba got up, still stroking his moustache, only to discover that his patent leather shoes had vanished. A great search was made for them, but they were nowhere to be found. There was nothing else to do but to borrow from the head of the house a pair of old slippers, which were sadly out of keeping with the rest of his attire.

When Apurba reached the lane by the side of the village pool, the same peal of laughter rang through the sky which he had heard the day before; and while he stood shamefaced and irresolute, looking about him, the culprit came out of her ambuscade and flung the patent leather shoes before him and tried to escape. Apurba rushed after her quickly and made her captive, holding her by the wrist. Mrinmayi writhed and wriggled, but could not set herself free. A sunbeam fell upon her mischievous face through a gap in the branches overhead, and Apurba gazed intently into her eyes, like a traveller peering through the limpid water of a rushing stream at the glistening pebbles below. He seemed to hesitate to complete his adventure, and slowly relaxed his hold and let his captive escape. If Apurba had boxed Mrinmayi's ears in anger, that would have seemed more natural to the girl than this silent incompleteness of punishment.

III

It is difficult to understand why a young man of culture and learning like Apurba should be so anxious to reveal his worth to this slip of a village girl. What harm would there be, if, in her pitiful ignorance, she should ignore him and choose that foolish poor Rakhal as her companion? Why should he struggle to prove to her that he wrote a monthly article in the journal Visvadip, and that a manuscript book of no mean size was waiting for publication in the bottom of his trunk, along with his scent bottles, tinted note-paper, harmonium lessons, etc.

In the evening Apurba's mother asked him, "Have you approved of your bride?"

Apurba said with a slight hesitation, "Yes, I like one of the girls."

"One of the girls!" she asked, "why, what do you mean?" After a great deal of beating about the bush she found out that her son had selected Mrinmayi for his bride. When she grasped this fact she greatly lost her respect for the B.A. degree. Then, followed a long struggle between them. At last the mother persuaded herself that Mrinmayi was not wholly impervious to improvement. She began to suspect also that the girl's face had a charm of its own, but the next moment the cropped head of hair came to her mind and gave her a feeling of disgust. Recognizing, however, "that hair is more amenable to reason than human nature, she felt consoled, and the betrothal was made.

Mrinmayi's father got the news. He was a clerk in an office at a small distant river station of a steamship company. He was engaged all day in selling tickets and loading and unloading cargo, living in a small hut with a corrugated iron roof. His eyes overflowed with tears when he got the letter telling him what had happened. How much was pleasure and how much was pain would be difficult to analyse.

Ishan applied to the head office in Calcutta for leave of absence. The reason of the betrothal seemed insufficient to the English manager of the company and the application was rejected. Ishan then, asked for a postponement of the marriage till the autumn holidays; but he was told by the mother of the bridegroom that the most auspicious day for the marriage that year fell in the last week of the current month. So Ishan went on selling tickets and loading and unloading cargo with a heavy heart – his petitions rejected from both sides. After this, Mrinmayi's mother and all the matrons of the village began to admonish the girl about the future household duties. She was warned that love of play, quickness of movement, loudness of laughter, companionship of boys and disregard of good manners in eating would not be tolerated in her husband's house. They were completely successful in proving the terrible cramped constraint of married life. Mrinmayi took the proposal of her marriage as a sentence of life-imprisonment, with hanging at the end of it. Like an unmanageable little pony, she took the bit between her teeth and said, "I'm not going to be married."

IV

But she had to marry after all. And then, began her lesson. The whole universe shrank for her within the walls of her mother-in-law's household. The latter began at once her reformation duties. She hardened her face and said,

"My child, you are not a baby. The vulgar loudness of your behaviour won't suit our family."

The moral which Mrinmayi learnt from these words was that she must find some more suitable place for herself and she became invisible that very afternoon. They went on vainly searching for her till her friend Rakhal played the traitor, and revealed her hiding place in a deserted, broken down wooden chariot once used for taking out the image of the god for an airing. After this, the atmosphere of her mother-in-law's home became intolerably hot. Rain came down at night.

Apurba, coming close to Mrinmayi in his bed, whispered to her, "Mrinmayi, don't you love me?" Mrinmayi broke out, "No, I shall never love you!"

"But what harm have I done you?" said Apurba.

"Why did you marry me?" was the reply. To give a satisfactory explanation to this question was difficult, but Apurba said to himself, 'I must win, in the end, this rebellious heart.'

On the next day, the mother-in-law observed some signs of petulance in Mrinmayi and shut her up in a room. When Mrinmayi could find no way to get out, she tore the bed sheet to rags with her teeth in vain anger, and flinging herself on the floor burst out weeping and calling in agony, "Father, father!"

Just then, somebody came and sat by her. He tried to arrange her dishevelled hair as she turned from side to side, but Mrinmayi angrily shook her head and pushed his hand away. Apurba (for it was he) bent his face to her ear and whispered,

"I have secretly opened the gate; let us run away by the back door."

Mrinmayi again violently shook her head and said, "No."

Apurba tried to raise her face gently by the chin saying, "Do look who is there." Rakhal had come and was standing foolishly by the door looking at Mrinmayi. But the girl pushed away Apurba's hand without raising her face.

He said "Rakhal has come to play with you. Won't you come?"

She said, "No!" Rakhal was greatly relieved to be allowed to run away from this scene.

Apurba sat still and silent. Mrinmayi wept and wept, till she was so tired that she fell asleep; then, Apurba went out silently and shut the door.

The next day Mrinmayi received a letter from her father, in which he expressed his regret for not being able to be present at the marriage of his darling daughter. He ended with his blessings. The girl went to her mother-in-law and said, "I must go to my father."

A scolding began at once, "Your father! What a thing to ask. Your father has no decent house for himself – how can you go to him?"

Mrinmayi came back to her room in despair and cried to herself, "Father, take me away from this place! I have nobody here to love me. I shall die if I am left here."

In the depth of the night, when her husband fell asleep, she quietly opened the door and went out of the house. It was cloudy, yet the moonlight was strong enough to show her the path. But Mrinmayi had no idea which was the way to reach her father. She had a belief that the road, which the post runners took, led to all the addresses of all the men in the world.

So she went that way, and was quite tired out with walking when the night was nearly ended.

The early birds doubtfully twittered their greetings to the morning, when Mrinmayi came to the end of the road at the river-bank where there was a big bazaar. Just then, she heard the clatter of the iron ring of the mail runner. She rushed to him and in her eager, tired voice cried, "I want to go to my father at Kushiganj. Do take me with you."

The postman told her hurriedly that he did not know where Kushiganj was and the next moment wakened up the boatman of the mail boat and sailed away. He had no time either to pity or to question.

By the time Mrinmayi had descended the landing stairs and called a boat, the street and the river-bank were fully awake. Before the boatman could answer, some one from a boat near at hand called out,

"Hallo, Mrinu! How on earth could you get here?" The girl replied in all eagerness, "Banamali, I must go to my father at Kushiganj. Please take me in your boat!"

This boatman belonged to her own village and knew all about the wild untameable girl. He said to her, "You want to go to your father? That's good. I'll take you."

Mrinmayi got into the boat. The clouds thickened and the rain came down in showers. The river, swollen by the monsoon, rocked the boat, and Mrinmayi fell asleep. When she woke up, she found herself in her own bed in her mother-in-law's house.

The maidservant began scolding her the moment she saw her awake. The mother-in-law came next. As she entered, Mrinmayi opened her eyes wide and silently looked in her face. But when the mother-in-law made a reference to the ill-breeding of Mrinmayi's family, the girl rushed out of her room and entered the next and shut the door from the inside.

Apurba came to his mother and said, "Mother, I don't see any harm in sending Mrinmayi for just a few days to her father's house."

The mother's reply was to scold Apurba in unmeasured terms for selecting this one girl from all the suitable brides who might have been had for the mere asking.

V

In the middle of the night, Apurba awakened Mrinmayi and said, "Mrinmayi, are you ready to go to your father?" She clutched his hand and said, "Yes."

Apurba whispered, "Then, come. Let us run away from this place. I have got a boat ready at the landing. Come." Mrinmayi cast a grateful glance at her husband's face, and got up and dressed, and was ready to go. Apurba left a letter for his mother, and then, both of them left the house together hand in hand.

This was the first time that Mrinmayi had put her hand into her husband's with a spontaneous feeling of dependence. They went on their journey along the lonely village road through the depth of the night.

When they reached the landing stage, they got into a boat, and in spite of the turbulent joy which she felt Mrinmayi fell asleep. The next day – what emancipation, what unspeakable bliss it was! They passed by all the different villages, markets, cultivated fields, and groups of boats at anchor near some ghat. Mrinmayi began to ply her husband with questions about every little trifle – where were those boats coming from, what were their cargoes, what was the name of that village? – questions whose answers were not in the text-books which Apurba studied in his college. His friends might be concerned to hear that Apurba's answers did not always tally with the truth. He would not hesitate for a moment to describe bags of sesame as linseed, and the village of Panchbere as Rainagar, or to point out the district magistrate's court as the landlord's office. Whatever answer she got, Mrinmayi was fully satisfied, never doubting its accuracy.

The next day the boat reached Kushiganj. Ishan, seated on his office stool, in his hut dimly lighted with a square oil-lantern, was deep in his accounts before his small desk, his big ledger open before him, when this young pair entered the room. Mrinmayi at once called out,

"Father!"

Such a word, uttered in so sweet a voice, had never sounded before in that corrugated iron room. Ishan could hardly restrain his tears and sat dumb for a moment, vainly seeking for some greeting. He was in great confusion how fitly to receive the young married couple in his office, crowded with bales of jute and piled up ledgers, which had also to serve him for a bedroom. And then, about the meals – the poor man had to cook for himself his own simple dinner, but how could he offer that to his guests? Mrinmayi said, "Father, let us cook the food ourselves."

And Apurba joined in this proposal with great zest. In this room, with all its lack of space for man and food, their joy welled up in full abundance, like the jet of water thrown up all the higher because the opening of the fountain is narrow.

Three days were passed in this manner. Steamers came to stop at the landing stage all day long with their noisy crowd of men. At last, in the evening, the river-bank would become deserted and then – what freedom! And the cooking preparations in which the art of cookery was not carried to its perfection – what fun it was! And the jokes and mock quarrels about the mock deficiencies in Mrinmayi's domestic skill – what absurd carryings on! But it had to come to an end at last. Apurba did not dare to prolong his French leave, and Ishan also thought it was wise for them to return.

When the culprits reached home, the mother remained sulkily silent. She never even blamed them for what they had done so as to give them an opportunity to explain their conduct. This sullen silence became at last intolerable, and Apurba expressed his intention of going back to college in order to study Law. The mother, affecting indifference, said to him, "What about your wife?"

Apurba answered, "Let her remain here."

"Oh, no, no!" cried the mother, "you should take her with you."

Apurba said in a voice of annoyance, "Very well."

The preparation went on for their departure to the town, and on the night before leaving Apurba, coming to his bed, found Mrinmayi in tears. This hurt him greatly and he cried, Mrinmayi, don't you want to come to Calcutta with me?" The girl replied, "No!"

Apurba's next question was, "Don't you love me?" But the question remained unanswered. There are times when answers to such questions are absolutely simple, but at other times they become too complex for a young girl to answer.

Apurba asked, "Do you feel unwilling to leave Rakhal behind?"

Mrinmayi instantly answered, "Yes". For a moment this young man, who was proud of his B.A. degree, felt a needle prick of jealousy deep down in his heart, and said,

"I shan't be able to come back home for a long time." Mrinmayi had nothing to say. "It may be two years or more," he added. Mrinmayi told him with coolness, "You had better bring back with you, for Rakhal, a Roger's knife with three blades."

Apurba sat up and asked,

"Then, you mean to stay on here?"

Mrinmayi said,

"Yes, I shall go to my own mother."

Apurba breathed a deep sigh and said,

"Very well, I shall not come home, until you write me a letter asking me to come to you. Are you very, very glad?" Mrinmayi thought this question needed no answer, and fell asleep. Apurba got no sleep that night.

When it was nearly dawn, Apurba awakened Mrinmayi and said,

"Mrinu, it is time to go. Let me take you to your mother's house."

When his wife got up from her bed, Apurba held her by both hands and said,

"I have a prayer to make to you. I have helped you several times and I want to claim my reward."

Mrinmayi was surprised and said,

"What?"

Apurba answered,

"Mrinu, give me a kiss out of pure love."

When the girl heard this absurd request and saw Apurba's solemn face, she burst out laughing. When it was over, she held her face for a kiss, but broke out laughing again. After a few more attempts, she gave it up. Apurba pulled her ear gently as a mild punishment.

VI

When Mrinmayi came to her mother's house, she was surprised to find that it was not as pleasant to her as before. Time seemed to hang heavily on her hands, and she wondered in her mind what was lacking in the familiar home surroundings. Suddenly it seemed to her that the whole house and village were deserted and she longed to go to Calcutta. She did not know that even on that last night the earlier portion of her life, to which she clung, had changed its aspect before she knew it. Now she could easily shake off her past associations as the tree sheds its dead leaves. She did not understand that her destiny had struck the blow and severed her youth from her childhood, with its magic blade, in such a subtle manner that they kept together even after the stroke; but directly she moved, one half of her life fell from the other and Mrinmayi looked at it in wonder. The young girl, who used to occupy the old bedroom in this house, no longer existed; all her memory hovered round another bed in another bedroom.

Mrinmayi refused to go out of doors any longer, and her laughter had a strangely different ring. Rakhal became slightly afraid of her. He gave up all thought of playing with her. One day, Mrinmayi came to her mother and asked her, "Mother, please take me to my mother-in-law's house." After this, one morning the mother-in-law was surprised to see Mrinmayi come and touch the ground with her forehead before her feet. She got up at once and took her in her arms. Their union was complete in a moment, and the cloud of misunderstanding was swept away leaving the atmosphere glistening with the radiance of tears.

When Mrinmayi's body and mind became filled with womanhood, deep and tender, it gave her an aching pain. Her eyes became sad, like the shadow of rain upon some lake, and she put these questions to her husband in her own mind – 'Why did you not have the patience to understand me, when I was late in understanding you? Why did you put up with my disobedience, when I refused to follow you to Calcutta?'

Suddenly she came to fathom the look in Apurba's eyes when, on that morning, he had caught hold of her hand by the village pool and then, slowly released her. She remembered, too, the futile flights of that kiss, which had never reached its goal, and was now like a thirsty bird haunting that past opportunity. She recollected how Apurba had said to her that he would never come back until he had received from her a message asking him to do so; and she sat down at once to write a letter. The gilt-edged notepaper which Apurba had given her was brought out of its box, and with great care she began to write in a big hand, smudging her fingers with ink. With her first word she plunged into the subject without addressing him,

Why don't you write to me? How are you? And please come home.

She could think of no other words to say. But though the important message had been given, yet unfortunately the unimportant words occupy the greatest space in human communication. She racked her brains to add a few more words to what she had written, and then, wrote,

This time don't forget to write me letters and write how you are, and come back home, and mother is quite well. Our black cow had a calf last night.

Here she came to the end of her resources. She put her letter into the envelope and poured out all her love as she wrote the name, Srijukta Babu Apurbakrishna Roy. She did not know that anything more was needed by way of an address, so the letter did not reach its goal, and the postal authorities were not to blame for it.

It was vacation time. Yet Apurba never came home. The mother thought that he was nourishing anger against her. Mrinmayi was certain that her letter was not well enough written to satisfy him. At last the mother said to her daughter-in-law, "Apurba has been absent for so long that I am thinking of going to Calcutta to see him. Would you like to come with me?"

Mrinmayi gave a violent nod of assent. Then, she ran to her room and shut herself in. She fell upon her bed, clutched the pillow to her breast, and gave vent to her feelings by laughing and excited movements. When this fit was over, she became grave and sad and sat up on the bed and wept in silence.

Without telling Apurba, these two repentant women went to Calcutta to ask for Apurba's forgiveness. The mother had a son-in-law in Calcutta, and so she put up at his house. That very same evening, Apurba broke his promise and began to write a letter to Mrinmayi. But he found no terms of endearment fit to express his love, and felt disgusted with his mother tongue for its poverty. But when he got a letter from his brother-in-law, informing him of the arrival of his mother and inviting him to dinner, he hastened to his sister's house without delay.

The first question he asked his mother, when he met her, was, "Mother, is everybody at home quite well?"

The mother answered, "Yes, I have come here to take you back home."

Apurba said that he thought it was not necessary on her part to have taken all this trouble for such a purpose, and he had his examination before him, etc., etc.

At dinner his sister asked him why he had not brought his wife with him when he returned to Calcutta this time. Apurba began to say very solemnly that he had his law examination to think of, etc., etc.

The brother-in-law cut in smiling,

"All this is a mere excuse, the real reason is that he is afraid of us."

His sister replied, "You are indeed a terrifying person! The poor child may well get a shock when she sees you." Thus, the laughter and jokes became plentiful, but Apurba remained silent. He was accusing his mother in his mind for not having had the consideration to bring Mrinmayi with her. Then, he thought that possibly his mother had tried, but failed, owing to Mrinmayi's unwillingness, and he felt afraid even to question his mother about it; the whole scheme of things seemed to him full of incorrigible blunders.

When the dinner was over, it came on to rain and his sister said, "Dada, you sleep here."

But Apurba replied, "No, I must go home. I have work to do."

The brother-in-law said, "How absurd! You have no one at home to call you to account for your absence, and you needn't be anxious."

Then, his sister told him that he was looking very tired, and it was better for him to leave the company and go to bed. Apurba went to his bed-room and found it in darkness. His sister asked him if he wanted a light, but he said that he preferred the dark. When his sister had left, he groped his way to the bedstead and prepared to get into bed.

All of a sudden a tender pair of arms, with a jingle of bracelets, were flung round his neck, and two lips soft as flower petals almost smothered him with kisses wet with tears.

At first it startled Apurba greatly, but then, he came to know that those kisses, which had been obstructed once by laughter, had now found their completion in tears.

32

The Parrot's Training

Once upon a time there was a bird. It was ignorant. It sang all right, but never recited scriptures. It hopped pretty frequently, but lacked manners.

Said the Raja to himself, 'Ignorance is costly in the long run. For fools consume as much food as their betters, and yet give nothing in return.'

He called his nephews to his presence and told them that the bird must have a sound schooling.

The pundits were summoned, and at once went to the root of the matter. They decided that the ignorance of birds was due to their natural habit of living in poor nests. Therefore, according to the pundits, the first thing necessary for this bird's education was a suitable cage.

The pundits had their rewards and went home happy.

A golden cage was built with gorgeous decorations. Crowds came to see it from all parts of the world.

"Culture, captured and caged!" exclaimed some, in a rapture of ecstasy, and burst into tears.

Others remarked, "Even if culture be missed, the cage will remain, to the end, a substantial fact. How fortunate for the bird!"

The goldsmith filled his bag with money and lost no time in sailing homewards.

The pundit sat down to educate the bird. With proper deliberation he took his pinch of snuff, as he said, "Textbooks can never be too many for our purpose!"

The nephews brought together an enormous crowd of scribes. They copied from books, and copied from copies, till the manuscripts were piled up to an unreachable height.

Men murmured in amazement, "Oh, the tower of culture, egregiously high! The end of it lost in the clouds!"

The scribes, with light hearts, hurried home, their pockets heavily laden.

The nephews were furiously busy keeping the cage in proper trim.

As their constant scrubbing and polishing went on, the people said with satisfaction, "This is progress indeed!" Men were employed in large numbers, and supervisors were still more numerous. These, with their cousins of all different degrees of distance, built a palace for themselves and lived there happily ever after.

Whatever may be its other deficiencies, the world is never in want of fault-finders; and they went about saying that every creature remotely connected with the cage flourished beyond words, excepting only the bird.

When this remark reached the Raja's ears, he summoned his nephews before him and said, "My dear nephews, what is this that we hear?"

The nephews said in answer, "Sire, let the testimony of the goldsmiths and the pundits, the scribes and the supervisors, be taken, if the truth is to be known food is scarce with the fault-finders, and that is why their tongues have gained in sharpness."

The explanation was so luminously satisfactory that the Raja decorated each one of his nephews with his own rare jewels.

The Raja at length, being desirous of seeing with his own eyes how his Education Department busied itself with the little bird, made his appearance one day at the great Hall of Learning.

From the gate rose the sounds of conch-shells and gongs, horns, bugles and trumpets, cymbals, drums and kettle-drums, tomtoms, tambourines, flutes, fifes, barrel-organs and bagpipes. The pundits began chanting mantras with their topmost voices, while the goldsmiths, scribes, supervisors, and their numberless cousins of all different degrees of distance, loudly raised a round of cheers.

The nephews smiled and said, "Sire, what do you think of it all?"

The Raja said, "It does seem so fearfully like a sound principle of Education!"

Mightily pleased, the Raja was about to remount his elephant, when the fault-finder, from behind some bush, cried out, "Maharaja, have you seen the bird?"

"Indeed, I have not!" exclaimed the Raja, "I completely forgot about the bird."

Turning back, he asked the pundits about the method they followed in instructing the bird.

It was shown to him. He was immensely impressed. The method was so stupendous that the bird looked ridiculously unimportant in comparison. The Raja was satisfied that there was no flaw in the arrangements. As for any complaint from the bird itself, that simply could not be expected. Its throat was so completely choked with the leaves from the books that it could neither whistle nor whisper. It sent a thrill through one's body to watch the process.

This time, while remounting his elephant, the Raja ordered his State Earpuller to give a thorough good pull at both the ears of the fault-finder.

The bird thus, crawled on, duly and properly, to the safest verge of inanity. In fact, its progress was satisfactory in the extreme. Nevertheless, nature occasionally triumphed over training, and when the morning light peeped into the bird's cage it sometimes fluttered its wings in a reprehensible manner. And, though it is hard to believe, it pitifully pecked at its bars with its feeble beak.

"What impertinence!" growled the kotwal.

The blacksmith, with his forge and hammer, took his place in the Raja's Department of Education. Oh, what resounding blows! The iron chain was soon completed, and the bird's wings were clipped.

The Raja's brothers-in-law looked black, and shook their heads, saying, "These birds not only lack good sense, but also gratitude!"

With text-book in one hand and baton in the other, the pundits gave the poor bird what may fitly be called lessons!

The kotwal was honoured with a title for his watchfulness and the blacksmith for his skill in forging chains.

The bird died.

Nobody had the least notion how long ago this had happened. The fault-finder was the first man to spread the rumour.

The Raja called his nephews and asked them, "My dear nephews, what is this that we hear?"

The nephews said, "Sire, the bird's education has been completed."

"Does it hop?" the Raja enquired.

"Never!" said the nephews.

"Does it fly?"

"No."

"Bring me the bird," said the Raja.

The bird was brought to him, guarded by the kotwal and the sepoys and the sowars. The Raja poked its body with his finger. Only its inner stuffing of book-leaves rustled.

Outside the window, the murmur of the spring breeze amongst the newly budded Asoka leaves made the April morning wistful.

33

The Trial of the Horse

Brahma, the creator, was very near the end of his task of creation when a new idea struck him.

He sent for the Store-keeper and said, "O keeper of the stores, bring to my factory a quantity of each of the five elements. For I am ready to create another creature."

"Lord of the universe," the Store-keeper replied, "when in the first flush of creative extravagance you began to turn out such exaggerations as elephants and whales and pythons and tigers, you took no count of the stock. Now, all the elements that have density and force are nearly used up. The supply of earth and water and fire has become inconveniently scanty, while of air and ether there is as much as is good for us and a good deal more."

The four-headed deity looked perplexed and pulled at his four pairs of moustaches. At last he said, "The limitedness of material gives all the more scope to originality. Send me whatever you have left."

This time Brahma was excessively sparing with the earth, water and fire. The new creature was not given either horns or claws, and his teeth were only meant for chewing, not for biting.

The prudent care with which fire was used in his formation made him necessary in war without making him warlike.

This animal was the Horse.

The reckless expenditure of air and ether, which went into his composition, was amazing. And, in consequence, he perpetually struggled to outreach the wind, to outrun space itself. The other animals run only when they have a reason, but the horse would run for nothing whatever, as if to run out of his own skin. He had no desire to chase, or to kill, but only to fly on and on till he dwindled into a dot, melted into a swoon, blurred into a shadow, and vanished into vacancy.

The Creator was glad. He had given for his other creatures habitations – to some the forests, to other the caves. But in his enjoyment of the disinterested spirit of speed in the Horse, he gave him an open meadow under the very eye of heaven.

By the side of this meadow lived Man.

Man has his delight in pillaging and piling things up. And he is never happy till these grow into a burden. So, when he saw this new creature pursuing the wind and kicking at the sky, he said to himself, "If only I can bind and secure this Horse, I can use his broad back for carrying my loads."

So one day he caught the Horse.

Then, Man put a saddle on the Horse's back and a spiky bit in his mouth. He regularly had hard rubbing and scrubbing to keep him fit, and there were the whip and spurs to remind him that it was wrong to have his own will.

Man also put high walls round the Horse, lest if left at large in the open the creature might escape him.

So it came to pass, that while the Tiger who had his forest remained in the forest, the Lion who had his cave remained in the cave, the Horse who once had his open meadow came to spend his days in a stable. Air and ether had roused in the horse longings for deliverance, but they swiftly delivered him into bondage.

When he felt that bondage did not suit him, the Horse kicked at the stable walls.

But this hurt his hoofs much more than it hurt the wall. Still some of the plaster came off and the wall lost its beauty.

Man felt aggrieved.

"What ingratitude!" he cried. "Do I not give him food and drink? Do I not keep highly-paid men-servants to watch over him day and night? Indeed he is hard to please."

In their desperate attempts to please the Horse, the men-servants fell upon him and so vigorously applied all their winning methods that he lost his power to kick and a great deal more besides.

Then, Man called his friends and neighbours together, and said to them exultingly, "Friends, did you ever see so devoted a steed as mine?"

"Never!" they replied. "He seems as still as ditch water and as mild as the religion you profess."

The Horse, as is well known, had no horns, no claws, nor adequate teeth, at his birth. And, when on the top of this, all kicking at the walls and even into emptiness had been stopped, the only way to give vent to his feelings was to neigh.

But that disturbed Man's sleep.

Moreover, this neighing was not likely to impress the neighbours as a paean of devotion and thankfulness. So Man invented devices to shut the Horse's mouth.

But the voice cannot be altogether suppressed so long as the mistake is made of leaving any breath in the body. Therefore, a spasmodic sound of moaning came from his throat now and then.

One day this noise reached Brahma's ears.

The Creator woke up from his meditation. It gave him a start when he glanced at the meadow and saw no sign of the Horse.

"This is all your doing," cried Brahma, in anger to Yama, the god of death, "You have taken away the Horse !" "Lord of all creatures!" Death replied, "All your worst suspicions you keep only for me. But most of the calamities in your beautiful world will be explained if you turn your eyes in the direction of Man."

Brahma looked below. He saw a small enclosure, walled in, from which the dolorous moaning of his Horse came fitfully.

Brahma frowned in anger.

"Unless you set free my Horse," said he, "I shall take care that he grows teeth and claws like the Tiger."

"That would be ungodly," cried man, "to encourage ferocity. All the same, if I may speak plain truth about a creature of your own make, this Horse is not fit to be set free. It was for his eternal good that I built him this stable – this marvel of architecture."

Brahma remained obdurate.

"I bow to your wisdom," said Man, "but if, after seven days, you still think that your meadow is better for him than my stable, I will humbly own defeat."

After this Man set to work.

He made the Horse go free, but hobbled his front legs. The result was so vastly diverting that it was enough to make even a frog burst his sides with laughter.

Brahma, from the height of his heaven, could see the comic gait of his Horse, but not the tragic rope which hobbled him. He was mortified to find his own creature openly exposing its divine maker to ridicule.

"It was an absurd blunder of mine", he cried, "closely touching the sublime."

"Grandsire," said Man with a pathetic show of sympathy, "what can I do for this unfortunate creature? If there is a meadow in your heaven, I am willing to take trouble to transport him thither."

"Take him back to your stable!" cried Brahma in dismay.

"Merciful God!" cried Man, "what a great burden it will be for mankind!"

"It is the burden of humanity," muttered Brahma.

34

THE OLD MAN'S GHOST

At the time of the Old Man Leader's death, the entire population wailed, "What will be our lot when you go?" Hearing this, the Old Man himself felt sad. "Who indeed," thought he, "will keep these people quiescent when I have gone?"

Death cannot be evaded, however. Yet the gods took pity and said, "Why worry? Let this fellow go on sitting on their shoulders even as a ghost. Man dies but a ghost does not."

The people of the country were greatly relieved.

For, worries come if only you believe in a future. Believing in ghosts you are freed from burden, all the worries enter the ghost's head. Yet the ghost has no head, so it does not suffer from headaches either, not for anybody's sake.

Those, who out of sheer wrong habit still attempt to think for themselves, get their ears boxed by the ghost. From this ghostly boxing you can neither free yourself nor can you escape it; against it is neither appeal nor any judgement at all.

The entire population, ghost-ridden, now walks with eyes shut. "The most ancient form of movement, this, with eyes shut," the philosophers assure them, "moving like blind fate, we call it.

Thus, moved the first eyeless amoeba. In the grass, in the trees, this habit of movement is still customary."

Hearing which, the ghost-ridden land feels its own primitive aristocracy. And it is greatly delighted.

The ghost's nayeb is the inspector of the prison. The walls of the prison-house are not visible to the eye. And so it is impossible to imagine how to pierce those walls and get free.

In the prison-house one has to slave at turning the oil-press night and day but not even an ounce of oil is produced which is marketable; only the energy of men goes out in extracting the oil. When their energy goes out, men become exceedingly peaceful. And thus, in that ghost's realm whatever else there might not be – food, or clothing or health – tranquillity remains.

How great is the tranquillity is proved by one example, in other lands excessive ghostly tyranny makes men restless and seek for a medicine-man. Here such a thought cannot arise. For the medicine-man himself has already been possessed by the ghost.

Thus, the days would have passed; nobody would have questioned the ghostly administration. Forever they could have taken pride that their future, like a pet lamb, was tied to the ghost's peg; such a creature neither bleated nor baa'd, it sprawled dumb on the dust, useless as dust.

Only, for a slight reason, some little trouble arose. It was that the other countries of the world were not ghost-ridden. Their oil-presses turned so that the extracted oil might be used for keeping the wheels of men's chariots moving forward, not for crushing the heart and pouring heart's blood into the paws of the ghost. So, men there have not yet been completely pacified. They were terribly wakeful.

All over the ghostly empire, *the baby sleeps; quiet is the neighbourhood.*

That is comforting for the baby, and for the baby's guardian too; as to the neighbourhood, we have already seen how it is.

But there is the other line, "the invaders enter the land." Thus, the rhythm is completed – otherwise for lack of one foot, this history would have been crippled.

The pedants and pundits are asked, "Why is it thus?" They toss their heads together and say, "Not the ghost's fault this, nor of the ghost-ridden land, the fault lies with the invader. Why does the invader come?"

"How right!" they all admit. And everyone feels exceedingly comforted.

Whosoever the fault might be, near the back-door of the house loiter the ghost's emissaries, and in the open street outside everywhere roam the non-ghost's emissaries; the householder can hardly stay in his house, to stir out of doors is also impossible. From one side they shout, "Pay the taxes?" and from the other also they shout, "Pay the taxes!"

Now the problem is, "How to pay the taxes?"

Up to now, from north, south, east and west, bulbulis of all species have come in large flocks, and gorged themselves with the corn, nobody was mindful. With all those who are mindful, these people avoid contact, lest they have to do prayashchitta for contamination. But those other folk who are mindful have a way of coming suddenly very near to them indeed and they do not observe any penance either.

The pedants and pundits open the text and say, "Pure are the unmindful, and impure the mindful ones; so be indifferent to these latter. Remember the sacred words, 'awake are those who sleepeth.'"

And hearing this the people are hugely delighted.

But, in spite of this, the query cannot be stopped, "How to pay the taxes?"

From the burning-ground, from the burial-ground the wild winds bring the loud answer, "Pay the taxes with the price of your modesty, with your honour, with your conscience, with your heart's blood."

The trouble with questions is, when they come they do not come singly. So, another question has arisen, "Will the ghostly reign itself remain for ever?"

Hearing this, all the lullaby-singing aunts and uncles put their hands on their ears in horror and exclaim, "Perdition! Never in our fathers' life have we heard of such a thing! What will then, have happened to our sleep, the most ancient sleep, the sleep which is earlier than all awakening?"

"That I see," the questioner persists, "but these most modern flocks of bulbulis and these very much present invaders – what about them?"

"To the bulbulis we shall repeat the name of Krishna," assert the aunts and uncles, "and so shall we do to the invaders."

The ignorant youths get impertinent and bluster out; "Drive the ghost out we shall – whatever the means."

The ghost's nayeb rolls his eyes in anger and shouts, "Shut up! The oil-press hasn't stopped grinding. No, not yet." Hearing which the baby of the land falls silent, and then, turns to sleep.

The great fact is, the Old Man is neither alive nor dead, but is a ghost. He neither stirs the country up nor ever relaxes his grip.

Inside the country, one or two men – those who never utter a word in daytime for fear of the nayeb – join their palms together and implore, "Old Man Leader, is it not yet time for you to leave us?"

"You fool," answers the Old Man, "I neither hold, nor let go; if you leave, then, I have also left."

"But we are afraid, Old Man Leader!"

"That is where the ghost enters," – comes the answer.

35

The Great News

Said Kusmi "You would give me all the big news – so you promised, didn't you, Dada Mashai, how else could I get educated?"

Answered Dada Mashai, "But such a sack of big news there would be to carry – with so much of rubbish in it."

"Why not leave those out?"

"Little else would remain, then. And that remainder you will think as small, news. But that would be the real news."

"Give it to me – the real news."

"So I will."

"Well, Dada Mashai let me see what skill you have. Tell me the great news of these days, making it ever so small."

"Listen."

Work was proceeding in peace.

In a mahajani boat there started a row between the sail and the oars.

The oars came clattering to the court of the Boatman, and said, "This cannot be endured any longer. That braggart sail of yours, swelling himself, calls us chhoto lok. Because we, tied night and day to the lower planks, must toil, pushing the waters as we proceed, while he moves by whim, not caring for the push of any one's hand. And so he is a boro lok. You must decide who is more worthy. If we are chhoto lok the inferior ones, we shall resign in a body. Let us see how you make your boat move."

The Boatman, seeing danger ahead, called the oars aside and whispered secretly, "Do not give ear to his words, brothers. He speaks an empty language, that sail. If you strong fellows did not work away, staking life and death, the boat would lie inert altogether. And that sail – he sits there in hallow luxury, perched on the top. At the slightest touch of stormy wind he flops, folds himself up, and lies low on the boat's thatch. Then, all his vain flutterings are silenced, not a word from him at all. But in weal and woe, in danger and in crisis, on the way to the market and the ghat, you are my constant support. It is a pity that you have to carry that useless burden of luxury, to and fro. Who says you are chhoto lok?"

But the Boatman was afraid, lest these words be overheard by the sail. So he came to him and whispered into his ear, "Mr. Sail, none ever can be compared with you. Who says that you drive the boat, that is the work of labourers. You move at your own pleasure, and your pals and comrades follow you at your slightest gesture and bidding. And whenever you feel out of breath, you would flop down easefully, and rest. Do not lend your ear, friend, to the parleying of those low-bred oars; so firmly have I tied them up, that splutter as they might, they cannot but work as slaves."

Hearing this, the sail stretched himself, and yawned mightily.

But the signs were not good. Those oars are hard-boned fellows, now they lie aslant but who knows when they will stand up straight, slap at the sail and shatter his pride into shreds. Then, the world would know that it is the oars who make the boat move, come storm come tornado, whether it be upstream or at ebb-tide.

Queried Kusmi, "Your big news, is it so small as this? You are joking."

Said Dada Mashai, "Joking it seems to be. Very soon this news will become big indeed."

"And then?"

"Then, your Dada Mashai will practise keeping time with the strokes of those oars."

"And I?"

"Where the oars creak too muck, you will pour a drop of oil."

Dada Mashai continued, "True news appears small, like the seeds. And then, comes the tree with its branches and foliage. Do you understand now?"

"So I do," said Kusmi. Her face showed that she had not understood. But Kusmi had one virtue, she would not easily admit it to her Dada Mashai that she would not understand. That she is less clever than Iru Mashi is better kept concealed.

36

The Supreme Night

I used to go to the same dame's school with Surabala and play at marriage with her. When I paid visits to her house, her mother would pet me, and setting us side by side would say to herself, "What a lovely pair!"

I was a child then, but I could understand her meaning well enough. The idea became rooted in my mind that I had a special right to Surabala above that of people in general. So it happened that, in the pride of ownership, at times I punished and tormented her; and she, too, fagged for me and bore all my punishments without complaint. The village was wont to praise her beauty; but in the eyes of a young barbarian like me that beauty had no glory – I knew only that Surabala had been born in her father's house solely to beat my yoke, and that therefore, she was the particular object of my neglect.

My father was the land-steward of the Chaudhuris, a family of zamindars. It was his plan, as soon as I had learnt to write a good hand, to train me in the work of estate management and secure a rent collectorship for me somewhere. But in my heart I disliked the proposal. Nilratan of our village had run away to Calcutta, had learnt English there, and finally became the Nazir of the District Magistrate; that was my life's ideal, I was secretly determined to be the Head Clerk of the Judge's Court, even if I could not become the Magistrate's Nazir.

I saw that my father always treated these court officers with the greatest respect. I knew from my childhood that they had to be propitiated with gifts of fish, vegetables, and even money. For this reason I had given a seat of high honour in my heart to the court underlings, even to the bailiffs. These are the gods worshipped in our Bengal – a modern miniature edition of the 330 millions of deities of the Hindu pantheon. For gaining material success, people have more genuine faith in them than in the good Ganesh, the giver of success; hence the people now offer to these officers everything that was formerly Ganesh's due.

Fired by the example of Nilratan, I too seized a suitable opportunity and ran away to Calcutta. There I first put up at the house of a village acquaintance, and afterwards got some funds from my father for my education. Thus, I carried on my studies regularly.

In addition, I joined political and benevolent societies. I had no doubt whatever that it was urgently necessary for me to give my life suddenly for my country. But I knew not how such a hard task could be carried out. Also, no one showed me the way.

But, nevertheless, my enthusiasm did not abate at all. We country lads had not learnt to sneer at everything like the precocious boys of Calcutta, and hence our faith was very strong. The "leaders" of our associations delivered speeches, and we went begging for subscriptions from door to door in the hot blaze of noon without breaking our fast; or we stood by the roadside distributing hand-bills, or arranged the chairs and benches in the lecture-hall, and, if anybody whispered a word against our leader, we got ready to fight him. For these things the city boys used to laugh at us as provincials.

I had come to Calcutta to be a Nazir or a Head Clerk, but I was preparing to become a Mazzini or a Garibaldi.

At this time Surabala's father and my father laid their heads together to unite us in marriage. I had come to Calcutta at the age of fifteen; Surabala was eight years old then. I was now eighteen, and in my father's opinion I was almost past the age of marriage. But it was my secret vow to remain unmarried all my life and to die for my country; so I told my father I would not marry before I had finished my education.

In two or three months I learnt that Surabala had been married to a pleader named Ram Lochan. I was then, busy collecting subscriptions for raising fallen India, and this news did not seem worth my thought.

I had matriculated, and was about to appear at the Intermediate Examination, when my father died. I was not alone in the world, but had to maintain my mother and two sisters. I had, therefore, to leave college and look out for employment. After a good deal of exertion I secured the post of second master in the matriculation school of a small town in the Noakhali District.

I thought, here is just the work for me! By my advice and inspiration I shall train up everyone of my pupils as a general for future India.

I began to work, and then, found that the impending examination was a more pressing affair than the future of India. The headmaster got angry whenever I talked of anything outside grammar or algebra. And in a few months my enthusiasm, too, flagged.

I am no genius. In the quiet of the home I may form vast plans; but when I enter the field of work, I have to bear the yoke of the plough on my neck like the Indian bullock, get my tail twisted by my master, break clods all day, patiently and with bowed head, and then, at sunset have to be satisfied if I can get any cud to chew. Such a creature has not the spirit to prance and caper.

One of the teachers lived in the school-house, to guard against fires. As I was a bachelor, this work was thrown on me. I lodged in a thatched shed close to the large cottage in which the school sat.

The school-house stood at some distance from the inhabited portion of the town, and beside a big tank. Around it were betel-nut, cocoa-nut, and madar trees, and very near to the school building two large ancient neem trees grew close together, and cast a cool shade around.

One thing I have forgotten to mention, and indeed I had not so long considered it worth mentioning. The local Government pleader, Ram Lochan Ray, lived near our school. I also knew that his wife – my early playmate, Surabala – lived with him.

I got acquainted with Ram Lochan Babu. I cannot say whether he knew that I had known Surabala in childhood. I did not think fit to mention the fact at my first introduction to him. Indeed, I did not clearly remember that Surabala had been ever linked with my life in any way.

One holiday I paid a visit to Ram Lochan Babu. The subject of our conversation has gone out of my mind; probably it was the unhappy condition of present-day India. Not that he was very much concerned or heart-broken over the matter; but the subject was such that one could freely pour forth one's sentimental sorrow over it for an hour or two while pulling at one's hookah.

While thus, engaged, I heard in a side-room the softest possible jingle of bracelets, crackle of dress, and footfall; and I felt certain that two curious eyes were watching me through a small opening of the window.

All at once there flashed upon my memory a pair of eyes, – a pair of large eyes, beaming with trust, simplicity, and girlhood's love – black pupils – thick dark eyelashes – a calm fixed gaze. Suddenly, some unseen force squeezed my heart in an iron grip, and it throbbed with intense pain.

I returned to my house, but the pain clung to me. Whether I read, wrote, or did any other work, I could not shake that weight off my heart; a heavy load seemed to be always swinging from my heart-strings.

In the evening, calming myself a little, I began to reflect, "What ails me?" From within came the question, "Where is your Surabala now?" I replied, "I gave her up of my free will. Surely, I did not expect her to wait for me for ever."

But something kept saying, "Then, you could have gotten her merely for the asking. Now you have not the right to look at her even once, do what you will. That Surabala of your boyhood may come very close to you; you may hear the jingle of her bracelets;

you may breathe the air embalmed by the essence of her hair, – but there will always be a wall between you two."

I answered, "Be it so. What is Surabala to me?"

My heart rejoined, "Today, Surabala is nobody to you. But what might she not have been to you?"

Ah! That's true. What might she not have been to me? Dearest to me of all things, closer to me than the world besides, the sharer of all my life's joys and sorrows, – she might have been. And now, she is so distant, so much of a stranger, that to look on her is forbidden, to talk with her is improper, and to think of her is a sin! – While this Ram Lochan, coming suddenly from nowhere, has muttered a few set religious texts, and in one swoop has carried off Surabala from the rest of mankind!

I have not come to preach a new ethical code, or to revolutionise society; I have no wish to tear asunder domestic ties. I am only expressing the exact working of my mind, though it may not be reasonable. I could not by any means banish from my mind the sense that Surabala, reigning there within shelter of Ram Lochan's home, was mine far more than his. The thought was, I admit, unreasonable and improper – but it was not unnatural.

Thereafter I could not set my mind to any kind of work. At noon when the boys in my class hummed, when Nature outside simmered in the sun, when the sweet scent of the neem blossoms entered the room on the tepid breeze, I then wished – I know not what I wished for; but this I can say, that I did not wish to pass all my life in correcting the grammar exercises of those future hopes of India.

When school was over, I could not bear to live in my large lonely house; and yet, if any one paid me a visit, it bored me. In the gloaming as I sat by the tank and listened to the meaningless breeze sighing through the betel-and cocoa-nut palms, I used to muse that human society is a web of mistakes; nobody has the sense to do the right thing at the right time, and when the chance is gone we break our hearts over vain longings.

I could have married Surabala and lived happily. But I must be a Garibaldi – and I ended by becoming the second master of a village school! And pleader Ram Lochan Ray, who had no special call to be Surabala's husband – to whom, before his marriage, Surabala was no wise different from a hundred other maidens – has very quietly married her, and is earning lots of money as Government pleader; when his dinner is badly cooked he scolds Surabala, and when he is in good humour he gives her a bangle! He is sleek and fat, tidily dressed, free from every kind of worry; he never passes his evenings by the tank gazing at the stars and sighing.

Ram Lochan was called away from our town for a few days by a big case elsewhere. Surabala in her house was as lonely as I was in my school building.

I remember it was a Monday. The sky was overcast with clouds from the morning. It began to drizzle at ten o'clock. At the aspect of the heavens our headmaster closed the school early. All day the black detached clouds began to run about in the sky as if making ready for some grand display. Next day, towards afternoon, the rain descended in torrents, accompanied by storm. As the night advanced the fury of the wind and water increased. At first the wind was easterly; gradually it veered, and blew towards the south and south-west.

It was idle to try to sleep on such a night. I remembered that in this terrible weather Surabala was alone in her house. Our school was much more strongly built than her bungalow. Often and often did I plan to invite her to the school-house, while I meant to pass the night alone by the tank. But I could not summon up courage for it.

When it was half-past one in the morning, the roar of the tidal wave was suddenly heard, – the sea was rushing on us! I left my room and ran towards Surabala's house. In the way stood one embankment of our tank, and as I was wading to it the flood already reached my knees. When I mounted the bank, a second wave broke on it. The highest part of the bank was more than seventeen feet above the plain.

As I climbed up the bank, another person reached it from the opposite side. Who she was, every fibre of my body knew at once, and my whole soul was thrilled with the consciousness. I had no doubt that she, too, had recognised me.

On an island some three yards in area stood we two; all else was covered with water.

It was a time of cataclysm; the stars had been blotted out of the sky; all the lights of the earth had been darkened; there would have been no harm if we held converse then. But we could not bring ourselves to utter a word; neither of us made even a formal inquiry after the other's health. Only we stood gazing at the darkness. At our feet swirled the dense, black, wild, roaring torrent of death.

Today, Surabala has come to my side, leaving the whole world. Today, she has none besides me. In our far-off childhood this Surabala had come from some dark primeval realm of mystery, from a life in another orb, and stood by my side on this luminous peopled earth; and today, after a wide span of time, she has left the earth, so full of light and human beings, to stand alone by my side amidst this terrible desolate gloom of Nature's death-convulsion. The stream of birth had flung the tender bud before me, and the flood of death had wafted the same flower, now in full bloom, to me and to none else. One more wave and we shall be swept away from this extreme point of the earth, torn from the stalks on which we now sit apart, and made one in death.

May that wave never come! May Surabala live long and happily, girt round by husband and children, household and kinsfolk! This one night, standing on the brink of Nature's destruction, I have tasted eternal bliss.

The night wore out, the tempest ceased, the flood abated; without a word spoken, Surabala went back to her house, and I, too, returned to my shed without having uttered a word.

I reflected, true, I have become no Nazir or Head Clerk, nor a Garibaldi; I am only the second master of a beggarly school. But one night had for its brief space beamed upon my whole life's course.

That one night, out of all the days and nights of my allotted span, has been the supreme glory of my humble existence.

37

In the Night

"Doctor, Doctor!"

I was startled out of my sleep in the very depth of night. On opening my eyes I saw it was our landlord Dokhin Babu. Hurriedly getting up and drawing out a broken chair, I made him sit down, and looked anxiously in his face. I saw by the clock that it was after half-past two.

Dokhin Babu's face was pale, and his eyes wide open, as he said, "To-night those symptoms returned – that medicine of yours has done me no good at all." I said rather timidly, "I am afraid you have been drinking again." Dokhin Babu got quite angry, and said, "There you make a great mistake. It is not the drink. You must hear the whole story in order to be able to understand the real reason."

In the niche there was a small tin kerosene lamp burning dimly. This I turned up slightly; the light became a little brighter, and at the same time it began to smoke. Pulling my cloth over my shoulders, I spread a piece of newspaper over a packing-case, and sat down. Dokhin Babu began his story,

"About four years ago I was attacked by a serious illness; just when I was on the point of death my disease took a better turn, until, after nearly a month, I recovered.

"During my illness my wife did not rest for a moment, day or night. For those months that weak woman fought with all her might to drive Death's messenger from the door. She went without food and sleep, and had no thought for anything else in this world.

"Death, like a tiger cheated of its prey, threw me from its jaws, and went off, but in its retreat it dealt my wife a sharp blow with its paw.

"Not long after my wife gave birth to a dead child. Then, came my turn to nurse her. But she got quite troubled at this, and would say, "For heaven's sake, don't keep fussing in and out of my room like that."

"If I went to her room at night when she had fever, and, on the pretence of fanning myself, would try to fan her, she would get quite excited. And if, on account of serving her, my meal-time was ten minutes later than usual, that also was made the occasion for all sorts of entreaties and reproaches. If I went to do her the smallest service, instead of helping her it had just the opposite effect. She would exclaim, "It's not good for a man to fuss so much."

"I think you have seen my garden-house. In front of it is the garden, at the foot of which the river Ganges flows. Towards the south, just below our bedroom, my wife had made a garden according to her own fancy, and surrounded it with a hedge of henna. It was the one bit of the garden that was simple and unpretentious. In the flower-pots you did not see wooden pegs with long Latin names flying pretentious flags by the side of the most unpretentious-looking plants. Jasmine, tuberose, lemon flowers, and all kinds of roses were plentiful. Under a large bokul tree there was a white marble slab, which my wife used to wash twice a day when she was in good health. It was the place where she was in the habit of sitting on summer evenings, when her work was finished. From there she could see the river, but was herself invisible to the travellers on the passing steamers.

"One moonlight evening in the month of April, after having been confined to her bed for many days, she expressed a desire to get out of her close room, and sit in her garden.

"I lifted her with great care, and laid her down on that marble seat under the bokul tree. One or two bokul flowers fluttered down, and through the branches overhead the chequered moonlight fell on her worn face. All around was still and silent. As I looked down on her face, sitting by her side in that shadowy darkness, filled with the heavy scent of flowers, my eyes became moist.

"Slowly drawing near her, I took one of her hot thin hands between my own. She made no attempt to prevent me. After I had sat like this in silence for some time, my heart began to overflow, and I said, "Never shall I be able to forget your love."

"My wife gave a laugh in which there were mingled some happiness, a trace of distrust, and also the sharpness of sarcasm. She said nothing in the way of an answer, and yet gave me to understand by her laugh that she thought it unlikely that I would never forget her, nor did she herself wish it.

"I had never had the courage to make love to my wife simply out of fear of this sweet sharp laugh of hers. All the speeches which I made up when I was absent from her seemed to be very commonplace as soon as I found myself in her presence.

"It is possible to talk when you are contradicted, but laughter cannot be met by argument; so I had simply to remain silent. The moonlight became brighter, and a cuckoo began to call over and over again till it seemed to be demented. As I sat still, I wondered how on such a night the cuckoo's bride could remain indifferent.

"After a great deal of treatment, my wife's illness showed no signs of improvement. The doctor suggested a change of air, and I took her to Allahabad."

At this point Dokhin Babu suddenly stopped, and sat silent. With a questioning look on his face he looked towards me, and Then, began to brood with his head resting in his hands. I too kept silence. The kerosene lamp flickered in the niche, and in the stillness of the night the buzzing of the mosquitoes could be heard distinctly. Suddenly breaking the silence, Dokhin Babu resumed his story,

"Doctor Haran treated my wife, and after some time I was told that the disease was an incurable one, and my wife would have to suffer for the rest of her life.

"Then, one day my wife said to me, "Since my disease is not going to leave me, and there does not seem much hope of my dying soon, why should you spend your days with this living death? Leave me alone, and go back to your other occupations."

"Now it was my turn to laugh. But I had not got her power of laughter. So, with all the solemnity suitable to the hero of a romance, I asserted, "So long as there is life in this body of mine – "

"She stopped me, saying, "Now, now. You don't need to say any more. Why, to hear you makes me want to give up the ghost."

"I don't know whether I had actually confessed it to myself then, but now I know quite well that I had, even at that time, in my heart of hearts, got tired of nursing the hopeless invalid.

"It was clear that she was able to detect my inner weariness of spirit, in spite of my devoted service. I did not understand it then, but now I have not the least doubt in my mind that she could read me as easily as a Children's First Reader in which there are no compound letters.

"Doctor Haran was of the same caste as myself. I had a standing invitation to his house. After I had been there several times he introduced me to his daughter. She was unmarried, although she was over fifteen years old. Her father said that he had not married her as he had not been able to find a suitable bridegroom of the same caste, but rumour said that there was some bar sinister in her birth.

"But she had no other fault, for she was as intelligent as she was beautiful. For that reason I used sometimes to discuss with her all sorts of questions, so that it was often late at night before I got back home, long past the time when I should have given my wife her medicine. She knew quite well that I had been at Doctor Haran's house, but she never once asked me the cause of my delay.

"The sick-room seemed to me doubly intolerable and joyless. I now began to neglect my patient, and constantly forgot to give her the medicine at the proper time.

"The doctor used sometimes to say to me, "For those who suffer from some incurable disease death would be a happy release. As long as they remain alive they get no happiness themselves, and make others miserable."

"To say this in the ordinary course might be tolerated, but, with the example of my wife before us, such a subject ought not to have been mentioned. But I suppose doctors grow callous about the question of life and death of men.

"Suddenly one day, as I was sitting in the room next to the sick chamber, I heard my wife say to the doctor, "Doctor, why do you go on giving me so many useless medicines? When my whole life has become one continuous disease, don't you think that to kill me is to cure me?"

"The doctor said, "You shouldn't talk like that."

"As soon as the doctor had gone, I went into my wife's room, and seating myself beside her began to stroke her forehead gently. She said, "This room is very hot, you go out for your usual walk. If you don't get your evening exercise, you will have no appetite for your dinner."

"My evening walk meant going to Doctor Haran's house. I had myself explained that a little exercise is necessary for one's health and appetite. Now I am quite sure that every day she saw through my excuse. I was the fool, and I actually thought that she was unconscious of this deception."

Here Dokhin Babu paused and, burying his head in his hands, remained silent for a time. At last he said, "Give me a glass of water," and having drunk the water he continued,

"One day the doctor's daughter Monorama expressed a desire to see my wife. I don't quite know why, but this proposal did not altogether please me. But I could find no excuse for refusing her request. So she arrived one evening at our house.

"On that day my wife's pain had been rather more severe than usual. When her pain was worse she would lie quite still and silent, occasionally clenching her fists. It was only from that one was able to guess what agony she was enduring. There was no sound in the room, and I was sitting silently at the bedside. She had not requested me to go out for my usual walk. Either she had not the power to speak, or she got some relief from having me by her side when she was suffering very much. The kerosene lamp had been placed near the door lest it should hurt her eyes. The room was dark and still. The only sound that could be heard was an occasional sigh of relief when my wife's pain became less for a moment or two.

"It was at this time that Monorama came, and stood at the door. The light, coming from the opposite direction, fell on her face.

"My wife started up, and, grasping my hand, asked, "O ke?" ("O ke?" is the Bengali for 'Who is that?') In her feeble condition, she was so startled to see a stranger standing at the door that she asked two or three times in a hoarse whisper, "O ke? O ke? O ke?"

"At first I answered weakly, "I do not know"; but the next moment I felt as though some one had whipped me, and I hastily corrected myself and said, "Why, it's our doctor's daughter."

"My wife turned and looked at me. I was not able to look her in the face. Then, she turned to the new-comer, and said in a weak voice, "Come in," and turning to me added, "Bring the lamp."

"Monorama came into the room, and began to talk a little to my wife. While she was talking the doctor came to see his patient.

"He had brought with him from the dispensary two bottles of medicine. Taking these out he said to my wife, 'See, this blue bottle is for outward application, and the other is to be taken. Be careful not to mix the two, for this is a deadly poison.'

"Warning me also, he placed the two bottles on the table by the bedside. When he was going the doctor called his daughter.

"She said to him, 'Father, why should I not stay? There is no woman here to nurse her.'

"My wife got quite excited and sat up saying, 'No, no, don't you bother yourself. I have an old maidservant who takes care of me as if she were my mother.'

"Just as the doctor was going away with his daughter, my wife said to him, 'Doctor, he has been sitting too long in this close and stuffy room. Won't you take him out for some fresh air?'

"The doctor turned to me, and said, 'Come along, I'll take you for a stroll along the bank of the river.'

"After some little show of unwillingness I agreed. Before going the doctor again warned my wife about the two bottles of medicine.

"That evening I took my dinner at the doctor's house, and was late in coming home. On getting back I found that my wife was in extreme pain. Feeling deeply repentant, I asked her, "Has your pain increased?"

"She was too ill to answer, but only looked up in my face. I saw that she was breathing with difficulty.

"I at once sent for the doctor.

"At first he could not make out what was the matter. At last he asked, "Has that pain increased? Haven't you used that liniment?"

"Saying which, he picked up the blue bottle from the table. It was empty!

"Showing signs of agitation, he asked my wife, 'You haven't taken this medicine by mistake, have you?' Nodding her head, she silently indicated that she had.

"The doctor ran out of the house to bring his stomach pump, and I fell on the bed like one insensible.

"Then, just as a mother tries to pacify a sick child, my wife drew my head to her breast, and with the touch of her hands attempted to tell me her thoughts. Merely by that tender touch, she said to me again and again, 'Do not sorrow, all is for the best. You will be happy, and knowing that I die happily.'

"By the time the doctor returned, all my wife's pains had ceased with her life."

Dokhin Babu, taking another gulp of water, exclaimed, "Ugh, it's terribly hot," and then, going on to the veranda, he paced rapidly up and down two or three times. Coming back he sat down, and began again. It was clear enough that he did not want to tell me; but it seemed as if, by some sort of magic, I was dragging the story out of him. He went on,

"After my marriage with Monorama, whenever I tried to talk effusively to her, she looked grave. It seemed as if there was in her mind some hint of suspicion which I could not understand.

"It was at this time that I began to have a fondness for drink.

"One evening in the early autumn, I was strolling with Monorama in our garden by the river. The darkness had the feeling of a phantom world about it, and there was not even the occasional sound of the birds rustling their wings in their sleep. Only on both sides of the path along which we were walking the tops of the casuarina trees sighed in the breeze.

"Feeling tired, Monorama went and lay down on that marble slab, placing her hands behind her head, and I sat beside her.

"There the darkness seemed to be even denser, and the only patch of sky that could be seen was thick with stars. The chirping of the crickets under the trees was like a thin hem of sound at the lowest edge of the skirt of silence.

"That evening I had been drinking a little, and my heart was in a melting mood. When my eyes had got used to the darkness, the grey outline of the loosely clad and languid form of Monorama, lying in the shadow of the trees, awakened in my mind an undefinable longing. It seemed to me as if she were only an unsubstantial shadow which I could never grasp in my arms.

"Suddenly, the tops of the casuarina trees seemed to be on fire. I saw the jagged edge of the old moon, golden in her harvest hue, rise gradually above the tops of the trees. The moonlight fell on the face of the white-clad form lying on the white marble. I could contain myself no longer. Drawing near her and taking her hand in mine, I said, 'Monorama, you may not believe me, but never shall I be able to forget your love.'

"The moment the words were out of my mouth I started, for I remembered that I had used the very same to some one else long before. And at the same time, from over the top of the casuarina trees, from under the golden crescent of the old moon, from across the wide stretches of the flowing Ganges, right to its most distant bank – Ha ha – Ha ha – Ha ha – came the sound of laughter passing swiftly overhead. Whether it was a heart-breaking laugh or a sky-rending wail, I cannot say. But on hearing it I fell to the ground in a swoon.

"When I recovered consciousness, I saw that I was lying on my bed in my own room. My wife asked me, 'Whatever happened to you?' I replied, trembling with terror, 'Didn't you hear how the whole sky rang with the sound of laughter – Ha ha – Ha ha – Ha ha?' "My wife laughed, as she answered, 'Laughter? What

I heard was the sound of a flock of birds flying past overhead. You are easily frightened!'

"Next day I knew quite well that it was a flock of ducks migrating, as they do at that time of year, to the south. But when evening came I began to doubt again, and in my imagination the whole sky rang with laughter, piercing the darkness on the least pretext. It came to this at last that after dark I was not able to speak a word to Monorama.

"Then, I decided to leave my garden-house, and took Monorama for a trip on the river. In the keen November air all my fear left me, and for some days I was quite happy.

"Leaving the Ganges, and crossing the Khore River, we at last reached the Padma. This terrible river lay stretched out like a huge serpent taking its winter sleep. On its north side were the barren, solitary sand-banks, which lay blazing in the sun; and on the high banks of the south side the mango groves of the villages stood close to the open jaws of this demoniac river, which now and again turned in its sleep, whereupon the cracked earth of the banks fell with a thud into its waters.

"Finding a suitable place, I moored the boat to the bank.

"One day we went out for a walk, on and on, till we were far away from our boat. The golden light of the setting sun gradually faded, and the sky was flooded with the pure silver light of the moon. As the moonlight fell on that limitless expanse of white sand, and filled the vast sky with its flood of brilliance, I felt as if we two were all alone, wandering in an uninhabited, unbounded dreamland, and without purpose. Monorama was wearing a red shawl, which she pulled over her head, and wrapped round her shoulders, leaving only her face visible. When the silence became deeper, and there was nothing but a vastness of white solitude all around us, then, Monorama slowly put out her hand and took hold of mine. She seemed so close to me that I felt as if she had surrendered into my hands her body and mind, her life and youth. In my yearning and happy heart, I said to myself, 'Is there room enough anywhere else than under such a wide, open sky to contain the hearts of two human beings in love?' Then, I felt as if we had no home to return to, that we could go on wandering thus, hand in hand, free from all cares and obstacles, along a road which had no end, through the moonlit immensity.

"As we went on, we came at last to a place where I could see a pool of water surrounded by hillocks of sand.

"Through the heart of this still water a long beam of moonlight pierced, like a flashing sword. Arriving at the edge of the pool, we stood there in silence, and Monorama looked up into my face. Her shawl slipped from off her head, and I stooped down and kissed her.

"Just then, there came, from somewhere in the midst of that silent and solitary desert, a voice, saying three times in solemn tones, 'O ke? O ke? O ke?'

"I started back, and my wife also trembled. But the next moment both of us realised that the sound was neither human nor superhuman – it was the call of some water-fowl, startled from its sleep at the sound of strangers so late at night near its nest.

"Recovering from our fright, we returned as fast as we could to the boat. Being late, we went straight to bed, and Monorama was soon fast asleep.

"Then, in the darkness it seemed as if some one, standing by the side of the bed, was pointing a long, thin finger towards the sleeping Monorama, and with a hoarse whisper was asking me over and over again, 'O ke? O ke? O ke?'

"Hastily getting up, I seized a box of matches, and lighted the lamp. Just as I did so, the mosquito net began to flutter in the wind, and the boat began to rock. The blood in my veins curdled, and the sweat came in heavy drops as I heard an echoing laugh, "Ha ha, Ha ha, Ha ha," sound through the dark night. It travelled over the river, across the sand-banks on the other side, and after that it passed over all the sleeping country, the villages and the towns, as though for ever crossing the countries of this and other worlds. Fainter and fainter it grew, passing into limitless space, gradually becoming fine as the point of a needle. Never had I heard such a piercingly faint sound, never had I imagined such a ghost of a sound possible. It was as if within my skull there was the limitless sky of space, and no matter how far the sound travelled it could not get outside my brain.

"At last, when it was almost unbearable, I thought, unless I extinguished the light, I should not be able to sleep. No sooner had I put out the lamp than once more, close to my mosquito curtain, I heard in the darkness that hoarse voice saying, 'O ke? O ke? O ke?' My heart began to beat in unison with the words, and gradually began to repeat the question, 'O ke? O ke? O ke?' In the silence of the night, from the middle of the boat my round clock began to be eloquent, and, pointing its hour hand towards Monorama, ticked out the question, 'O ke? O ke? O ke?' As he spoke, Dokhin Babu became ghastly pale, and his voice seemed to be choking him. Touching him on the shoulder, I said, 'Take a little water.' At the same moment the kerosene lamp flickered and went out, and I saw that outside it was light. A crow cawed, and a yellow-hammer whistled. On the road in front of my house the creaking of a bullock-cart was heard.

"The expression on Dokhin Babu's face was altogether changed. There was no longer the least trace of fear. That he had told me so much under the intoxication of an imaginary fear, and deluded by the sorcery of night, seemed to make him very much ashamed, and even angry with me. Without any formality of farewell he jumped up, and shot out of the house.

Next night, when it was quite late, I was again wakened from my sleep by a voice calling, 'Doctor, Doctor.'"

38

Master Mashai

I

Adhar Babu lives upon the interest of the capital left him by his father. Only the brokers, negotiating loans, come to his drawing room and smoke the silver-chased hookah, and the clerks from the attorney's office discuss the terms of some mortgage or the amount of the stamp fees. He is so careful with his money that even the most dogged efforts of the boys from the local football club fail to make any impression on his pocket.

At the time this story opens a new guest came into his household. After a long period of despair, his wife, Nanibala, bore him a son.

The child resembled his mother, – large eyes, well-formed nose, and fair complexion. Ratikanta, Adharlal's protégé, gave verdict – "He is worthy of this noble house." They named him – Venugopal.

Never before had Adharlal's wife expressed any opinion differing from her husband's on household expenses. There had been a hot discussion now and then, about the propriety of some necessary item and up to this time she had merely acknowledged defeat with silent contempt. But now Adharlal could no longer maintain his supremacy. He had to give way little by little when things for his son were in question.

II

As Venugopal grew up, his father gradually became accustomed to spending money on him. He obtained an old teacher, who had a considerable repute for his learning and also for his success in dragging impassable boys through their examinations. But such a training does not lead to the cultivation of amiability. This man tried his best to win the boy's heart, but the little that was left in him of the natural milk of human kindness had turned sour, and the child repulsed his advances from the very beginning. The mother, in consequence, objected to him strongly, and complained that the very sight of him made her boy ill. So the teacher left.

Just then, Haralal made his appearance with a dirty dress and a torn pair of old canvas shoes. Haralal's mother, who was a widow, had kept him with great difficulty at a District school out of the scanty earnings which she made by cooking in strange houses and husking rice. He managed to pass the Matriculation and determined to go to College. As a result of his half-starved condition, his pinched face tapered to a point in an unnatural manner – like Cape Comorin in the map of India; and the only broad portion of it was his forehead, which resembled the ranges of the Himalayas.

The servant asked Haralal what he wanted, and he answered timidly that he wished to see the master.

The servant answered sharply, "You can't see him." Haralal was hesitating, at a loss what to do next, when Venugopal, who had finished his game in the garden, suddenly came to the door. The servant shouted at Haralal, "Get away." Quite unaccountably Venugopal grew excited and cried, "No, he shan't get away." And he dragged the stranger to his father.

Adharlal had just risen from his mid-day sleep and was sitting quietly on the upper verandah in his cane chair, rocking his legs. Ratikanta was enjoying his hookah, seated in a chair next to him. He asked Haralal how far he had got in his reading. The young man bent his head and answered that he had passed the Matriculation. Ratikanta looked stern and expressed surprise that he should be so backward for his age. Haralal kept silence. It was Ratikanta's special pleasure to torture his patron's dependants, whether actual or potential.

Suddenly it struck Adharlal that he would be able to employ this youth as a tutor for his son on next to nothing. He agreed, there and then, to take him at a salary of five rupees a month with board and lodging free.

III

This time the post of tutor remained occupied longer than before. From the very beginning of their acquaintance Haralal and his pupil became great friends. Never before did Haralal have such an opportunity of loving any young human creature. His mother had been so poor and dependent, that he had never had the privilege of playing with the children where she was employed at work. He had not hitherto suspected the hidden stores of love which lay all the while accumulating in his own heart.

Venu, also, was glad to find a companion in Haralal. He was the only boy in the house. His two younger sisters were looked down upon, as unworthy of being his playmates. So his new tutor became his only companion, patiently bearing the undivided weight of the tyranny of his child friend.

IV

Venu was now eleven. Haralal had passed his Intermediate, winning a scholarship. He was working hard for his B.A. degree. After College lectures were over, he would take Venu out into the public park and tell him stories about the heroes from Greek History and Victor Hugo's romances. The child used to get quite impatient to run to Haralal, after school hours, in spite of his mother's attempts to keep him by her side.

This displeased Nanibala. She thought that it was a deep-laid plot of Haralal's to captivate her boy, in order to prolong his own appointment. One day, she talked to him from behind the purdah, "It is your duty to teach my son only for an hour or two in the morning and evening. But why are you always with him? The child has nearly forgotten his own parents. You must understand that a man of your position is no fit companion for a boy belonging to this house."

Haralal's voice choked a little as he answered that for the future he would merely be Venu's teacher and would keep away from him at other times.

It was Haralal's usual practice to begin his college study early before dawn. The child would come to him directly after he had washed himself. There was a small pool in the garden and they used to feed the fish in it with puffed rice. Venu was also engaged in building a miniature garden-house, at the corner of the garden, with its Lilliputian gates and hedges and gravel paths. When the sun became too hot they would go back into the house, and Venu would have his morning lesson from Haralal.

On the day in question Venu had risen earlier than usual, because he wished to hear the end of the story which Haralal had begun the evening before. But he found his teacher absent. When asked about him, the door-servant said that he had gone out. At lesson time Venu remained unnaturally quiet. He never even asked Haralal why he had gone out, but went on mechanically with his lessons. When the child was with his mother taking his breakfast, she asked him what had happened to make him so gloomy, and why he was not eating his food. Venu gave no answer. After his meal his mother caressed him and questioned him repeatedly. Venu burst out crying and said – "Master Mashai." His mother asked Venu – "What about Master Mashai?" But Venu found it difficult to name the offence which his teacher had committed.

His mother said to Venu, "Has your Master Mashai been saying anything to you against me?" Venu could not understand the question and went away.

V

There was a theft in Adhar Babu's house. The police were called in to investigate. Even Haralal's trunks were searched. Ratikanta said with meaning, "The man who steals anything, does not keep his thefts in his own box."

Adharlal called his son's tutor and said to him, "It will not be convenient for me to keep any of you in my own house. From today you will have to take up your quarters outside, only coming in to teach my son at the proper time."

Ratikanta said sagely, drawing at his hookah, "That is a good proposal – good for both parties."

Haralal did not utter a word, but he sent a letter saying that it would be no longer possible for him to remain as tutor to Venu.

When Venu came back from school, he found his tutor's room empty. Even that broken steel trunk of his was absent. The rope was stretched across the corner, but there were no clothes or towel hanging on it. Only on the table, which formerly was strewn with books and papers, stood a bowl containing some gold-fish with a label on which was written the word "Venu" in Haralal's handwriting. The boy ran up at once to his father and asked him what had happened. His father told him that Haralal had resigned his post. Venu went to his room and flung himself down and began to cry. Adharlal did not know what to do with him.

The next day, when Haralal was sitting on his wooden bedstead in the Hostel, debating with himself whether he should attend his college lectures, suddenly he saw Adhar Babu's servant coming into his room followed by Venu. Venu at once ran up to him and threw his arms round his neck asking him to come back to the house.

Haralal could not explain why it was absolutely impossible for him to go back, but the memory of those clinging arms and that pathetic request used to choke his breath with emotion long after.

VI

Haralal found out, after this, that his mind was in an unsettled state, and that he had but a small chance of winning the scholarship, even if he could pass the examination. At the same time, he knew that, without the scholarship, he could not continue his studies. So he tried to get employment in some office.

Fortunately for him, an English Manager of a big merchant firm took a fancy to him at first sight. After only a brief exchange of words the Manager asked him if he had any experience, and could he bring any testimonial. Haralal could only answer, "No"; nevertheless a post was offered him of twenty rupees a month and fifteen rupees were allowed him in advance to help him to come properly dressed to the office.

The Manager made Haralal work extremely hard. He had to stay on after office hours and sometimes go to his master's house late in the evening. But, in this way, he learnt his work quicker than others, and his fellow clerks became jealous of him and tried to injure him, but without effect. He rented a small house in a narrow lane and brought his mother to live with him as soon as his salary was raised to forty rupees a month. Thus, happiness came back to his mother after weary years of waiting.

Haralal's mother used to express a desire to see Venugopal, of whom she had heard so much. She wished to prepare some dishes with her own hand and to ask him to come just once to dine with her son. Haralal avoided the subject by saying that his house was not big enough to invite him for that purpose.

VII

The news reached Haralal that Venu's mother had died. He could not wait a moment, but went at once to Adharlal's house to see Venu. After that they began to see each other frequently.

But times had changed. Venu, stroking his budding moustache, had grown quite a young man of fashion. Friends, befitting his present condition, were numerous. That old dilapidated study chair and ink-stained desk had vanished, and the room now seemed to be bursting with pride at its new acquisitions, – its looking-glasses, oleographs, and other furniture. Venu had entered college, but showed no haste in crossing the boundary of the Intermediate examination.

Haralal remembered his mother's request to invite Venu to dinner. After great hesitation, he did so. Venugopal, with his handsome face, at once won the mother's heart. But as soon as ever the meal was over he became impatient to go, and looking at his gold watch he explained that he had pressing engagements elsewhere. Then, he jumped into his carriage, which was waiting at the door, and drove away. Haralal with a sigh said to himself that he would never invite him again.

VIII

One day, on returning from office, Haralal noticed the presence of a man in the dark room on the ground floor of his house. Possibly he would have passed him by, had not the heavy scent of some foreign perfume attracted his attention. Haralal asked who was there, and the answer came,

"It is I, Master Mashai."

"What is the matter, Venu?" said Haralal. "When did you arrive?"

"I came hours ago," said Venu. "I did not know that you returned so late."

They went upstairs together and Haralal lighted the lamp and asked Venu whether all was well. Venu replied that his college classes were becoming a fearful bore, and his father did not realise how dreadfully hard it was for him to go on in the same class, year after year, with students much younger than himself. Haralal asked him what he wished to do. Venu then, told him that he wanted to go to England and become a barrister. He gave an instance of a student, much less advanced than himself, who was getting ready to go. Haralal asked him if he had received his father's permission. Venu replied that his father would not hear a word of it until he had passed the Intermediate, and that was an impossibility in his present frame of mind. Haralal suggested that he himself should go and try to talk over his father.

"No," said Venu, "I can never allow that!"

Haralal asked Venu to stay for dinner and while they were waiting he gently placed his hand on Venu's shoulder and said,

"Venu, you should not quarrel with your father, or leave home."

Venu jumped up angrily and said that if he was not welcome, he could go elsewhere. Haralal caught him by the hand and implored him not to go away without taking his food. But Venu snatched away his hand and was just leaving the room when Haralal's mother brought the food in on a tray. On seeing Venu about to leave she pressed him to remain and he did so with bad grace.

While he was eating the sound of a carriage stopping at the door was heard. First, a servant entered the room with creaking shoes and then, Adhar Babu himself. Venu's face became pale. The mother left the room as soon as she saw strangers enter. Adhar Babu called out to Haralal in a voice thick with anger,

"Ratikanta gave me full warning, but I could not believe that you had such devilish cunning hidden in you. So, you think you're going to live upon Venu? This is sheer kidnapping, and I shall prosecute you in the Police Court."

Venu silently followed his father and went out of the house.

IX

The firm to which Haralal belonged began to buy up large quantities of rice and daal from the country districts. To pay for this, Haralal had to take the cash every Saturday morning by the early train and disburse it. There were special centres where the brokers and middlemen would come with their receipts and accounts for settlement. Some discussion had taken place in the office about Haralal being entrusted with this work, without any security, but the Manager undertook all the responsibility and said that a security was not needed. This special work used to go on from the middle of December to the middle of April. Haralal would get back from it very late at night.

One day, after his return, he was told by his mother that Venu had called and that she had persuaded him to take his dinner at their house. This happened more than once. The mother said that it was because Venu missed his own mother, and the tears came into her eyes as she spoke about it.

One day Venu waited for Haralal to return and had a long talk with him.

"Master Mashai!" he said. "Father has become so cantankerous of late that I cannot live with him any longer. And, besides, I know that he is getting ready to marry again. Ratikanta is seeking a suitable match, and they are always conspiring about it. There used to be a time when my father would get anxious, if I were absent from home even for a few hours. Now, if I am away for more than a week, he takes no notice, – indeed he is greatly relieved. If this marriage takes place, I feel that I cannot live in the house any longer. You must show me a way out of this. I want to become independent."

Haralal felt deeply pained, but he did not know how to help his former pupil. Venu said that he was determined to go to England and become a barrister. Somehow or other he must get the passage money out of his father, he could borrow it on a note of hand and his father would have to pay when the creditors filed a suit. With this borrowed money he would get away, and when he was in England his father was certain to remit his expenses.

"But who is there," Haralal asked, "who would advance you the money?"

"You!" said Venu.

"I!" exclaimed Haralal in amazement.

"Yes," said Venu, "I've seen the servant bringing heaps of money here in bags."

"The servant and the money belong to someone else."

Haralal explained why the money came to his house at night, like birds to their nest, to be scattered next morning.

"But can't the Manager advance the sum?" Venu asked.

"He may do so," said Haralal, "if your father stands security."

The discussion ended at this point.

X

One Friday night a carriage and pair stopped before Haralal's lodging house. When Venu was announced Haralal was counting money in his bedroom, seated on the floor. Venu entered the room dressed in a strange manner. He had discarded his Bengali dress and was wearing a Parsi coat and trousers and had a cap on his head. Rings were prominent on almost all the fingers of both hands, and a thick gold chain was hanging round his neck, there was a gold-watch in his pocket, and diamond studs could be seen peeping from his shirt sleeves. Haralal at once asked him what was the matter and why he was wearing that dress.

"My father's marriage," said Venu, "comes off tomorrow. He tried hard to keep it from me, but I found it out. I asked him to allow me to go to our garden-house at Barrackpur for a few days, and he was only too glad to get rid of me so easily. I am going there, and I wish to God I had never to come back."

Haralal looked pointedly at the rings on his fingers. Venu explained that they had belonged to his mother. Haralal then, asked him if he had already had his dinner. He answered, "Yes, haven't you had yours?"

"No," said Haralal, "I cannot leave this room until I have all the money safely locked up in this iron chest."

"Go and take your dinner," said Venu, "while I keep guard here, your mother will be waiting for you."

For a moment Haralal hesitated, and then, he went out and had his dinner. In a short time he came back with his mother and the three of them sat among the bags of money talking together. When it was about midnight, Venu took out his watch and looked at it and jumped up saying that he would miss his train. Then, he asked Haralal to keep all his rings and his watch and chain until he asked for them again. Haralal put them all together in a leather bag and laid it in the iron safe. Venu went out.

The canvas bags containing the currency notes had already been placed in the safe, only the loose coins remained to be counted over and put away with the rest.

XI

Haralal lay down on the floor of the same room, with the key under his pillow, and went to sleep. He dreamt that Venu's mother was loudly reproaching him from behind the curtain.

Her words were indistinct, but rays of different colours from the jewels on her body kept piercing the curtain like needles and violently vibrating. Haralal struggled to call Venu, but his voice seemed to forsake him. At last, with a noise, the curtain fell down. Haralal started up from his sleep and found darkness piled up round about him. A sudden gust of wind had flung open the window and put out the light. Haralal's whole body was wet with perspiration. He relighted the lamp and saw, by the clock, that it was four in the morning. There was no time to sleep again; for he had to get ready to start.

After Haralal had washed his face and hands his mother called from her own room – "Baba, why are you up so soon?"

It was the habit of Haralal to see his mother's face the first thing in the morning in order to bring a blessing upon the day. His mother said to him, "I was dreaming that you were going out to bring back a bride for yourself." Haralal went to his own bedroom and began to take out the bags containing the silver and the currency notes.

Suddenly his heart stopped beating. Three of the bags appeared to be empty. He knocked them against the iron safe, but this only proved his fear to be true. He opened them and shook them with all his might. Two letters from Venu dropped out from one of the bags. One was addressed to his father and one to Haralal.

Haralal tore open his own letter and began reading. The words seemed to run into one another. He trimmed the lamp, but felt as if he could not understand what he read. Yet the purport of the letter was clear. Venu had taken three thousand rupees, in currency notes, and had started for England. The steamer was to sail before day-break that very morning. The letter ended with the words, "I am explaining everything in a letter to my father. He will pay off the debt; and then, again, my mother's ornaments, which I have left in your care, will more than cover the amount I have taken."

Haralal locked up his room and hired a carriage and went with all haste to the jetty. But he did not know even the name of the steamer which Venu had taken. He ran the whole length of the wharves from Prinsep's Ghat to Metiaburuj. He found that two steamers had started on their voyage to England early that morning. It was impossible for him to know which of them carried Venu, or how to reach him.

When Haralal got home, the sun was strong and the whole of Calcutta was awake. Everything before his eyes seemed blurred. He felt as if he were pushing against a fearful obstacle which was bodiless and without pity. His mother came on the verandah to ask him anxiously where he had gone. With a dry laugh he said to her – "To bring home a bride for myself," and then, he fainted away.

On opening his eyes after a while, Haralal asked his mother to leave him. Entering his room he shut the door from the inside while his mother remained seated on the floor of the verandah in the fierce glare of the sun. She kept calling to him fitfully, almost mechanically – "Baba, Baba!"

The servant came from the Manager's office and knocked at the door, saying that they would miss the train if they did not start out at once. Haralal called from inside, "It will not be possible for me to start this morning."

"Then, where are we to go, Sir?"

"I will tell you later on."

The servant went downstairs with a gesture of impatience.

Suddenly, Haralal thought of the ornaments which Venu had left behind. Up till now he had completely forgotten about them, but with the thought came instant relief. He took the leather bag containing them, and also Venu's letter to his father, and left the house.

Before he reached Adharlal's house he could hear the bands playing for the wedding, yet on entering he could feel that there had been some disturbance. Haralal was told that there had been a theft the night before and one or two servants were suspected. Adhar Babu was sitting in the upper verandah flushed with anger and Ratikanta was smoking his hookah. Haralal said to Adhar Babu, "I have something private to tell you." Adharlal flared up, "I have no time now!" He was afraid that Haralal had come to borrow money or to ask his help. Ratikanta suggested that if there was any delicacy in making the request in his presence he would leave the place. Adharlal told him angrily to sit where he was. Then, Haralal handed over the bag which Venu had left behind. Adharlal asked what was inside it and Haralal opened it and gave the contents into his hands.

Then, Adhar Babu said with a sneer, "It's a paying business that you two have started – you and your former pupil! You were certain that the stolen property would be traced, and so you come along with it to me to claim a reward!"

Haralal presented the letter which Venu had written to his father. This only made Adharlal all the more furious.

"What's all this?" he shouted, "I'll call for the police! My son has not yet come of age – and you have smuggled him out of the country! I'll bet my soul you've lent him a few hundred rupees, and then, taken a note of hand for three thousand! But I am not going to be bound by this!"

"I never advanced him any money at all," said Haralal.

"Then, how did he find it?" said Adharlal, "Do you mean to tell me he broke open your safe and stole it?"

Haralal stood silent.

Ratikanta sarcastically remarked, "I don't believe this fellow ever set hands on as much as three thousand rupees in his life."

When Haralal left the house he seemed to have lost the power of dreading anything, or even of being anxious. His mind seemed to refuse to work. Directly he entered the lane he saw a carriage waiting before his own lodging. For a moment he felt certain that it was Venu's. It was impossible to believe that his calamity could be so hopelessly final.

Haralal went up quickly, but found an English assistant from the firm sitting inside the carriage. The man came out when he saw Haralal and took him by the hand and asked him, "Why didn't you go out by train this morning?" The servant had told the Manager his suspicions and he had sent this man to find out.

Haralal answered, "Notes to the amount of three thousand rupees are missing."

The man asked how that could have happened.

Haralal remained silent.

The man said to Haralal, "Let us go upstairs together and see where you keep your money." They went up to the room and counted the money and made a thorough search of the house.

When the mother saw this she could not contain herself any longer. She came out before the stranger and said, "Baba, what has happened?" He answered in broken Hindustani that some money had been stolen.

"Stolen!" the mother cried, "Why! How could it be stolen? Who could do such a dastardly thing?" Haralal said to her, "Mother, don't say a word."

The man collected the remainder of the money and told Haralal to come with him to the Manager. The mother barred the way and said,

"Sir, where are you taking my son? I have brought him up, starving and straining to do honest work. My son would never touch money belonging to others."

The Englishman, not knowing Bengali, said, "Achcha! Achcha!" Haralal told his mother not to be anxious; he would explain it all to the Manager and soon be back again. The mother entreated him, with a distressed voice,

"Baba, you haven't taken a morsel of food all morning." Haralal stepped into the carriage and drove away, and the mother sank to the ground in the anguish of her heart.

The Manager said to Haralal, "Tell me the truth. What did happen?"

Haralal said to him, "I haven't taken any money."

"I fully believe it," said the Manager, "but surely you know who has taken it."

Haralal looked on the ground and remained silent.

"Somebody," said the Manager, "must have taken it away with your connivance."

"Nobody," replied Haralal, "could take it away with my knowledge without taking first my life."

"Look here, Haralal," said the Manager, "I trusted you completely. I took no security. I employed you in a post of great responsibility. Everyone in the office was against me for doing so. The three thousand rupees is a small matter, but the shame of all this to me is a great matter. I will do one thing. I will give you the whole day to bring back this money. If you do so, I shall say nothing about it and I will keep you on in your post."

It was now eleven o'clock. Haralal with bent head went out of the office. The clerks began to discuss the affair with exultation.

"What can I do? What can I do?" Haralal repeated to himself, as he walked along like one dazed, the sun's heat pouring down upon him. At last his mind ceased to think at all about what could be done, but the mechanical walk went on without ceasing.

This city of Calcutta, which offered its shelter to thousands and thousands of men had become like a steel trap. He could see no way out. The whole body of people were conspiring to surround and hold him captive – this most insignificant of men, whom no one knew. Nobody had any special grudge against him, yet everybody was his enemy. The crowd passed by, brushing against him, the clerks of the offices were eating their lunch on the road side from their plates made of leaves, a tired wayfarer on the Maidan, under the shade of a tree, was lying with one hand beneath his head and one leg upraised over the other, The up-country women, crowded into hackney carriages, were wending their way to the temple, a chaprassi came up with a letter and asked him the address on the envelope – so the afternoon went by.

Then, came the time when the offices were all about to close. Carriages started off in all directions, carrying people back to their homes. The clerks, packed tightly on the seats of the trams, looked at the theatre advertisements as they returned to their lodgings. From today, Haralal had neither his work in the office, nor release from work in the evening. He had no need to hurry to catch the tram to take him to his home. All the busy occupations of the city – the buildings – the horses and carriages – the incessant traffic – seemed, now at one time, to swell into dreadful reality, and at another time, to subside into the shadowy unreal.

Haralal had taken neither food, nor rest, nor shelter all that day.

The street lamps were lighted from one road to another and it seemed to him that a watchful darkness, like some demon, was keeping its eyes wide open to guard every movement of its victim. Haralal did not even have the energy to enquire how late it was. The veins on his forehead throbbed, and he felt as if his head would burst. Through the paroxysms of pain, which alternated with the apathy of dejection, only one thought came again and again to his mind; among the innumerable multitudes in that vast city, only one name found its way through his dry throat – Mother!

He said to himself, "At the deep of night, when no one is awake to capture me – me, who am the least of all men – I will silently creep to my mother's arms and fall asleep, and may I never wake again!"

Haralal's one trouble was lest some police officer should molest him in the presence of his mother, and this kept him back from going home. When it became impossible for him at last to bear the weight of his own body, he hailed a carriage. The driver asked him where he wanted to go. He said, "Nowhere, I want to drive across the Maidan to get the fresh air." The man at first did not believe him and was about to drive on, when Haralal put a rupee into his hand as an advance payment. Thereupon the driver crossed, and then, re-crossed, the Maidan from one side to the other, traversing the different roads.

Haralal laid his throbbing head on the side of the open window of the carriage and closed his eyes. Slowly all the pain abated. His body became cool. A deep and intense peace filled his heart and a supreme deliverance seemed to embrace him on every side. It was not true – the days despair which threatened him with its grip of utter helplessness. It was not true, it was false. He knew now that it was only an empty fear of the mind. Deliverance was in the infinite sky and there was no end to peace. No king or emperor in the world had the power to keep captive this nonentity, this Haralal. In the sky, surrounding his emancipated heart on every side, he felt the presence of his mother, that one poor woman. She seemed to grow and grow till she filled the infinity of darkness. All the roads and buildings and shops of Calcutta gradually became enveloped by her. In her presence vanished all the aching pains and thoughts and consciousness of Haralal. It burst – that bubble filled with the hot vapour of pain. And now there was neither darkness nor light, but only one tense fulness.

The Cathedral clock struck one. The driver called out impatiently, "Babu, my horse can't go on any longer. Where do you want to go?"

There came no answer.

The driver came down and shook Haralal and asked him again where he wanted to go.

There came no answer.

And the answer was never received from Haralal, where he wanted to go.

39

The Fugitive Gold

I

After his father's death, Baidyanath settled down on the proceeds of the Government stock which had been left to him. It never even occurred to him to look for work. His manner of spending time was to cut off branches of trees, and with minute care and skill he would polish them into walking-sticks. The boys and young men of the neighbourhood were candidates for these, and his supply of them never fell short of the demand.

By the blessing of the God of Fruition, Baidyanath had two boys and one daughter who had been given in marriage at the proper time.

But his wife Sundari bore a grievance against her lot, because there was not the same surplus in the resources of her husband as in those of their cousin across the road. The dispensation of Providence struck her as unnecessarily imperfect, when she could not show the same glitter of gold in her house, and tilt her nose as superciliously as her neighbour.

The condition of her own house gave her continual annoyance, where things were not only inconvenient but humiliating. Her bedstead, she was sure, was not decent enough to carry a corpse, and even an orphan bat who for seven generations had been without relatives would have scorned to accept an invitation within such dilapidated walls; while as for the furniture, why, it would have brought tears to the eyes of the most hardened of ascetics. It is impossible for a cowardly sex like man to argue against such palpable exaggerations, so Baidyanath merely retired on to his veranda, and worked with redoubled energy at polishing his walking-sticks.

But the rampart of silence is not the surest means of self-defence. Sometimes the wife would break upon her husband at his work, and, without looking at him, say, "Please tell the milkman to stop delivering milk."

At which Baidyanath, after his first shock of speechlessness, might possibly stammer out, "Milk? How can you get on if you stop the supply? What will the children drink?"

To this his wife would answer, "Rice water." On another day she would use quite the opposite method of attack, and, suddenly bursting into the room, would exclaim, "I give it up, you manage your own household."

Baidyanath would mutter in despair, "What do you wish me to do?"

His wife would reply, "You do the marketing for this month," and then, give him a list of materials sufficient for reckless orgies of feasting.

If Baidyanath could summon up courage to ask, "What is the necessity of so much?" he would get the reply,

"Indeed it will be cheaper for you to let the children die of starvation, and me also for that matter."

II

One day after finishing his morning meal Baidyanath was sitting alone, preparing the thread for a kite, when he saw one of those wandering mendicants, who are reputed to know the secret of transmuting the baser metals into gold. In a moment there flashed to his mind the surest chance of unearned increment to his funds. He took the mendicant into his house, and was surprised at his own cleverness when he secured the consent of his guest to teach him the art of making gold. After having swallowed an alarming amount of nourishment, and a considerable portion of Baidyanath's paternal inheritance, the ascetic at last encouraged Baidyanath and his wife with the hope that the next day they would see their dream realised.

That night no one had any sleep. The husband and wife, with astounding prodigality, began to build golden castles in the air and discuss the details of the architecture. Their conjugal harmony was so unusually perfect for that night that in spite of disagreements they were willing to allow compromises in their plans for each other's sake.

Next day the magician had mysteriously disappeared, and with him the golden haze from the atmosphere in which they had been living. The sunlight itself appeared dark, and the house and its furniture seemed to its mistress to be four times more disgraceful than before.

Henceforth, if Baidyanath ventured even a truism on the most trifling or household matters, his wife would advise him with withering sarcasm to be careful of the last remnant of his intelligence after the reckless expenditure from which it had suffered.

Sundari in the meantime was showing her hand to every palmist that came her way, and also her horoscope. She was told that in the matter of children she would be fortunate, and that her house would soon be filled with sons and daughters. But such prospect of overgrowth of population in her house did not produce any exhilaration in her mind.

At last one day an astrologer came and said that if within a year her husband did not come upon some hidden treasure then, he would throw his science to the winds and go about begging. Hearing him speak with such desperate certainty, Sundari could not entertain a moment's doubt as to the truth of his prophecy.

There are certain recognised methods for acquiring wealth, such as agriculture, service, trade, and the legal and illegal professions. But none of these points out the direction of hidden wealth. Therefore, while his wife spurred him on, it more and more perplexed him to decide upon the particular mound which he should excavate, or the part of the river-bed where he should send down a diver to search.

In the meantime the Puja festival was approaching. A week before the day, boats began to arrive at the village landing laden with passengers returning home with their purchases, baskets full of vegetables, tin trunks filled with new shoes, umbrellas and clothes for the children, scents and soap, the latest story-books, and perfumed oil for the wives.

The light of the autumn sun filled the cloudless sky with the gladness of festival, and the ripe paddy fields shimmered in the sun, while the cocoa-nut leaves washed by the rains rustled in the fresh cool breeze.

The children, getting up very early, went to see the image of the goddess which was being prepared in the courtyard of the neighbouring house. When it was their meal-time, the maid-servant had to come and drag them away by force. At that time Baidyanath was brooding over the futility of his own life, amidst this universal stir of merriment in the neighbourhood. Taking his two children from the servant, he drew them towards him, and asked the elder one, "Well, Obu, tell me what do you want for a present this time?"

Obu replied without a moment's hesitation, "Give me a toy boat, father."

The younger one, not wishing to be behindhand with his brother, said, "Oh, father, do give me a toy boat too."

III

At this time an uncle of Sundari's had come to his house from Benares, where he was working as an advocate, and Sundari spent a great part of her time going round to see him.

At last one day she said to her husband, "Look here, you will have to go to Benares."

Baidyanath at once concluded that his wife had received from an astrologer a positive assurance of his impending death, and was anxious for him to die in that holy place, to secure better advantage in the next world.

Then, he was told that at Benares there was a house in which rumour said there was some hidden treasure. Surely it was destined for him to buy that house and secure the treasure.

Baidyanath, in a fit of desperation, tried to assert his independence, and exclaimed, "Good heavens, I cannot go to Benares."

Two days passed, during which Baidyanath was busily engaged in making toy boats. He fixed masts in them, and fastened sails, hoisted a red flag, and put in rudders and oars. He did not even forget steersmen and passengers to boot. It would have been difficult to find a boy, even in these modern times, cynical enough to despise such a gift. And when Baidyanath, the night before the festival, gave these boats to his boys, they became wild with delight.

On hearing their shouts Sundari came in, and at the sight of these gifts flew into a fury of rage, and, seizing the toys, threw them out of the window.

The younger child began to scream with disappointment, and his mother, giving him a resounding box on the ears, said, "Stop your silly noise."

The elder boy, when he saw his father's face, forgot his own disappointment, and with an appearance of cheerfulness said, "Never mind, father, I will go and fetch them first thing in the morning."

Next day Baidyanath agreed to go to Benares. He took the children in his arms, and kissing them good-bye, left the house.

IV

The house at Benares belonged to a client of his wife's uncle, and for that reason perhaps the price was fairly high. Baidyanath took possession of it, and began to live there alone. It was situated right on the river-bank, and its walls were washed by the current.

At night Baidyanath began to have an eerie feeling, and he drew his sheet over his head, but could not sleep. When in the depth of night all was still he was suddenly startled to hear a clanking sound from somewhere. It was faint but clear – as though in the nether regions the treasurer of the god Mammon was counting out his money.

Baidyanath was terrified, but with the fear there mingled curiosity and the hope of success. With trembling hand he carried the lamp from room to room, to discover the place where the sound had its origin, till in the morning it became inaudible among the other noises.

The next day at midnight the sound was heard again, and Baidyanath felt like a traveller in a desert, who can hear the gurgle of water without knowing from which direction it is coming, hesitating to move a step, for the fear of taking a wrong path and going farther away from the spring.

Many days passed in this anxious manner, until his face, usually so serenely content, became lined with anxiety and care. His eyes were sunk in their sockets, and had a hungry look, with a glow like that of the burning sand of the desert under the mid-day sun.

At last one night a happy thought came to him, and locking all the doors, he began to strike the floors of all the rooms with a crowbar. From the floor of one small room came a hollow sound. He began to dig. It was nearly dawn when the digging was completed.

Through the opening made Baidyanath saw that underneath there was a chamber, but in the darkness he had not the courage to take a jump into the unknown. He placed his bedstead over the entrance, and lay down. So morning came. That day, even in the day-time, the sound could be heard. Repeating the name of Durga, he dragged his bedstead away from the cavity in the floor. The splash of lapping water and the clank of metal became louder. Fearfully peeping through the hole into the darkness, he could see that the chamber was full of flowing water, which, when examined with a stick, was found to be about a couple of feet deep. Taking a box of matches and a lantern in his hand, he easily jumped into the shallow room. But lest in one moment all his hopes should collapse, his trembling hand found it difficult to light the lantern. After striking almost a whole box of matches, he at last succeeded.

He saw by its light a large copper cauldron, fastened to a thick iron chain. Every now and then, when the current came with a rush, the chain clanked against the side, and made the metallic sound which he had heard.

Baidyanath waded quickly through the water, and went up to this vessel, only to find that it was empty.

He could not believe his eyes, and with both hands he took the cauldron up and shook it furiously. He turned it upside down, but in vain. He saw that its mouth was broken, as though at one time this vessel had been closed and sealed, and some one had broken it open.

Baidyanath began to grope about in the water. Something struck against his hand, which on lifting he found to be a skull. He held it up to his ear, and shook it violently – but it was empty. He threw it down.

He saw that on one side of the room towards the river the wall was broken. It was through this opening that the water entered, and he felt sure that it had been made by his unknown predecessor, who had a more reliable horoscope than his own.

At last, having lost all hope, he heaved a deep sigh, which seemed to mingle with the innumerable sighs of despair coming from some subterranean inferno of everlasting failures.

His whole body besmeared with mud, Baidyanath made his way up into the house. The world, full of its bustling population, seemed to him empty as that broken vessel and chained to a meaningless destiny.

Once more to pack his things, to buy his ticket, to get into the train, to return again to his home, to have to wrangle with his wife, and to endure the burden of his sordid days, all this seemed to him intolerably unreasonable. He wished that he could just slide into the water, as the broken-down bank of a river into the passing current.

Still he did pack his things, buy his ticket, get into the train, and one evening at the end of a winter day arrive at his home.

On entering the house, he sat like one dazed in the courtyard, not venturing to go into the inner apartments. The old maid-servant was the first to catch sight of him, and at her shout of surprise the children came running to see him with their glad laughter. Then, his wife called him.

Baidyanath started up as if from sleep, and once more woke into the life which he had lived before. With sad face and wan smile, he took one of the boys in his arms and the other by the hand and entered the room. The lamps had just been lighted, and although it was not yet night, it was a cold evening, and everything was as quiet as if night had come.

Baidyanath remained silent for a little, and then, in a soft voice said to his wife, "How are you?"

His wife, without making any reply, asked him, "What has happened?"

Baidyanath, without speaking, simply struck his forehead. At this Sundari's face hardened. The children, feeling the shadow of a calamity, quietly slipped away, and going to the maidservant asked her to tell them a story.

Night fell, but neither husband nor wife spoke a word. The whole atmosphere of the house seemed to palpitate with silence, and gradually Sundari's lips set hard like a miser's purse. Then, she got up, and leaving her husband went slowly into her bedroom, locking the door behind her. Baidyanath remained standing silently outside. The watchman's call was heard as he passed. The tired world was sunk in deep sleep.

When it was quite late at night the elder boy, wakened from some dream, left his bed, and coming out on to the veranda whispered, "Father."

But his father was not there. In a slightly raised voice he called from outside the closed door of his parents' bedroom, "Father," but he got no answer. And in fear he went back to bed.

Next morning early the maid-servant, according to her custom, prepared her master's tobacco, and went in search of him, but could find him nowhere.

40

The Editor

As long as my wife was alive, I did not pay much attention to Probha. As a matter of fact, I thought a great deal more about Probha's mother than I did of the child herself.

At that time my dealing with her was superficial, limited to a little petting, listening to her lisping chatter, and occasionally watching her laugh and play. As long as it was agreeable to me I used to fondle her, but as soon as it threatened to become tiresome I would surrender her to her mother with the greatest readiness.

At last, on the untimely death of my wife, the child dropped from her mother's arms into mine, and I took her to my heart.

But it is difficult to say whether it was I who considered it my duty to bring up the motherless child with twofold care, or my daughter who thought it her duty to take care of her wifeless father with a superfluity of attention. At any rate, it is a fact that from the age of six she began to assume the role of housekeeper. It was quite clear that this little girl constituted herself the sole guardian of her father.

I smiled inwardly but surrendered myself completely to her hands. I soon saw that the more inefficient and helpless I was the better pleased she became. I found that even if I took down my own clothes from the peg, or went to get my own umbrella, she put on such an air of offended dignity that it was clear that she thought I had usurped her right. Never before had she possessed such a perfect doll as she now had in her father, and so she took the keenest pleasure in feeding him, dressing him, and even putting him to bed. Only when I was teaching her the elements of arithmetic or the First Reader had I the opportunity of summoning up my parental authority.

Every now and then, the thought troubled me as to where I should be able to get enough money to provide her with a dowry for a suitable bridegroom. I was giving her a good education, but what would happen if she fell into the hands of an ignorant fool?

I made up my mind to earn money. I was too old to get employment in a Government office, and I had not the influence to get work in a private one. After a good deal of thought I decided that I would write books.

If you make holes in a bamboo tube, it will no longer hold either oil or water, in fact its power of receptivity is lost; but if you blow through it, then, without any expenditure it may produce music. I felt quite sure that the man who is not useful can be ornamental, and he who is not productive in other fields can at least produce literature. Encouraged by this thought, I wrote a farce. People said it was good, and it was even acted on the stage.

Once having tasted of fame, I found myself unable to stop pursuing it farther. Days and days together I went on writing farces with an agony of determination.

Probha would come with her smile, and remind me gently, "Father, it is time for you to take your bath."

And I would growl out at her, "Go away, go away; can't you see that I am busy now? Don't vex me."

The poor child would leave me, unnoticed, with a face dark like a lamp whose light has been suddenly blown out.

I drove the maid-servants away, and beat the men-servants, and when beggars came and sang at my door I would get up and run after them with a stick. My room being by the side of the street, passers-by would stop and ask me to tell them the way, but I would request them to go to Jericho. Alas, no one took it into serious consideration that I was engaged in writing a screaming farce.

Yet I never got money in the measure that I got fun and fame. But that did not trouble me, although in the meantime all the potential bridegrooms were growing up for other brides whose parents did not write farces.

But just then, an excellent opportunity came my way. The landlord of a certain village, Jahirgram, started a newspaper, and sent a request that I would become its editor. I agreed to take the post.

For the first few days I wrote with such fire and zest that people used to point at me when I went out into the street, and I began to feel a brilliant halo about my forehead.

Next to Jahirgram was the village of Ahirgram. Between the landlords of these two villages there was a constant rivalry and feud. There had been a time when they came to blows not infrequently. But now, since the magistrate had bound them both over to keep the peace, I took the place of the hired ruffians who used to act for one of the rivals. Everyone said that I lived up to the dignity of my position.

My writings were so strong and fiery that Ahirgram could no longer hold up its head. I blackened with my ink the whole of their ancient clan and family.

All this time I had the comfortable feeling of being pleased with myself. I even became fat. My face beamed with the exhilaration of a successful man of genius. I admired my own delightful ingenuity of insinuation, when at some excruciating satire of mine, directed against the ancestry of Ahirgram, the whole of Jahirgram would burst its sides with laughter like an over-ripe melon. I enjoyed myself thoroughly.

But at last Ahirgram started a newspaper. What it published was starkly naked, without a shred of literary urbanity. The language it used was of such undiluted colloquialism that every letter seemed to scream in one's face. The consequence was that the inhabitants of both villages clearly understood its meaning.

But as I was hampered in my style by my sense of decency, my subtlety of sarcasm very often made but a feeble impression upon the power of understanding of both my friends and my enemies.

The result was that even when I won decidedly in this war of infamy my readers were not aware of my victory. At last in desperation I wrote a sermon on the necessity of good taste in literature, but found that I had made a fatal mistake. For things that are solemn offer more surface for ridicule than things that are truly ridiculous. And therefore, my effort at the moral betterment of my fellow-beings had the opposite effect to that which I had intended.

My employer ceased to show me such attention as he had done. The honour to which I had grown accustomed dwindled in its quantity, and its quality became poor. When I walked in the street people did not go out of their way to carry off the memory of a word with me. They even went so far as to be frivolously familiar in their behaviour towards me – such as slapping my shoulders with a laugh and giving me nicknames.

In the meantime my admirers had quite forgotten the farces which had made me famous. I felt as if I was a burnt-out match, charred to its very end.

My mind became so depressed that, no matter how I racked my brains, I was unable to write one line. I seemed to have lost all zest for life.

Probha had now grown afraid of me. She would not venture to approach me unless summoned. She had come to understand that a commonplace doll is a far better companion than a genius of a father who writes comic pieces.

One day I saw that the Ahirgram newspaper, leaving my employer alone for once, had directed its attack on me. Some very ugly imputations had been made against myself. One by one all my friends and acquaintances came and read to me the spiciest bits, laughing heartily. Some of them said that however one might disagree with the subject-matter, it could not be denied that it was cleverly written. In the course of the day at least twenty people came and said the same thing, with slight variations to break its monotony.

In front of my house there is a small garden. I was walking there in the evening with a mind distracted with pain. When the birds had returned to their nests, and surrendered themselves to the peace of the evening, I understood quite clearly that amongst the birds at any rate there were no writers of journalism, nor did they hold discussions on good taste. I was thinking only of one thing, namely, what answer I could make. The disadvantage of politeness is that it is not intelligible to all classes of people. So I had decided that my answer must be given in the same strain as the attack. I was not going to allow myself to acknowledge defeat.

Just as I had come to this conclusion, a well-known voice came softly through the darkness of the evening, and immediately afterwards I felt a soft warm touch in the palm of my hand. I was so distracted and absent-minded that even though that voice and touch were familiar to me, I did not realise that I knew them.

But the next moment, when they had left me, the voice sounded in my ear, and the memory of the touch became living. My child had slowly come near to me once more, and had whispered in my ear, "Father," but not getting any answer she had lifted my right hand, and with it had gently stroked her forehead, and then, silently gone back into the house.

For a long time Probha had not called me like that, nor caressed me with such freedom. Therefore, it was that today at the touch of her love my heart suddenly began to yearn for her. Going back to the house a little later, I saw that Probha was lying on her bed. Her eyes were half closed, and she seemed to be in pain. She lay like a flower which has dropped on the dust at the end of the day.

Putting my hand on her forehead, I found that she was feverish. Her breath was hot, and her pulse was throbbing.

I realised that the poor child, feeling the first symptoms of fever, had come with her thirsty heart to get her father's love and caresses, while he was trying to think of some stinging reply to send to the newspaper.

I sat beside her. The child, without speaking a word, took my hand between her two fever-heated palms, and laid it upon her forehead, lying quite still.

All the numbers of the Jahirgram and Ahirgram papers which I had in the house I burnt to ashes. I wrote no answer to the attack. Never had I felt such joy as I did, when I Thus, acknowledged defeat.

I had taken the child to my arms when her mother had died, and now, having cremated this rival of her mother, again I took her to my heart.

41

The Lost Jewels

My boat was moored beside an old bathing ghat of the river, almost in ruins. The sun had set.

On the roof of the boat the boatmen were at their evening prayer. Against the bright background of the western sky their silent worship stood out like a picture. The waning light was reflected on the still surface of river in every delicate shade of colour from gold to steel-blue.

A huge house with broken windows, tumbledown verandas, and all the appearance of old age was in front of me. I sat alone on the steps of the ghat, which were cracked by the far-reaching roots of a banyan tree. A feeling of sadness began to come over me, when suddenly I was startled to hear a voice asking, "Sir, where have you come from?"

I looked up, and saw a man who seemed half-starved and out of fortune. His face had a dilapidated look such as is common among my countrymen who take up service away from home. His dirty coat of Assam silk was greasy and open at the front. He appeared to be just returning from his day's work, and to be taking a walk by the side of the river at a time when he should have been eating his evening meal.

The new-comer sat beside me on the steps. I said in answer to his question, "I come from Ranchi."

"What occupation?"

"I am a merchant."

"What sort?"

"A dealer in cocoons and timber."

"What name?"

After a moment's hesitation I gave a name, but it was not my own.

Still the stranger's curiosity was not satisfied. Again he questioned me, "What have you come here for?" I replied, "For a change of air."

My cross-examiner seemed a little astonished. He said, "Well, Sir, I have been enjoying the air of this place for nearly six years, and with it I have taken a daily average of fifteen grains of quinine, but I have not noticed that I have benefited much."

I replied, "Still, you must acknowledge that, after Ranchi, I shall find the air of this place sufficient of a change."

"Yes, indeed," said he. "More than you bargain for. But where will you stay here?"

Pointing to the tumble-down house above the ghat, I said, "There."

I think my friend had a suspicion that I had come in search of hidden treasure. However, he did not pursue the subject. He only began to describe to me what had happened in this ruined building some fifteen years before.

I found that he was the schoolmaster of the place. From beneath an enormous bald head, his two eyes shone out from their sockets with an unnatural brightness in a face that was thin with hunger and illness.

The boatmen, having finished their evening prayer, turned their attention to their cooking. As the last light of the day faded, the dark and empty house stood silent and ghostly above the deserted ghat.

The schoolmaster said, "Nearly ten years ago, when I came to this place, Bhusan Saha used to live in this house. He was the heir to the large property and business of his uncle Durga Saha, who was childless.

"But he was modern. He had been educated, and not only spoke faultless English, but actually entered Sahebs' offices with his shoes on. In addition to that he grew a beard; thus, he had not the least chance of bettering himself so far as the Sahebs were concerned. You had only to look at him to see that he was a modernised Bengali.

"In his own home, too, he had another drawback. His wife was beautiful. With his college education on the one hand, and on the other his beautiful wife, what chance was there of his preserving our good old traditions in his home? In fact, when he was ill, he actually called in the assistant surgeon. And his style of food, dress, and his wife's jewels were all on the same extravagant scale.

"Sir, you are certainly a married man, so that it is hardly necessary to tell you that the ordinary female is fond of sour green mangoes, hot chillies, and a stern husband. A man need not necessarily be ugly or poor to be cheated of his wife's love, but he is sure to lose it if he is too gentle.

"If you ask me why this is so, I have much to say on this subject, for I have thought a good deal about it. A deer chooses a hardwood tree on which to sharpen its horns, and would get no pleasure in rubbing its horns against the soft stem of a plantain tree. From the very moment that man and woman became separate sexes, woman has been exercising all her faculties in trying by various devices to fascinate and bring man under her control. The wife of a man who is, of his own accord, submissive is altogether out of employment. All those weapons which she has inherited from her grandmothers of untold centuries are useless in her hands, the force of her tears, the fire of her anger, and the snare of her glances lie idle.

"Under the spell of modern civilisation man has lost the God-given power of his barbaric nature, and this has loosened the conjugal ties. The unfortunate Bhusan had been turned out of the machine of modern civilisation an absolutely faultless man. He was therefore, neither successful in business nor in his own home.

"Mani was Bhusan's wife. She used to get her caresses without asking, her Dhaka muslin saris without tears, and her bangles without being able to pride herself on a victory. In this way her woman's nature became atrophied, and with it her love for her husband. She simply accepted things without giving anything in return. Her harmless and foolish husband used to imagine that to give is the way to get. The fact was just the contrary.

"The result of this was that Mani looked upon her husband as a mere machine for turning out her Dhaka muslins and her bangles – so perfect a machine, indeed, that never for a single day did she need to oil its wheels.

"Though Bhusan's birthplace was Phulbere, here was his place of business, where, for the sake of his work, he spent most of his time. At his Phulbere house he had no mother, but had plenty of aunts and uncles and other relatives, from which distraction he brought away his wife to this house and kept her to himself alone. But there is this difference between a wife and one's other possessions, that by keeping her to oneself one may lose her beyond recovery.

"Bhusan's wife did not talk very much, nor did she mix much with her neighbours. To feed Brahmins in obedience to a sacred vow, or to give a few pice to a religious mendicant, was not her way. In her hands nothing was ever lost; whatever she got she saved up most carefully, with the one exception of the memory of her husband's caresses. The extraordinary thing was that she did not seem to lose the least atom of her youthful beauty. People said that whatever her age was, she never looked older than sixteen. I suppose youth is best preserved with the aid of a heart that is an ice-box.

"But as far as work was concerned Mani was very efficient. She never kept more servants than were absolutely necessary. She thought that to pay wages to any one to do work which she herself could do was like playing the pickpocket with her own money.

"Not being anxious about any one, never being distracted by love, always working and saving, she was never sick nor sorry.

"For the majority of husbands this is quite sufficient, – not only sufficient, but fortunate. For the loving wife is a wife who makes it difficult for her husband to forget her, and the fatigue of perpetual remembrance wears out life's bloom. It is only when a man has lumbago that he becomes conscious of his waist. And lumbago in domestic affairs is to be made conscious, by the constant imposition of love, that you have such a thing as a wife. Excessive devotion to her husband may be a merit for the wife but not comfortable for the husband – that is my candid opinion.

"I hope I am not tiring you, Sir? I live alone, you see; I am banished from the company of my wife, and there are many important social questions which I have leisure to think about, but cannot discuss with my pupils. In course of conversation you will see how deeply I have thought of them."

Just as he was speaking, some jackals began to howl from a neighbouring thicket. The schoolmaster stopped for a moment the torrent of his talk. When the sound had ceased, and the earth and the water relapsed into a deeper silence he – opened his glowing eyes wide in the darkness of the night, and resumed the thread of his story.

"Suddenly a tangle occurred in Bhusan's complicated business. What exactly happened it is not possible for a layman like myself either to understand or to explain. Suffice it to say that, for some sudden reason, he found it difficult to get credit in the market. If only he could, by hook or by crook, raise a lakh and a half of rupees, and only for a few days rapidly flash it before the market, then, his credit would be restored, and he would be able to sail fair again.

"But the money did not come easily. If the rumour got about that he was borrowing in the market where he was known, then, he feared that his business would suffer even more seriously. So he began to cast about to see whether he could not raise a loan from some stranger. But, in that case, he would be bound to give some satisfactory security.

"The best security of all is jewelry, for that saves the signing of all sorts of complicated documents. It not only saves time but is a simple process.

"So Bhusan went to his wife. But unfortunately he was not able to face his wife as easily as most men are. His love for his wife was of that kind which has to tread very carefully, and cannot speak out plainly what is in the mind; it is like the attraction of the sun for the earth, which is strong, yet which leaves immense space between them.

"Still, even the hero of a high-class romance does sometimes, when hard pressed, have to mention to his beloved such things as mortgage deeds and promissory notes. But the words stick, and the tune does not seem right, and the shrinking of reluctance makes itself felt. The unfortunate Bhusan was totally powerless to say, "Look here, I am in need of money; bring out your jewels."

"He did broach the subject to his wife at last, but with such extreme delicacy that it only excited her opposition without bending it to his own purpose. When Mani set her face hard, and said nothing, he was deeply hurt, yet he was incapable of returning the hurt back to her. The reason was that he had not even a trace of that barbarity which is the gift of the male. If any one had upbraided him for this, then, most probably he would have expressed some such subtle sentiment as the following, "If my wife, of her own free choice, is unwilling to trust me with her jewelry, then, I have no right to take them from her by force."

"Has God given to man such forcefulness only for him to spend his time in delicate measurement of fine-spun ideals?

"However this may be, Bhusan, being too proud to touch his wife's jewels, went to Calcutta to try some other way of raising the money.

"As a general rule in this world, the wife knows the husband far better than the husband ever knows the wife; but extremely modern men in their subtlety of nature are altogether beyond the range of those unsophisticated instincts which womankind has acquired through ages. These men are a new race, and have become as mysterious as women themselves. Ordinary men can be divided roughly into three main classes; some of them are barbarians, some are fools, and some are blind; but these modern men do not fit into any of them.

"So Mani called her counsellor for consultation. Some cousin of hers was engaged as assistant steward on Bhusan's estate. He was not the kind of man to profit himself by dint of hard work, but by help of his position in the family he was able to save his salary, and even a little more.

"Mani called him and told him what had happened. She ended up by asking him, "Now what is your advice?"

"He shook his head wisely and said, "I don't like the look of things at all." The fact is that wise men never like the look of things. Then, he added, "Babu will never be able to raise the money, and in the end he will have to fall back upon that jewelry of yours."

"From what she knew of humanity she thought that this was not only possible but likely. Her anxiety became keener than ever. She had no child to love, and though she had a husband she was almost unable to realise his very existence. So her blood froze at the very thought that her only object of love, the wealth which like a child had grown from year to year, was to be in a moment thrown into the bottomless abyss of trade. She gasped, "What, then is to be done?"

"Modhu said, "Why not take your jewels and go to your father's house?" In his heart of hearts he entertained the hope that a portion, and possibly the larger portion, of that jewelry would fall to his lot.

"Mani at once agreed. It was a rainy night towards the end of summer. At this very ghat a boat was moored. Mani, wrapped from head to foot in a thick shawl, stepped into the boat. The frogs croaked in the thick darkness of the cloudy dawn. Modhu, waking up from sleep, roused himself from the boat, and said, "Give me the box of jewels."

"Mani replied, "Not now, afterwards. Now let us start."

"The boat started, and floated swiftly down the current. Mani had spent the whole night in covering every part of her body with her ornaments. She was afraid that if she put her jewels into a box they might be snatched away from her hands. But if she wore them on her person, then, no one could take them away without murdering her. Mani did not understand Bhusan, it is true; but there was no doubt about her understanding of Modhu.

"Modhu had written a letter to the chief steward to the effect that he had started to take his mistress to her father's house.

The steward was an ancient retainer of Bhusan's father. He was furiously angry, and wrote a lengthy epistle, full of misspellings, to his master. Although the letter was weak in its grammar, yet it was forcible in its language, and clearly expressed the writer's disapproval of giving too much indulgence to womankind. Bhusan on receiving it understood what was the motive of Mani's secret departure. What hurt him most was the fact that, in spite of his having given way to the unwillingness of his wife to part with her jewels in this time of his desperate straits, his wife should still suspect him.

"When he ought to have been angry, Bhusan was only distressed. Man is the rod of God's justice, to him has been entrusted the thunderbolt of the divine wrath, and if at wrong done to himself or another it does not at once break out into fury, then, it is a shame. God has so arranged it that man, for the most trifling reason, will burst forth in anger like a forest fire, and woman will burst into tears like a rain-cloud for no reason at all. But the cycle seems to have changed, and this appears no longer to hold good.

"The husband bent his head, and said to himself, "Well, if this is your judgment, let it be so. I will simply do my own duty." Bhusan, who ought to have been born five or six centuries hence, when the world will be moved by psychic forces, was unfortunate enough not only to be born in the nineteenth century, but also to marry a woman who belonged to that primitive age which persists through all time. He did not write a word on the subject to his wife, and determined in his mind that he would never mention it to her again. What an awful penalty!

"Ten or twelve days later, having secured the necessary loan, Bhusan returned to his home. He imagined that Mani, after completing her mission, had by this time come back from her father's house. And so he approached the door of the inner apartments, wondering whether his wife would show any signs of shame or penitence for the undeserved suspicion with which she had treated him.

"He found that the door was shut. Breaking the lock, he entered the room, and saw that it was empty.

"It seemed to him that the world was a huge cage from which the bird of love had flown away, leaving behind it all the decorations of the blood-red rubies of our hearts, and the pearl pendants of our tear-drops.

"At first Bhusan did not trouble about his wife's absence. He thought that if she wanted to come back she would do so. His old Brahmin steward, however, came to him, and said, "What good will come of taking no notice of it? You ought to get some news of the mistress." Acting on this suggestion, messengers were sent to Mani's father's house. The news was brought that up to that time neither Mani nor Modhu had turned up there.

"Then, a search began in every direction. Men went along both banks of the river making inquiries. The police were given a description of Modhu, but all in vain. They were unable to find out what boat they had taken, what boatman they had hired, or by what way they had gone.

"One evening, when all hope had been abandoned of ever finding his wife, Bhusan entered his deserted bedroom. It was the festival of Krishna's birth, and it had been raining incessantly from early morning. In celebration of the festival there was a fair going on in the village, and in a temporary building a theatrical performance was being given. The sound of distant singing could be heard mingling with the sound of pouring rain. Bhusan was sitting alone in the darkness at the window there which hangs loose upon its hinges. He took no notice of the damp wind, the spray of the rain, and the sound of the singing. On the wall of the room were hanging a couple of pictures of the goddesses Lakshmi and Saraswati, painted at the Art Studio; on the clothes-rack a towel, and a bodice, and a pair of saris were laid out ready for use. On a table in one corner of the room there was a box containing betel leaves prepared by Mani's own hand, but now quite dry and uneatable. In a cupboard with a glass door all sorts of things were arranged with evident care – her china dolls of childhood›s days, scent bottles, decanters of coloured glass, a sumptuous pack of cards, large brightly polished shells, and even empty soapboxes. In a niche there was a favourite little lamp with its round globe. Mani had been in the habit of lighting it with her own hands every evening. One who goes away, leaving everything empty, leaves the imprint of his living heart even on lifeless objects. Come, Mani, come back again, light your lamp, fill your room with light once more, and, standing before your mirror, put on your *sari* which has been prepared with such care. See, all your things are waiting for you. No one will claim anything more from you, but only ask you to give a living unity once more to these scattered and lifeless things, by the mere presence of your imperishable youth and unfading beauty. Alas, the inarticulate cry of these mute and lifeless objects has made this room into a realm of things that have lost their world.

"In the dead of night, when the heavy rain had ceased, and the songs of the village opera troupe had become silent, Bhusan was sitting in the same position as before. Outside the window there was such an impenetrable darkness that it seemed to him as if the very gates of oblivion were before him reaching to the sky – as if he had only to cry out to be able to recover sight of those things which seemed to have been lost for ever.

"Just as he was thinking thus, a jingling sound as of ornaments was heard. It seemed to be advancing up the steps of the ghat. The water of the river and the darkness of the night were indistinguishable. Thrilling with excitement, Bhusan tried to pierce and push through the darkness with his eager eyes, till they ached, – but he could see nothing. The more anxious he was to see, the denser the darkness became, and the more shadowy the outer world. Nature, seeing an intruder at the door of her hall of death, seemed suddenly to have drawn a still thicker curtain of darkness.

"The sound reached the top step of the bathing ghat, and now began to come towards the house. It stopped in front of the door, which had been locked by the porter before he went to the fair. Then, upon that closed door there fell a rain of jingling blows, as if with some ornaments. Bhusan was not able to sit still another moment, but, making his way through the unlighted rooms and down the dark staircase, he stood before the closed door. It was padlocked from the outside, so he began to shake it with all his might. The force with which he shook the door and the sound which he made woke him suddenly. He found he had been asleep, and in his sleep he had made his way down to the door of the house. His whole body was wet with sweat, his hands and feet were icy cold, and his heart was fluttering like a lamp just about to go out. His dream being broken, he realised that there was no sound outside except the pattering of the rain which had commenced again.

"Although the whole thing was a dream, Bhusan felt as if for some very small obstacle he had been cheated of the wonderful realisation of his impossible hope. The incessant patter of the rain seemed to say to him, "This awakening is a dream. This world is vain."

"The festival was continued on the following day, and the doorkeeper again had leave. Bhusan gave orders that the hall-door was to be left open all night, but the porter objected that there were all sorts of suspicious characters about who had come from other places to the fair, and that it would not be safe to leave the door open. But Bhusan would not listen, whereupon the porter said that he would himself stay on guard. But Bhusan refused to allow him to remain. The porter was puzzled, but did not press the point.

"That night, having extinguished the light, Bhusan took his seat at the open window of his bedroom as before. The sky was dark with rain-clouds, and there was a silence as of something indefinite and impending. The monotonous croaking of the frogs and the sound of the distant songs were not able to break that silence, but only seemed to add an incongruity to it.

"Late at night the frogs and the crickets and the boys of the opera party became silent, and a still deeper darkness fell upon the night. It seemed that now the time had come.

"Just as on the night before, a clattering and jingling sound came from the ghat by the river. But this time Bhusan did not look in that direction, lest, by his over-anxiety and restlessness, his power of sight and hearing would become overwhelmed. He made a supreme effort to control himself, and sat still.

"The sound of the ornaments gradually advanced from the ghat, and entered the open door. Then, it came winding up the spiral staircase which led to the inner apartments. It became difficult for Bhusan to control himself, his heart began to thump wildly, and his throat was choking with suppressed excitement. Having reached the head of the spiral stairs, the sound came slowly along the veranda towards the door of the room, where it stopped just outside with a clanking sound. It was now only just on the other side of the threshold.

"Bhusan could contain himself no longer, and his pent-up excitement burst forth in one wild cry of 'Mani', and he sprang up from his chair with lightning rapidity. Thus, startled out of his sleep, he found that the very window-panes were rattling with the vibration of his cry. And outside he could hear the croaking of the frogs and patter of rain. Bhusan struck his forehead in despair.

"Next day the fair broke up, and the stall-keepers and the players' party went away. Bhusan gave orders that that night no one should sleep in the house except himself. The servants came to the conclusion that their master was going to practise some mystic rites. All that day Bhusan fasted.

"In the evening, he took his seat at the window of that empty house. That day there were breaks in the clouds, showing the stars twinkling through-the rain-washed air. The moon was late in rising, and, as the fair was over, there was not a single boat on the flooded river. The villagers, tired out by two nights' dissipation, were sound asleep.

"Bhusan, sitting with his head resting on the back of his chair, was gazing up at the stars. He was thinking of the time when he was only nineteen years old, and was reading in Calcutta; how in the evening he used to lie in College Square, with his hands behind his head, gazing up at those eternal stars, and thinking of the sweet face of Mani in his father-in-law's house. The very separation from her was like an instrument whose tense-drawn strings those stars used to touch and waken into song.

"As he watched them, the stars one by one disappeared. From the sky above, and from the earth beneath, screens of darkness met like tired eyelids upon weary eyes. Tonight, Bhusan's mind was full of peace. He felt certain that the moment had come when his heart's desire would be fulfilled, and that death would reveal his mysteries to his devotee.

"The sound came from the river ghat just as on the previous nights and advanced up the steps. Bhusan closed his eyes, and sat in deep meditation. The sound reached the empty hall. It came winding up the spiral stairs. Then, it crossed the long veranda, and paused for a long while at the bedroom door.

"Bhusan's heart beat fast; his whole body trembled. But this time he did not open his eyes. The sound crossed the threshold. It entered the room. Then, it went slowly round the room, stopping before the rack where the clothes were hanging, the niche with its little lamp, the table where the dried betel leaves were lying, the almirah with its various knick-knacks, and, last of all, it came and stood close to Bhusan himself.

"Bhusan opened his eyes. He saw by the faint light of the crescent moon that there was a skeleton standing right in front of his chair. It had rings on all its fingers, bracelets on its wrists and armlets on its arms, necklaces on its neck, and a golden tiara on its head – in fact its whole body glittered and sparkled with gold and diamonds. The ornaments hung loosely on the limbs, but did not fall off. Most dreadful of all was the fact that the two eyes which shone out from the bony face were living – two dark moist eyeballs looking out with a fixed and steady stare from between the long thick eyelashes. As he looked his blood froze in his veins. He tried hard to close his eyes but could not; they remained open, staring like those of a dead man.

"Then, the skeleton, fixing its gaze upon the face of the motionless Bhusan, silently beckoned with its outstretched hand, the diamond rings on its bony fingers glittering in the pale moonlight.

"Bhusan stood up, as one who had lost his senses, and followed the skeleton, which left the room, its bones and ornaments rattling with a hollow sound. The skeleton crossed the veranda and, winding down the pitch-dark spiral staircase, reached the bottom of the stairs. Crossing the lower veranda, they entered the empty lampless hall and, passing through it, came out on to the brick-paved path of the garden. The bricks crunched under the tread of the bony feet. The faint moonlight struggled through the thick network of branches, and the path was difficult to discern. Making their way through the flitting fireflies, which haunted the dark shadowy path, they reached the river ghat.

"By those very steps, up which the sound had come, the bejewelled skeleton went down step by step, with a stiff gait and hard sound. On the swift current of the river, flooded by the heavy rain, a faint streak of moonlight was visible.

"The skeleton descended to the river, and Bhusan, following it, placed one foot in the water. The moment he touched the water he woke with a start. His guide was no longer to be seen. Only the trees on the opposite bank of the river were standing still and silent, and overhead the half moon was staring as if astonished. Starting from head to foot, Bhusan slipped and fell headlong into the river. Although he knew how to swim, he was powerless to do so, for his limbs were not under his control. From the midst of dreams he had stepped, for a moment only, into the borderland of waking life – the next moment to be plunged into eternal sleep."

Having finished his story, the schoolmaster was silent for a little. Suddenly, the moment he stopped, I realised that except for him the whole world had become silent and still. For a long time I also remained speechless, and in the darkness he was unable to see from my face what was its expression.

At last he asked me, "Don't you believe this story?"

I asked, "Do you?"

He said, "No; and I can give you one or two reasons why. In the first place, Dame Nature does not write novels, she has enough to do without –"

I interrupted him and said, "And, in the second place, my name happens to be Bhusan Saha."

The schoolmaster, without the least sign of discomfiture, said, "I guessed as much. And what was your wife's name?"

I answered, "Nitya Kali."

42

EMANCIPATION

"Theft from the king's treasury!" The cry ran through the town. The thief must be found, or there will be trouble for the officer of the guards.

Vajrasen, a stranger from a foreign port, came to sell horses in the town, and, robbed by a band of robbers of all his earnings, was lying in a ruined temple outside the walls. They charged him with the theft, chained him, and led him through the streets to the prison.

Proud Shyama, of a perilous charm, sat in her balcony idly watching the passing crowd. Suddenly she shuddered, and cried to her attendant, "Alas, who is that godlike young man with a noble face, led in chains like a common thief? Ask the officer in my name to bring him in before me."

The chief of the guards came with the prisoner, and said to Shyama, "Your favour is untimely, my lady; I must hasten to do the king's bidding." Vajrasen quickly raised his head, and broke out, "What caprice is this of yours, woman, to bring me in from the street to mock me with your cruel curiosity?"

"Mock you!" cried Shyama, "I could gladly take your chains upon my limbs in exchange for my jewels."

Then, turning to the officer, she said, "Take all the money I have, and set him free."

He bowed, and said, "It cannot be. A victim we must have to stay the king's wrath."

"I ask only two days' respite for the prisoner," urged Shyama. The officer smiled, and consented.

On the end of his second night in prison, Vajrasen said his prayers, and sat waiting for his last moment, when suddenly the door opened, and the woman appeared with a lamp in her hand, and at her signal the guard unchained the prisoner.

"You have come to me with that lamp, merciful woman,' said he, 'like the dawn with her morning star after a night of delirious ever."

"Merciful indeed," Shyama cried, and broke out in wild laughter, till tears came with a burst, and she sobbed, and said, "There is no stone brick in this prison-tower harder than this woman's heart." And clutching the prisoner's hand she dragged him out of the gates.

On the Varuna's bank the sun rose. A boat was waiting at the landing. "Come to the boat with me, stranger youth," Shyama said. "Only know that I have cut all bonds, and I drift in the same boat with you."

Swiftly the boat glided on. Merrily sang the birds. 'Tell me, my love,' asked Vajrasen, 'what untold wealth did you spend to buy my freedom?'

"Hush, not now," said Shyama.

Morning wore on to noon. Village women had gone back home with their clothes dripping from their bath, and pitchers filled with water. Marketing was over. The village path glared in the sun all lonely.

In the warm gusts of the noontide wind Shyama's veil dropped from her face. Vajrasen murmured in her ears, "You freed me from a bond that was brief to bind me in a bond everlasting. Let me know how it was done." The woman drew her veil over her face, and said, "Not now, my beloved."

The day waned, and it darkened. The breeze died away. The crescent moon glimmered feebly at the edge of the steel-black water.

Shyama sat in the dark, resting her head on the youth's shoulder. Her hair fell loose on his arms.

"What I did for you was hard, beloved,' she said in a faint whisper, but it is harder to tell you. I shall tell it in a few words. It was the love-sick boy Uttiya who took your place, charging himself with the theft, and making me a present of his life. My greatest sin has been committed for the love of you, my best beloved."

While she spoke the crescent moon had set. The stillness of the forest was heavy with the sleep of countless birds.

Slowly the youth's arm slipped from the woman's waist. Silence round them became hard and cold as stone.

Suddenly the woman fell at his feet, and clung to his knee crying, 'Forgive me, my love. Leave it to my god to punish me for my sin.'

Snatching his feet away, Vajrasen hoarsely cried, "That my life should be bought by the price of a sin! That every breath of mine should be accursed!"

He stood up, and leapt from the boat on the bank, and entered the forest. He walked on and on till the path closed and the dense trees, tangled with creepers, stopped him with fantastic gestures.

Tired, he sat on the ground. But who was it that followed him in silence, the long dark way, and stood at his back like a phantom?

"Will you not leave me?" shouted Vajrasen.

In a moment the woman fell upon him with an impetuous flood of caresses; with her tumbling hair and trailing robes, with her showering kisses and panting breath she covered him all over.

In a voice choked with pent-up tears, she said, "No, no; I shall never leave you. I have sinned for you. Strike me, if you will; kill me with your own hands."

The still blackness of the forest shivered for a moment; a horror ran through the twisting roots of trees underground. A groan and a smothered breath rose through the night, and a body fell down upon the withered leaves.

The morning sun flashed on the far-away spire of the temple when Vajrasen came out of the woods. He wandered in the hot sun the whole day by the river on the sandy waste, and never rested for a moment.

In the evening he went back aimlessly to the boat. There on the bed lay an anklet. He clutched it, and pressed it to his heart till it bruised him. He fell prone upon the blue mantle left lying in a heap in the corner, hid his face in its folds, and from its silken touch and evasive fragrance struggled to absorb into his being the memory of a dear living body.

The night shook with a tense and tingling silence. The moon disappeared behind the trees. Vajrasen stood up, and stretched out his arms towards the woods, and called, "Come, my love, come." Suddenly a figure came out of the darkness, and stood on the brink of the water.

"Come, love, come."

"I have come, my beloved. Your dear hands failed to kill me. It is my doom to live."

Shyama came, and stood before the youth. He looked at her face, he moved a step to take her in his arms – then, thrust her away with both hands, and cried, "Why, oh why did you come back?"

He shut his eyes, turning his face, and said, "Go, go; leave me."

For a minute the woman stood silent before she knelt at his feet and bowed low. Then, she rose, and went up the river-bank, and vanished in the vague of the woods like a dream merging into sleep; and Vajrasen, with aching heart, sat silent in the boat.

43

The River Stairs

If you wish to hear of days gone by, sit on this step of mine, and lend your ears to the murmur of the rippling water.

The month of Ashwin (September) was about to begin. The river was in full flood. Only four of my steps peeped above the surface. The water had crept up to the low-lying parts of the bank, where the kochu plant grew dense beneath the branches of the mango grove. At that bend of the river, three old brick-heaps towered above the water around them. The fishing-boats, moored to the trunks of the babla trees on the bank, rocked on the heaving flow-tide at dawn. The path of tall grasses on the sandbank had caught the newly risen sun; they had just begun to flower, and were not yet in full bloom.

The little boats puffed out their tiny sails on the sunlit river. The Brahmin priest had come to bathe with his ritual vessels. The women arrived in twos and threes to draw water. I knew this was the time of Kusum's coming to the bathing-stairs.

But that morning I missed her. Bhuban and Swarno mourned at the ghat. They said that their friend had been led away to her husband›s house, which was a place far away from the river, with strange people, strange houses, and strange roads.

In time she almost faded out of my mind. A year passed. The women at the ghat now rarely talked of Kusum. But one evening I was startled by the touch of the long familiar feet. Ah, yes, but those feet were now without anklets, they had lost their old music.

Kusum had become a widow. They said that her husband had worked in some far-off place, and that she had met him only once or twice. A letter brought her the news of his death. A widow at eight years old, she had rubbed out the wife's red mark from her forehead, stripped off her bangles, and come back to her old home by the Ganges. But she found few of her old playmates there. Of them, Bhuban, Swarno, and Amala were married, and gone away; only Sarat remained, and she too, they said, would be wed in December next.

As the Ganges rapidly grows to fulness with the coming of the rains, even so did Kusum day by day grow to the fulness of beauty and youth. But her dull-coloured robe, her pensive face, and quiet manners drew a veil over her youth, and hid it from men's eyes as in a mist. Ten years slipped away, and none seemed to have noticed that Kusum had grown up.

One morning such as this, at the far end of a far-off September, a tall, young, fair-skinned sannyasi, coming I know not whence, took shelter in the Shiva temple in front of me. His arrival was noised abroad in the village. The women left their pitchers behind, and crowded into the temple to bow to the holy man.

The crowd increased day by day. The sannyasi's fame rapidly spread among the womenkind. One day he would recite the *Bhagvad,* another day he would expound the *Gita,* or hold forth upon a holy book in the temple. Some sought him for counsel, some for spells, some for medicines.

So months passed away. In April, at the time of the solar eclipse, vast crowds came here to bathe in the Ganges. A fair was held under the babla tree. Many of the pilgrims went to visit the sannyasi, and among them were a party of women from the village where Kusum had been married.

It was morning. The sannyasi was counting his beads on my steps, when all of a sudden one of the women pilgrims nudged another, and said, "Why! He is our Kusum's husband!" Another parted her veil a little in the middle with two fingers and cried out, "Oh dear me! So it is! He is the younger son of the Chattergu family of our village!" Said a third, who made little parade of her veil, "Ah! He has got exactly the same brow, nose, and eyes!" Yet another woman, without turning to the sannyasi, stirred the water with her pitcher, and sighed, "Alas! That young man is no more; he will not come back. Bad luck to Kusum!"

But, objected one, "He had not such a big beard"; and another, "He was not so thin"; or "He was most probably not so tall." That settled the question for the time, and the matter spread no further.

One evening, as the full moon arose, Kusum came and sat upon my last step above the water, and cast her shadow upon me.

There was no other at the ghat just then. The crickets were chirping about me. The din of brass gongs and bells had ceased in the temple – the last wave of sound grew fainter and fainter, until it merged like the shade of a sound in the dim groves of the farther bank. On the dark water of the Ganges lay a line of glistening moonlight. On the bank above, in bush and hedge, under the porch of the temple, in the base of mined houses, by the side of the tank, in the palm grove, gathered shadows of fantastic shape. The bats swung from the chhatim boughs. Near the houses the loud clamour of the jackals rose and sank into silence.

Slowly, the sannyasi came out of the temple. Descending a few steps of the ghat he saw a woman sitting alone, and was about to go back, when suddenly Kusum raised her head, and looked behind her. The veil slipped away from her. The moonlight fell upon her face, as she looked up.

The owl flew away hooting over their heads. Starting at the sound, Kusum came to herself and put the veil back on her head. Then, she bowed low at the sannyasi's feet.

He gave her blessing and asked, "Who are you?"

She replied, "I am called Kusum."

No other word was spoken that night. Kusum went slowly back to her house which was hard by. But the sannyasi remained sitting on my steps for long hours that night. At last when the moon passed from the east to the west, and the sannyasi's shadow, shifting from behind, fell in front of him, he rose up and entered the temple.

Henceforth, I saw Kusum come daily to bow at his feet. When he expounded the holy books, she stood in a corner listening to him. After finishing his morning service, he used to call her to himself and speak on religion. She could not have understood it all; but, listening attentively in silence, she tried to understand it. As he directed her, so she acted implicitly. She daily served at the temple – ever alert in the god's worship – gathering flowers for the puja, and drawing water from the Ganges to wash the temple floor.

The winter was drawing to its close. We had cold winds. But now and then, in the evening the warm spring breeze would blow unexpectedly from the south; the sky would lose its chilly aspect; pipes would sound, and music be heard in the village after a long silence. The boatmen would set their boats drifting down the current, stop rowing, and begin to sing the songs of Krishna. This was the season.

Just then, I began to miss Kusum. For some time she had given up visiting the temple, the ghat, or the sannyasi.

What happened next I do not know, but after a while the two met together on my steps one evening.

With downcast looks, Kusum asked, "Master, did you send for me?" "Yes, why do I not see you? Why have you grown neglectful of late in serving the gods?"

She kept silent.

"Tell me your thoughts without reserve."

Half averting her face, she replied, "I am a sinner, Master, and hence, I have failed in the worship."

The sannyasi said, "Kusum, I know there is unrest in your heart."

She gave a slight start, and, drawing the end of her sari over her face, she sat down on the step at the sannyasi's feet, and wept.

He moved a little away, and said, "Tell me what you have in your heart, and I shall show you the way to peace."

She replied in a tone of unshaken faith, stopping now and then, for words, "If you bid me, I must speak out. But, then I cannot explain it clearly. You, Master, must have guessed it all. I adored one as a god, I worshipped him, and the bliss of that devotion filled my heart to fulness. But one night I dreamt that the lord of my heart was sitting in a garden somewhere, clasping my right hand in his left, and whispering to me of love. The whole scene did not appear to me at all strange. The dream vanished, but its hold on me remained. Next day when I beheld him he appeared in another light than before. That dream-picture continued to haunt my mind. I fled far from him in fear, and the picture clung to me. Thenceforth, my heart has known no peace – all has grown dark within me!"

While she was wiping her tears and telling this tale, I felt that the sannyasi was firmly pressing my stone surface with his right foot.

Her speech done, the sannyasi said,

"You must tell me whom you saw in your dream."

With folded hands, she entreated, "I cannot."

He insisted, "You must tell me who he was."

Wringing her hands she asked, "Must I tell it?"

He replied, "Yes, you must."

Then, crying, "You are he, Master!" she fell on her face on my stony bosom, and sobbed.

When she came to herself, and sat up, the sannyasi said slowly, "I am leaving this place to-night that you may not see me again. Know that I am a sannyasi, not belonging to this world. You must forget me.

Kusum replied in a low voice, "It will be so, Master."

The sannyasi said, "I take my leave."

Without a word more Kusum bowed to him, and placed the dust of his feet on her head. He left the place.

The moon set; the night grew dark. I heard a splash in the water. The wind raved in the darkness, as if it wanted to blow out all the stars of the sky.

44

Two Sisters

SARMILA

Women are of two kinds, the mother-kind and the beloved-kind – so I have heard some learned men say. If a comparison may be drawn with the seasons, the mother is the rainy season. She brings the gift of water and of fruit, tempers the heat, and dissolving from the heights drives away the drought. She fills with plenty. The beloved, on the other hand, is the Spring. Deep its mystery, sweet its enchantment. Its restlessness rocks the blood into waves and swings over into the jewel-chamber of the mind where the solitary string of the golden veena is lying mute, waiting for the vibration to set the body and the mind ringing in some wordless melody.

Sasanka's wife Sarmila was the mother-kind. Her large, gentle eyes had a deep, steady look. The dark, well-rounded limbs had the comely grace of the first rain-laden clouds. The vermilion mark at the parting of her hair, the broad black border of her sari, the thick bangles on her wrists bespoke homely grace rather than elegance of style.

There was no outlying region in the territory of her husband's life over which her empire was not actively exercised. The extreme solicitude with which she had surrounded his life had made him careless. If by any chance the fountain pen was so misplaced on the table as not to be readily at hand the moment he needed it, his wife would have to discover it for him. If he could not remember where he had left his wrist-watch before going to bathe, his wife was sure to know where it was. So, too, she must be there to repair his error when, having put on socks of different shades, he was ready to go out. He mixed up English dates with Bengali months and sent out invitations to friends accordingly, and when the unexpected guests made their untimely appearance, it was his wife who had to bear the brunt of it. He knew full well that any negligence in the day's routine would be set right by her. To perpetrate negligences, therefore, had become second nature with him.

"It's the limit," his wife would complain, half, derisively, half lovingly. "Will you never learn?"

If he had learnt, Sarmila's days would have lain idle as untilled land.

One day, Sasanka was at some friend's, playing bridge. It was getting rather late at night. Suddenly, his friends burst out laughing. "Ah! Here comes your bearer with the summons! Your time is up." Sure enough, there was the inevitable Mahesh, with his moustache gone grey and the hair still black on his head, wearing a vest, with a coloured duster on his shoulder, and a bamboo rod in his hand.

"The mistress has sent me to inquire if the master is here. She is afraid of some mishap to the master on his way back in the dark night. She has sent a lantern as well."

Irritated, Sasanka threw down the cards and got up. The friends taunted, "Ah, the lonely, unguarded male!"

On reaching home Sasanka addressed his wife in no gentle terms or peaceful manner. Sarmila quietly accepted the scolding. What was she to do? She simply could not get rid of her fear that when her husband was not with her, all sorts of impossible perils were conspiring to waylay him.

Another day, some stranger had called on business. Every now and then a chit would be handed in. "You know you were indisposed yesterday. Do come in early to dinner." Sasanka lost his temper, but yielded, nevertheless.

Once in extreme exasperation he had told his wife. "For goodness' sake, get hold of some god or deity like that Chakravarty wife. It's too much for me to withstand your attentions all by myself. Sharing them with a god would make it easier. The gods can stand excesses, but man is frail."

"Indeed!" retorted Sarmila. "Have you forgotten your condition that time when I went to Haridwar with my uncle?"

He had himself related to his wife, adding embellishment for effect, how very pathetic his condition had been in her absence. He knew that such exaggeration would make her feel at once penitent and happy. How could he now go back on his own immoderate version! And so, he swallowed the retort and kept quiet. Nor did it end there. Fancying that in the morning he had a slight touch of cold, she made him swallow ten grains of quinine as well, with juice of tulsi leaves in tea. He dared not object, for, having refused to take quinine on a previous occasion, he had developed fever – which incident had remained ineffaceably engraved in the domestic annals.

As she was solicitous of her husband's well-being and comfort at home, so was Sarmila jealously mindful of his dignity abroad. Let me recall an incident.

Once, they were going to Nainital on holiday and had their compartment reserved "through". At a junction where they changed trains, they went out to dine. Returning they found a villainous looking figure in livery actively occupied in dispossessing them of their berths. The station-master came and explained that the compartment had been actually reserved for a certain celebrated general, though through inadvertence their name had been affixed to it. Opening his eyes wide, flabbergasted, Sasanka made ready to shift, when up jumped Sarmila into the compartment and standing against the door challenged:

"Let me see who dares pull me down! Call your General here!"

Sasanka, who was a government servant, and was well accustomed to keeping a safe distance from the path of the superior official tribe, grew nervous and began to protest: "But what's the use? There are plenty of other carriages – "

But Sarmila would not heed. In the end the General who had returned from the refreshment room, cigar in mouth, and was witnessing this spectacle of feminine wrath, himself retired to another compartment. Sasanka turned to his wife: "Do you know how big that man is?"

"Don't care to know. In a compartment reserved for us, he is no bigger than you."

"What if he had insulted us?" ventured Sasanka

"What are you for then?" retorted Sarmila.

Sasanka was a graduate of the Sibpur Engineering College. However irresponsible he might be in the other walks of his life, he was careful enough in his official duties; the main reason being that the planet presiding over his official world was not his wife but the ruthless eye of the "Bara Saheb".

When he was acting as the district engineer his newly won promotion was suddenly reversed and he was superseded, despite his superior claim, by an inexperienced English youth, with the mere down of a moustache – an unsuspected proof of what right connections in high quarters can achieve. Sasanka knew that he would still have to carry on the real work, while that white booby would be installed in the chair. The big boss patted him on the back and said consolingly:

"Very sorry, Mazumdar. As soon as feasible, we'll push you up."

Both of them were Freemasons.

But despite this hope and consolation, the whole affair was exceedingly unpleasant for Mazumdar. At home he found cause for quarrel with every little thing. Suddenly, he noticed soot in a corner of his office room; suddenly, he felt that he couldn't bear the sight of the green cover of his sofa. He thundered at the office-boy who was sweeping the verandah for blowing dust in his direction. The inevitable specks of dust blew daily, but the master's thunder was something new.

He kept the news of his humiliation from his wife, afraid she would only add one more complication to the already complicated affairs of his service. She might even go and pick a quarrel with his boss, in no pleasant language, specially as she already nursed a grudge against Donaldson. Once, while engaged in suppressing the monkey pest in the garden of the circuit house, he had instead marked holes in Sasanka's sola hat. Fortunately, there was no accident, but an accident there might easily have been. People blamed Sasanka, which only added to Sarmila's wrath against Donaldson. What inflamed her wrath most was that Sasanka's enemies made much of the joke that a bullet aimed at a monkey had landed on Sasanka.

However, she herself found out all about the reverse in her husband's official status. She had suspected from his manner that somewhere a thorn was pricking. It did not take long to discover the cause. Rejecting the way of 'constitutional agitation', she went straight for 'self-determination'. She told her husband:

"Have done with it. Hand in your resignation immediately." Resignation would no doubt remove the leech of humiliation from his breast. But then, there stretched before his mind's eye the rich field of regular monthly income and beyond that the golden prospect of a pension.

In the very year in which Sasankamauli had topped the pinnacle of the M.Sc. degree, his father-in-law, unwilling to delay the auspicious event, married him off to Sarmila. With the wealthy father-in-law's help he passed the engineering course. Seeing his speedy rise in service, Rajaram Babu had felt assured of his son-in- law's steady progress in prosperity. The daughter, too, never suspected till now that the contrary could happen. Not that any want was actually felt in the house; the ways of her father's house had been maintained here, too, the reason being that in the domestic dyarchy all management was in Sarmila's control. She had no child, nor any longer the hope of one. Whatever her husband earned was delivered into her hands to the last copper. If any special need arose he had no alternative but to go and beg from the Annapurna of his home. If the demand was unreasonable, it was refused; he accepted the decision, scratching his head. But there was always some other sweet compensation to make up for this disappointment.

"To give up the job," said Sasanka, "matters little to me. It's for your sake that I hesitate. You'll be put to hardship."

"It's a worse hardship to try to swallow injustice which sticks in the throat."

"But," remonstrated Sasanka, "one must work. If I give up the certain, where shall I go about looking for the uncertain?"

"Where you don't care to look now. You jokingly call your government service your luchusthan – beyond the arid wastes of Baluchisthan, and you are so obsessed with it that you ignore the whole wide world outside it."

"Good Heavens! The whole world is too big for me. Who is going to survey all its highways and byways? Where am I to find a telescope big enough for that?"

"No big telescope is needed. My cousin Mathurdada is a big contractor in Calcutta. If you join him as a partner, we'll manage to make both ends meet."

"It would be an unfair sharing, for the weight on this side of the scale would not be enough. To hobble in such partnership seems too undignified."

"The weight on this side of the scale would be not one whit too light. You know the amount father had deposited in the bank in my name – well, it's there, only bloated with interest. You would not have to feel small before your partner."

"How can I take that? That money is yours." Saying which Sasanka got up. There were visitors waiting outside. Sarmila caught hold of his dress and pulled him back into the seat.

"I too am yours," she said. And added: "Pull out that fountain- pen from your pocket, here's the paper, write out your resignation. I can have no peace till I have posted that letter."

"Nor can I have any peace either, it seems." He wrote the letter of resignation.

The very next day, Sarmila went to Calcutta and straight to Mathurdada's house. Petulantly she greeted him:

"Not once have you cared to inquire after your sister."

One of her own sex would have retorted: "Nor have you." But the male brain could think of no such retort. Mathurdada admitted his fault:

"Have I even the time to breathe? Sometimes, I even forget whether or not I exist. Besides, you two are always on tour."

"I read in the papers," said Sarmila, "that you have secured the contract for building a bridge at Mayurbhanj or Mathurganj or some such place. I was so delighted that I thought, let me go and congratulate Mathurdada in person."

"Wait a little, Khuki. It's not time yet."

The trouble was that liquid capital was needed for which he had offered to enter into partnership with a wealthy Marwari. In the end it turned out that the Marwari's conditions were such that while the Marwari would have all the juice, he would be left only the refuse. So, he was trying to back out.

"Impossible," cried Sarmila excitedly. "It can't be allowed. If you needs must enter into partnership, then let it be with us. It would be too bad to let such business slip from your hands. I simply will not allow it, say what you will."

It did not take long to render all this into a written deed. Mathurdada's heart too was touched.

The business went ahead. Formerly, Sasanka's work had been 'service', it limits were well defined. Working under a boss, his responsibility ended with the demand made on it. Now, however, he was his own boss, subject to no will but his own. The claim of duty and his response to it were now merged in one. The days were no longer woven in a network of work-days and holiday, but became one compact whole. Because he was now free to ignore his responsibility, its hold on his mind became all the more tenacious. If nothing else, he must at least pay back his debt to his wife; after that there would be time enough to set the pace slow and easy. And so, in khaki pants, his leather belt fastened tight, wearing thick- soled shoes, a sola hat on his head, his sleeves rolled up, a watch strapped to his left wrist, and sunglasses to protect his eyes, Sasanka plunged headlong into his work. Nor, was the pressure of the steam relaxed, even when the debt had been wellnigh liquidated; the mind was still in full heat.

Formerly, his income and expenditure had flowed through one single channel; now they branched into two, one flowing bankwards, the other homewards. Sarmila continued to receive her old portion and dispensed it as before, Sasanka remaining a stranger to its mysteries. On the other hand, Sasanka's leather-bound ledger of business accounts was to her inaccessible, incomprehensible. There was no harm in that. But the fact that this path of her husband's business life ran outside her domestic orbit did, however, mean that her jurisdiction to that extent had suffered.

"Don't overdo it please," she pleaded, "your health will break down."

To no avail. Strangely enough, his health did not break down. Impetuously ignoring all pleadings of conjugal solicitude, her anxiety for his health, her complaints at his lack of rest, her fussy concern over the details of his comfort, et cetera, Sasanka left the house early in the morning, blowing the horn of his second-hand Ford, himself at the wheel; returned at about two or half-past two, received a scolding and then his food which he gulped down.

One day, his car ran into another. He was unhurt, but the car was damaged and had to be sent to the garage for repairs. Sarmila was greatly upset.

"You must not drive anymore," she beseeched, her voice hoarse.

"An accident at another's hands can be equally fatal," replied Sasanka, laughingly dismissing her concern.

One day, while he was supervising some repair work, a packing- box nail pierced through the shoe right into his foot. At the hospital the wound was bandaged and he was given an anti-tetanus injection. That day, Sarmila was all tears.

"Stay in bed for a day or two at least," she pleaded. But Sasanka replied laconically: "Work."

It is not possible to improve on such brevity of expression.

"But," remonstrated Sarmila, – but Sasanka had left, without even a word, and with bandage on.

Sarmila dared not test her powers anymore. The man's masterfulness in his own field was now evident. Beyond all argument, entreaty, pleading, was the one phrase, "I've work to do."

For no reason Sarmila was uneasy, anxious. The slightest delay in returning home and she thought of an accident to the car. When she saw her husband's face flushed with the sun's heat, she thought it must surely be influenza. Timidly, she would suggest the doctor – and immediately stop, seeing the reaction on him. Nowadays, she was afraid even to express her anxiety fully and freely.

In no time Sasanka became sun-burnt and dry. His dress, like his leisure, was cut short to tightness; his movements became hurried; his speech abrupt like sparks. To this quick rhythm Sarmila's ministry strove to adjust its motions. Some food must always be kept ready and warm near the stove – for who knew when the husband might suddenly and untimely declare: "I'm off. Shall be late in returning." A provision of soda water and dry food-stuff in a tin was neatly stored in his car; a bottle of eau de cologne carefully concealed from view – in case of headache. She looked into them carefully each time the car returned home, only to find that nothing had been used. It was distressing. Every day a clean change of clothes, neatly folded, was prominently displayed in his bedroom, nevertheless, at least four days in the week he found no time to change. Domestic consultation reduced to the briefest, in the staccato style of an express telegram, had to be carried out in a most casual manner, standing, walking or calling from behind, "Just a word, dear." The little connection which Sarmila had with his business also came to an end with the repayment of her loan, interest and all. The interest, too, had been paid to the penny and a formal receipt taken.

"What a pity!" wailed Sarmila. "Even in love men cannot wholly lose themselves. A portion of themselves they needs must set apart for the exercise of their masculine ego."

From his share of the profits Sasanka built a house in Bhowanipore, after his own heart. To astound Sarmila he planned the latest devices of hygiene, comfort and order. Sarmila too, was not remiss in allowing herself to be properly astounded. There was the laundry machine installed by the engineer. Sarmila looked at it from this side and that and praised it profusely; but to herself she added: "Nevertheless, the clothes will continue to be sent to the dhobi as they have been till this day. I've known the donkey carry soiled clothes, but have not known science take its place yet."

Seeing the potato-peeling machine she was all amazement. "Three- fourths of the drudgery of cooking potatoes is gone now," she declared. Later on, it was rumoured that this machine had earned its liberation from toil in some limbo of oblivion, alongside many a leaking pot and broken kettle.

When the house was completed, Sarmila's repressed affection found a stable object for its exercise. The infinite patience of a brick- and-mortar body makes it a convenient object of affection. The endless pother of setting and fitting, furnishing and arranging drove the two bearers to the end of their tether; one of them gave notice. The interior decoration was for Sasanka's benefit. He hardly ever sat in the drawing room; yet cushions of various patterns were devotedly spread for his tired back-bone; tables and teapoys were there, with fringed covers embroidered with flowered patterns; and many a flower-vase. He no longer entered the bedroom during the day, the reason being that in his current calendar Sunday had been adopted as twin-brother of Monday. Even on other holidays when the office was closed he managed to find some little work or other to do and went and sat in his study with his files or with his tracing cloth. Nevertheless, in the bedroom the old order persisted. In front of the spacious, cushioned sofa were the knitted slippers; beside it the pans ready as of old in the betel box; on the rack a punjabi of fine silk and a dhoti, pleated and crinkled, ready for wear.

It was a risky business to meddle with Sasanka's study; despite the risk Sarmila ventured in with a duster when he was not there. With unremitting diligence she strove to bring order and harmony in the medley of things useful and useless.

Thus, Sarmila continued to be serviceable, but her service went a great deal unobserved. Her devotion which was once offered directly to its object was now directed to its symbols –

in looking after the house and the garden, in knitting a cover for Sasanka's sofa, embroidering flower patterns on his pillow-case, in setting on a corner of his office-table bouquets of tuberoses in blue crystal vases. It cost her no little pain to worship her deity from so great a distance. She was still bathing with her secret tears the wound inflicted on her only the other day. It was the 29th of Karthik, Sasanka's birthday, the most festive day in her life. And usual, invitations had been sent out to friends and the house and the gate specially decorated with flower and leaf. Returning from work just before noon, Sasanka inquired: "What's the matter? A doll's wedding, I suppose!"

"Dear me! You have even forgotten it's your birthday today. But say what you will, you must stay in this evening."

"Business bends its head before no day, save the day of death."

"I won't ever ask you again, but today I have already sent out the invitations."

"Look here, Sarmila, don't you ever try to set me up as a plaything and call in the crowd to watch you play."

Saying which Sasanka hurriedly left. Shutting the bedroom door, Sarmila cried awhile.

In the afternoon the guests arrived. They readily acknowledged the paramount claim of 'business'. Had it been Kalidasa's birthday instead, the plea that he had to finish Act III of *Sakuntala* would have been dismissed by them as too frivolous to be seriously entertained as an excuse for his absence. But business! However, there was enough of amusement and gaiety. Nalu Babu made everyone laugh by his caricatures of the current stage-acting; even Sarmila joined in the hilarity. Sasanka's birthday, bereft of Sasanka, prostrated itself before the business presided over by him. Even Sarmila's heart, aggrieved as it was, made its distant obeisance to the flying banner on the racing chariot of that business.

Unbending was this work, which cared for none, which ignored everything, the wife's entreaties, the invitations to friends, his own comfort even. Such faith in his work gives man faith in himself; it is the homage of self to its own power. Standing on one bank of their river – the bank of daily domestic routine – Sarmila watched with awe Sasanka's work on the other bank which made itself felt far and wide, beyond the boundaries of the household, in distant lands, on the shores of distant seas, gathering in the net of its authority men both known and unknown.

Man is at daily war with his fate; if the soft entwining arms of woman hinder him in his rugged onward march, it is but natural that he should ruthlessly break away. With loving faith Sarmila had accepted this ruthlessness. But there were times when she could not help herself, and impelled by love, her tender solicitude trespassed on forbidden ground. Rebuffed, she acknowledged the rebuff as well-merited and sorrowfully retraced her steps, praying to the Deity to watch her husband's steps where access to her was barred.

NIRAD

When the prosperity of this family, riding on bank investments, was running into six figures, Sarmila was attacked and laid prostrate by a disease which could not be diagnosed. It is necessary to explain why this fact caused so much consternation.

Sarmila's father, Rajaram Babu, had owned a considerable estate in Barisal, near the mouth of the Ganges, besides holding shares in a ship-building yard at Salimar. He was born at the junction of the old times and the new. He could wrestle, hunt, wield a lathi like an expert, and was also famous for his skill at pakhawaj. He could recite from memory passages from The Merchant of Venice, Julius Caesar and Hamlet, held Macaulay's English as his ideal, and was an ardent admirer of Burke's orations. His appreciation of Bengali literature extended as far as *Meghnadbadh Kabya*. In his middle age he had looked upon the taking of alcoholic drinks and proscribed food as a sine qua non of modern culture. In his old age, however, he gave it up. Handsome and dignified in appearance, of tall and sturdy build, he dressed with meticulous care, and was of a hearty and sociable disposition. He never could say 'no' to needy importunity. Though he himself was indifferent to religious forms, they were nevertheless, observed in his house with great pomp, for such impressive observances add to the prestige of the family. As regards the actual worship of the deity there were the ladies of the house and many others to look after it. Had he been keen, he could easily have secured the title of a Raja for himself. If anyone asked him why he was indifferent to it, Rajaram laughingly replied that his father having already conferred on him the name Raja, it would be belittling that honour to add a duplicate to it. At the Government House he was honoured with entry by the special gate. On the occasion of the customary Jagadhatri Puja in his house, champagne used to flow freely and high English officials had their fill of it.

After Sarmila's marriage, his widowed home was left with only his eldest son Hemanta and his youngest daughter Urmimala. "Brilliant!" – That is how the teachers had always spoken of the boy. His appearance was such that when one had passed him one turned to look at him again. There was no subject in which he did not secure the highest marks at every examination. In athletic achievements, too, he promised to live up to his father's reputation. It is superfluous to state that he was constantly besieged by eager agents of prospective brides, but he was averse to marriage as yet. For the present his heart was bent on the prospect of a degree at a European University, with which object he had even begun to study French and German. Meanwhile, for want of anything better, he began the study of law as well, though there was hardly any necessity for it.

About this time, however, Hemanta was suddenly attacked by a disease, whether of the intestines or of some other organ, the doctors failed to diagnose. The mysterious ailment was lodged in his robust body as in a citadel; it was as difficult to locate it as to attack it. Rajaram Babu had implicit faith in an English doctor, who enjoyed at that time high reputation as a surgeon. The surgeon began an exploration of his patient's body and, as is the way of surgeons, came to the conclusion that the trouble was rooted in some inaccessible organ which must therefore be uprooted. But when, accordingly, his skilful instruments cut open the outer layer of the flesh and exposed the interior, neither the alleged enemy nor any trace of its havoc was discovered. The mischief was irremediable and the boy died. The father was disconsolate with bitter grief. It was not the death so much as the picture of a strong, beautiful and palpitating body being mutilated which, like a black bird of prey, dug its piercing claws into his mind, and sucking his vitals day and night, brought him to the very verge of death.

Dr. Nirad Mukherjee, an old classmate of Hemanta's, who had recently qualified as a doctor and was helping in the nursing of his friend, had protested from the very beginning that the case was being wrongly treated. He had given his own diagnosis and had advised a change of climate and a long stay in some dry place. But the prejudices of an older generation were too firmly fixed in the mind of Rajaram, who believed that only an English doctor could effectively combat the fierce onslaught of death. But after this experience his affection for Nirad and confidence in him rose disproportionately high. His young daughter Urmi too suddenly realised that here was a man of uncommon genius and said to her father:

"So young in years, father, and yet how strong his confidence in himself! See, how boldly and without any hesitation or doubt he asserted his judgement even against that of such a big and hefty foreign doctor!"

The father replied: "A doctor does not learn from books alone. Some are endowed with a rare, God-given insight – which I find Nirad has."

Thus, under the impact of sorrow and in the pain of remorse, a slight proof of merit was sufficient to give rise to their loving admiration which, once born, went on growing without waiting for any further evidence of worth.

One day, Rajaram called his daughter and said:

"Urmi, I almost hear Hemanta calling to me, – calling upon me to alleviate the suffering of diseased humanity. I have decided to found a hospital in his name."

"Excellent!" exclaimed Urmi exultingly, carried away by her natural enthusiasm. "Send me to Europe. Let me return as a doctor and take charge of the hospital."

The suggestion appealed to Rajaram.

"This hospital will be a Debottar property," he said, "and you shall be the shebait. Great pain was Hemanta's portion; he loved you much; your devoted service will bring him peace in the other world. You served him day and night on his sick bed; now that service will attain a larger scope in your hands."

It did not strike him as preposterous that a girl of aristocratic family should take to medicine as a profession; for he had now deeply realised what it meant to rescue life from the clutches of disease. His own son could not survive, but the sons of others might; which would be some compensation for his loss, some lightening of the weight of his sorrow. He said to his daughter:

"Finish your science course at the University here, and then proceed to Europe."

From now on, one thought constantly recurred to Rajaram's mind, the thought of that boy Nirad. A veritable piece of gold. The more he saw him, the more he liked him. Having covered the tedious course of examinations, how smoothly he was swimming his way through the deep ocean of medical knowledge! Despite his young years, he was unmoved by the pleasures of light-hearted gaiety, deeply absorbed in the latest discoveries, discussing them, analysing them and putting them to the test, even at the risk of his professional career. He had great contempt for those who had only built up a practice, and would say: "The foolish achieve success, the worthy glory." An epigram taken from a book.

At last, Rajaram told Urmi one day: "I've been thinking that it would be best for the success of the mission if you and Nirad join hands in this work. I too, would feel reassured. It's rare to come across a boy like that."

Whatever else Rajaram could do, he could not be indifferent to Hemanta's opinions; and Hemanta used to say that it was barbarous of parents to ignore the daughter's wishes in the matter and to force on her a marriage of their own choice. Rajaram had once argued that marriage was not a mere personal affair but involved the whole family, and that therefore, in its making not only desire but experience also should count. But argue as he might, and despite his own likes and dislikes, so great was his affection for Hemanta that in this family it was really the latter's will that prevailed.

Nirad Mukherjee had always been a frequent visitor. Hemanta had nicknamed him the Owl. When invited to explain the significance, Hemanta used to say: "This man is mythological; he has no age, only learning; hence I call him Minerva's mount." Nirad was a frequent guest at their tea-table, where he would often enter into a terrific argument with Hemanta. No doubt, Urmi was in his mind; if his behaviour gave no indication of the fact, it was because his nature had not fitted him for the ways appropriate to such expression. He could discuss, but could not converse. Even if the heat of youth was in him, he was without its glow. Hence, he took a particular delight in running down those in whom the exuberance of youth was self-evident. Naturally, therefore, no one had reckoned him as a suitor for Urmi's hand, though now it so happened that this very apparent indifference raised Urmi's respect for him to the point of veneration.

When Rajaram had made it quite clear that, provided his daughter had no objection, it would make him happy to see her wedded to Nirad, Urmi signified her consent by a nod of her head; only adding that the wedding would have to wait till she had completed her course of education, both here and in Europe.

"That's as it should be," replied the father, "as long as the engagement is accepted and made definite by both the parties."

It did not take long to get Nirad's consent, though his manner implied that for a scientist marriage was a kind of self-abnegation, almost amounting to suicide. Perhaps, as a partial alleviation of this calamity, he made it a condition that in education as in other matters Urmi would be guided entirely by him, so that he might gradually mould and fashion her as his future wife. This training would be scientific, rigidly prescribed and regulated, infallible as a laboratory process.

"The birds and beasts," explained Nirad to Urmi "come out ready-made from Nature's workshop. But human life is in a raw, unformed state. It's for man to put it into shape."

Urmi gently replied: "You may by all means experiment. I'll make no difficulties."

"The life-force in you is dispersed," went on Nirad. "It has to be mobilised and marshalled round one single object of your life. Then will your life gain a meaning. When that which is scattered is gathered and concentrated towards a single aim and becomes intense and dynamic, then alone can we call it a moral organism."

Urmi was thrilled. So many young men frequented their tea-table and their tennis court, but not one ever said anything thought-provoking or did anything but yawn, if someone else happened to say it.

Indeed, Nirad did have a way of imparting the utmost profoundity to anything he uttered. In whatever he said Urmi discovered a wonderful depth of meaning. Amazingly intellectual!

Rajaram would often invite his elder son-in-law to his house and tried to encourage intimacy between the two sons-in-law.

"What an insufferably cheeky blighter!" remarked Sasanka to Sarmila. "He thinks we are all his pupils – and that too., at the very bottom of the very lowest Form."

"That is your jealousy," replied Sarmila laughing. "Why, I rather like him."

"Why not change places with your younger sister?" asked Sasanka.

"That might mean a great relief to you," replied Sarmila, "but to me – it is different."

Nirad, too, did not seem to feel any particularly brotherly regard for Sasanka. "A mason – not a scientist!" he said to himself. "He has hands – but what of the brain?"

Sasanka would often chaff his sister-in-law about Nirad.

"It is time you changed your name."

"In the English manner?"

"No, in the pure Sanskrit way."

"Let's hear the new name."

"Vidyut-lata. Nirad will like it. He is familiar with this thing in his laboratory. Now, he will have it harnessed at home."

To himself he said: 'Indeed, the name does suit her.' A secret pang pricked him. 'Pity that such a girl should fall into the hands of so great a prig.' In whose hands it would have consoled and pleased Sasanka to see her fall, it is hard to say.

Shortly after, Rajaram died. The future rightful master of Urmi now wholeheartedly took upon himself the responsibility of guiding her mind to its full maturity.

Good looking as Urmimala was, she seemed even better looking than she was; the luminous intensity of her mind scintillated in the lively movements of her body. She was eager about everything: interested in science, even more so in literature; greatly excited at the prospect of witnessing a football match on the maidan; not indifferent to the cinema; must be present when the physicist from Europe lectured at the Presidency College; listened to the radio and though she might now and again ejaculate an "ugh!" was nevertheless interested; ran out to the verandah to watch a wedding party pass- by, with its bride-groom and the fanfare of trumpets; was a frequent visitor to the Zoo which she enjoyed greatly, especially when she stood watching the monkeys in their cage; would accompany her father and sit by his side when he went angling; played tennis; was particularly good at badminton. All these interests she had derived from her brother. Slender and delicate as a frail creeper, she swayed with every breath of the wind. She dressed simply but elegantly; knew how to bring out the full beauty of the figure in a sari by a slight turn here, a right twist there, a little tightening here and a little loosening there – in a way whose secret no one could catch. Though she could not sing well, she could play on the sitar. When she played, it was difficult to say whether it was a thing to hear or a sight to see – it seemed as though her wild unruly fingers were in an uproar. She was never in want of a topic for conversation, never waited for a proper excuse for laughter. She had an inexhaustible talent for creating company out of dullness and filling emptiness with her mere presence. Only in Nirad's presence she became an altogether different person, as though the wind had left the sail and the boat had to be slowly and gently towed.

Everyone said that Urmi's nature was like her brother's, full of vitality and liveliness. Urmi knew that it was her brother who had released the current of her mind. Hemanta used to say: "Our homes are like moulds for fashioning human beings of clay, which is why the foreign juggler has succeeded so long in keeping thirty-three crores of puppets dancing to his tune. When the time comes, I'll break into this puppet-dom and wreak the havoc of a Kalapahar." The time never came – but he left Urmi's mind very living, indeed.

What caused all the trouble was the extreme rigidity of Nirad's method of work. He prescribed a course of study for her, and admonished her thus: "Look here, Urmi, if you let your mind spill over in its onward march, what will be left in your pitcher at the end of the journey?" He added: "You are like a butterfly, restlessly flitting about without gathering anything. You should be like a bee. Every moment is of account. Life is not dalliance."

Of late, Nirad had been studying books on Pedagogy borrowed from the Imperial Library. All these maxims were to be found in them. His very language was of the books, for he did not know how to put things in simple and natural words of his own. Urmi was left in no doubt that she was at fault. Great was her mission and yet every now and then her mind wandered away from it, leaving her in a state of perpetual self-reproof. Before her was the example of Nirad. How amazingly steadfast, how single-minded of purpose! How sternly he had set his face against all fun and frivolity! If any work of fiction or light literature caught his eye on Urmi's table, it was immediately forfeited. One day, when he came to pay his supervisory call, he learnt that she had gone to spend the evening at an English theatre to see Gilbert and Sullivan's Mikado. She had never missed such chances while her brother lived. She was severely taken to task by Nirad. He spoke in English in a tone of the utmost gravity:

"Have you already begun to forget that you have dedicated your life to the mission of making your brother's death fruitful in service?"

The words stung Urmi with extreme remorse. She said to herself: "What an uncommon power of seeing through the mind this person has! Indeed, it does seem that my grief is losing its intensity – I myself couldn't realise it. Shame on this fickleness in my character!'

She began a strict watch on herself, removing every trace of attractiveness from her dress. The sari was now coarse, its colour all gone. The chocolates were still in the drawer, but the desire for them was gone. She leashed her unchained mind to the dry post of duty within a severely restricted orbit. Her elder sister scolded her; as for Sasanka, the bitter epithets he showered on Nirad were too strong and too foreign to be found in the dictionary – they were not exactly pleasant to hear.

Sasanka and Nirad had one thing in common: both took to English – Sasanka when in a furiously abusive temper, and Nirad when he was discoursing on something profound. Nirad disliked it most when Urmi was invited to her sister's house. It was not that she merely went – she was most eager to go. This intimacy of blood relationship seemed to cut through his own rights over her.

One day, with a grave countenance he said to Urmi:

"Please, don't mind the unpleasant words which my sense of responsibility towards you obliges me to say. I must warn you that this intimacy is injurious to the development of your character. Family attachment makes you blind – but I can see quite clearly the likelihood of degradation."

The first mortgage deed of the thing called Urmi's character being in Nirad's strong box, the loss would naturally be his if anything happened to that character. As a result of Nirad's ban, Urmi, on various pretexts, made her visits to Bhowanipore very rare. This imposition of restraint on herself she regarded as a sort of repayment of her huge debt. For, what sacrifice could be greater for a votary of science than that which Nirad had made by encumbering his work for his own ideal with this life-long charge of her life?

Though in a sense Urmi had got used to the unhappy strain of withholding herself from every enjoyment, now and again her mind was seized with a painful yearning which she could not wholly suppress as a mere frivolity. Nirad merely directed her – why did he never for a moment woo her? For such an expression of ardour on his part her heart ever waited, and for want of it, remained unfulfilled; her very acts of duty became dry and lifeless. Sometimes, when she suddenly caught a look of wistfulness in Nirad's eyes, it seemed to her that the deep secret of his heart would now be laid bare. But, God knows, even if deep yearning was in him anywhere, its language was not known to him. And because he could not express himself, he found fault with the urge for self-expression and prided himself on the very dumbness of his agitated heart, which he thought was but a proof of his strength of character. "Sentimentality is not in my grain," he declared. On such occasions Urmi felt like crying, but so hypnotised was she by her own devotion that she too thought that this indeed, was manliness. And then she would begin again ruthlessly chastising her 'weak' mind. But try as she might, she could not get away from the consciousness that the spontaneous readiness with which, under the impact of great sorrow, she had at first undertaken her arduous mission had steadily flagged until now it had to cling for support to another's will.

Nirad put it quite plainly to her: "You had better understand, Urmi, that it is no good expecting from me the kind of adulation which girls commonly hope for from men. What I give you is something far more true and valuable than all their made-up pretty talk."

With bent head Urmi silently wondered: "Can't anything ever remain hidden from him?"

She is unable to fix her mind on anything. On the roof-terrace she paces about alone. The afternoon fades into dusk. Across the uneven heights of the city mansions, the sun sinks to its rest beyond the distant masts of ships on the Ganges. The clouds with their many-coloured bars raise barricades at the day's frontier. Gradually, the barricades fade out of sight. The moon climbs above the church spire. In the misty light the city looks like a dream, like an enchanted land. She wonders, is life really so uncompromisingly severe? Can it be so niggardly as to allow no holiday, no gift of joy? And then, a maddening impulse seizes her, a desire to do something wicked, to shout at the top of her voice, 'I don't care!'

URMIMALA

Nirad finished the piece of research he had taken in hand, and sent the thesis to a scientific association in Europe. It brought him recognition as well as a scholarship. He made up his mind to cross the seas for a degree at a European university.

The moment of parting was not marked by any tender words. He merely kept on repeating "Now that I am leaving, I am afraid you will slacken in your efforts."

"Have no fear," replied Urmi.

"I am leaving detailed instructions in writing," said Nirad, "to guide your future conduct and studies."

"I shall follow them faithfully."

"I'll remove these books from your almirah," went on Nirad, "and leave them locked up in my house."

"You may take them," said Urmi handing him the key.

He glanced once at her sitar but hesitated and said nothing. But he felt obliged by his sense of responsibility to utter the last admonition.

"My only fear is that if you start once more frequenting Sasanka Babu's house your steadiness will again falter. There's no doubt of it. Please, don't imagine that I am out to malign Sasanka Babu. He is an excellent man. I've seen very few Bengalis with his zeal and aptitude for business. His only drawback is that he acknowledges no ideals. To tell you the truth, at times I feel very apprehensive about him."

This led to further elaboration of Sasanka's many drawbacks. Nirad could not help giving vent to his grave concern at the several other shortcomings in Sasanka's character which, though dormant then, were bound to become more active with age. But that, nevertheless, he was an excellent man, Nirad was anxious vociferously to admit, adding in the same breath that it was imperative for Urmi to guard herself against his house. It would be a sure degradation for Urmi if her mind ever came down to their level.

"But why are you so apprehensive?" asked Urmi.

"Shall I tell you why? You won't resent it?"

"You have taught me to bear the truth. I will stand it though I know it won't be easy."

"Then, listen. I've observed a sort of likeness between your temperament and Sasanka Babu's. It's this very light-heartedness of his that appeals to you, isn't it?"

'Is this man omniscient?' Urmi wondered. Undoubtedly, she liked her brother-in-law very much – and mainly for his capacity for rollicking laughter, his pleasantries and his waggish pranks. Then, also he knew just what flower Urmi loved best and what colour pleased her most in a sari.

"Yes, that's true, I like it," she admitted.

"Sarmila-didi's love," proceeded Nirad, "is serene and deep; her care and devotion are like an act of religious merit; her duty knows no holiday. It's by virtue of these that Sasanka Babu is enabled to give his whole mind to his work. But the day you go to Bhowanipore the mask falls off his face – there he is with his tomfooleries, pulling out your hair-pins and letting loose your coiffure, snatching your book and hiding it on the almirah-top. His interest in tennis suddenly becomes overwhelming despite other engagements."

Urmi could not help admitting to herself that it was this very naughtiness of Sasankada's which drew her to him. Her own irresponsible girlishness surged up in her when she was with him, and he too was no less a victim of her pranks. Her Didi would smile her gentle, serene smile at their wild frolics. Sometimes, she would mildly chide, though the chiding was but a pretence.

"You should stick only to that," said Nirad, winding up, "which gives the least scope to your own nature. There was little fear so long as I was there, for my nature is the exact contrary of yours. While I was your guardian it was impossible that any of my acts should ever vitiate your mind."

"I'll always bear in mind what you have said," said Urmi, her head bent low.

"I am leaving behind some books for you," said Nirad. "Read especially the chapters I have marked. You will find them useful."

Urmi needed this tutoring. Of late she had been assailed by doubts that perhaps, she had been misled by the first fervour of her enthusiasm in selecting medicine as her line, that perhaps she had no aptitude for it. The books marked by Nirad would act like a rope tied to her, towing her upstream.

After Nirad's departure, Urmi subjected herself to even harder severities. Except that she went to college, she practically shut herself up as if in a zenana. Returning home at the end of the day, she would again ruthlessly chain her mind to study, however much the tired mind yearned for rest. She made no progress whatsoever, her listless wandering mind vainly lingering over the same page. But she would not admit defeat. Because Nirad was not there, his will from its distance began to work all the more effectively on her.

She particularly despised herself when in the midst of work she was haunted by memories of the past. Many were her admirers among the young men; to some she had been indifferent, towards some she had felt drawn. Though in no case had it yet matured into love, the longing to love, like the sweet and gentle breeze of spring, played about her mind; so that now she would be humming a tune all by herself, now copying a poem that had caught her fancy, now playing on the sitar, if the mind were stirred a little too deeply. Nowadays, it was not uncommon that as she sat in the evening, her eyes fixed on the pages of her book, she was suddenly startled to discover that her mind was haunted by the memory of a face and of a day which had moved her but little at the time. Sometimes, the face would be of one whose persistent wooing had actually irritated her, though today that very memory seemed to stir in her mind a pang of discontent, as the light, fleeting wings of the butterfly leave on the flower a touch of spring.

The more fiercely she tried to fling these thoughts away from her mind, the more surely they boomeranged back into it. She had placed a photograph of Nirad on her desk at which she would look long and steadily. The light of intellect was in that face, but no trace of the heart's ardour. If that face did not call, to what was her spirit to respond? All she could do was to work up her mind into a state of exalted contemplation of his genius, his heroic striving, his unblemished character and her own undreamt-of good fortune.

We might as well state here that in one respect Nirad had triumphed. At the time of his engagement to Urmi, Sasanka, as well as several other skeptics, had laughed and had mockingly declared: "The simple-minded Rajaram Babu has convinced himself that Nirad is an idealist. An idealist, indeed! No pious platitudes can hide the fact that his idealism is secretly worming its way into Urmi's purse. True, he has 'sacrificed' himself – but to the deity enthroned in the Imperial Bank. Where we would plainly and bluntly tell our father- in-law that we need money, which won't be wasted but will, on the contrary, be used for his daughter's benefit, this great man condescends to marry only for the sake of a great mission! And then, he will daily translate that mission into figures in his father-in-law's cheque book."

Knowing that such comments were inevitable, Nirad had told Urmi that the one condition of his marriage was that he would not touch a penny of her money, but would depend entirely on his own earnings. When the would-be father-in-law proposed to send him to Europe, Nirad did not agree, even though it meant that he would have to wait long. He had moreover told Rajaram Babu: "Whatever money you choose to donate for the founding of the hospital should be put down in the name of your daughter. When 1 take charge of the hospital I'll draw no remuneration for my work. I am a doctor. I don't have to worry about my livelihood."

Such extreme disinterestedness only confirmed Rajaram Babu's love and admiration for Nirad and gave Urmi cause for much pride. On the other hand, the fact that this pride had a legitimate cause turned Sarmila's mind against Nirad. 'Pshaw! Let's see how long these heroics last!' Henceforth, whenever Nirad was in the midst of one of his usual, profound discourses, Sarmila would suddenly get up and walk out of the room, her head mockingly cocked sideways, her steps audible from a considerable distance. For Urmi's sake she said nothing but her silence by its very irony was withering enough.

At first, every mail brought from Nirad four or five pages of long- winded counsel. After some time, however, there came a startling telegram, demanding a considerable sum of money, urgently needed for his study. Though the pride which Urmi had cherished as her supreme treasure received a blow, the telegram was also in a way secretly comforting. For, as the days passed and Nirad's absence was prolonged, her original nature had begun to seek ways of escape from the barricade of duty she had erected round it. Under various pretexts she would deceive herself and then reproach herself. Nirad's appeal for money, therefore, came as a consolation to her contrite mind.

Handing the telegram to the estate manager, Urmi said hesitatingly, "Kaka-babu, the money – "

"I can't make out what it means," said the manager. "All along we have been under the impression that your money was unacceptable to him." The manager did not like Nirad.

"But in a foreign land – " Urmi faltered, unable to finish the sentence.

"That the foreign soil can change our native character, 1 know well enough," said Kaka-babu. "But how are we going to keep pace with such changes?"

"But he might be landed in difficulties if the money is not sent to him," protested Urmi.

"Very well then, I'll send it. Don't be anxious. But mark my words, this is only the beginning, not the end of it."

That this was not the end was speedily proved when another call arrived for a still bigger sum – this time for reasons of health.

"I had better consult Sasanka Babu," said the manager, looking grave.

"Please, do not let Didi and others come to know of it," pleaded Urmi greatly flustered.

"I don't like to take all the responsibility on my shoulders."

"But all this money will in any case be his, one day."

"Before that we must see to it that it is not thrown away."

"But we must also consider his health."

"Ill-health is of various sorts. Exactly what he is suffering from is not known. Maybe, if he returned here the change of climate would restore him to health. We might arrange his passage back."

The proposal to get Nirad back greatly perturbed Urmi. She attributed it to her concern for his studies.

The Kaka was saying: "Well, let the money be sent this time, – though I fear it will only aggravate the doctor's malady."

Radhagovinda was a near relation of Urmi's. The innuendo in his words stirred a faint breath of suspicion in her mind. "Maybe, it's better to let Didi know." On the other hand, the question kept recurring to her, poking her:

"Why don't I feel dejected – as I should?"

About this time Sarmila's disease had begun to cause anxiety, the tragedy of her brother's case adding alarm to anxiety. A number of doctors were set on the trail of its mysterious source. Smiling her wearied smile, Sarmila remarked: "The culprit will elude the C.I.D., only the innocent will be harassed to death."

"Let the Inspectors carry on their legitimate investigation – but third degree methods, no, never!" Sasanka assured her.

Sasanka had two heavy contracts on hand, one with a jute mill on the Ganges' bank, the other at Tollygunge in the garden house of the Mirpur zamindar. The workers' tenements at the jute mill which had to be completed within three months, besides the several tube-wells in different localities he had taken in hand, left him no time to spare. Between the pressure of his work and the frequent claims of Sarmila's illness on his time, he was in a state of constant anxiety.

In the many years of their married life he had never had to worry on account of his wife's health, with the result that this time the strain of her illness drove him into a state of almost childish flurry. Leaving his work unattended he would return home and sit helplessly by her side. Gently caressing her hair he would inquire how she felt that day.

"I'm alright," Sarmila would promptly answer. "Please, don't worry unnecessarily."

Encouraged by his own wishful thinking, Sasanka believed the obviously unbelievable and felt greatly relieved.

"I've been entrusted with a huge contract by the Raja of Dhenkanal, and have to discuss the plan with the Dewan. I'll return at the earliest – before the doctor comes."

"I beg of you," pleaded Sarmila anxiously, "don't let unnecessary hurry spoil your work. Don't I understand that your presence is needed there! Of course, you must go. If you don't, I'll only get worse. There are enough people to attend to me."

To build up a magnificent fortune had become Sasanka's obsession day and night. It was not wealth but the magnificence of it which drew him on. Man is made that way; he responds to the call of glory. One may despise wealth only when it barely and meagrely suffices; but the moment its summit is raised high, men flock to admire it. Not that they are any the better for it, but because they delight in watching the splendour of eminence. As Sasanka sat by his wife's side, his uneasy mind could not help apprehending where lay a possible obstacle to his career of achievement. Sarmila knew that this apprehension in her husband's mind was not due to any miserly greed but was rooted in a manly ambition to build up from the very bottom a tower of triumph. Considering his glory as her own, she did not like him to neglect his work in order to attend to her, however pleasing such attentions in themselves. She, therefore, constantly urged him to return to his duty.

Her own duties caused her endless anxiety. Now that she was laid up in bed, who knew what mess the servants were making – no doubt using bad ghee in cooking, neglecting to keep hot water in the bath at the appointed hour or to change the bed linen in time; no one to see if the drains had been properly cleaned. Well, she knew what confusion it meant if the clothes from the washer-man were not properly received and checked. Unable to bear the strain she would secretly leave her bed to see things for herself. The pain would increase, the temperature shoot up, and the doctor would be puzzled.

At last, she sent for her sister Urmimala. "Never mind your college for a few days – come to the rescue of my household, otherwise I can't even die in peace."

Those who have read the story so far will at this stage smile knowingly and declare, "We know the rest." Indeed, it does not need much intelligence to anticipate. What must happen does happen, and no more need happen. Nor, is it necessary to imagine that in the game of life Fortune will necessarily keep back her cards, throwing dust into Sarmila's eyes.

Urmi was enthusiastic at this opportunity of serving her sister and was ready, since there was no alternative, to set aside all other tasks. Moreover, so she argued, nursing a patient was quite in line with her future medical career. She got ready a leather-bound book of charts for recording graphically the daily variations of disease. She also made up her mind to read up from books all she could gather about her sister's illness, lest the attending physician look down upon her for her ignorance. Physiology being her subject in M.Sc., she would have no difficulty in following the therapeutic terminology. In short, having convinced herself that attending on her sister would mean no snapping of the thread of duty but would rather help her to pursue it the more arduously and steadfastly, she packed all her books and papers in a bag and presented herself at the Bhowanipore residence. She did not have to pore over the bulky medical manuals, for not even the specialists were able to diagnose the disease.

Imagining herself as the sole warden of the sick room, she very gravely announced to her sister: "Since I am here to see that the doctor's instructions are strictly carried out, you will have to listen to whatever I say."

Amused at the elaborate earnestness of her attitude, Sarmila replied, smiling: "Indeed, what teacher has coached you in such earnestness – this fanaticism of a new convert? As a matter of fact, I have called you here only because I must have someone to carry out my instructions. Your hospital is not yet ready, but my household is in full swing; so meanwhile, take charge of it so that your Didi may have some relief."

And so, she was relieved of her duty in the sick room at her Didi's own insistence.

Now, Urmi became the vice-regent in the kingdom of her sister's household. Things were in chaos there and needed immediate measures. In the scheme of this household every activity of each member, high and low, was directed and subordinated to one great purpose, namely, the comfort and convenience of the gentleman who presided over it. That this gentleman was utterly helpless and pathetically incapable of looking after his own physical needs – this impression was too firmly rooted in Sarmila's mind to be ever dislodged. When she found that he had not even noticed the hole which his cigar had burnt in his sleeve, she was not a little amused, but was at the same time filled with a great tenderness. The engineer would bustle off in the morning to his duty in such a great hurry as to forget to turn the tap off after his wash, only to find on his return the bedroom floor one sheet of water and the carpet in a mess. At the very outset when the tap was being installed, Sarmila had objected, knowing that a tap so near the bed would only result in his hands in a daily recurrence of an all-round mess in the room. But the great engineer must set up every sort of complicated nuisance in the name of scientific amenities. Once, in a fit of originality he had contrived an entirely original model of a stove, with shutters and funnels on all sides for conserving heat and for the speedy discharge of ash, and fitted inside with a variety of special devices of cells and shelves for baking, grilling, boiling and what not. If, in the interest of peace and goodwill, the invention was accorded a warm domestic welcome, the reception was in words and manner only, not in any use made of it. Adult babies have their hobbies, which they forget in a day but which, if resisted, lead only to friction. Bored with the monotony of daily usage, they break into something spectacular, to which women need pay no more than lip- service, while free to do as they choose. This responsibility of husband- tending Sarmila had long enjoyed.

A long time, indeed. It was impossible for Sarmila to conceive of Sasanka's world without herself in it. But now, she was afraid that the courier of Death would intervene between that world and its presiding goddess. She even feared that after death her bodiless spirit would have no peace if Sasanka's bodily comforts were not well looked after. Fortunately, there was Urmi. Though not so gentle as her sister, Urmi could nevertheless, carry on the work, for after all hers was a woman's touch. Without the tender grace of such a touch the daily provision of a man's life is left dry and flavourless, devoid of charm. And so, as she watched Urmi's beautiful hands peel and cut an apple, rind and slice an orange, neatly pick out the seeds of a pomegranate and tastefully set everything on a plate of white stone, Sarmila seemed to realise her own self in her sister. A stream of directions would issue ceaselessly from her sick bed:

"Do fill his cigarette case, Urmi."

"Can't you see it won't occur to him to change his soiled kerchief?"

"He won't have the sense to ask the bearer to clean his shoes – see how stiff they look with their coating of cement and sand!"

"Do have the pillow cases changed, dear."

"Put away these paper scraps in the wastepaper basket."

"Do peep into his study, Urmi, I'm sure he has left the key of his cash box on the desk."

"Don't forget it's time to transplant the cauliflower seedlings."

"Please, ask the mali to prune the rose plants."

"Look at those daubs of lime on the back of his coat! Do wait a moment, why this hurry? Please, Urmi dear, brush them off."

Though Urmi was used to books rather than to domestic work, she thoroughly enjoyed her new duties. Having broken away from the rigid discipline of her life, these varied ministrations gave her a sense of freedom. The under-current of anxiety and devotion beneath the smooth running of this household was little realised by her, for the strain of its direction was borne by her sister. To Urmi it all seemed a play, a kind of holiday, occupation without an aim. Here was a world in itself, wholly different from her own old world; here no aim, no object to be achieved held up its warning finger before her; and yet the day was full of activity, delightfully varied. She had not to account for each mistake, each shortcoming. If her Didi tried to chide her, ever so mildly, Sasanka would laugh it all away, as though the very shortcomings of Urmi added a special relish to his enjoyment. Indeed, the fact that their little world had now lost its look of earnest responsibility, that in the new atmosphere of laxity, mistake and inadvertence no longer mattered, was to Sasanka a source of great relaxation and amusement. Life seemed a picnic now. The fact that Urmi never seemed worried, never looked miserable, never felt ashamed of little mishaps, but always overflowed with enthusiasm in whatever she did helped considerably to lighten the strain on Sasanka's mind of his own heavy responsibility of work. Nowadays, he was always eager to return home as soon as his work was over – sometimes, even when the work was not over.

It must be confessed that Urmi was no expert at household management. Nevertheless, it was evident that, if not by virtue of her work, by the charm of her personality she filled a great and longstanding void in this house. What this void was, it is difficult to define in words. And so, when Sasanka returned home these days, he experienced the buoyancy of a playful, holiday spirit in the atmosphere. This enjoyment was not of domestic comfort, nor was it merely in the atmosphere. It had a rapturous embodiment. Indeed, it was Urmi's own holiday spirit which filled the void in this house, making day and night radiant with her liveliness, sending waves of blood pulsing through the work-weary Sasanka. On the other hand, the unmistakable consciousness that she was a source of joy to Sasanka made Urmi happy. For the satisfaction that her mere presence could make another happy had long been denied to her, causing her no little humiliation.

The care and attention to his personal needs to which the master of the house had been so long accustomed, now began to seem to him of but secondary importance. He was pleased with everything now, delighted almost without any cause. He remonstrated with his wife:

"Why do you worry over trifles? An occasional change of routine does not necessarily mean inconvenience – in fact, it is quite a relief."

Sasanka's mind was now like a river in the interval between ebb and flow. The pressure of work had slowed down. The tempestuous protests that the work would suffer, the loss would be serious, et cetera, which had been so frequent before, were hardly audible now. At any such manifestation Urmi would blow out the solemnity with her laughter. If she found him looking unusually serious, she would inquire: "Has your bogey been here today – that green-turbaned broker, from God knows where – has he been frightening you?"

"How on earth did you know of him?" asked Sasanka in surprise.

"Oh, I know him very well. I found him sitting in the verandah that day. You had gone out, so I kept him engaged in conversation. He is from Bikaner; his wife was burnt to death when her mosquito-net caught fire. He is looking for another."

"In that case he will come here daily at the right time – just when I am out. As long as he has not discovered a wife, the dream will grow on him."

"Just let me know what you want of him. I believe I can get it out of him."

If nowadays, the fat figure of profit in Sasanka's income-ledger came for a while to a standstill in its numerical progress, he was not greatly perturbed. Never before had Sasanka Mazumdar's enthusiasm for listening-in to the evening radio been so pronounced. When Urmi dragged him to it, he did not spurn it as frivolous, nor think the time wasted. He even went to Dum Dum one early morning to watch the aeroplanes take off. Nor, was scientific curiosity the main attraction.

He learnt for the first time to go shopping in the New Market. It was Sarmila who used occasionally to visit the Market to buy fish, meat, fruits and vegetables. She looked upon this work as her own special responsibility and never dreamt nor even desired that Sasanka should accompany her on such errands. But Urmi never bought anything, she merely picked up things, handled them, looked them over and haggled with the shopkeeper. If Sasanka attempted to buy anything for her, she snatched away his purse and locked it up in her bag.

Urmi did not in the least share Sasanka's concern for his work. Sometimes, when she wasted too much of his time, he lost his temper with her; the result was so disastrous that to retrieve the tragedy he had to sacrifice twice as much time. Between the imminence of tears in Urmi's eyes and the urgent claims of his work he did his best to finish as much of his work as he could in his office before returning home. But even there he found it difficult to stay beyond the afternoon. If sometimes he was detained for any reason, he found awaiting him on return Urmi's stony, impenetrable silence. Sasanka was secretly thrilled at this expression of aggrieved affection in Urmi's eyes misty with suppressed tears.

Very innocently he would plead: "If you have sworn not to talk to me, I must respect your satyagraha, but for heaven's sake, Urmi, don't give up playing – it was not included in your vow." And forthwith he brought the tennis rackets. When about to win the set, he deliberately chose to lose it. Next morning on waking up, he would be seized with remorse for having wasted his time the previous day.

In the afternoon of a holiday, as he sat at his desk deeply absorbed in some difficult problem, a red-and-blue pencil in his right hand, the fingers of his left hand needlessly ruffling his hair, Urmi came and announced: "I've fixed it up with that broker of yours – he'll take me to see the Temple of Pareshnath. Come with me – please!"

"No, not today, please," pleaded Sasanka, "it's impossible to get away."

But Urmi was undaunted by the majesty of work.

"How can you," she protested, "without any compunction leave a young, helpless and unprotected girl in the hands of that green- turban? Is that what you call your chivalry?"

In the end, unable to resist, Sasanka left his desk and drove the car.

If Sarmila came to learn of any such outrage, she was greatly annoyed, for she considered it an unforgivable liberty on the part of a woman to intrude on man's field of activity. She had always treated Urmi as a child and thought her so even now; nevertheless, in no case was she going to let her turn her husband's office into a play-room. She sent for Urmi and talked to her severely. Her words might have borne fruit, if Sasanka, overhearing his wife's angry tone, had not come and stood behind the door, winking encouragingly at Urmi and beckoning to her with a pack of cards to slip away to his office to learn poker from him. It was no time for playing cards, nor had any such idea been in his mind. It was only to spare Urmi the painful humiliation of her sister's bitter scolding which hurt him almost more than it hurt Urmi. He himself might, by pleading, cajoling or mild reproof, restrain her from interfering with his work, but that Sarmila should take Urmi to task for it was more than he could bear.

Sarmila sent for him and remonstrated. "Why must you indulge her so much – at all hours of the day? Your work is bound to suffer."

"Ah, the poor lonely child," commiserated Sasanka, "if she finds no playmate, how can she live in this lonely house?"

So much for her childish pranks. But it also happened that when Sasanka sat engrossed in some architectural plan, Urmi would pull up a chair by his side and ask him to explain it to her. She was quick of understanding and could steer through mathematical formulae. Sasanka was delighted and would set her problems which she solved. She insisted on accompanying him when he went out on inspection in the steam launch of the jute company. And she not merely accompanied him, but challenged his figures and conclusions, thrilling him with her arguments, which Sasanka found more delightful than any poetry. So that now he was not afraid of bringing some of his office work home. Whether drafting plans or working out problems, she was at his side, listening to his explanation and following his arguments. Though the progress in Sasanka's work was rather slow, it seemed to him that the long hours spent at it were fruitfully employed.

Sarmila was scandalised. While she could appreciate Urmi's childish waywardness and might affectionately tolerate her shortcomings in the management of the household, she could not but strongly disapprove of her unrestrained frequent excursions into her husband's workaday world which she herself had looked upon as absolutely beyond the reach of the feminine mind. Sheer impertinence, it seemed to her – directly contravening the teaching of the *Bhagavad Gita* which enjoined that one should keep within the limits of one's own nature, one's *dharma*.

Unable to restrain herself, she asked Urmi one day: "Can it be that you really enjoy all this tracing and drafting and calculating?"

"I do indeed – greatly, Didi."

"Really!" exclaimed Sarmila skeptically. "Or, is it only to please him that you pretend this interest?"

Well, why not? We might ask, since all that Sarmila desired was to make Sasanka happy. But while she would have done it by attending to his personal comforts, this particular way of making him happy did not accord with her conception of happiness. She would repeatedly send for her husband and expostulate:

"Why do you waste so much of your time with her? Your work suffers. She's a child, what will she understand of all this?"

"She understands no less than I do," replied Sasanka, thinking that praise of her sister must please his wife. The simpleton!

In the beginning, when in the excitement and pride of his work Sasanka had cooled in his attentions to his wife, Sarmila had not only accepted the fact as inevitable but had actually felt pride in it, and had steadily taught her devoted heart to restrain the ardour of its solicitude, saying, "Man belongs to the race of kings; he must perpetually extend his empire of heroic achievements, otherwise he would be less than woman; for while the natural grace and sweetness of woman, her inborn wealth of love, are sufficient in themselves for the fulfilment of her function in this world, man has to vindicate himself by constant battle and strife. In the old days kings marched out to new conquests, not always out of greed of territory, but to vindicate over again their proud claim to manliness. Far be it from woman to stand in the way of this pride!"

And so, Sarmila had not stood in the way; of her own accord she had effaced herself completely from the path to which he had set himself. Once, she had held him tight in the net of her devoted attachment, but gradually, at no little cost to her happiness, she had loosened the bonds, until she had learnt to serve him from behind the scenes.

And now, alas! She was shocked to see him sink lower day-by-day. From her sick bed she could not watch everything, but what she could sense was sufficient. Looking into Sasanka's face she could see that he was always in a kind of trance. That this mere slip of a girl should in a few days have shaken that stern worker out of his arduous striving – the ignominy was more agonising to Sarmila than the actual pain of her disease.

There was no doubt that the little details of his personal comfort to which Sasanka had been used so long were being neglected; for example, it would be suddenly noticed that his favourite dish was missing at the table. Some sort of excuse would, of course, be offered. But in the old days no excuse was ever tolerated in this house, no such inadvertence was ever overlooked, but was severely rebuked. What a great revolution, indeed, that in this very same disciplined household the direst negligence was now looked upon as more amusing than reprehensible! Whom to blame! If Urmi did as her sister desired and sat on her cane stool in the kitchen, supervising the culinary operations – while at the same time carrying on her investigations into the life-history of the cook – suddenly Sasanka would storm into the kitchen with his peremptory, "Come along! Have done with all this!"

"Why, what do you want me to do instead?"

"I'm off duty now. Come along, let's go and see the Victoria Memorial. I'll explain to you why it looks so ludicrously pretentious."

Urmi's impressionable mind found it hard to stick to her duties in face of so great a temptation. Sarmila was well aware that her sister's absence would make little material difference to the excellence of the cuisine, nevertheless, the solicitude of a feminine touch did impart grace and charm to a man's comfort. But what was the use of worrying when each day it became clearer that comfort hardly mattered to him any longer – he was so happy!

Thus, a sort of uneasiness grew upon and possessed Sarmila's mind. Tossing about in her sick-bed she kept on repeating to herself: 'This much I have learnt before death – whatever else I could do, I could not make him happy. I thought I should see myself in Urmi, but Urmi is not myself, she has her own individuality.' She looked through the window and thought: 'She cannot replace me, nor could I replace her. My absence would make some difference, but hers would create a void.'

In the midst of these thoughts she suddenly remembered that winter was approaching, and it was time for the warm clothing to be put out to dry in the sun. She sent for Urmi who was playing table-tennis with Sasanka.

"Here's the key, Urmi. Please, have all the winter clothes taken out and spread on the roof in the sun."

Hardly had Urmi turned the key in the lock when Sasanka turned up and said: "There's plenty of time for all that. Come and finish the game first."

"But Didi-"

"Alright, I'll get you your Didi's permission."

Didi did give her permission – with a deep sigh. Calling the maidservant she asked her to put a cold compress on her head.

Although this spell of sudden freedom after a long confinement had tended to make Urmi forgetful of herself, there were times when she was suddenly reminded of her life's stern mission. She knew that she was not free; she was bound by her own self-imposed vow, bound also by that very vow to another individual, bound to his guardianship, bound to follow the daily routine he had set for her. She could in no way refute his life-long claim over her. It was easy enough to acknowledge this claim when Nirad was there. She seemed to draw strength from him. But now, while the heart was estranged, only the conscience was insistent, making the heart still more rebellious. The very difficulty of excusing her transgression made it possible for her to indulge it. In order, as it were, to drug this uneasiness with opium, she tried constantly to forget herself in fun and frolic with Sasanka, saying: "It'll be all right in the end. Let me make the most of this little holiday."

Another day, she would suddenly shake her head and taking out all her books and papers from the trunk sit and pore over them. Now, it was Sasanka's turn to snatch the books from her hands, shove them back into the trunk, and sit tight on the lid.

"How wicked of you, Sasankada!" Urmi protested. "Please, don't waste my time."

"I can't waste your time," retorted Sasanka, "without wasting my own as well. So, we are quits."

After a little pushing and jostling, Urmi had to give in. It didn't seem that she very much resented the fact either. Thus thwarted, her conscience, after a brief offensive of four or five days, gradually flagged.

"Please, don't imagine I am weak-minded," she warned Sasanka. "What 1 have resolved upon I shall carry out."

"That is?"

"That is, after getting my degree here, I shall proceed to Europe for medical study."

"And then?"

"And then, I shall found and maintain a hospital."

"Whom else will you maintain? That fellow Nirad Mukherjee, that insufferable – "

"Shut up!" cried Urmi, literally shutting his mouth with her palm. "If you talk like this, we'll fall out."

She struggled hard to keep her faith. 'I must be true, true to myself.' She thought that if she failed in the relationship which her father had established between her and Nirad, she would prove herself faithless. Her real trouble was lack of adequate inspiration from the other party. She was like a tree, well rooted in the soil, but bereft of any light of the sun, its leaves turning yellow. Sometimes, she found it intolerable and cried out:

"Why can't the fellow write as men write?"

Having received her early school training for many years in a convent, Urmi, whatever the other defects in her education, knew English well. Nirad was aware of it and was therefore, all the more keen to dazzle her with his mastery of that language. It would have been better if he had written in Bengali, for the poor fellow did not know how little English he knew. His sentences, packed with long, cumbrous words and phrases culled from books, creaked along like overloaded bullock-carts. Urmi felt like laughing but was too ashamed to do so and would reprove herself:

'It's snobbish to find fault with the English of a Bengali.'

When formerly Nirad used to lecture to her, as he always did, his presence and manner lent weight and dignity to his words, which struck her imagination as even mightier than they sounded. But there is little room for such effects in a long letter. His long-winded pomposities sounded silly and easily betrayed their lack of substance. All that she had grown used to while he was with her now began to jar upon her from a distance. The fellow was utterly devoid of any sense of humour. His letters exposed this want most glaringly and she could not help contrasting him with Sasanka.

What happened one day only emphasised this contrast. As she was rummaging for some clothes in her trunk, she discovered an unfinished knitted slipper at the bottom, which brought back to her the memory of an episode that had happened four years ago. Her brother Hemanta was living then. They had all gone up to Darjeeling. There was no end of fun. Hemanta and Sasanka between them seemed to have released a regular cataract of gaiety. Urmi, who had just learnt knitting from an aunt, had begun a pair of slippers intended as a birthday gift to her brother. It was a subject of constant chaffing by Sasanka. "Whatever else you may give to your brother, please, don't give him slippers. That way one insults one's elders, says Lord Manu."

"For whom has Lord Manu prescribed them then?" asked Urmi with a mischievous side-long glance.

"The ancient prescriptive right to be insulted," replied Sasanka gravely, "is the brother-in-law's. Moreover, you owe it to me, interest and all."

"Owe it to you? I don't remember."

"Nor can you. You were a mere child then and hardly of age to play Puck in your sister's bridal chamber on the auspicious occasion of our wedding. The privilege your tender hands then missed of pulling the ears of this lucky chap now waits to be exercised in fashioning a pair of slippers for him."

The debt was, however, never paid, for that particular pair of slippers found its way to the feet of Urmi's brother.

Soon after, Urmi received a letter from Sasanka which caused her considerable amusement. The letter was still in the box. She opened it and re-read:

"You left yesterday. Before the memory of your visit could fade, a scandal has been associated with your name which it would be wrong of me to conceal from you.

"Many eyes have observed the slippers I habitually wear. What they have observed even better is the way my toe-nails jut out of the holes – like a wreath of moons breaking out of clouds. (vide Bharat Chandra's 'Annada Mangal'. In case of doubt as to the authenticity of the simile, refer to Didi.) This morning in the office as Brindaban Nandi took the dust of my slippered feet, the dilapidated state of their dignity was exposed. Shocking! I asked my servant Mahesh what had happened to my new pair of slippers. On whose holy usurping feet had it found its refuge? He replied, scratching his head: 'When you went to Darjeeling with Urmi Mashi, the pair went with you. On your return only one slipper came back, the other – 'here Mahesh grew red in the face. I also thundered at him to shut up, for there were other persons in the room. Stealing a pair of slippers is a base thing to do, but the human mind is weak and the temptation too great. Let us hope God forgives. Of course, when the theft is ingeniously carried out, it wipes away much of its shame. But to steal one slipper! Fie!

"I have suppressed the name of the thief. But if she allows her own natural sauciness to be provoked by this charge, she will only publicise it the more widely. If her conscience is clear, it may be worth while to create a scene even over one slipper. If now, you want to shut the mouth of that vile calumniator Mahesh, you had better have immediate recourse to a pair of hand-embroidered slippers. Fancy the fellow's cheek! Herewith, is enclosed the measure of my foot."

Urmi, delighted with the letter, had immediately set her hands to knitting a pair for Sasanka, but she could not finish it as she soon lost interest in knitting. Today when she discovered this unfinished slipper in her trunk, she resolved to present it, as it was, to Sasanka to mark the anniversary of their journey to Darjeeling, which was only a few weeks ahead. A deep sigh escaped her. Where were those light-winged days under that laughter-lit sky? All that lay in front of her was a prospect of a dreary life of duty, bleak and unrelieved like a desert.

It was the 26th of Falgun, the day of the Holi festival. Busy with his work, Sasanka had no time for this play and the day had been forgotten. Urmi went to where her sister lay in bed and putting the ceremonial mark of the red powder on her feet, pranaam'd her. Then, she went in search of her brother-in-law and found him at his desk immersed in his work. Creeping behind him she smeared his head with the colour, which fell profusely on his file of papers as well. A regular skirmish ensued. The ink-pot being handy on the desk, Sasanka threw the red ink over Urmi's sari, and then catching hold of her hand, he snatched the powder wrapped in an end of her sari and rubbed it over her face. Then began an uproar of chasing and scuffling. Though it was getting late for lunch and Sasanka had not yet had his bath, the house went on ringing with the notes of Urmi's pealing laughter. It was only when Sarmila, concerned for Sasanka's health, began to send message after message that the hilarity came to an end.

The day had long receded, the night was far advanced. Overtopping the flowering branches of the krishnachura tree, the moon rose clear in the unclouded sky. In the sudden gusts of the spring breeze, the green denizens of the garden murmured and swayed, the web of light and shade at the foot of the trees blending in the harmony. Urmi sat by the window, silent and still. Sleep was not in her eyes, for the waves of excitement had not yet quieted down in her blood. The scent of the flowering mango tree filled her mind with its intoxication. The madhavi creeper thrilled with pain in the creative agony of its sap to burst into flower. Urmi's whole being too seemed filled with the same ecstasy. She went into the bathroom and poured water on her head and cooled the burning flesh with a wet towel. Then, she lay on her bed, tossing about, until sleep dragged her down into the world of dreams.

At about three in the morning she suddenly woke up. The moon was no longer visible from the window. The room was in darkness; outside, the row of areca palms seemed caught in a network of light and darkness. Urmi broke into a fit of sobbing. Unable to control it, she threw herself on her bed and hid her face into the pillow. It was the wail of the spirit; language cannot lend it either words or meaning. If asked, could she have explained from where came this flood of sorrow that overwhelmed her mind, sweeping away the day's record of duties, the night's repose of sleep?

When she woke in the morning, the sun was already in the room. She had missed her morning duty. Sarmila had excused her absence, attributing it to the strain of fatigue. What was this regret that had overcome and dejected Urmi and filled her with a sense of defeat! She went to her sister and said: "Didi, since I am not of much use to you here, I might as well return home, if you would permit me." Sarmila could no longer protest: 'No you can't go – please, don't!' She readily agreed. "Alright! You may go – since your studies suffer. Come and see us now and again when you have leisure."

Sasanka was out on duty. Taking advantage of his absence, Urmi left for her home that very day. When Sasanka returned from office he brought with him a set of instruments for mechanical drawing he had bought for Urmi, having promised to teach her the technique. Not finding her in her usual place, he came and asked Sarmila: "Where on earth has Urmi disappeared?"

Sarmila replied: "It was not convenient for her studies here, so she's gone home."

"But she had come prepared to put up with this inconvenience for a few days. Why then this objection today, all of a sudden?"

From her husband's tone, Sarmila divined that he suspected her as the cause. Without wasting any words on that score, she merely said: "Please, bring her back here – tell her I want her to return. I'm sure she won't object."

Returning home Urmi found awaiting her a long-overdue letter from Nirad. She was afraid to open it, knowing what a pile of guilt she had accumulated. So long, she had been citing her sister's illness as her excuse for indiscipline. The excuse had very nearly lost its validity, ever since Sasanka had insisted on engaging trained nurses for Sarmila both for day and night. In accordance with the doctors' instructions the nurses did not allow the relatives to frequent the patient's room. Urmi knew that her sister's illness would not carry weight with Nirad who would dismiss it with, "That's no excuse." Indeed, it was not, since her attendance was not needed. Full of repentance, she made up her mind to confess her wrongdoing and to beg for Nirad's forgiveness. She would swear never to go astray again, nor take any more liberties with the discipline of her life.

Before opening the letter, she took out again that photograph of Nirad which she had not seen for so long, and placed it on her desk. She knew that if Sasanka saw it he would jeer at it. Never mind, she would remain unaffected by his ridicule. That would be her expiation. While in her sister's house, she had hitherto refrained from raising the topic of her impending marriage with Nirad, nor did anyone else there ever allude to it. The engagement had met with no one's approval in that house. Urmi now resolved, with clenched fists, to proclaim the fact in every act of hers. She put on her finger the engagement ring which she had so far kept hidden. It was a very cheap ornament which Nirad, by way of flaunting the pride of his "honest poverty", had valued far above any diamond. His manner had said: "The price of the ring is no measure of my value; it's my worth that lends value to the ring."

Having thus made due amends, Urmi very slowly opened the envelope. No sooner had she perused its contents than she gave a leap of joy. She felt like dancing, but not being used to that art, she snatched the sitar lying on her bed and, without bothering to tune it, began to draw all sorts of frenzies out of it. Just at that moment Sasanka entered the room. "What on earth is the matter?" he asked. "It seems the date of the wedding is fixed, after all!"

"Indeed, Sasankada, it's fixed."

"Fixed beyond any possibility of change?"

"Beyond all possibilities of change."

"Let me send for the pipers then and order sweets at Bhimnag's."

"You don't have to bother."

"What! Will you arrange everything yourself? Bravo Amazon! What about the wedding gifts?"

"The wedding gifts have gone from my own pocket."

"The fish being fried in its own oil, eh? I don't quite understand."

"Here, take this letter and read it."

She gave him the letter to read. Having finished it, Sasanka roared with laughter. Nirad had written that having discovered that it was not feasible to carry on in India the highly difficult line of research to which he had dedicated his life, it had become necessary for him to make a supreme sacrifice. He had no alternative but to release himself from his engagement to Urmi. A European lady had agreed to marry him and to devote herself to his work. But, of course, the mission was the same, whether it was carried on in India or over there. Hence, it would be no injustice to the spirit of Rajaram Babu's will if part of the money he had set apart for the mission were to be handed over to him. Indeed, such an act would but bring honour to the deceased.

"At any rate, it wouldn't be bad," commented Sasanka, "to help to keep this creature alive in that distant land. If you stop sending him money, there's the danger of the fellow turning up here one day, driven by hunger."

"If you are afraid of that," laughed Urmi, "you had better send him the money yourself. I won't give a penny."

"Sure, you won't change your mind anymore?" asked Sasanka. "Will the pride of the proud one last?"

"If I should change my mind, what's that to you, Sasanka-da?"

"To answer that question truthfully would only add to your conceit. For your own good, therefore, I'll keep quiet. But really, I wonder at the fellow's impertinence – what the English call cheek."

A great weight seemed to have been lifted off Urmi's mind – a burden of long standing. She hardly knew what to do with this joy of freedom. She tore up and threw away the programme of study. She flung the ring out of the window to the beggar in the lane who was asking for alms.

"Will any hawker buy these fat books with their pencil annotations?" she asked.

"First, let's hear what would happen, if no one bought them."

"The ghost of the dead and buried days may reside in them and may come and stand by my bed at dead of night, pointing its dread finger at me."

"If there be any such fear, I'll buy the books right away, without waiting for any hawker."

"What will you do with them?"

"Perform their last rites according to the Hindu Shastras. I would go as far as Gaya to consecrate their ashes, if that would set your mind at rest."

"No, that would be going too far."

"Very well, I'll build a pyramid in a corner of my library to lodge their mummy."

"But let me tell you, you can't go to your work today."

"Not at all?"

"Not at all."

"What am I to do instead?"

"Let's get into a car and just vanish."

"Go and get your sister's permission."

"I'll tell her after we return – though I'll get a good scolding. But then it won't matter."

"Right! I too am willing to stand your sister's scolding. I'll sweep you along at the rate of forty-five miles an hour, and won't mind bursting a tyre or running over a couple of our own species, even if it takes us as far as the jail – provided you promise thrice that at the end of our chariot-drive you will return to our house."

"Agreed, agreed, agreed!"

After the drive they returned to the Bhowanipore house, but the excitement of forty-five miles an hour still ran hot in their blood and would not subside. This turbulence of blood made them blind to all sense of responsibility, fear or shame.

For some days, Sasanka's work fell into a state of complete disorder. He knew that what he was doing was not right and that the price of neglect might prove to be very heavy. At night, he was haunted in bed by fearsome apprehensions in which all ominous possibilities seemed greatly exaggerated. But next day, he was once again "heedless of his trust", like the Yaksa of *Meghaduta*.

Alcohol taken once has to be taken again to drown the regret.

SASANKA

Thus, time passed. The eyes were frenzied, the mind infatuated. Urmi took long to realise what was happening to her, but one day she was rudely awakened to the reality.

For some unknown reason Urmi was afraid of Mathur-dada and had always avoided him. One day, Mathur came to her sister's room in the morning and stayed there till noon. Soon after, Sarmila sent for Urmi and with an expression at once calm and stern said to her: "Do you realise what havoc you have caused by distracting him from his work day after day?"

"Why, what has happened, Didi?" asked Urmi frightened.

"Mathur-dada has just informed me that your brother-in-law has grossly neglected his duties, leaving everything to Jawaharlal who has been helping himself to the building materials with both hands. It has come to light that large godowns have been so badly roofed that the rain pours through them as through a sieve, damaging the goods stored inside. Owing to the high reputation of our firm, the clients did not have the construction tested. And now, we are faced not only with the loss of our firm's reputation but with considerable financial loss as well. Mathur-dada is severing the partnership."

Urmi's heart sank, her face grew ashen. In a moment, as by a lightning flash, her heart's hidden secret was revealed to her. She realised now the full measure of intoxication which had unconsciously robbed her of her senses, of her power of discrimination. She had looked upon Sasanka's work as a sort of rival who must be thwarted, and from whose clutches she was ever impatient to snatch him away, to have him all to herself. Many a time when Sasanka was bathing, she had thoughtlessly dismissed visitors on business with a curt, "He can't see anybody now," – only because she was afraid lest Sasanka should again after his bath get engrossed in work and Urmi's day be rendered fruitless for want of his leisure. The terrible picture of her infatuation rose full and clear before her eyes. Instantly, she flung herself at her sister's feet and began to repeat in hoarse and broken tones: "Kick me away from your house, drive me away from your presence, now, this very minute!"

The sister had made up her mind on no account to forgive Urmi, but now her heart melted. Gently caressing Urmi's head she said: "Don't worry. Some way out of the difficulty shall be found."

Urmi rose. "Why should you bear all the loss?" she cried. "I too have some means."

"Are you crazy?" broke in Sarmila. "Do you suppose I'm such a pauper as that? I have requested Mathur-dada not to make a fuss over this matter. I'll make up the loss. And now, listen, see that your brother-in-law does not come to know that I know anything about it."

Urmi again fell at her sister's feet. "Forgive me, Didi, please, forgive me!" she cried, beating her head.

"Who is to forgive whom, sister?" wearily murmured Sarmila wiping her tears. "Life is so perplexing! We are baffled in our hopes, cheated of our loves."

After this incident Urmi did not leave her sister's side even for a moment, personally attending to every one of her needs, ministering medicine, serving food, helping her bathe, putting her to sleep. Once more she took to her books, poring over them, seated by her sister's bed. She dared not trust herself or Sasanka any more.

The result was that Sasanka took to visiting the sick-room. Only a male can be so clumsy in his infatuation as not to notice that his wife could plainly see through the motive of his frequent visits. Each time he bustled in Urmi blushed hot with shame. He invited Urmi to a football match to see the Mohun Bagan team play; the temptation did not work. He then brought the newspaper where in the advertisement column he had underlined Charlie Chaplin's name, but that also bore no fruit. When Urmi was less remote Sasanka did make an effort to attend to his work, but now even that was impossible.

However painful to her the sight of this unfortunate man, suffering so uselessly, Sarmila at first drew a secret pleasure from it. But she gradually noticed that his suffering was gaining on him, his face drying up, the black marks deepening under his eyes. It was obvious that with Urmi absent from the dining table, he did not relish his food and was slowly starving himself. The recent flood of gaiety that had inundated the house had suddenly ebbed, carrying away with it even the easy and peaceful tenor of their former days.

Once, Sasanka had been indifferent to his appearance. He used to have his hair cropped so short as almost to render the service of a comb superfluous. After many vehement attempts at remonstrating, Sarmila had in the end given him up as hopeless. But lately, Urmi's brief verdict couched in the form of a loud laugh had not been without effect. For the first time in his life Sasanka had begun to apply scented hair-oils to the new growth of hair on his head. But nowadays, his heart's wretchedness was so pitifully obvious in the unkempt state of his hair that it was no longer possible to make fun of it, open or secret. Love's tenderness proving stronger than its bitterness, Sarmila was torn with pity for him and contempt at her own callousness; the torment of her illness was intensified.

There was to be military tattoo on the Maidan of the troops stationed at the Fort. Timidly, Sasanka inquired: "Will you come, Urmi? I have booked good seats." Before Urmi could reply, Sarmila said: "Of course, she'll go. She's dying for a little outing."

Thus encouraged, Sasanka proposed after a couple of days: "Circus?" Urmi seemed only too eager. And then, "Botanical Gardens?" She hesitated, unwilling to leave her sister's side for so long. But the sister now advocated Sasanka's cause. Drudging with the masons the whole long day, getting messed all over with dust and sand – it was enough to drive one crazy. His health would break down if he didn't go out for a little fresh air. This plea was deemed sufficient to justify a trip as far as Rajganj.

'He cannot afford to lose her, for whose sake he does not mind risking the ruin of his work,' said Sarmila to herself.

Though no one ever told him in so many words, it seemed to Sasanka that what he was doing had the silent approval of all around him. He had convinced himself that Sarmila was in no way unhappy, that on the contrary, she felt happy in watching the happiness of this pair. This might have been impossible in the case of an ordinary woman, but then Sarmila was no ordinary woman. During the days of his government service, an artist had made a pencil sketch of his wife, which had till now remained buried in his portfolio. He now took it out and had it expensively framed by a European firm and hung it on the wall in his office, facing his desk. The gardener filled the vase in front with fresh flowers everyday.

At last, a day came when Sasanka, taking Urmi round the garden to see the sunflowers in bloom, suddenly seized her hand and confessed: "Surely, you know that I love you. As for your sister, she is a veritable goddess. I worship her as I could worship none else in this life. She is no creature of this earth, so infinitely superior is she to us."

Her sister had repeatedly confided to Urmi that her greatest consolation was that Urmi would be there to fill her place. Painful, no doubt, it was to imagine another woman in her place; on the other hand, she could not bear the thought of Sasanka dragging on a forlorn, wretched existence, without a woman to look after his comfort. She had also said that if he was thwarted in love, it would react even more ruinously on his business. Once the hunger of his heart was appeased, his work would resume its old order.

Sasanka's mind was in a delirium of exhilaration. He felt transported to a fairyland where all sense of responsibility faded in a stupor of happiness. Nowadays, he observed the sanctity of the Sunday as a holiday with the scrupulous adherence of a Christian. One day, he came and told Sarmila: "I've secured the steam-launch for the day from the Jute Sahebs. Tomorrow being Sunday, I propose to take Urmi to Diamond Harbour. We'll leave before day-break and return before dusk."

Something seemed to wring the very veins of Sarmila's heart; her forehead was wrinkled with pain. Sasanka noticed nothing.

"What about the food?" she mildly inquired.

"I've ordered it at a hotel."

There was a time when she had looked after such details. Then, Sasanka had been indifferent. Now it all seemed changed, topsy-turvy.

"Alright. You may go," she said. No sooner had the words left her mouth than Sasanka turned and hurriedly left, without caring to waste a moment. A desire to sob aloud overpowered Sarmila. She hid her face in the pillow and murmured over and over again: 'Why am I lingering?'

The next day, Sunday, was the anniversary of their wedding day, a day whose observance had never suffered a breach so far. This time, too, lying in her bed, she had planned all the arrangements, unknown to her husband. Nothing much. She would have made him put on the red Benaras dhoti he had worn at his wedding, herself clad in her wedding sari. She would have put a garland round his neck and made him sit and eat in front of her. Incense burning in the room, the gramophone in the adjoining room playing the familiar wedding music of the sanai – that was all. Every year on this day Sasanka had surprised her with some charming gift. This time too, she had felt sure that he had brought something to give her on the morrow.

But everything had turned bitter today. All alone in the room, she kept on murmuring: "False, false, all is false. What's the use of this farce!"

She had no sleep that night. Early in the morning she heard the car drive away from the gate. She broke into sobs. "Thou art but a myth, Lord!" she cried.

From now on, Sarmila's condition grew steadily and speedily worse. One day when the disease showed very grave symptoms, she sent for her husband. It was evening, the light in the room was faint. She motioned to the nurse to leave them alone. She made her husband sit beside her and, taking his hand in hers, said: "I have looked upon you as the Heaven-sent boon of my life. God did not grant me the power to prove worthy of you. I have done the best I could. For my many shortcomings I beg your forgiveness."

Silencing Sasanka, who was about to say something, she continued: "No, don't interrupt me. I leave Urmi to your care. She is my own sister; in her you will find me, and much else besides that you could not find in me. No, please keep still, don't say anything. That I have brought about your happiness before dying is to me the fulfilment of my good fortune."

From outside the nurse called: "The doctor has come." "Please, bring him in," answered Sarmila.

The conversation stopped.

Sarmila's maternal uncle was an enthusiastic patron of all sorts of unorthodox systems of healing. Recently, he had become attached to a sannyasi. When the doctors gave up Sarmila's case as hopeless, he insisted that the prescription of his Himalaya-returned sannyasi should be given a trial. The medicine consisted of a powder made of a Tibetan root, to be taken with plenty of milk. Sasanka, who could never stand quacks, objected, but Sarmila pleaded: "It'll do no good, of course. But at any rate it'll please Uncle."

But the medicine did bear fruit. Her breathing trouble subsided and she no longer spat blood. Gradually, after a fortnight's treatment she was able to sit up. The doctors explained it by saying that sometimes, the imminence of death provokes so desperate a reaction in the body that the life is saved. However that might be, Sarmila's life was saved.

'How embarrassing!' thought Sarmila. 'What's to be done? Will life saved prove in the end a greater calamity than death?'

Urmi was busy packing. Her term of stay had drawn to its end. Sarmila went up to her.

"You can't leave," she said.

"Why, what do you mean?"

"I mean – is it so rare in our Hindu society for sisters to be co-wives?"

"Hush – for shame!"

"Afraid of a scandal? Are people's tongues of greater consequence than the voice of Fate?"

She sent for Sasanka and told him: "Let's migrate to Nepal. You were once offered job at the Royal Court there. You may get it now if you try. No one will malign us there."

Without giving anyone time to oppose her suggestion, Sarmila began to make preparations for departure. Morose and downcast, Urmi went about the house as though she would have liked to hide herself. Sasanka said to her: "If you abandon me now, you may well imagine what will happen to me."

"I'm unable to think, to decide for myself," replied Urmi. "Whatever you two decide, I'll accept."

The preparations took some days. When the day of departure drew near, Urmi said: "Please, wait a week longer, while I go and consult uncle on a matter of business."

She left.

In her absence Mathur came to Sarmila looking very glum, and said: "You are going away at the right moment. After my last conversation with you, 1 arrived at a settlement with Sasanka of our mutual business relations, dividing the business without sharing liabilities. Lately, Sasanka has been going through the accounts with a view to winding up his own share of the business and it has come to light that not only has all your money been used up but it seems that this house too may have to be sold, to meet the liability."

"Did it never strike him that the crash was so imminent?" asked Sarmila.

"Some crashes," explained Mathur, "like the crash of lightning, are difficult to predict. They strike without a moment's warning. He was aware of his losses and could have repaired them in time, if the silly notion had not possessed him of resorting to quick expedients to restore his losses. Without consulting me he began to speculate in coal. The result was that he was in the end obliged to sell off in a falling market the goods bought when the market was soaring. Now, he has suddenly discovered that all he had has blown up like a rocket, leaving behind nothing but ashes. If now by God's grace he gets a job in Nepal, it may still be alright."

Sarmila was not afraid of poverty. On the contrary she knew that in the house of a needy husband her place would be all the more assured, for she was confident that she knew how to soften the rigours of want. Her ornaments would go a long way to keep off the starkness of poverty for some time. Urmi's portion, too, would be at the disposal of her husband if he married her – a faint suggestion of this thought did peep into her mind. But merely to exist is not enough. The fortune which her husband had built up so long by his own prowess, for whose sake she had, day after day, voluntarily suppressed many a claim of her heart, this embodiment of the joint dream of their lives now vanished like a mirage – the humiliation of it made her crumble into dust. She wished that death had spared her this dishonour.

'I have resigned myself to my fate,' she said to herself, 'but will he reconcile himself to the inexorable emptiness of poverty and dishonour? Will it not plant the bitterness of regret in his heart? He may find it hard one day to forgive her whose infatuation brought this all about; the very food served by her will taste like poison in his mouth. Chocked with shame by the stench of his own sottishness, he will only find fault with the alcohol. And if in the end he is driven to dependence on Urmi's income, the bitterness of his humiliation will turn every moment of her life into a hell.'

In the process of clearing his accounts with Mathur, Sasanka suddenly discovered that every penny of Sarmila's had been lost in his business, and that, without telling him anything about it, she had paid up the debt to Mathur. He recalled how, when he had resigned his Government post, he had built up his business with her money. Now again, leaving the ruin of his business behind, he was entering the harness of service, with the load of that same debt to Sarmila on his back. How would he ever repay the debt with the meagre income of a salaried post?

In about ten days' time they would be leaving for Nepal. That night he had not a wink of sleep. Before the day broke, he flung himself out of bed and bringing his fist down on the dressing table with all his might, cried out: "I will not go to Nepal." He swore: "Here in Calcutta we will stay on, the two of us along with Urmi – facing the full malicious glare of frowning, scowling society. And here in this very Calcutta I will build up once again the ruined edifice of my business."

Sarmila was busy making a list of articles to be taken on the journey or to be left behind. Suddenly, she heard her name called out, and ran to her husband, throwing the list down. Apprehensive of some sudden calamity she asked with a trembling heart, "Why, what's the matter?"

"1 will not go to Nepal," came the reply. "I will defy society and stick it out here."

"Why, what has happened?" she inquired.

"Work," he replied.

Work! The same old word! Her heart began to beat fast.

"Don't think I am a coward, Sarmi. Could you imagine me so degraded as to run away from my responsibility?"

Drawing closer, Sarmila took his hand in hers.

"Do make your meaning clear," she said.

"Don't conceal the fact from me," cried Sasanka, "that I am once again in your debt."

"Alright, I won't," submitted Sarmila.

"From this very day," went on Sasanka, "I'll begin discharging the debt – as I did once before. Mark my words. I'll recover and drag up again what I have flung away into the abyss. Trust me again as you once gave me your trust."

Sarmila's head sank on her husband's breast.

"Let me also have your full trust," she murmured. "Teach me, train me, mould me so that I may become worthy of sharing your task."

From outside came the cry: "Letter!" Two letters came in, written in Urmi's hand. One of them was addressed to Sasanka:

"I am on my way to Bombay en route for Europe. I shall carry out father's wishes and return a doctor in about six or seven years' time. In the meantime the havoc I have caused in your home will have had time to repair itself. Don't worry about me. I can't help worrying about you."

The other letter was for Sarmila.

"Didi, a thousand pranaams at your feet. Forgive me the wrong I have done you unwittingly. If no wrong has been done – then that very knowledge will make me happy. I dare not hope for any greater happiness, nor indeed, do I know for certain wherein lies happiness. If happiness is not in store for me, let it be so. Let me only not err."